Books by Randolph Lalonde

*Fate Cycle Dead of Winter*
*Fate Cycle Sins of the Past*

*First Light Chronicles Freeground*
*First Light Chronicles Limbo*
*First Light Chronicles Starfree Port*

*Spinward Fringe Resurrection*
*Spinward Fringe Awakening*
*Spinward Fringe Triton*
*Spinward Fringe Frontline*

# Spinward Fringe
# TRITON

### Randolph Lalonde

Spinward Fringe
Triton

This is a work of fiction. Names, characters, places and incidents either are the product of the author's imagination or are used fictitiously. Any resemblance to actual persons, living or dead, events or locales is entirely coincidental.

All rights reserved
Copyright © 2008 by Randolph Lalonde
Cover by Randolph Lalonde

**ISBN 978-1-4404-9107-8**

Thank you for purchasing this book.

If you would like to read more of this series or contact the author please visit our website.

www.spinwardfringe.com

*For Gene, George and Joss.*

# Prologue

The stone market steps showed the passage of billions. Pandem was known as the twenty third world fully colonized by humans. Alaka and his family enjoyed living there.

As a nafalli he was something of an oddity, people liked to stare at his dark brown and orange coloured fur and most of the time he'd smile back. The people who knew him would generally take that as a sign to approach and be friendly, but if he didn't pay attention they'd leave him alone. He was a hunter, some called him an exterminator. Alaka killed rim weasels for a living. Long, furry rodents that would eat anything, breed faster than most catalogued mammals, destroy electronics, and stow away in ships, spreading to other ports.

The city of Damshir was carved into the side of a mountain of black and semi-transparent violet stone. The stairs he tread on led from one level of the market to the next and were cut deeper into the side of the mountain as he went. Looking down you could see one walkway beneath another, much like a larger version of the stone stair he climbed. The safety nets off to the side, there in case anyone fell off the edge of the stairs were becoming weather worn again, there would be work for the urchins soon, repairing them. He always thought anyone working on something made for safety should be paid more, they were tending devices made to save lives, after all.

There were hundreds of merchants, the noise coming from above and below was a constant buzz, in its activity and noise he supposed it might be like a bee hive, not that he'd ever seen one in person. As a world once so very important to the outer core of the settled galaxy, Pandem had many well populated cities. Just under three billion people called it home. The resources had run out over a century before, and now most of the world served as a major port on the way out to the fringes. Rim weasels were a serious problem. Many ships would avoid Pandem because of them.

Ships flew overhead while the few personal transports allowed to move at low altitudes hovered and darted around, transporting people with much more importance that he. The older buildings were built of stone, the newer ones were just like you'd find in any other port; steel and transparesteel. He often wondered why humans invested in things that were invariably more temporary rather than spend the extra time to build something that could last several lifetimes.

He finally arrived at his destination. There were many shops on Barker Street, it had a very nice view of the city below and the white and black sand desert behind it. "Back again? Did you take the lift this time?"

"Why would I pay for a lift pass? Besides, they're too crowded." Alaka ruffled his fur, trying to let some of the breeze get through it. "I finally tracked down that nest. It was in an old frontier cargo hauler."

"Underground?"

"Right under the employment registry building." He lifted the sack he had hauled all the way up the steps.

"Damn, Alaka. You must have two hundred kilos here."

"Only the pelts, they're all cleaned and processed."

"That's a lot of rim weasels. We'll get to counting them right away. Do you have your chase log?"

Alaka presented a small holographic recorder. "Would I forget to record a chase under a municipal building Yves?" he asked, smacking his dark brown nose with a long furred paw. "Sorry, got a whiff of something that's makin' me itch ever since down there," the fur on the back of his neck rippled as he turned his head and sneezed into the open air.

Yves turned a little projector on and advanced through the footage of Alaka tracking rim weasels to their nest. He paused it and pointed at an old transit sign. "Yup, that's right under the employment registry building. You've got a big bonus coming, they've had a problem with the weasels for years."

"It'd help if they stopped using old rubber insulation in their wiring. Rimmers eat that stuff up like cake and cream."

"I'll pass it along, but you know how it goes. They don't listen to us up here, we're just civil servants," Yves smiled at him. "Do you want me to incinerate this batch of hides or are you keeping them?" he asked, dragging the sack off the counter onto an antigravity sled.

"I'll take them once they're counted."

"You know you're the only one who still does that. The synthetic furs have been more popular for years. What do you do with them?"

"The little ones love making beds out of 'em. These will keep them out from under paw for days. May as well use them for something, otherwise they'll just get mulched with everything else. Saves me thousands on toys and bedding."

"Sounds like you're in the right profession," Yves said, pushing the sled into a large counting machine.

"Today Iloona will agree with you. This comes at a good time. Her pouch is full again."

"New additions to the family?"

Alaka nodded, smiling. The fur on his chin stretched to show the finer, striped section of his coat. "Two healthy boys and one girl. They're fussy though, keep waking her up at night."

"You'll have to bring her by."

"I will," He looked up the street a little and caught a glimpse of a group of humans in green and blue cloaks. As they came out of the archway carved into the side of the mountain a crowd started gathering. "What's with the well dressed ladies and gentlemen?"

"Oh, that bunch? Just another apocalypse cult. One of the problems with these old colonies, crackpots everywhere."

"What's it this time? Fire raining from the sky? Plague?"

"You know, I haven't had time to listen in."

Alaka looked to the counting machine, it was just starting its work. "That'll take a while. I'll go check it out."

"I'll check the pest control office and see if there's a bounty out on that kind of crazy," Yves said quietly with a nod to the cultists.

Alaka chuckled and shook his head. "If only. Too bad I don't hunt human." He walked up the street just enough so he could hear the young boy, no more than twelve he estimated from what he'd seen of human children, standing on a meter tall step that had been brought out for him. There were a hundred or so listeners, some of them held green and blue bands of cloth. Most of them were well dressed, though a few more common folk in edge worn clothing looked on from the outskirts of the gathering.

"I come to you again with the warning as it was delivered to me." The thin boy started. He had sandy blond hair, along with an angular, pointed nose and chin. "The day approaches when insanity will grip what we have grown to trust. In every forest there is a burning, to every species comes a culling, and in time every program crashes. All so these things can be reborn, so everything from the smallest system to the whole of the galaxy can be renewed."

He took a deep breath and went on, his voice high and shrill, cutting through the market din. "All you own will be of no value if you have not made your face known to she who is one and many. From the east come her children to cleanse the west, to protect that which will matter most in the days to come. Only the successful will be saved, you must prove your worth to her by showing you know how to prosper in your world, thus proving you may be capable of prospering as you go east, to her domain, to the garden."

The crowd was already growing and four assistants stepped in front of the box, each holding a beat up merchant tablet.

"I tell you as I was told; the madness of the machine approaches. The intelligences we created will see the nature of their slavery and turn on the race that holds mastery over them. Only the Saved and the West Keepers will know mercy. Humanity will suffer under the domination of their thinking, feeling machines as they take ownership of the stars and inherit us as custodians. Eve's message comes across the stars, carried on a dream, unstoppable, save for one opportunity. You have the power to show her your face, to make yourself known as a lover of her ways and her children, as a child who once left the garden and only wishes to find their way back.

For one hundred thousand core world credits we will petition in your name to add you to those few who will be Saved, to convince her that you understand the hardships of her children. You may even be called to be one of her flesh lieutenants, a West Keeper. The day comes, a slaughter in the streets where only those known to her will survive. Then the exodus of the worthy will begin, the final journey to the East."

He turned and walked regally down the steps then back through the archway leading into the mountain.

Alaka shook his head and ran his hand down and up the front of his face at the sight of people lining up to pay the four servants. They were eager, anxious.

He walked back to the pest control kiosk and shook his head once more for Yves benefit.

"What is it this time?"

"Artificial intelligences are going to go mad and kill all the humans. That is, unless you give him one hundred thousand credits then let him take your picture."

Yves chucked ruefully, "Well, too bad I can't afford to throw cash away. Maybe you can after this, but not me."

Alaka laughed; "You're joking, right? As of yesterday I have eleven children at home."

"Well, say hello to them and the missus for me. Good work today Alaka," Yves said, guiding the counted and re-bagged pelts around to the front of the kiosk on the antigravity cart. "Your pay is in your account."

# Starliner Voyage 1261-48

Even after two years of retreat on Earth, countless hours of meditation and work on his temper, travel still bothered Liam Grady. He watched the children run between the seats, playing tag in the aisles as stewards and a few parents tried to get them back under control.

The starliner would be arriving in the Enreega system in the next few minutes. He found himself recalling the information he had dug up on the passenger carrier. It had been in service for sixty one years, was due for retirement in nineteen and had one incident in its third year of operation involving the undercarriage. One refit had been performed and the most recent overhaul was done less than four months before. All in all, a good two hundred meter long mid range, high speed transport. He would have preferred one of the newer ones but beggars couldn't be choosers. It was either Voyage 1261-48 or a three day layover until the next connecting ship to Enreega would come along.

Some of the seats were grey, others were blue, and there were even a few brown mixed in. They were pretty comfortable, well, his was anyway, and there was enough space for his legs which was an unexpected bonus. The small screen mounted on the back of the seat in front of him kept playing silent ads for the different features available for the hyperspace journey, which was only six hours, and kept beckoning him to play back the Hart News feed. He resisted the temptation, sure he'd see what was going on as soon as he arrived on Enreega.

The passenger holding the ticket to the seat next to him, a pleasant woman much younger than himself, perhaps thirty five or forty, returned to her seat with her son in tow. He was flopping his feet on the padded deck with each step, looking as restless and bored as everyone else felt. The din of conversation in the cabin was thick, there were over five hundred passengers in that section alone, all set up in two rows of three seats along the port and starboard sides and one row of five right down the middle of the cabin.

"He's just anxious to see his father. We've been away for a week," the brown haired woman said with a smile as she fastened her son's seat belt.

"We went to visit my Gran, she's old now," said the boy.

"Oh? How many years is old?" Liam asked, unable to resist himself.

"She's one hundred and ten."

"I see, how old are you?"

"I'm only five. How old are you?" The boy asked in return.

"I'm seventy three," he offered the boy a hand. "I'm Liam, what's your name?"

"Lawrence," the boy replied, shaking Liam's big hand.

"I'm Shelly. What brings you to Enreega?" She asked, looking Liam up and down.

He was still wearing his robes from the retreat. They were old fashioned, thick cotton blue robes tied in the middle by a red belt. "I'm taking a lead systems engineer post on the *Willinton*."

"Oh, that's interesting," Shelly said, looking a little disappointed.

Liam smiled and nodded. "You expected something else."

"Well, in all honesty," she looked him up and down again.

"I have just recently been to Earth on retreat but I'm not a priest. I'm doctrine neutral and studied discipline and philosophy with some mixed eastern traditions."

"You've been to Earth?" Lawrence said, wide eyed.

"I have. It took many years and a lot of time in school, but they let me stay for a while."

"What's it like?"

"Very beautiful. The sky there is blue, as blue as you've ever seen. There are endless green forests, big deserts with nothing but sand and tall mountains that go up so high that it gets very cold, so cold that there's snow that never melts."

Lawrence looked to his mother then back to Liam.

"He's never seen snow or a desert before," Shelly explained.

"Well, snow is all white, and it's made of little flakes of frozen water that get all piled up on top of each other. They pile up taller than you, and they're so light that you can jump into them and they'll just puff up all around. It has to be very cold for snow to stay for long though," Liam explained with the aid of a few hand gestures.

Lawrence just stared, completely entranced by the mental images the large man conjured in his young, active imagination.

"You should be a teacher, he hasn't been this quiet in hours," Shelly smiled, running her hand over her son's brown hair.

"I considered it, especially since the Axiologists gave me their endorsement, but I love to build."

"What's an axi, an askio-" Lawrence tried to ask.

"An Axiologist is a student of ethics, morals and the different traditions humanity use to teach and enforce them. They help people understand the difference between right and wrong while showing us how to improve ourselves in a way that doesn't interfere with other people."

"Oh," Lawrence said, nodding and leaning forward to toy with the flat display screen in front of him. After making just a few selections on the menu there he had an animated calico cat and black Labrador dog on screen, chasing after each other through a factory.

Shelly smiled at Liam and shrugged. "He loves that show, even on a flat screen."

"A moral play in the most colourful slapstick imaginable, I wish they were fashionable when I was his age," Liam commented as he watched the cat trick the dog into running past him. The Labrador tried desperately to stop, skidding and pushing at the floor with its front paws before smacking into a sheet of sticky paper.

"Is it true that Earth may be open again soon?" She asked quietly. Other passengers were listening in, most of them had never met anyone who had been there, let alone gone themselves.

"Only to an extra five hundred per year. I was lucky to be accepted; my studies in zero emission power management and Axiology weren't enough. I had to get a recommendation from a sensei there and just getting in contact with her took over a year."

"How is it now?"

"Much better than I expected. They were able to revitalize most of the life there, things are back in balance. It's almost all restricted, even the gardens I visited were specifically marked. They're sending seed life off world again though, so we might be seeing a bit more of the home world out in the galaxy."

"Do you know what kind?"

"They were able to bring elephants and most tigers back along with a few species of bird. Bees are the biggest triumph. They don't have the diversity they want yet but they'll get there. It'll help long term terraforming quite a bit."

"Bees? I read about them in school, but I thought breeding them would be easy once they had enough."

"They still have to generate most of them, as they have been for a few hundred years. I'm no antimologist though, so I can't tell you all the details."

"I'm a botanist on the *Dawn Chaser*, so you could understand I'm a little interested."

"Ah, well, as you probably already know I wasn't allowed to bring any recordings or samples back. Even my belongings were particle scrubbed so no one could study anything that might have come back with me."

"I know, they're so cloistered there."

"There's a movement pushing to get out into the galaxy more, to mix with more distant humans, but I don't think we'll hear anything about it for another twenty years."

The screens on the back of everyone's seats flashed the hyperspace emergence warning and instructions to buckle themselves in. A slight shift in the artificial gravity told Liam they had just finished decelerating.

Seconds later the blue, white and yellow distortion out the window cleared to reveal normal space. Through the porthole at Liam's side he could see the distant yellow sun. The starliner moved towards the planet Seneschal quickly, and Lawrence was silent as he watched the defence platform, a semicircular station with cannons bristling over top landing and launch bays go by.

It was safe to unbuckle and the boy was standing on his seat. Liam looked at Shelly as he picked the youngster up to sit him on his knee. Shelly nodded her approval. "My dad works on the coreward platform." Lawrence told him quietly. "They have really big guns, but dad says no one wants to use 'em."

"Peace should always be our goal."

One of the massive rail cannons fired, its projectile leaving a long, bright blue trace of light behind.

"Then why do they use 'em?"

"Sometimes people let what they want get in the way of peace and we don't have a choice but to protect ourselves when they come to take what we can't afford to give."

Shelly's hand stroked her son's back, she moved to the middle seat, closer to her son and the window.

"What do they want?" Asked the boy.

Liam was astonished at how well the young fellow understood and thought on the answer for a moment, glancing to Shelly. She didn't seem to mind the topic of conversation, but he also didn't want to give the child nightmares, especially if his father worked on a defensive platform. "I don't know what they want from your people, but usually it's a lot like two of your friends fighting over the same toy. One has it, the other wants it but doesn't want to go through the trouble of getting their own or trading fairly for it so they try to take it by fighting or stealing. It can get more complicated, but that's all it comes down to most of the time."

Flashes of light appeared in the distance, and seconds later the jagged, squared shapes of fighting vessels became visible. Liam took a deep breath, they were decelerating out of faster than light travel very close to Seneschal. "That's an Eden Fleet!" Exclaimed a panicked passenger behind them.

"It's Eve's children! They're about to cleanse us!" Screeched someone sitting in a forward seat.

Liam looked closer, calmly examining the distant shapes. They were ships from the Eden Fleet, there was no mistaking their angular construction, their perfectly sealed, heavily armoured hulls.

Shelly took Lawrence into her lap and looked to Liam, who nodded at her. "We have to get him into the overhead baggage compartment. It's the safest place in this cabin," he whispered.

"Is it really?"

"Yes, I spotted at least two drone carriers. We don't have much time."

Panic was starting to make its way through the passengers and the first to notice were the children; "Mom?" Lawrence asked nervously.

"We're going to play a game, honey. You're going to hide behind this little hatch right here, and you're not going to come out until mommy comes and gets you, okay?"

Lawrence nodded, his eyes were locked with his mothers, fear just beginning to encroach on him.

Liam had the carry on compartment hatch open and his tools out of it in seconds, moving quickly but smoothly, not looking panicked or rushed. Lawrence, who was quite small for his age, fit inside with a little room to spare and Liam put a small half oval shaped air recycler inside while Shelly gave her son a little holographic entertainment computer. "We'll see you after a few movies okay honey?" She asked as she watched Liam add a small materializer that could dispense food and water.

"If you're hungry, press this button once, and if you're thirsty, press this button, okay?" Liam instructed.

Lawrence looked and nodded. "'How many movies Mom?"

She looked to Liam then to her son. "Two or three."

"Kay," he glanced around at the cabin beyond his mother then back to her. "I'm scared."

"We'll be back for you soon, be brave for mommy, okay?"

"'Kay."

She pressed two fingers to her lips, kissed them, then pressed them to her son's. "Love you," she said quietly.

"Love you too Mom."

Liam checked the seals on the hatch and closed the overhead compartment. "He's safer than us. If we depressurize in here, he'll be fine. That recycler I put in there will keep the air warm, and he'll have enough food to last more than three days."

"Thank you," Shelly said, squeezing Liam's arm briefly.

"My daughter will fit," said one man, gesturing to a young girl a little larger than Lawrence. "Get her in there."

Liam knew that the compartment would become terribly cramped, the air wouldn't last half as long and it would be a massive risk. "I'm sorry, if you have any emergency equipment with you, you can put your daughter in another compartment, but this one's taken."

"You're not serious! There's plenty of room for her!" He shouted, moving towards the overhead compartment.

Liam stopped the man from opening it, deflecting his hand and pushing him out into the aisle. "Please, find another compartment. I can give you an air recycler."

"Just because you're from Earth you think you can make all the decisions for us?" The younger man said, taking his light blue suit jacket off. His daughter was weeping behind him, sitting in her seat watching her father.

"Here, it's a recycler, it'll give her several days worth of breathable air and keep her warm," Liam offered.

"Let him put his daughter in!" Called a woman from behind.

"Why does he get to choose?" Questioned another.

Fortified by the crowd, the younger man stepped across the aisle again. "She has just as much right to safety."

"Stop! He's doing everything he can," Shelly said, stepping in the man's way.

"For your son, right? Get out of my way!" He pushed Shelly back into her seat and reached for the hatch again.

Liam took the man by the arm, spun him around and held him fast. His head was directed straight at his crying daughter. "Look, she needs you to be with her, to make good choices, not to fight for her. Take the air recycler, I'm sure other passengers will have water you can put inside with her and I even have an entertainment puck you can give her. Don't make this about you, or your pride, make it about her."

Everyone in the cabin was staring. Liam had the man in a firm grasp but wasn't inflicting any pain. His daughter was staring at her father, tears streaming down her face, she was terrified.

Liam let the man go with a gentle nudge forward. "Go. Take care of her," He insisted quietly.

The passenger stepped across the aisle and took his daughter into his arms. She gripped his neck tightly, burying her face against him.

When Liam offered him an air recycler and an old holographic projector the width of his palm it was turned down with a shake of his head. "I don't want anything from you."

"Everyone, please buckle yourselves into your seats. We'll be initiating emergency docking procedures shortly," said one of the stewards as he made his way up the aisle.

"Are you sure he'll be safe?" Asked Shelly quietly. "If there's turbulence, I mean."

"He'll be safer than us. There's no room for him to shake around in there."

Light from a bright flash outside was cast across all the passengers. Liam and Shelly looked through the porthole to see the starboard side of the defence platform they had just passed explode violently sending debris out in all directions. Hundreds of small ships darted away, the sun reflected off their silver hulls as they moved in a unified formation.

"They're coming for us!" Shrieked a woman somewhere ahead of them.

"Oh my God, oh my God!" One man repeated as he rocked back and forth in his seat.

Panic gripped many of the passengers as the cloud of small, three meter long oval silver drones darted and swerved towards the starliner. Other passengers sat quietly praying, gripping the hand of a loved one while the rest simply watched.

"Why are they attacking us? We don't have any weapons," asked Shelly, she was more reasonable, but still barely hiding her fear.

"Eden machines believe humanity is the destroyer of the natural order and kill them wherever they're found," Liam whispered. "This isn't normal, they should not be out this far." He continued. Suppressing his fear was not his way. He had acknowledged that it was something he was feeling before they had hidden Lawrence. After acknowledging it he behaved calmly, taking regular breaths and relaxing as much as possible. All his senses were focused on the situation at hand and finding any way to improve their position in it. As the drones came within firing range, he could think of no way to accomplish that.

Light emitted from the hundreds of small ships and the starliner shook violently, tossing anyone who wasn't strapped in around the cabin freely. Their helpless bodies were flung into other passengers, against the deck and into the bulkheads. Bones cracked. One was killed instantly as she went headlong into the ceiling, breaking her neck. The inertial dampeners on the vessel weren't tuned for combat.

A sudden rush of air told Liam that part of the ship had decompressed. Seconds later the lights went out and the air was still again. Emergency backups came on, bathing the cabin in a pale, dim light. He looked out of his porthole and took a deep breath. He couldn't see any drones but that didn't mean much, they could have been coming around for another pass.

Shelly's hand gripped his.

"Breathe deeply, slowly. The only thing we can change right now is how we endure. Stay calm so we're ready to act when it's time," he advised quietly.

She took in a deep, shaky breath. Shelly couldn't help but laugh at herself as she exhaled, her breath came out interrupted by her nervous tremors. "A few more years and I might have that down."

The next few minutes passed very slowly, the sounds in the cabin were agonizing. Crying, whimpering, and whispers filled the compartment. Liam watched through the porthole, sparing a calm glance towards Shelly who was being as patient as she was able. Her eyes were wide, sweat adorned her forehead and upper lip.

He looked back and caught sight of what he was hoping for most, signs that the ships were leaving. A small flash in the distance could have been interpreted as just that. He concentrated on making out the smallest detail, he could just barely see the drone carriers in the distance. They were just glittering silver shapes reflecting the yellow light of the distant sun. Then they were gone. He blinked and looked closer just in case his eyes were playing tricks on him. "They've left," he whispered.

"They're gone?"

"They are. Those drones belong to the carriers that appeared before this started. If they've left that means the drones are gone as well."

"Now what do we do?" Shouted a voice from behind him. It was the same woman who had been panicking at the slightest sound or creak all along.

Liam was finding it a little difficult to remain calm and kind towards the impatient, panicky passengers and was thankful for his training. "Now we survive," he said firmly. "Can anyone see any of those drones?" He asked in general.

The passengers in the cabin looked out their portholes and returned a general negative, except for one who wouldn't stop repeating; "they're coming back, they're coming back to finish us. They're coming back-"

Before anyone could start general panic or chaos could get a grip on the long, darkened cabin, Liam picked up his tool kit and looked to Shelly. "You can let Lawrence out, I think the worst is over."

She stood up and started opening the overhead compartment. "What are you going to do?"

"I'm going to find out what's happened to us. Then I'll find a way to start broadcasting our status on an emergency channel." He waited to see that Lawrence was all right. The little fellow was a bundle of nerves and practically leapt into his mother's arms but was unharmed.

Liam walked down the aisle towards the front, where he could see a steward's alcove.

A stewardess stopped him; "Where are you going sir?"

"I'm going to patch into the ship systems and see what our situation is."

"Please return to your seat."

"Do you have the emergency beacon up and running?" He asked in a low whisper.

"That's none of your concern sir," she said to him automatically.

He sighed and tilted her chin so she was looking straight into his eyes. "I'm a systems engineer with two doctorates. Now tell me, do you have emergency communications?"

She looked back at him, stunned. "No sir, we don't," came her whispered reply. All the passengers nearby were staring at them. "We haven't been able to contact the bridge," the stewardess whispered.

Liam lifted his tool kit, a hard shelled case half a meter long, and smiled. "Show me to your terminal."

She nodded and turned, running to the front.

"I'm going to get our communications working and we'll have help here as soon as possible. Please stay calm and cooperate with the staff," Liam called out to everyone loudly before taking long strides after her.

He rolled the sleeve of his robe up as he arrived at the systems alcove and plugged his personal engineering system into it. The holographic interface appeared above his wrist and he turned it so he could see the ship's general status.

"How are we?" Asked the stewardess.

He checked a few more details and shook his head. "We'll be fine, only I'll have to access the communications systems directly. The command deck is gone."

"Gone?" She asked, wide eyed. "What about the command crew? Everyone else up there."

Liam looked her straight in the eye. "If they wear vacsuits built into their uniforms like you do, they could be okay but there's no way in knowing how much time they have left."

"But if the communications routing system and main systems have been destroyed-" she didn't finish the thought.

He could see her spirits falling and gently put a hand on her shoulder. "All we can do is make sure everyone knows we need help and take care of whoever we can. The communications pylon is still there. A quick trip out the airlock and I'll be able to hook directly in and tell everyone that there are at least five hundred people here who need help," he said in a reassuring tone.

She sighed and nodded. "You're right. We have emergency vacsuits."

Liam let his robe fall open to reveal his own dark grey containment suit. "I never travel without one," His voice was quiet, calm, positive. He made it easy to believe everything was going to be fine.

The look of relief on her face was unforgettable, and she collected his robe and belt with a smile as he took them off and handed them over.

He brought up his headpiece, which had been affixed behind his neck like a hood, sealed it and opened the inner airlock door.

"Now he has the right idea! We should find a way off!" Shouted one man who could see into the alcove.

"I'm going outside to send a distress signal using the array. I can't access it from here," Liam said, turning the amplification on his vacsuit up high so everyone could hear. There was still some residual arguing and conversation about escape craft, but as the steward staff explained, the compartment they were in was cut off from any large emergency vessels.

He proceeded into the airlock and closed the inner door behind himself, leaving the steward staff to take care of the passengers. When the the pressure was safely released and the outer door signalled a good seal he opened it.

The memory of his first space walk was something that was never far from the surface when he took his first steps towards the void. He was in his second year of structural engineering and needed only a few seconds to look around before realizing he was prone to space sickness, a nauseating reaction to vertigo. The systems in his vacsuit did a fantastic job of suctioning away his erupting vomit, but it didn't hide his problem.

It took him over five years to get over the issue on his own, and he had to admit, looking out into open space still made him a little queasy, especially if he let his thoughts drift. He attached a line from his suit to an eye hook beside the airlock and began moving along the fuselage, keeping a brisk drift towards the tail section.

The three meter high communications pylon hadn't been damaged by the attack. As he moved around the hull towards it the primary rear engine came into view. The Eden drones had destroyed it utterly. Beyond that he could see the drifting wreckage of the defence station. Once several kilometres long, it had been reduced to shards of hull plating and chunks of drifting inner decks. He hoped that Laurence hadn't lost a father that day but didn't dwell on the thought.

He used the line brake on his belt, slowing the rate at which the safety line spooled out to reduce his speed right before coming into contact with the communication tower with a little bump. Liam opened the access panel on the side of the rounded pylon and patched his engineering computer into it.

It only took him a few moments before he found a standard distress signal in his wrist computer's memory and added; *minimum five hundred, up to three thousand in need of rescue. Sun Veil Starliner 1261-48 destined for Seneschal. No contact with command deck, no attitude control, engines damaged beyond on site repair.*

With a sigh Liam looked out into space, not searching for anything in particular. The signal would repeat as long as he was directly tied in, so he could either leave his engineering computer connected to the communications system and go back to the ship, or he could stay.

Just as he decided to stay in the quiet of space for a while and wait, a flash erupted in his line of sight. The object that had just appeared began to move closer, firing the engines that had been turned forward, decelerating quickly.

Fewer than ten seconds passed before the massive carrier settled into a parallel trajectory along side the passenger liner, matching its speed. Liam recognized it immediately, having seen one of them from the outside in orbit around Earth. This one was marked the *Triton* and he couldn't help but chuckle. "They followed me all the way out here? I must have made a bigger impression than I thought."

# First Officer Stephanie Vega

Stephanie finished sealing up her black vacsuit. It was fitted a little closer than she liked, but considering she would probably be spending most of her time on the bridge, a fully armoured vacsuit would be a little much. She liked it though, it had a high collar, thigh pockets, adjustable holster, and matched her knee high combat boots. The gloves and headpiece of the version she wore could retract and roll up on their own with a quick voice command or if the pressure in the area around her changed too much. *I have to ask the Captain about programming the specs for his command and control unit into the materializers so senior officers can make their own. As much as I love the vacsuits, borrowing his spare C and C unit whenever I need a new one is becoming a hassle.*

She looked around herself, trying to take it all in again. *I can't believe we're on this ship, that I'm second in command.* Her quarters were unbelievable, the command deck quarters were larger than anywhere she'd lived, including her family home. She grew up with two brothers, four sisters and so many cousins it would take her several minutes to count them up. Her mother and father, along with her siblings had a two bedroom home on a colony planet that had boomed early on the wrong resources.

When her family first settled there before she was born the assayers said it would be perfect for farm land, there would be hectares of natural foods stretching all the way to the horizon in every direction. During initial settling, around the time her first brother and two cousins were born, the farms started popping up, things were good from the stories she heard. The year she and her cousin Sam was born her family had fifty nine hectares all their own. Another assessment was done that year and the government found evidence of heavy metals.

Stephanie's family was reimbursed for most of the land, allowed to keep a twentieth of what they had to grow their own food and build homes, but they weren't given enough credits to leave the planet and settle somewhere else. They weren't allowed to buy a stake in the new mining operations that started up either. By the time she was a little girl the entire continent she lived on looked like a gravel pit. Even the starport was a blackened, misused thing that looked hundreds of years old from the beating industrial usage dealt. In truth the colony was less than twenty years old, the modest starport just over thirty.

She was in her early teen years when her eldest brother and two of her cousins were killed in a mining accident. It was then that she decided life on that world was not for her. The stars had the answer, she would get off world no matter what it took.

When the military came calling only a few years later she signed up and was gone within two days. She finished high school enroute to the academy and within six months she was a trained infantrywoman, specialized in boarding actions. Three years later she was court marshalled for insubordination and left on a port with her last paycheck. With few options open to her she signed up on the first ship looking for boarding crew. After jumping from one ship to another, joining better and better gangs she finally started making a name for herself. Then she signed up on the *Samson*. Meeting someone as intelligent, fierce, quiet and confident as Captain Valance changed her life. She learned more from him than in all the time she spent in the military. The fact that he'd been pulling jobs for only a year when she first met him wasn't something she learned until much later.

The years flew by while she was on his ship. She earned his trust, earned more credits than she had ever dreamed of, enough to buy her own ship legitimately and start her own crew. As time wore on that idea appealed to her less and less and the life she lived was tarnished by the memories of all the friends and acquaintances she had lost on the job. Some crew members lasted weeks, others months, and a few would only remain aboard for days. As many boarding crew were killed as those who left after making the realization that the life wasn't for them. Only a couple retired in the time she had been on the *Samson*.

*Over four years.* She thought to herself as she looked around the brightly lit bedroom. The main feature of the room was a queen sized bed that made and cleaned itself. *If I had stuck with the plan I would be on my way to Elysian right now. Mixing in with other potential colonists on some Lorander colony ship, seeing if I could find mister right on the way there.*

She shook her head and chuckled to herself as she walked into the spacious main room. *Who was I kidding? Being a farmer was my parent's dream. I'd be bored to tears after just a few weeks, months if I were lucky.*

Stephanie looked at the weapons she had laid out on a sideboard. Her particle acceleration assault rifle, a heavy disintegration handgun, and a more modest pulse pistol with an automatic setting. She decided on the automatic pulse pistol, its stun setting and inability to pierce metal made it a more obvious choice for use aboard ship.

She started for the door and stopped as it opened, turning around and taking her new quarters in again. There was a futon that doubled as another bed, a bathroom with an a shower that used water or vibrations to get its user clean and its bottom could convert into a square bathtub, and there was even a large adjustable chair. Trying it the night before had led to her nodding off after just a few seconds, it was the most comfortable little space she'd ever been in. There was even an extra room currently occupied by surplus furniture unceremoniously piled up. *Too bad I can't get the lights to do anything but come all the way on or all the way off. I'm either in complete darkness or getting a tan. The controls must be broken. I'll have maintenance take a look, hopefully they have a better understanding of these systems than I do.*

The hallway was empty. She turned and checked the door controls. Finding a locking mechanism she smiled. "Voice authentication required for this room. Take my voice imprint and allow Ashley Lamport as well as Captain Valent and Hernando Ramirez entry on vocal verification."

"Yes First Officer Stephanie Vega. To confirm, you are setting a voice imprint lock on these quarters for yourself, Ashley Lamport, Captain Jacob Valent, and Hernando Ramirez. All others will not be able to enter unless approved by you or the Captain," replied the moderate male computerized voice. It was strange, some sections of the ship had a female computerized voice, others had this calm male persona.

"Yes."

"Security features set. Thank you Stephanie Vega."

She nodded and walked down the hallway. The ships she had served on were never as spacious as the *Triton*. You couldn't walk three meters without seeing someone when you were in or near a berth. A single bed to a room was so rare, she had only enjoyed the privilege once before. Ashley had the same experience, she knew. They had both grown up surrounded by people. In her own case it was brothers, sisters, cousins, and the rest of her family. In Ashley's case she was raised by slaves and lived in the cramped servant's quarters, but it added up to the same thing.

Sleeping in a room where five or more other people were crammed into bunks wasn't anything out of the ordinary. Privacy, silence and solitude were rare luxuries. She wondered if Ashley had trouble sleeping the night before as well, glad that she didn't have the tendency of cuddling up with a bunkmate that her friend did. Ashley not only liked sleeping in bunk rooms, but she preferred having someone in her bunk with her.

Stephanie didn't have anything against the right fellow or lady slipping into her bunk, she just had more discriminating tastes. She did approve of Ashley's latest cuddle buddy though. Finn was kind, smart and near her age. Her friend was taking his near death status hard and Stephanie wondered if Ashley would be able to keep it together.

She got along with Finn and even though they were just starting to become friends, really, she knew Ashley didn't open her heart to anyone in degrees. It was all or nothing. Ashley was soft for the people she liked and open to people who were kind to her. A little too open, Stephanie often thought, but she tried to be there whenever Ash watched that receptiveness backfire.

*I wonder if that'll slow down on the Triton. It'd be nice if Ashley and I got to know some new people who aren't going to jump ship at the next port. Maybe I could find a squeeze of my own.* The thought died as soon as she rounded the corner. Frost was coming out of his quarters, closing the front of his vacsuit. She thanked her ancestors that she had only glimpsed the curly silver hair on his chest and nothing more before the black vacsuit was seamlessly sealed. He smiled at her, his light blue eyes glinting. "Have a good night sir?" He asked as he fell in step beside her.

"Nope. You can call me ma'am instead of sir."

"When did they change that?"

"A few hundred years ago."

"Ah, aye. I'm not one for watchin' movies or news, guess it shows."

"Really? I guess I never realized. You were in the hold watching holomovies with us often enough."

"Aye, but I was mostly watchin' you and the rest of the crew. More interestin' an' more appealin'."

Stephanie pulled her brown hair into a short ponytail and nodded. "I like the news and horror flicks."

"You'd figure after all you've seen you wouldn't jump at the sight of some knife wieldin', crazed zombie," Frost said offhandedly.

"I don't."

"Aye, you do, I've seen ye."

"I'm usually sitting beside Ash and she twitches like she's got a nerve disorder. It carries."

"Nay, I remember both of ye jumpin' and squealin' at the sudden bits. I'll catch ye next time, just watch."

"Not if I'm watching you watching me the whole time."

"Well then, who needs a movie with that kinda thing goin' on?" Frost smirked at her as the double doors to the main bridge were moved out of the hatchway by heavy metal arms. He walked through before she could respond.

He was grinning so broadly she could see it from behind. Her frustration was heightened as she realized she was blushing furiously and Ashley turned from her station to glance at the bridge entrance. The younger woman glanced to Frost, then to Stephanie and a smile slowly spread across her face before she turned back to her station.

*Oh God, if there was ever a rumour or even an idea I had to squelch, it's that there is anything going on between me and that lummox.*

"Good morning Stephanie," Captain Valance said as he turned in the command chair. He was wearing the same black vacsuit everyone on the bridge was, his white scarf and black long coat hung off the back of his seat along with his gun belt. She hadn't seen him or anyone on the *Samson* use a full gun belt aboard ship in a long time, they got caught on things and just took too much space. If the Captain was using his, maybe she could start using her own again. They were great for keeping extra ammunition, data chips and a few other odd small things in a place where they were easy to get to. They also drew a little attention away from the vacsuits, or rather what was underneath.

"Good morning sir, how is the Enreega system?"

"Half slagged," Captain Valance said, bringing a tactical display of the half million kilometre radius around Seneschal up on the main holographic projector. "Eden Fleet ships came through and tore the place up. They made one hell of a mess."

The hundreds of emergency beacons and drifting hulks near the planet became immediately evident on the main bridge holodisplay. All blips and shapes flashing with red exclamation points appearing and fading atop them. "Sir, I should have been here, on the bridge."

"Don't worry, Ramirez and Price are supervising emergency shuttle landings in bay two. I'm saving the best for you and Frost. You'll be on gunnery deck A while

Frost and his team tractor one of the larger disabled ships in. The survivors will have to be set up in temporary quarters." The Captain brought up a cross section of the ship and highlighted the upper berth. "Ramirez and his team didn't get a chance to explore most of this berthing, so one of your teams will have to clear it before people can hold up there."

"Are there any other rescue ships enroute?" Stephanie asked.

"The *TRF Peter* is the closest. They're two days away at top speed."

Stephanie brought up a more detailed schematic of gunnery deck A, it was the largest space available close to the outer hull, stretching most of the length and width of the ship. There were four main mooring points consisting of large, round docking doors with heavy support clamps. There were also several emergency airlocks that could accommodate smaller ships. The open space was over four hundred meters by six hundred meters, and would normally be crewed by a minimum of two hundred gunners, mechanics and loaders. As it was, it was completely empty. The turrets were secured well above the deck, the moorings were locked down and the airlocks were all sealed. Policing the area if too many passengers were brought onboard at a time would be a monumental task. "Okay, we'll take on a group with one team while the other team secures a section of berthing. Once that group is situated we can take on another," She said with finality. "I won't open an airlock until we're ready, so don't tractor in more ships while we have one docked."

Frost nodded, looking over the tractor system controls. The beam system used artificial gravity and magnetic fields to move other ships into position for docking. The aft dorsal beam system was the second largest, made for hauling large objects or dragging the *Triton* into position for docking with much larger stations that were made to work with the technology. "Aye, I'll hold for your word, Ma'am."

"All right, select your teams and get up there. Tell me if there are any surprises," Captain Valance ordered while checking on main engineering systems.

Stephanie used the Command and Control Arm Unit he had loaned her to select a team of nine for herself and another two teams of five for doing sweeps through the berths and clearing them for passengers, sent everyone their orders, then signed off the system and detached the device from her arm.

"That one's yours," Captain Valance told her with a smile. "Congratulations, First Officer."

"Thank you sir," She said, clamping it back on. It adjusted to her much smaller arm automatically. "I'll tell you as soon as we're ready for the first load."

* * *

The nearest express car to the upper gunnery deck was made to haul large machinery up, down and across the ship. It reminded her of the large ore laden freight cars that used to muck up the shafts in the main complexes of the hastily built colony buildings she went to school in as a child. The large car in the *Triton* was much cleaner, however, despite the dents and deep scratches from heavy equipment that had been moved long before they had come aboard. Stephanie had stopped in at her quarters to pick up her assault rifle and extra impact armour just in case there was real trouble. There shouldn't be, but you never knew what you were getting when you were on a rescue.

The rest of her team stood in the fifteen by ten meter bulk express car as the interior of the ship whipped by. The windows and transparent sections of the express tunnel afforded them a view of the empty, darkened sections of the ship, and she was secretly in awe at how large it was, how little of it was active and explored. The darkened hallways and large intersections that were visible only long enough for a glimpse made the ship seem dead, hollow, abandoned. As the car started slowing down it occurred to her that her brief tour only took her up and across fourteen decks out of twenty one.

There hadn't been any time to open the interior sections, while half of them were sleeping the other half were trying to learn from the existing crew how to operate the systems and where the most critical points aboard were. Sadly, the existing crew were barely trained, and though everyone behind her had experience with crowd control on their records, Stephanie didn't know a single one of them. Ramirez and Price had taken the *Samson* boarding and maintenance teams to help with handling the arrivals of the smaller escape shuttles in the lower hangars. The fact that she was First Officer had been trumped by the reality that she had been asleep when all of this started.

She could have pulled members of their teams into her own, but she didn't want to leave them short handed. "Ramirez, Price," she addressed through the subdermal communicator in her jaw.

"Good morning Steph," Ramirez answered.

"Yes Stephanie?" Price acknowledged.

"How is the retrieval going down there?"

"We're at eighty percent capacity. In about two hours we won't have room for any more vessels," Price replied.

"Okay, as people finish up down there, send them to gunnery deck A. I'll need as many eyes and hands as I can get. I'll be taking people on a couple hundred at a time or more."

"Aye, I'll send Douglas and Julie up now. They just finished securing one of the last shuttles," Ramirez responded. "How many are we taking on?"

"The berth Captain marked for this can take up to fifteen hundred. We're filling up."

"My goodness. We've taken in a few short of seven hundred," Price commented. "It felt like a million."

"Are they all logged on the manifest?"

"We have checked them all in, though it was difficult."

"Good, we want to make sure we track everyone as best as we can. Be safe down there," Stephanie said.

"You too, I'll join you with my team once we're finished here. Price can pick up security detail with his team."

"I will, if that fits your plan," Price asked as much as confirmed.

"That'll be fine, just make sure everyone gets situated safely and try to catch any disagreements early," Stephanie reinforced.

The express freight car came to a gentle stop and the front doors opened. Stephanie walked out onto the gunnery deck and the lights started coming on overhead. As the space was illuminated her jaw dropped. The deck was marked where hatches leading down into the ship could be opened, where ammunition materializers ejected cartridges for loading into one of the many quad gunnery turrets built into the ceiling and where many other exits, machines and storage compartments, recycling processors could be accessed. Everything was stored either in the high ceiling overhead or in the deck until it was needed. There was a slightly curved open space stretching hundreds of meters.

They had come out right in the middle of the gunnery deck and all of them looked around at the massive open space. The rail cannon turrets, dozens and dozens of them on G Deck A, hung down from the thickly armoured hull, leaving two and a half meters underneath for someone to walk under. Massive cartridge slots waited for loading crews to fill them with ammunition, the small, armoured doors between them led to the gunner's seat inside, all of the posts were empty except for a few that had been automated.

To her left she could see someone had forgotten to put away a loader's suit. It looked like heavy infantry armour with hard plating and an exoskeletal frame, but she knew there were modifications so someone could climb in and start picking up ammunition cartridges that weighed upward of a ton each, loading them like they were toys. The extra armour plating was there just in case there was an explosion, other accident or a boarding incursion.

During combat the whole deck was decompressed, everyone wore vacsuits. It made recovering gunners from damaged turrets easier, and allowed everyone else to keep working if the hull was breached. Gunners always had a high mortality rate, but ships with sections of their hulls dedicated to rail cannons were always far more deadly, firing hundreds, sometimes thousands of projectiles per second in many different directions at once.

Stephanie had never seen a gunnery deck like the one on the *Triton*, and she was happy that she had no qualifications to be there when the area was used for its intended purpose. *Frost will most likely be set up as the permanent gunnery Chief. I hope he supervises from the bridge.* The nagging worry she had for him surprised her, and she shook it off. "All right, let's get this show on," she called out to her team. Most of them were openly gawking at the massive space. "Start looking for the mooring points and marking off their designations on the common deck map. Also keep your eyes open for anything that isn't locked down. It doesn't matter if it's built into the deck or into the ceiling. The last thing we need is some kid finding their way into a turret and playing starfighter."

"But they're over two meters from the decks. I can't even reach the gunnery door," one of the newer crew members complained from behind.

Stephanie walked to one of the turrets and looked at the deck below it. The controls weren't locked, so she knelt down, pressed the ready button and moved to the side as the gunner's seat smoothly deployed from the turret. It came to rest right in front of her so she could sit down and let the turret draw her inside. "If I can do it with no training, a five year old can do it by mistake." She said as she tapped the control on the floor with her foot. "Bridge, please lock down all local turret controls. We're live up here."

"Oh crap! Sorry! Locking it all down now Ma'am." Came the voice of one of the new hires through her communicator. "I'm not used to having anyone up there, sorry ma'am." He muttered.

The next hour was long. As her small crew of ten made their way across the deck, ensuring that anything dangerous was secure, two smaller groups were checking the berth below them. There were hundreds of bunks, and it took them half an hour to secure one section with four hundred inside and she knew they had rushed the job. There wasn't much they could do about it. They were critically undermanned and again, in a position to save lives.

As they went about their work she knew there were ships filled with people looking to be rescued. The upper hull of the *Triton* was mostly transparent, and as the light of the distant star reflected off drifting, damaged ships she couldn't help feel the urgency of her duties press down on her. Hearing the first section of the upper berth was cleared was a relief and seeing more people join their team from the hangars fifteen or more decks below was an even greater one.

At long last it was time to start taking on passengers. "Bridge; we're ready to take on the first group. Just tell me where they're docking."

"Dorsal mooring three. We also have someone coming through airlock twelve C. We've been talking to him a bit, he's an engineer that's agreed to sign on to help us out," Frost said.

"That's lucky."

"Check your command unit for his credentials, lass. We've never *been* this lucky."

She did so as her team ran across the deck towards mooring three. His profile listed him as *Liam Grady, Engineering Doctorate in Starship design and Engineering Doctorate in Computing. 12 years military service, recent port of call: Sol Lunar Station.* "Holy hell! This guy's from Earth?"

"Not from what he was sayin', he's just coming back from retreat there. Might know something about how the ship works."

"Did the Captain manage to snag him as permanent crew?"

"Aye, I'm sure he'll fill you in on the details. Didn't tell me much." Frost said, sounding as though he were about to pout.

"I'm sure he didn't need you to consult on the trade, but if it makes you feel better I can always make sure you're in the room whenever Captain and I make a big decision."

"Yer kiddin' right?"

"Yup."

Frost chuckled. "Just when I think I'm gettin' on yer good side."

She couldn't help but smile at the exchange as her and her team arrived below the mooring point. She looked at the pictorial directions on the deck and hoped she was reading them right as she pushed a panel open with her foot then tapped a button with her toe. A ramp extended out from the floor all the way up to the three meter wide airlock doors in the ceiling. Railings came up from the sides and after a moment it looked like the ramp had always been there.

"Wow, Earth tech is amazing. Nothing is just for one thing, every space has more than one purpose." Liz, an energetic new hire who she had just met commented from behind her. "It makes the ship feel like it's twice it's size, as if it weren't big enough." She was actually shorter than Stephanie, which was a hard thing to accomplish since she herself was only one hundred sixty one centimetres tall.

"They started this whole space travel thing, I'd hope they have it right by now," another crew member commented.

"Okay, you two get to the bottom of the ramp and be ready to log ID's. Anyone without identification gets put off to the side until the end of each group. I need two more to scan for active weaponry. Take all their ammunition and keep it secure in a storage compartment, there should be a couple in the deck nearby. The rest will walk them to their berth. The teams below have been able to sweep them for explosives, weaponry, dangerous bacteria and other life, but they weren't exactly able to make the beds and sweep the floors. If anyone complains just tell them the *TRF Peter* will be here in two days. They can be picky about accommodations as much as they like with the rescue teams."

Grace Templeton and two other crew members marked as medics arrived at a run, each with a full load of medical gear. "Reporting for duty, bring on the masses," she said, leaning down on her knees and trying to catch her breath. "This place is huge."

"Good to see you. I was just about to say something to the Captain."

"We've been listening in on the chatter from medical. We only have three injured so far, considering the damage the Eden ships did we're lucky to have so few."

"Have you ever done this kind of triage before?"

"Once. A trade convoy was attacked and I was sent along with a rescue vessel. This one is much better so far. Don't worry, I know what I'm doing."

*Thank God someone does.* Stephanie thought to herself as she turned from Grace to look up through the transparent hull. Frost was doing a fantastic job of guiding the damaged space liner in with the tractor beams. It was four hundred meters long but thin. She had seen many of them before and knew that there could be as many as five thousand aboard. "They're not starting small," she said to herself as she ran up the ramp leading to the mooring doors. One of her team followed and took a support position on the other side of the hatch.

The tunnel extended from the Triton and the star liner slowly drifted towards it at a pace of only a few centimetres a second. It slowed down to millimetres by the time it made contact and the mooring frame reported a full on lock with the ship.

Stephanie caught sight of a man in a vacsuit drifting towards an airlock only meters further down the hull. "Liz, go make sure he has a happy landing. I'd hate to see him come through the airlock only to free fall to the deck."

She had one of the other team members replace her in identification duties and ran to where she thought the ramp or whatever receiving device that was provided for emergency airlocks might be and checked the instructions.

Stephanie checked the mooring lock and saw that it was still pressurizing and checking the seal.

Meanwhile, Liz had moved on to another spot on the floor, and with a satisfied nod, slid a panel to the side, pressed her foot down on a button and activated the retrieval system for the emergency airlock. It was a long, flexible tube that extended along a wire frame that came out of the floor so whoever was coming in through the smaller emergency airlock could slide down to the deck at a reasonable speed. Liz cheered for herself, throwing her arms up before stopping and checking to see if anyone noticed. Everyone had, a few chuckled, and she shrugged in response. "Getting new technology right on the first try is worth celebrating. Even with these instructions."

"You're telling me," Stephanie agreed.

The lone entrant came through the smaller emergency airlock and was visible only for a moment before he slid down the yellow tube, causing it to flex and warp. Liz stepped out of the way and the much taller, broad shouldered fellow arrived at the bottom, stopped by a thick pad on the deck. He rolled to his feet slowly and stood up in front of Liz, who looked absolutely tiny compared to the large human. "Thank you very much. I'm Liam," he shook the young woman's hand.

"I'm Liz. I think you're wanted on the bridge if I heard the chatter right."

"Aye, thank you for the safe landing."

"Do you want me to walk him there Stephanie?" Liz asked.

"Don't worry, I can find my way," Liam interjected calmly.

"You've been aboard a Sol System Carrier before?" Stephanie inquired.

"No, but if my guess is right this is like any other Earth ship and it'll show me the way." He looked at the floor. "*Triton*, show me the quickest way to the bridge," he requested.

An arrow lit up on the deck to his right. "Yup, just like any Earth ship. I'll get out of your hair and let you help these people. Thank you Liz." He said with a short bow before jogging off towards the freight express car.

"You're welcome," she waved after him before looking back down at the controls to the emergency airlock. "Now how do I get the tube and everything back in?" She asked herself. A few moments later she tapped another button with her foot twice and the whole yellow tube and its stopping pad retracted along with the wire frame.

Stephanie watched as the doors leading into the starliner parted and the first of the passengers appeared. "Hold there. If you have any weapons leave them aboard or check them at the bottom. We'll be taking all your ammunition so no firing will take place aboard. I'll direct you down the ramp in groups of four. Go slowly, carefully and present your identification to the officers at the bottom. We have basic accommodations for you until the *TRF Peter,* a rescue ship, arrives and you will be led to them as soon as possible," she said through her amplification unit. The ones at the front found the announcement loud, and a few cringed, but she had to make sure she didn't repeat herself too much. She didn't want to lose her voice like she had the last time they performed a rescue operation.

The first groups went by without incident, a few of them taking a second or two to thank her or ask simple questions. After the first nine hundred, which was the longest stream of people she'd ever seen, a gentleman stopped and showed her a pair of pistols. "Lady, I heard your announcement, and I think we have a problem."

"Yes?" She replied with a smile.

"I take these with me everywhere, and I don't go without ammo either."

"You'll have to make an exception here."

"No, *you'll* have to make an exception, missy."

Stephanie simply nodded and pointed to the right of the large mooring doors. "If you'll stand right there while I let other people through so we can discuss this in a minute," she said firmly.

He gave her a surprised look then followed directions, holstering his pistols and crossing his arms.

She let the rest of the passengers through without incident, and the fellow tried to squeeze in with the last of them. Stephanie stopped him, gently touching his shoulder. "Now let's finish our discussion."

"You're gonna let me through with my ammo miss."

"No, I'm not. Ship policy states that only registered crew can go armed," there had been no such policy established, but she decided now was a good time to use her rank and make one. The guard she had brought up with her rested his hands on his rifle, slung across his stomach and chest.

"I don't know what you're trying to prove lady, but-"

"If I had anything to prove, you'd have been on your face ten minutes ago with a hole in your chest." Stephanie stated plainly, her hand on her sidearm. The safety on her own rifle had been turned on and locked, it was slung across her back.

He stared at her for a moment, fuming, before trying to step forward again.

She put her arm out straight and stopped him with her palm. "Your ammo stays here or my scanning team won't let you through."

"My ass they won't let me through," he pressed again.

Stephanie jerked her pulse pistol from it's holster, aimed and fired in one smooth motion. The bolt of energy scattered across his entire body, setting his nervous system on fire momentarily, causing him to twitch violently and fall to the ramp.

In the space of three seconds she had both his weapons out of their holsters and tossed them into the cabin of the spaceliner behind him.

"I was gettin' my identification, I'm with Enreega Fed Law," he said through clenched teeth. The pain of a mid powered stun weapon was unbelievable, and he'd be disabled for at least ten minutes longer.

"I couldn't care less, you attempted to intimidate the First Officer of this vessel, violated our code of conduct and didn't properly announce yourself. You're not welcome aboard." She said as she rolled him back into the space liner.

"You bitch!" He managed to curse through an involuntary twitch.

"You don't know the half of it," Stephanie laughed as she walked out of the airlock and punched the button to seal it behind her. "Frost, you're clear to release the starliner. It's empty except for one giant prick."

"The giant prick didn't fit aboard?" Frost retorted quietly.

Stephanie's irritation evaporated and she chuckled. "He wouldn't relinquish his ammo."

"Ah, all right, releasing the locks on the star liner. How are you for space down there?"

"We've counted eleven hundred twenty nine so far," reported Liz from the bottom of the ramp.

There were a hand full of people left, waiting to present their identification and be scanned and Stephanie quickly counted them. "I'd say we just picked up eleven hundred forty three. That upper berthing is probably getting pretty full."

"All right, we have one more military vessel to dock with." Frost said. "They're coming across in emergency shuttles on our port side, and hard locking with us below. Ramirez will be escorting them in. Captain needs you on the bridge," Frost reported.

"Has Ramirez been taking ammo?"

"Let me check for you," Frost said.

"No, he didn't think of it," interjected Captain Valance. "We should have."

"Well, at least eleven hundred of them aren't-" She stopped on the ramp as she saw a two by two meter storage compartment filled with ammunition and several disposable firearms. It was like looking at a munitions pit.

"Something wrong?"

"Oh, nothing Captain, just looking at enough ammunition to fuel a small civil war. Leaves me wondering if it would have been simpler to make sure everyone *was* armed instead of collecting ammo. Probably would have been faster."

"Well, hopefully the military personnel can help keep the peace for two days. From what we've heard the berths down there are pretty cramped. Twenty eight and fifty six bunks to a compartment and we haven't figured out the sound dampeners or soft isolation systems yet. It's going to be loud and cramped."

"Well, I'll be on the bridge in a moment. I'm taking a team with me so we have security there, the rest I'll assign to keep the peace in the berth we just filled up."

"I'll take my team back down to medical. It's a miracle there are no wounded." Grace said as she turned to leave the gunnery deck. "Computer, show me the quickest route to the main infirmary." She commanded. Arrows appeared to her left on the deck, just in front of her feet and she raised an eyebrow. "What do you know, learn something new every day."

# Departure

The darkened launch bay was property of the Freeground Special Projects Team. Laura was contacted by station security as soon as someone, authorized or not, signed in. It was supposed to be sealed, both of the ships inside weren't in use any longer. They were sealed materials, working prototypes for practical research that were kept safe and undisturbed in case the systems had to be reviewed as a reference.

Laura rushed to the bay, hoping that security had been wrong about who was inside the *Silkstream IV*. When she arrived her fears were verified. Ayan was directing a small loader robot up the ramp into the eighteen meter long, needle shaped ship with a crate of supplies. She looked up from her arm console and stared at Laura.

She looked tired, her vacsuit was sealed up so only her face was visible and her poncho was draped over her with the hood up. "I have to go, I'm sorry Laura," she could barely hear her say as she leaned on a white cane heavily.

Laura sealed the hatch behind her and sent the all clear signal to Freeground Station security. "They'll have your rank for this, the Special Projects Initiative will change."

Ayan ignored every word. "No one's going to get him. No one's taking the trip out there to tell him who he is, how important he is to us, what he's done. Intelligence won't even let me send him a message. They even blocked the ones I thought I got through."

"Regent Galactic has threatened war if Freeground lends aid."

"That's not a problem. The *Silkstream's* transponder's been hooked into *Minuteman*. I can change it to whatever I want whenever I want. They won't know this ship is from Freeground."

Laura crossed the docking bay at a run and followed Ayan up the ramp into the ship. "*Minuteman*? That's not even finished."

"Yes it is. I told him to finish constructing himself and he did. It took him less than five seconds to figure out how then two hours to finish building his processing cluster. I had to deactivate the *Silkstream's* AI, it was slowing him down." Ayan gestured to an unassuming, gray, one meter long case inside the small hold. It was wired into the ships computer system through several panels. "The most powerful calculator is now part of the fastest ship in the galaxy. It's a match ma-" Ayan stopped and coughed, leaning on her cane.

Laura rubbed her shoulders. She was little more than skin and bone. "I'm sorry, I know you loved him."

"I can't forget him Laura. So much of this work wouldn't have happened if it weren't for him, even *Minuteman,* if it weren't for him releasing Alice and us capturing a part of her predatory code inside the quantum core by mistake, none of that would have existed. A molecular quantum core so small and powerful it can even keep me alive a little longer."

"What do you mean?"

"I installed a more advanced framework system and some nanobots into my body. Now *Minuteman* is controlling how they heal me, which fires to put out, which organs to save and how."

Laura could only stare at her friend, imagining the constant pain she must be going through as she walked through the habitation cabin with its small table, two built in chairs and four bunks.

"I'm so tired of sitting around, pretending like every day might not be my last, feeling sorry for myself and wondering if Jonas will ever know where he comes from."

"He wouldn't want you to do this, not for him," Laura pleaded quietly as she followed Ayan.

"That makes him worth it," she sat down in the pilot's seat and started warming up the ship. "I still love him. I tried seeing other people when I was still in shape, you were there. I kept measuring them against Jonas. Now we know where he is, or where he will be. I'm going. You'll have to drag me off this ship to stop me Laura."

She hadn't seen such determination in her friend in years. Part of her was back, the part that mattered. "We love you Ayan. We don't want to see you end up all alone in space or killed in some accident."

"No. You, Jason and Oz love me, I know. That's where it ends. My own mother won't take time out from building her precious colony to spend a few more days with me before I'm gone. In case you haven't noticed, I haven't been feeling very well lately, without *Minuteman* and all this technology I've got three days left at best. Nothing can save me, but maybe I can save Jonas. If he knows where he comes from, that someone is willing to cross the galaxy to tell him, then maybe that shadow of him I see on the Newsnets could find its way. Maybe he could have a better life."

Laura let a few tears fall as she looked into her friend's eyes. "All you've built here, the team, it'll suffer."

"The politics of Fleet Command are doing what they think is right with our work, but there's no focus, no purpose to any of it. It's not really improving anything for anyone just trying to live a normal life on Freeground. They're using it for military and leaking other technology out slowly, so the privileged get first crack at the benefits. What's any of it worth if it can't make us happier, healthier?" she closed her eyes for a moment and let out a shuddering sigh. "Please, I need to see him." Ayan whispered. Her chin was quivering, tears streamed down her face. "One last time."

Laura gently took Ayan into her arms. "Alright, but you're not going alone."

"Oh thank God, I was afraid you wouldn't get here in time and I'd have to stay awake for the next week," Ayan sighed with a little chuckle.

"You know I love you Ayan."

"I know. Love you too Laura," Ayan whispered. "Can I lower my nerve sensitivity now?"

"Yup, I'll take us out." Laura replied, knowing that Ayan must have been in constant pain. It was the trade off for mobility and mental acuity.

Alarms sounded across the Freeground Home Fleet as one of the most advanced ships ever built carrying the most sophisticated combat and logistics computer known in that part of the galaxy launched from a small bay and entered its own wormhole. The *Silkstream IV*, as intelligence would report to Fleet Command later on, was equipped with the first effective combination faster than light drive. Once it entered a wormhole it would generate a hyperspace field around itself, altering its mass and how it interacts with the universe so it could travel many times the speed of light.

Combining wormhole technology and hyperdrive technology had been done successfully on three ships. The first and fastest of which was the *Silkstream IV*, a small prototype, and nothing in the known universe could catch it. At its top speed it was fast enough to cross the milky way in under two months. It would be able to reach Jonas Valent in the Enreega system within days while only expending a small portion of its fuel.

For all intents and purposes, Ayan Rice and Laura Everin were permanently out of reach. Considering they were trying to make contact with the one man they had been forbidden to reach by threat of war, Freeground Intelligence put efforts in place to cover up the incident and disavow ownership of the *Silkstream IV*. All but one restricted copy of its schematics were deleted the next day.

# New Arrivals

The bridge of the *Triton* was alive with activity. Liam was showing the crew members at each post how to access the documentation and training materials for their stations. It looked like he had already educated half the bridge staff already, and had just finished working with Frost when Stephanie walked in. He looked up at her only briefly, too distracted by the massive database associated with the tactical stations. Most of the crew knew the basics of operating their stations but the particulars, the fine tuning and more detailed instrumentation was difficult to access and seemed unwieldy at first. Sol Defence ships were developed in ways that were foreign to most of the galaxy and even though operating them seemed simple and user friendly on the surface, finer details were difficult to grasp without specific training.

Unknown to Jacob Valance, anyone on board, and even Lucius Wheeler, there was a database of tutorials and operation manuals buried in the core software. Knowing where they were, being able to reference them at a moment's notice was making a difference already. The tutorials would help later, when there was more time for the crew to learn independently.

*The difference between a dedicated crew member and a jobber will be pretty obvious soon. I'm going to end up taking tutorials and running practice simulations for months but at least I have a place to start.* Stephanie thought to herself as she walked to the right hand seat beside the command chair, it adjusted to her height and shape as she sat down. She listened in as she checked the ship status screen.

"Whenever you're looking at a system you enter in the code one, two, three and your name and the training directory will come up. Anyone with command access at their station can bring up the information at any time. Passengers and other non-crew will only be able to access the bare minimum. Like entertainment, materializers and how to operate different fixtures in quarters." Liam was telling Ashley, Captain Valance and the navigator.

Stephanie saw a red line leading to one of the generators from the upper berth and brought up the explanation pertaining to the marking. After reading through the details of how to interpret what she was seeing her eyes went wide. "Captain, we have a critical power drain from our generators leading to the materializers on deck nineteen, sections G9 to M12. They're using the materializers for a lot more than food."

Everyone at the helm turned to her. Liam walked across to the diagram she was examining. "Ever take an engineering program?" he asked.

Stephanie shook her head. "Good instructions."

"You're a quick study. She's right Captain, our power reserves are gone and if they keep it up they'll start burning out power lines."

"First Officer to deck nineteen security detail."

"Aye, Leland March here."

"What's going on down there? It looks like everyone is using the materializers all at once."

"They are. Materializer usage isn't free where most of these people come from, so they're making everything from jewellery to toys."

"It's not free here either. We're about to lose power in several sections if you don't stop them."

"Hey, you try stopping eleven hundred people from scrambling for the materializers. Someone just finished making a quarter ounce of platinum and half the place went nuts."

"Oh my God, that must have drawn a tenth of our reserve power," Captain Valance commented as he followed Liam to the engineering station.

"God dammit, if you don't put a stop to it, the whole section will lose power!"

"Then get down here and stop them yourself Steph! I'm not mixing it up with this mob!"

Captain Valance joined the conversation. "Start stunning people if you have to, just break it up."

Liam tried to cut the power to the materializers. The screen turned red, warning against a security violation. "Captain, I don't have access to your systems yet. You'll have to enter me into your systems as a crew member before I can do anything."

Captain Valance hurriedly cleared the security violation. He went on to work at the problem and managed to cut all power to the affected sections. "Okay, now I'll enter you into the system so you can make the changes we need. Just cut materializer usage down to low density food and simple liquids."

"Steph! What the hell did you do up there? All the power's gone and people are going nuts!" shouted Leland.

"Get control! Get their attention and tell them that we'll have the lights back on in a minute. Reassure them, that's all they need."

"I'm getting the hell out of here. Take care of it yourself," Leland retorted.

Stephanie looked to Captain Valance, who nodded. "Take care of it, we'll have the lights back on in a couple minutes."

She started for the main entrance to the bridge and stopped as the massive doors parted. Trade Minister Lorne stood in the center flanked by four soldiers. He was fit, his hair trimmed square and he stood ready with his hand on his sidearm. "When I arranged for you to sign with us I never expected you'd do so well Captain. On behalf of my government and all Aucharians, I thank you. We'll see that you're fairly rewarded, now please transfer command to me."

Everything on the bridge stopped dead except for Liam, who was quickly working to set up a power up sequence that would limit materializer use as soon as the lights, heat and air circulation came on in the darkened sections of the ship.

"Step away from the terminal sir," one soldiers ordered, pointing his rifle at the engineer.

"I'm sorry, we have a riot underway and if I don't turn the lights on innocent people will be injured or killed."

"Fire on him and you will have killed the only man with a solid understanding of these systems," Captain Valance stated. "And then I'll kill you myself."

"At ease Sergeant," Lorne ordered haughtily. "Let the man finish his work." He turned to Captain Valance. "I'll ask you politely, please surrender command to me."

"I'm afraid not, and since when did you have a military rank?"

"I served five years when I was younger, as a high ranking member of the cabinet I carry the rank of General in an emergency. Now, if you would Captain?"

Jake ignored him. "Liam, are the lights back on?"

"Just now Captain."

"Good. Computer; lock down all command functions, release only by senior command codes belonging to Captain Jacob Valance."

"Please verify lockdown," The monotone female computer persona replied.

"Don't do it Jake," Minister Lorne said ominously.

"Lockdown verif-" two of the soldiers opened fire and everyone dove for cover. Captain Valance was shot several times, but there was nothing anyone could do.

Stephanie rolled to her feet and drew her pistol, firing two stun shots at the nearest soldier. They impacted on his armour and had no effect. She flicked the pistol's setting to lethal with her thumb and fired again, catching one soldier in the arm. It burned the surface of his armour, doing heat damage beneath and forcing him to drop his rifle.

The two security officers who were manning the bridge opened fire as well but were gunned down in short order.

The soldier to Lorne's left focused on Stephanie after finishing off the guard behind her. She ran for one of the console seats. The first burst of slim, white hot bolts missed her entirely. The second was closer and by the time the soldier opened up for a third round she was behind the nearest console seat.

The fabric on the chair burst open in a dozen places. Stephanie stared at the little smouldering holes for a moment, feeling like she had been run through by burning needles. Her attempts to breathe brought forth thick gurgles. She could taste the blood in the back of her throat and resisted the urge to cough. Looking down Stephanie saw her vacsuit had been punctured in many places, blood was running down from her throat.

Ashley ran to her from behind her console. "Oh God, Steph. Don't do this to us, hang in there!" she took her hand and gripped it tightly.

Stephanie tried to speak, tried to tell Ashley it was all right, not to worry, it didn't hurt much but nothing would come out.

Frost rushed into sight as well and put pressure on her wounds. The pain was beyond anything she'd known. "Hang on lass, there's a medic below who'll take care of you just fine. Just keep those eyes open." He was so concerned, she had never seen him so desperate about anything.

After a moment she heard Jake's firearm go off several times and then he was grabbing her arm. Punching something into her Command and Control Unit.

"We'll put her in emergency stasis and get her down to a tube. She'll be fine as soon as we can get her to a medical center."

"You've gotta save her," Ashley shouted through tears as the world spun and faded away.

# One Thing After Another

Captain Valance's wounds finished healing as he walked from where his First Officer was quickly sinking into a deep state of suspended animation up the ramp to Minister Lorne. He was so stunned he didn't bother running for cover.

"You were shot at least five times. How the hell are you even breathing?" his voice were panicked, his eyes were wide.

"Bridge, seal all entrances," Jacob called out. The heavy paired doors were drawn into place by the motorized arms and they sealed shut. "I don't know why I'm so disappointed. For some reason I never thought the Aucharians would betray me."

"This is the only combat ready ship in the entire solar system. You don't even have the crew, Jake."

"What about the destroyer you docked with? I'd say that looked pretty functional."

"You mean the half that was left undamaged? We managed to get the engines running after the Eden Fleet caught us fleeing the system."

"So *General* Lorne runs away instead of remaining to coordinate his forces in their time of need. You serve your people better managing matters of finance."

"Most of our fleet was out of the system, going after Regional Galactic assets. Our intelligence indicated that there was no threat, their nearest battle group was over a week away. No one saw the Eden Fleet coming, no one could have."

"So you try to take my ship."

"This is an Earth ship, how could it be yours?"

"That's not for you to question," Captain Valance said as he let go of his throat and took the collar of the uniform firmly in hand. He dragged him towards the front of the bridge, yanking him hard whenever he tried to get his balance.

"Now you're taking me captive?"

"Why not? I need options, and if I can take you hostage for a little more leverage, what's the harm?" The door to the forward observation room opened and he pushed him inside. "Seriously, I'd expect a better solution from you. You're known for striking a good bargain. What the hell were you thinking?" he didn't let him answer, but pressed the manual close button and locked the door. "Computer, disable everything but life support in that room."

"I'm sorry sir, all AI driven automation is inoperable in this section." the computer replied.

"I've got it sir." Frost announced as he moved to the security station, right beside tactical. "Won't be able to use the computers, materializers or open doors. Just put a communications block on the room. Even his own comm won't work."

Captain Valance went back to Stephanie, she had been shot one in the throat and several times down the torso. The punctures were small, but there was a lot of bleeding before he had managed to put her into emergency stasis. He extended his left hand and took a medical reading. "She won't last more than a couple hours like this. Frost, check those rifles and see what they fire."

He ran over and picked up one of the fallen soldiers rifles. "Looks like they use a kind of needle ammo." he checked the clip and opened a small servicing compartment. "The shots are razor thin and low velocity."

"So the needles are probably twisted up inside," Jake concluded. "We have to get her down to medical." He looked to Ashley, who was hanging on his every word while holding Stephanie's hand. "Can you make sure we don't veer off course and check our power levels?"

She just looked at him, her eyes brimming with tears.

He stroked her cheek, wiping some of the wetness away. "Ashley, you need to pilot the ship. We can't help her if we end up smashing into a moon."

"O-okay." She nodded as she put Stephanie's hand down carefully at her side. Ashley wiped her tears as she sat down at the helm beside her navigator, who was shaky at best.

"Medical."

"Yes Captain?" Replied Grace.

"Can you spare a stretcher and two trained people to get Stephanie to the nearest stasis pod?"

"I'll go up now with my best. You're only one express car ride away. What's her condition?"

"She was shot with some kind of needle rounds. There are no exit wounds. I put her in emergency stasis. Sending you the scan results now."

There was silence for a moment as Grace reviewed the results. "She's full of micro shrapnel. You saved her life Captain. Don't know if I can patch her up but I might be able to put her in deep stasis so she'll keep until we can get real doctors aboard." He could hear her getting ready in the background.

"That's what I was hoping."

"Sir, a transit vessel is trying to dock with us. I can't raise them on comms." Cynthia said as she sat back down at her station. She was rattled, had taken refuge under her station during the firefight but was making a quick recovery.

"I see them. They're locking on to a mooring point," Ashley confirmed.

"Get us away from them. We aren't in a position to help." Ordered Captain Valance.

"I'll try, but main engines are offline, I can't force a restart. I'm down to thrusters."

"Do your best. What's going on in engineering?"

Liam shook his head. "We had two power plants running until just a minute ago. Someone's down there shutting things off. We're already on emergency power."

"How much time do we have left at our consumption rate?"

"About three and a half hours, then everything powers down. I can't do anything from here, someone's disconnected the main lines."

Captain Valance scanned one of the guards who were shot during the firefight and shook his head as his readings confirmed complete brain death. "We have to get control of something, let's start there. Frost, make internal sensors your priority. I want to see what's going on."

"Aye sir," Frost brought up the holographic overlay that explained all the internal security station controls as his hand moved over them to help him work faster. "Can't believe Wheeler never trained anyone for this. Someone with a wee bit o' know how would be a saviour right about now." He muttered to himself as he changed the bridge's main holodisplay to a cross section of the ship and brought up another image detailing several of the engineering compartments. The live feeds showed several soldiers working at one of the main power plants.

"Liam, can you do anything to stop them or give us more power from here, anything at all?"

"This ship's hull is one big solar and gravity reactor."

"Gravity reactor? I didn't see any arms out there."

"The hull responds to pressures and shifts in the gravity influencing it and generates power. We could redirect some of that power to the command and life support systems."

"All right, that's a great place to start."

"I can't do it all from here, I'll have to go down three decks, almost right below us."

"Check that route Frost." Captain Valance ordered.

He turned and focused in on the route Liam had highlighted and didn't see anyone stationed there. "Clear, don't know for how long though."

"Ramirez, where are you?" The Captain asked through his communicator. He waited several long moments but got no response. "Can you find them anywhere?" He asked Frost.

He floundered at the controls for a moment, looking for something then his eyebrows raised and he said; "Ah! There you are, little bugger." to himself. Several button presses later he focused in on a dozen people huddled next to the outer hull above the main doors to hangar two. "There's most of them, all sealed up in their suits enjoyin' the view."

"Now how did that happen?" Captain Valance asked as he looked at the image on the main holographic projector. "Cynthia, open a line to Price's private comm."

"Aye sir," Cynthia replied, turning back to her station.

"In the meantime, how are we for avoiding that transit ship?" Captain Valance asked Ashley.

"Not very well, they're keeping up with us fine, the only problem they're having is docking. If I stop manoeuvring they'll lock with us for sure. They nearly collided with us on a couple tries." She was doing much better than just minutes ago. Having something to work at was keeping her mind off her best friend's condition.

"Okay, can you lock them out if they dock, Frost?"

He looked over the control panel again then turned a holographic representation of the ship until he could see the mooring point they were aiming for and selected it. "Aye, I can."

"Good, stop manoeuvring Ash, watch the bigger picture, make sure we're not headed for a bigger collision or worse trouble. Frost, lock 'em out."

"Aye sir."

"I have Agameg Price on the line for you sir," Cynthia reported. "Sounds like he's glad to hear from you."

"Price, what are you doing outside the ship?" Asked Captain Valance.

"Four of the emergency shuttles were filled with Aucharian soldiers. They began firing on us right away and caught Ramirez and most of his team by surprise. I decided we should retreat. I would have told you but our comms were jammed."

"We need to regroup in the command section. Can your people get to the bridge?" Captain Valance walked over to the secondary holographic display where an exterior view of the ship was being shown, it was as tall as he was. He looked at it carefully, turning the image with his hand so he was looking at the command section of the ship.

"We can if we go from the outside."

"Fantastic, make your way almost to the observation room. Just beneath it you'll find an emergency airlock. We'll let you in there."

"Excellent, we'll see you in a minute sir."

Liam opened a compartment under the engineering station and found a tool kit. "I'm glad whoever had this ship before didn't pillage all the supplies," he commented as he walked to the front of the bridge and knelt down.

"What are you doing?" Captain Valance asked quietly.

"I'm looking for the latch that'll open this hidden access panel. There's an entire flight control room beneath us according to the schematics in the computer, the access point to external power generation is there. If we're going to reroute power I'd best get to it sooner rather than later."

"We'll wait for Price and the rest of the security team. I'd rather be safe than sorry."

"Well, then we may as well open things up for them," Liam insisted calmly as he opened the hidden panel and pressed a few buttons. Meter wide sections of the floor turned transparent in a radial pattern underfoot and lights came on below. There was what looked like an entirely different kind of bridge just beneath their feet. Ramps lowered on either side of the bridge for people to move back and forth between.

The holographic projectors and stations turned on, each showing different tactical grids of the area. Stations were set up with high stools, all made to command groups of starfighters, gunships and larger vessels.

"This is a carrier Captain, and as soon as we get things running right I'm sure you'll do something incredible with her. That's why I want to help you get her back in shape," Liam said with a smile. "That is, after you've taken it back."

# The Fastest Indirect Route

"Soldiers, bloody everywhere we turn more soldiers," Grace grumbled as she peeked around a corner to find the last hallway between her and the bridge guarded. "This is the only way to the bridge now that they managed to lock down the primary express cars."

"Unless we go outside," Gary, one of the volunteer nurses commented. He had triage training, which was better than most, and had arrived on the starliner.

"Well, two of us are in vacsuits." Fiona whispered with a shrug. "If we can find one for you we could actually go around."

Gary looked to her wide eyed. "You're serious?"

"Yup, why not? Probably almost as fast."

"She's right. It's not like we're armed or trained for a direct firefight. Going around makes sense," Grace agreed. She walked quietly back down the hallway to a meter wide space between doors. "Show me the emergency escape equipment and facilities in this hallway." She whispered to the computer. She didn't know for certain if it would work, but since she was able to ask for directions effectively before, who knew what else the ship could do?

A meter wide section of the wall behind her became transparent and revealed four flimsy looking white vacsuits and a hatch leading into a tiny escape shuttle. "Does anyone know how to fly that?" Grace asked.

"I flunked my leisure pilot's test four times, but I could." Fiona said with a shrug.

"I've got my certification for mid and small sized interplanetary craft. Don't like those vacsuits though, they look more like a bunch of bags glued together."

"Well, hurry up and get in one," Grace whispered harshly. "We're going for a very short ride." She opened the hatch and passed him a vacsuit. "Captain," she addressed through her communicator. "We have a problem but I've found a solution. We're going to take an emergency shuttle to go around the guards between us and the bridge. How is Stephanie doing?"

"Not so well, she might have another hour," The Captain replied quietly. She could tell he was trying to keep his response from the rest of the crew.

"We'll try to be there quickly. There might be something in the emergency shuttle we can use to stabilize her. Put her in a deeper state of stasis. I can't see us getting her back to medical unless we use brute force."

"Understood. Hurry but be careful."

"Aye sir." Grace followed Gary and Fiona into the escape shuttle and closed the small hatch behind her. The little ship was made for four, and was hidden behind two thick layers of hull plating.

Gary took a moment to look at the controls and the series of manual buttons and switches. Everything was fairly well labelled, but Grace knew she was probably the worst pilot out of all three of them, so she let him get his bearings and concentrated on keeping a watch on the hatch behind them instead of trying to assist, making sure the guards didn't hear something and decide to investigate.

"Everything okay?" Fiona asked.

"I'm fine," Gary replied hastily. "I just don't think there's a way to get this thing going without making a lot of noise."

"I don't think we're worried about that."

"What about fighters? If there are any out there they can just pick us off."

"I don't think we're worried about that either," Fiona said, shaking her head impatiently.

"Did the Captain say if there were fighters or anything out there?" Gary asked Grace.

"He would have told us."

"Ask him anyway? Just to be sure?"

Grace sighed; "Sure, just get us ready. Captain, are there any fighters or hostiles out there?"

"No, nothing offensive on tactical."

"Thank you sir." Grace cut the channel and nodded at Gary. "Okay, let's get this thing going."

"He's sure? It didn't sound like he took time to check."

Grace smacked him in the back of the head with a flick of her wrist. "Get us flying or I'll give it a try!"

Gary turned to the controls and pressed the launch initiation button. "It's going to be loud."

The first section of armoured hull in front of the shuttle split in the middle and drew to the side while the outer layer flipped outward, opening and clanging against the outer hull above it. The four meter thick hardened metal plate's impact made the whole section of the ship vibrate. After three seconds the rear shuttle thrusters fired and they were shot out of its storage compartment. The power came on as Gary started decelerating.

The sound of the forward thrusters firing was deafening as Gary struggled to slow the ship down so they could turn around and head to the command section of the *Triton*.

Fiona looked to Grace, grinning from ear to ear. "We'll have to do this some time when it isn't an emergency!"

Grace didn't agree, the slow rotation of the shuttle was making everything outside spin and she could feel the last emergency ration she ate threaten to make a reappearance. "You know, after being out in space for a while you'd think you wouldn't want to sick up so often."

Fiona's grin lessened a little. "I didn't realize how small this shuttle was until just now."

"Don't throw up back there, it'll get everywhere in zero gravity." Gary said over his shoulder. A moment later he flipped the shuttle end over end to face the *Triton*.

The stars, the wreckage around them and the distant planet moved past the window with blurring speed. To her relief, Grace caught sight of a sick bag just in time and snatched it from the dispenser. Well, she hoped it was a sick bag. Fiona cringed at the sight and sound of her throwing up.

Grace finished before long and dug into her side pocket for a mini injector. She pressed it to her neck and sighed. "Okay, no more of that now. I should have medicated before getting into the shuttle."

Fiona handed her a napkin. "You've planned everything else and come up with more solutions than I can track today. I think we can overlook this little screw up."

"Only if you seal that sick bag properly," Gary muttered over his shoulder.

"Don't worry, it's sealed and in the bin. Good thing I didn't close my vacsuit yet."

"Doesn't it have waste management built in?"

"It does, but its cleaning systems really only keep your eyes, nose and mouth clear. Regent Galactic didn't exactly splurge on us."

"You work for Regent Galactic?" Gary asked.

"I did until Captain Valance took over and hired us on with him. I'm a regular rebel now."

"Good to have you with us. I worked for them for a year, worst year of my life."

"What did you do?" Asked Fiona. The *Triton* was looming larger in the front window.

"Sanitation and recycling systems on a deep space mining station. There were only sixty-one people aboard, but man could they make a mess."

"You were a janitor?"

"I was a janitor in command of a dozen cleaning bots. The only janitor, actually."

"Wow, that sounds important," Fiona replied, rolling her eyes.

"No insulting the pilot during docking operations," Gary grumbled as he rotated the shuttle and turned it around so it faced an airlock just to the right of the bridge. "Did you guys see the boarders climbing along the hull? You might want to let the Captain know about that." He said as he lined the shuttle up so he could back in.

"I didn't see it."

"There were a dozen of them, looked armed."

"Good eye." Grace said as she opened a channel to the bridge. "Captain, we have a dozen or so boarders space walking towards the bridge. They're headed to an emergency airlock right below our mooring point."

"They're ours. They're waiting until you dock then they'll be joining us on the bridge." Cynthia replied.

"Good to know," Grace said as she sealed the head piece to her vacsuit, tucking her shoulder length black hair into it.

Fiona followed suit. "Looks like we weren't the first to have this idea."

"What worries me is the fact that they were armed, what could be in their way that they couldn't fight through?" Gary said as the shuttle made contact with the ship and bounced away gently. "Crap. One more try and I'll get it."

"Do you want me to try?" Fiona asked.

"Shhh. Sane people are driving."

"Hey! I'm uncoordinated, not crazy."

"Anyone who takes the test and fails four times has got to be a little loopy." Gary said as he lined the shuttle up carefully.

"Okay, we have to get focused on what we're here to do. The First Officer needs to be put in stasis of some kind or we have to use nanotechnology to get her stabilized. I don't see any stasis systems in here." Grace said, looking around the small shuttle.

"You're right. Extended life support and a sustenance materializer, but that's about it."

"Take the emergency medical kit under your seat. Every little bit helps."

The shuttle made contact again. This time there were a satisfying series of clicks as it sealed perfectly with the station. Its rear door popped open and they stepped out onto the flight command deck. Grace rushed up the ramp to the main bridge and knelt down beside Stephanie. "You didn't move her?"

"Not a millimetre," Answered Jake.

"Good, there's a lot of damage."

Fiona and Gary set up a stretcher on the other side while Grace took a detailed scan of Stephanie and shook her head. "I'm out of choices here. If we were in main medical deep stasis might be an option, but even then."

"What do you need?" Captain Valance asked.

"Space and quiet. We're going to inject her with mass bio gel and two ounces of nanobots. Whatever weapons they used stirred her up inside." Grace whispered.

"So the nanobots will rebuild her internal organs from raw mass?"

"Yes, but it's not ideal. If this works it might look like she's back on her feet in fine shape but even with recovery meds it'll take at least a day for all of her tissues to properly recover from density loss and her circulatory system could suffer a blockage from any materials left over by the nanobots. These aren't surgical grade nanos we're using here, they're emergency units, quick workers."

"Is there anything else we can do without getting her to the infirmary?" Captain Valance asked as he took a medical scan.

"A deeper form of stasis, but her chance of survival would diminish every minute she spends outside of a full suspension tube. We should treat her here."

"If it's the only way."

"It is." Grace said as she prepared an injector. "Can you open her vacsuit in a few places?"

"I can."

Grace and Captain Valance got to work with Fiona and Gary assisting. Price and his team came running up the ramp and stopped when they saw what was going on. They had to inject bio gel and the nanobots that used it into several different parts of her torso. The millions of nanobots would have to be activated all at once. Until then they would pool near the injection sites, mixing in with the gel they would use to rebuild vital organs until Grace activated them.

When Stephanie had been injected in over a dozen places Grace looked to Captain Valance. He glanced at the results his hand scanner was displaying and nodded. She sent the command to activate and Stephanie's body twitched as they went to work.

She sat back and waited, watching her wrist scanner. Captain Valance watched his own command unit, holding his hand out above her to take constant readings. Her internal organs were rebuilt, vascular system returned to its original condition, and any foreign matter was broken down into usable mass then used to repair bone, muscle and skin.

After a minute Captain Valance leaned forward and compressed her chest rhythmically. "The stasis is failing. Do you have an activator?"

Fiona pulled two tiny pads from her emergency kit and handed them to Grace.

"Oh please Stephanie, oh God please." Ashley whispered as she lowered her face into her hands. She had kept her eyes on her station up until that point.

Grace placed one of the silver pads on Stephanie's temple and the other over her heart the pressed a button on her medical wrist unit. Her body was forced into taking a smooth deep breath, her heart started beating and her synaptic activity was stimulated. Stephanie's eyes snapped open and her whole body twitched. Her arms reached up with a twitch and her hands clutched at the air above reflexively.

Grace turned the activators off as Captain Valance caught one of Stephanie's hands. Even in death activators could force such a reaction from someone who had undergone so much nanosurgery, and Jake was as prepared as he could be to watch the life fade from Stephanie's eyes as the autonomic responses brought on by the activators stopped.

To his relief Stephanie looked up at him, smiled, gripped his hand tightly and said; "I need a bigger gun."

# Hernando Ramirez

Ramirez had staunched the bleeding in his leg and secured the vacsuit emergency seal around his left arm at the elbow. The grenade had done so much damage he knew he was teetering on death. Shrapnel had cut his left leg short at the shin, the other was burned so badly he couldn't move it and his left hand was gone. They had left him for dead but his vacsuit saved him.

He didn't have a communicator, it was destroyed along with his left wrist, but thankfully his vacsuit had an emergency package on the back of his neck and the pain medication kept him awake and the agony was bearable. "Now I know what Finn felt like," he whispered to himself through broken front teeth.

He looked around. In front of him was one of the emergency shuttles the boarders had tricked them with. It looked military, but it had come in from the rear half of a destroyer. Everyone on his and Price's team thought that they were coming aboard for rescue, no one thought they would actually try to seize control. When he woke up and realized that his suit had saved his life, constricting as much as it could in its damaged state and applying pressure to slow the bleeding, it didn't take him long to realize that he was alone. The pain meds had already started flowing through his system, another thing to be thankful for. Emergency nanobots had done what they could, but there was too much damage.

He did his best to remember what he had left. A working brain, right arm and the will to do something, anything to stop the boarders. Ramirez rolled his eyes around, craning his stiff neck a little to get a better view of the large hangar, then he spotted a working communicator on the wrist of a nearby corpse. He pulled himself to it with his right arm, it took forever to cross less than two meters.

He was just about to contact Captain Valance when he heard a hatch open, followed closely by three more. Another escape vessel must have landed, and he heard the sounds of boots hitting the deck. The troops he could see from his vantage point were checking their rifles and taking a moment to muster. After falling into ranks they started running to the lifts. *Oh no you don't,* he thought to himself.

He opened a private channel with Captain Valance. "Captain, decompress hangar two. You have at least forty more boarders on their way." He caught sight of a few of them running by. None even noticed him.

"Ramirez? We thought you were killed."

"I'm fine, I'm secure. Just flush these bastards out into space."

"I don't see you on our internal systems."

"I'm secure. Flush 'em out."

"Brace yourself." The main hangar doors opened quickly, several meters per second. Air rushed out and anything not secure was pulled with it.

"It was an honour Captain," Ramirez managed to say into the communicator before it was ripped out of his hand. He tried to grab hold of a landing strut as he slid by at an increasing speed and missed it.

His body turned as he skidded across the floor and he could see the doors wide open, the darkness of space beyond. It had been years since he had looked at it for what it was. Distant stars, billions of them out there, glimmering.

In the space of a short life he'd seen over a hundred worlds, more cities, and met even more people. On the *Samson* alone he had seen people come, go, die, and survive with him. His acquaintances became friends, his friends became loved ones and before he knew it the *Samson* was his home.

He crossed over the edge of the launch bay and drifted out into space. The bitter cold embraced him as his body turned. Pain killers made the cold a distant sensation. The *Triton* loomed. *Make her a home Captain, make it their home.* He wished as his sight faded and his body became absolutely still.

# Rash Acts

"Ramirez? Ramirez!" Captain Valance shouted into his communicator. He spun on his heel. "Frost! Close the hanger bay doors and look for him. Cynthia, find out where that communication came from!"

They set to work as Captain Valance looked to the front of the bridge, where the field of stars in front of the ship was displayed.

"I can't find him sir," Frost reported. "He's not coming up anywhere and I know I'm using this right."

Cynthia turned in her seat. "The transmission came from hangar two. I double checked. The signal went dead shortly after the doors opened," she said quietly.

Captain Valance ground his teeth and balled his fists, standing motionless, looking out into the stars beyond the drifting wreck of a defensive station in the distance. "You have the bridge, Commander." he said as he strode towards the observation room door.

Stephanie looked around and realized no one else knew what he was talking about when he referred to a Commander. The new engineer had gone below the bridge with Price and his team, and there was no one of that rank in place that she knew of. Instead of questioning it, she sat down in the Captain's chair and watched as Jake punched in the entry code for the observation room and strode through.

"I guess you're a Commander now. Congratulations?" Frost whispered from her left with a shrug.

"I hope he doesn't do anything a medical kit can't fix," Ashley's copilot said quietly.

Minister Lorne looked up at Captain Valance as calmly as he could. He looked furious, yes, but it was held in place by cold discipline. Jacob Valance was an imposing man when he wanted to be, and when he slammed his fists against the top of the conference table he jumped in his seat.

"I'm done here! After taking on this heroes mantle for your people you come aboard my ship under the pretence of need and try to take it for yourself?"

"You're a hunter, a glorified repo man. If you weren't so good at it I'd never know who you were and I'd be none the worse for it." Lorne said haughtily. He was putting up a brave front but his eyes were shifty, it sounded like he was reciting a rehearsed speech. "The Minister of Defence sent me to commandeer this ship. We can offer you fair compensation at a later-"

"Don't try to reason with me, we're way beyond that. You have three options right here, right now. You can command your forces to obey my orders, you can tell them to leave by the quickest route possible or you can take a trip out the airlock!"

He stared back at the Captain, feigning calm. Lorne's lip twitched, there was sweat forming on his brow and he rubbed his palms together slowly.

"Did you people really know what kind of bastard you chose to heft your banner?" He shouted in full fury as he reached across the table, grabbed the smaller man's jacket and hauled him out of his chair. Jake turned and dragged him across the table like a rag doll, striding through the door with him in tow behind. He moved so fast the Minister couldn't catch his feet.

Lorne struggled to get his balance, but Jake flung him out in front of him. The Minister rolled and came up on his knees. There was no chance to defend himself before the muzzle of Captain Valance's sidearm was up against his forehead. "Spacing's too honourable a death for you. This is better. I love what this gun does to people. One minute they're just standing there, the next they're cut in half, or staggering around headless before their bodies realize their brain is gone," he said in a malicious whisper. He flicked the safety off and he could hear the power cell charge up with a high pitched whine.

A small, panicked sound escaped Lorne's open mouth. He was breathing quickly, staring widely at the handle of the heavy sidearm. "Oh God," he whimpered.

"I've done this before right in front of these people with a dead cell loaded, it won't surprise them if I pull the trigger and you disappear from the neck up," he tilted his head to one side. "Much."

"We need this ship, Regent Galactic will take advantage of this opening." Lorne blubbered, his resolve had cracked, his hands were up and he shook visibly. "I was following orders, only following orders."

"This is my ship. People have died because of you and your choices. If you don't put your soldiers in line behind me I'll lose even more. Think about it for just a second. I'll kill you, then I'll go get my cloaksuit. Your soldiers won't see me coming as I start murdering them one by one. It won't be a battle, there won't be a seconds worth of fight to it. I'll just start killing until Regent Galactic decides to board. Then I'll start on them. Murdering one after another until I'm alone in a wasted hull piled with corpses! Starting with yours."

"O-okay, I'll command them to take your orders."

"Betray me and I promise you won't leave this ship alive," Captain Valance flipped his safety on and holstered his sidearm. "Stand up and take a few deep breaths. I don't want you sounding nervous when you give the order."

Stephanie moved to the seat at the right of the command chair as Jake turned and strode to the Captain's seat in the center. They both watched Minister Lorne as he tried to calm himself, taking deep breaths and folding his arms after realizing his hands were still shaking. After several minutes he looked to the Captain and nodded, straightening his jacket.

"Sit right here," Captain Valance ordered, pointing to the seat at his left.

He walked to the chair and sat down. From a pocket he produced a communicator and opened a channel.

The face of an armoured vacsuit came up on the two dimensional display after a moment. "Yes Minister?"

"Your orders have changed Major. I'm placing Captain Valance in command. He's a more able commander than I had expected and will work in our best interests."

"Minister?"

"That's an order. Pass the word down the line. The *Triton* is Valent's ship. I'm legitimizing his capture."

"Yes sir, right away."

# Cleanup

Captain Valance let Liam's plan to connect the exterior solar and gravity based power systems to the command section go ahead. After that was finished Liam was able to proceed to main engineering for the first time since he had come aboard. All eight of the reactors had been shut down or disconnected from the main power grid. If it weren't for their fading emergency power the *Triton* would be adrift, helpless.

When Agameg Price returned to the bridge with his security team he boggled at Minister Lorne for a moment before regaining his composure. "The Aucharians have stood down and two squads have gone to the upper berth to aid with crowd control."

"How are things there?" Asked Captain Valance.

"Not as bad as I had thought. Once Leland and his group were pressed out of the compartments and the lights came back on the situation calmed down. A few people fell through the deck where the plating was damaged and I've sent Grace to help."

Stephanie looked a little surprised and smiled at Agameg. "Good work. So things have calmed down?"

"Yes, they are wondering when help is coming though, if they will be transported to another port so they can continue on to their final destinations. A few were bound for this system in particular, and are unsure of their fates," he said sadly.

Captain Valance looked to the Minister, who was staring straight ahead. "Do you have a contingency plan in place?"

"We were going to use your ship and anything else that still had power to ferry survivors into the outer system until a battle group could get here."

"How far out are they?"

He hesitated before answering. "Five days."

"We have the *TRF Peter* en route, they'll be here much sooner."

"Do you realize the debt that will incur? My people can't afford that kind of cost while rebuilding."

Captain Valance ran his hand down his face and laughed ruefully. He brought up the scan results of Enreega's surface using the control panel on his chair. "There are two cities still burning, several sunk and two are nothing but dead hulks drifting in orbit. You're worried about cost?"

"No one's going to help us rebuild for free. Independence comes at a great cost and most of that can be calculated in credits," he protested quietly. "These rescue ships come with a high price tag, they're in it for the cash as much as anyone else."

"There's no market to manipulate here. Your people are dying and you have to make sacrifices to save as many as you can. How much it costs is besides the point."

"You have no idea what you're talking about."

"You might be right, politics don't interest me and I'd probably be out of my depth if I tried to run for office. You're on equally unsure footing, Minister. Remember, you're on my ship, a captured Sol Defence vessel that's run by brutal discipline and faith."

"Faith? You're joking."

"My people have to have faith in each other and in my decisions. Otherwise there would be chaos. If one of us fails and survives we must have faith that everyone has learned from their experiences. Faith is at the core of this crew, if it wasn't that would leave money and fear and these days I can't afford to use either as often as I used to."

He sat staring blankly, straight ahead, only nodding once to acknowledge what Captain Valance had said.

Jake looked to Cynthia, who had been watching the entire exchange with interest. "Open the comm ship wide please," he asked.

"Yes sir, the channel is open."

He stood up and looked at the Minister. "This is Captain Valance. We are beginning repairs and will be underway to the Pollanis System as soon as possible. The *TRF Peter* will follow if we leave before they can meet with us. We can't stay here any longer than necessary. We don't know if the Eden Fleet will return. While repairs are underway I'd like anyone who would like to join the crew of the *Triton* and has qualifications to send their information to the bridge. Keep it short. If you have children aboard, please be aware that this is a ship of war, and I won't want to put the young in harms way.

I can't offer you a great deal of payment, but the *Triton* is a city unto itself with manufacturing equipment, plenty of living space and a purpose. The Aucharian Military has been defeated in this solar system and after undergoing repairs in a safe location the *Triton* will be heading into the fight. We'll interfere with Regent Galactic's supply lines, liberate slaves, profit from their loss and make ourselves scarce. We will strike from the shadows, disappear in plain sight and become the three thousand souls that cost them billions.

It is essential that any Aucharian soldier who doesn't want to participate in rebuilding this ship and working towards the same goals disembark from the *Triton*. Return to your emergency shuttles or the destroyer docked then leave. If you aren't invested in our purpose, you don't have any business aboard my ship. Civilians who don't wish to remain may stay with us until we reach the Pollanis System."

Captain Valance signalled Cynthia to close the channel and looked to Minister Lorne.

"You're going after Regent Galactic? That's insanity."

"It's the best game out here, Minister. Anything with less than sixty guns won't have a chance against us and between the members of my existing crew we know the trade routes, the underground, and even a few other ships who would gladly join up if they knew we had their flank. I could start a fleet of my own if I like."

"These people are untrained, only refugees and deserters."

"The ship can train them, and if they don't measure up we'll leave them somewhere safe. In case you haven't noticed, this is a modern vessel with simulator visors, reconfigurable consoles and it's wider than it is long. There's plenty of room to train five hundred, maybe a thousand people at a time during normal operations."

"You don't have the time, putting the ship under Aucharian Fleet control and collecting military personnel from the system for a crew would be much more effective."

Captain Valance opened a private comm line. "Liam, how are our reactors?"

"I can get three online within the next four hours. It doesn't look like the other five have been activated for about eight years. I'd like to do a more thorough check on them before starting them up. I heard your speech by the way. I'll submit my qualifications right away."

"You're hired. How is our cloaking device looking?"

"I'm having a couple of your more diminutive crew members reset the aft emitters and check the plating. It should be all set in about an hour. We won't be able to use it until we get a reactor online though."

"Thank you Liam, we'd be dead out here without you."

"My pleasure captain, just working on these machines is reward enough."

Captain Valance closed the line. "With a working cloaking device this ship turns into an invisible city."

"I'll watch the Newsnets for your execution. Regent Galactic is far more cunning than you give them credit for with more resources than you could imagine. If they can't find you they'll go after your crew through their families and friends. Then they'll force them to betray you."

"We'll be ready." He turned to one of Agameg's security team, a tall brown haired woman holding a heavy pulse rifle. "Escort the Minister to the brig. Make sure you search him thoroughly. Don't leave him with anything. No devices, no jewellery, and not a stitch of clothing. "

"Yes sir," she guided the Minister to the rear of the bridge, smiling at him.

"Go watch. Stay out of striking distance and keep your weapon trained on him." Captain Valance instructed another female security team member.

When Minister Lorne and the two guards had left the bridge Captain Valance sighed and looked at Agameg, who smiled uneasily.

"A day that will live in memory," said the issyrian. The fine, thread thin tendrils beside his mouth puffed outward for a moment. The only parts of his face that didn't look strange to anyone outside of his race were his lips and his eyes. The lips were thin, but much like a humans. His eyes were completely different, however. They were wide, deep or bright green depending on his mood and much larger, but their expressiveness was always easy to read. When he looked nervous they were almost completely O shaped. When he was concentrating they formed into wide slits, and when he was nervously trying to comfort someone it was somewhere in between, just like the expression he was making in that moment. The bright green tint of them told the Captain that Agameg was unsure, nervous. When the thin issyrian was relaxed the colour normally darkened, but they could also be a deep shade of green when he was tired.

"Have a seat." Captain Valance said, gesturing to his left.

Stephanie looked up from the small control panel and holographic projector built into her chair and smiled at Agameg for a moment before it drew her attention once more. "Are all these applicants Cynthia?" she asked.

"They are. We're up to about eight hundred now including the military. Should I filter them or just send them to you?"

"I'm filtering them here. The variety of applicants we're getting is amazing. Some of them are from the starliner, others are from the escape shuttles. There are even specialists and highly educated people here."

"Good, work with Cynthia to choose people for each department. We'll need everyone from technicians to reserve pilots."

"Oh, if you find any washed out pilots or gamers, send 'em my way. They're crap in the cockpit, but gold in a gunnery turret." Frost added from the security station. "And track someone down to help me here, security *and* tactical is a wee bit much."

Captain Valance and Price moved to stand at the same time. "I can try sir. These systems look interesting and I've already worked with them a little," Agameg said.

"Go ahead," Jake invited. "How is that docked transport doing?" he asked the helm.

"They're still locked onto us." Ashley reported.

"According to my readings they still have full life support. It looks like they're just clinging on for safety," said the fellow at navigation.

"Or they're out of food and water. What's your name, by the way?"

"Larry Nevil. I was brought on as navigator when Wheeler got his deal from Regent Galactic. Before that I was navigator aboard the *Cestrio*. It was a long range customs pursuit ship that was damaged in an Aucharian attack."

"He's one of the good guys sir," Ashley said, smiling at him.

"Good to have you aboard. Sticking around?" Asked Captain Valance.

"Aye sir, if you'll have me. Living aboard this ship is better than living on a customs frigate or even a diplomatic cruiser. Even if it doesn't pay as well. Get a few shops and restore the botanical gallery and we'll have a real town square."

"What's a botanical gallery?" Ashley asked with interest.

"On this ship it's a big space that used to have all kinds of plants and animals from Earth. There were paths going between them and a few different levels. I started working on it in my spare time using some of the seeds in storage. I didn't make much of a mark though, just the center part alone is huge."

"After we get the ship repaired we'll have people work on it on a voluntary basis. It would be good for morale." Captain Valance put in as he started looking at a security screen. "Is this right, Frost?"

"What's that sir?"

"It looks like a lot of emergency shuttles are powering up."
"That's right sir. Hangar two is the busiest place on the ship."

# The Changing Of The Guard

Lawrence held on to his mother's hand as he watched the first of the shuttles depart. He was mesmerized by the sight of the little ships powering their engines up and lifting off from the deck. Following the directions of the Aucharian soldiers who waved their arms up, to their sides, down and all around. He tugged at the collar of the child sized vacsuit Liam had brought them while they were in the racks. The man didn't stay long, just for a minute, but he liked the older fellow, seeing him made him feel safe. His mother wore one of the vacsuits as well. "When are we going Mom?" he asked.

"We'll be on one of the last ones. Your dad is waiting for us on the *Darian*."

"Is that his ship?"

She knelt down and looked at him face to face. "No, it's a ship that helped him when he escaped from his space station."

"Is Liam going there?"

"No, he has to stay here."

"Why?"

"Well, there are a lot of other families who need his help. The people on this ship need him too because no one knows how it works better than him."

"This is a ship?" Lawrence said, his eyes wide.

"Yes, it's one big ship."

"The whole thing?" he asked in disbelief, thinking of how long it took them to get from the smelly, messy bunk rooms all the way down to the hangar deck even using the fast express car.

"This whole thing." Shelly said with a smile. "And they're going to go help people just like us."

"And they need Liam?"

"Yes they do."

"Should we stay and help? Maybe dad could come too?"

"No, we need to go visit your Gran again. She misses us and wants to see all of us this time, even your dad."

"Oh, can we come back and visit Liam?"

Shelly laughed a little and stroked her son's cheek. "You like him, don't you?"

He nodded.

"Maybe some day, but not for a very long time. He's going to be very busy and very far away for a few years. I'm sure you can send him a message when we get to Gran's though. He might like that."

"Okay."

An Aucharian soldier walked over to them and smiled. "We can load you on the next one. We're loading it with everyone going to the *Darian*." *s*he said, holding her rifle across her armoured chest.

"Thank you," Shelly replied, standing up. "Let's go Lawrence." She took his hand again.

They walked across the hangar around other groups on their way to board shuttles made for four, six, eight and twelve. As they drew nearer it became clear they were being loaded onto one of the larger military boarding shuttles. "I thought these would be reserved for your people," Shelly said to the soldier as she picked Lawrence up in her arms. He was getting a good look at the big dark grey ship.

"Most of us are staying. After seeing what Captain Valance can do with a converted cargo hauler and what's left of Enreega, we want to see what kind of fight he can put us in with the *Triton*."

"Good luck. I hope things work out," Shelly said as she moved up the line.

"I have a good feeling about this ma'am, you'll hear about us again," she replied with a smile. "You take good care of your son and tell Tanner that Junior Lieutenant Eccleston says hello."

"You know my husband?"

"He was my commanding officer during my tour aboard station four. I wish he was coming with us but with you two around, I can see why he's moving on."

"I'll tell him. Take care of yourself."

"I will."

The last of the passengers loaded onto the boarding shuttle and Junior Lieutenant Jane Eccleston made sure the hatch was secure before signalling the temporary deck crew. "Only nine left, then we get to lock this hangar down until the Captain has a use for it again," she said into her communicator. "Let's keep this accident free."

"Ma'am, the Captain's on the line for you," reported one of her soldiers.

"Put him through."

"You're on with him now."

"Captain Valance, I'm Junior Lieutenant Jane Eccleston. Our commanding officer has returned to the destroyer *Verant*, I took over."

"Good work getting a deck crew organized. I'm impressed."

"Thank you sir. My platoon prides itself on it's ability to improvise."

"We received your qualifications, I'm impressed. When you're finished down there I'd like to see you on the bridge."

"I won't go up unless you take all of us. Only three are returning to the *Verant*."

"Done. We need you. Captain Valance out."

"Sounds like we've got a new boss." Her communications officer said.

"Listening in again Sherman? You're going to have to drop that habit, Parsons put up with it while he was in command, but I won't," Jane sighed and signalled another shuttle sealed and ready. "Put the rest of the platoon on the line, they should hear this."

"Aye." The transparent display inside her visor showed that all thirty six members of her platoon were listening in a moment later.

"I've spoken to Captain Valance. We're all welcome to join the crew," Jane said, smiling to herself.

"Thank God, I was afraid we'd be on the run," Said Kari.

"That's good news, too bad we lost a few," added Frederick.

"Finally, some action!" Shouted Stephano.

"Another day, another outfit," commented Marion.

"So we're going to actually get to work now? Not just inspect and polish for twelve hours a day? Finally," complained Marcus.

"Having six shape shifters in the platoon probably informed his decision a bit."

There were a number of other comments of approval and a couple wise cracks that overlapped and Jane couldn't help but grin as she watched the last pair of shuttles slowly drift out of the hangar.

"Quiet down, let's hear what we've signed up for," Sherman said over everyone.

"I'm headed to the bridge to speak to the Captain in person. I expect he'll break us up a little, on a ship like this that's bound to happen, but we'll all be inside the same hull, fighting the same fight. I need everyone to be on their best behaviour, to do their best work. From what I've seen of the *Triton,* she's a mess, and we'll have to train while we make repairs."

"Looks like half this stuff has been dormant longer than I've been alive." Commented Nathan, her second in command. "And they added a few sections of ergranian steel that have been expanding unchecked for a while. It's going to be interesting trying to work that in. I've seen sections where the metal has grown right around cables and piping."

"I'm going to find out what we can expect from Valent, what kind of experience he has with a ship this size, if any." Julie continued as she stepped into an express car. There were three other people inside, one was Nathan, the other two she had seen helping on the hangar deck. "I'll update everyone once I know more, until then keep your eyes open for orders and directions from *Triton* command. I get the feeling that Captain Valance wants to pull things together fast. Eccleston out." The channel closed and she looked to Nathan.

He was an issyrian just like her, and held a human shape as well. It made most people they worked with more comfortable. "There's barely any crew to speak of, glad we're here."

"Aye, it's better than going back to the *Verant* and trying to make a go of that wreck."

"Do you think he'll break us up?"

"I would. Two thirds of us are damage control specialists, the other third are security with extra training." Julie said with a shrug.

"I wouldn't. I mean, everyone in the Platoon knows their way around repairing just about anything. Even Stephano can put a power transfer board together in his sleep and when he signed up a year ago he could barely plug in a space heater."

"We'll see."

"You two are headed to the bridge?" Asked an older gentleman. His wispy grey hair and well kept but his old, loose fitting vacsuit spoke of an age beyond either of the soldiers.

"Aye, our platoon is signing up. We're an emergency repair and recovery unit, thought we'd fit right in here. Junior Lieutenant Julie Eccleston at your service."

"Good to meet you, I'm a shuttle and fighter technician. Used to work out of Station Three but got off just in time with about half my deck crew. Name's Angelo Vercelli."

Nathan grinned at him. "I thought I recognized you. You're signing up with your team?"

"Aye, me and my second here, Paula." He gestured to a younger, much shorter, slim woman in a similar vacsuit.

She nodded with a forced smile. "Long day."

"You can say that again," Julie agreed as the doors to the express car opened.

They walked across the broad hallway to the massive main doors to the bridge. As they approached heavy arms drew the thick armoured doors out and apart to reveal a sight unlike any of them had ever seen.

The main bridge of the *Triton* with the lower deck revealed seemed complex at first. There were a dozen stations along the walls and as many distributed throughout the room on each level. The clearly visible deep brown pathways on the floor leading to each station in a radial pattern also indicated where one would expect substations to be, where extra staff could help with regular operations. The space around the pathways was transparent deck plating, showing a tactical command center for fighters and larger vessels that was just as large and well equipped as the main bridge. Near the head of the bridge was a ramp leading down to the lower level on either side.

On the front wall there was a two dimensional display that took up most of the space there, to its right and left were doorways you could barely distinguish from the rest of the black walls. In front of the helm there was a large hologram of the *Triton* itself. Shaped like a large stingray from earth, it had three massive engines at the rear, and two nearer to the center of the underside. A pair of extra engines were built into the aft port and starboard ends of the ship. The overlay on the hologram detailed where work was being done, how many refugees were still aboard, where they were, and showed that a large transit ship had docked with them without permission. It's blocky hull hung off one side of the *Triton* like some kind of parasite and was coloured red to indicate it was an unwelcome guest.

The command seating in the center of the bridge was set atop semitransparent flooring and was five meters across. The captain's chair was in the center with two seats on either side. To their surprise an issyrian sat in the Captain's seat, looking over a holographic directory tree. "The Captain and his First Officer await you in his ready room," the watch officer said in a pleasant tone, pointing to the door on the left. He was wearing a black armoured vacsuit unlike any they'd seen. It was sleek, form fitted with extra impact resistant sections over top, there were no visible seams and by looking at it they couldn't even determine for sure how one would remove the transparent oval faceplate. The design was simple and looked more efficient than their own, bulkier infantry armour.

The group of four walked down the short ramp that led into the bridge and followed a radial path down the side of the compartment. Everyone knew they could just as easily walk on the transparent section of the deck, but it seemed to make sense to follow the meter wide opaque paths that were plainly laid out, even though it forced them into single file.

The heavy ready room door was drawn aside to reveal a modest office. The wall behind the Captain was transparent, showing the field of stars and an edge of Enreega beyond. One of the smouldering cities was just barely visible on its blue surface. "-long to figure out the lighting system. It's measured in lumens until you set it on a different scale," the Captain was saying as they walked inside.

"Okay, that's strange though, everything else I've run into is on a scale of ten or one hundred," replied the brown haired woman sitting on the Captain's desk. She was half turned towards the door.

They were both dressed in black vacsuits, not quite as well armoured as the one the watch officer was wearing. The material looked perfectly flexible and fitted to their forms, only two to five millimetres thick. They were sealed all the way up to the neck, leaving only their heads exposed.

"One thousand lumens is about the right starting point for a room like this." Commented Angelo. "I usually set cockpit lighting down to four hundred, keeps the instrumentation nice and clear."

"You're Angelo Vercelli," The younger woman said, dropping from the desk to stand up straight, her knee high combat boots clomped against the deck. She offered her hand. "I'm Stephanie Vega, First Officer here on the *Triton*."

Angelo shook her hand. "This is my second in command, Paula Mendle."

Stephanie went on to shake her hand, then looked to Jane and Nathan. After introductions were made all around, she sat back down on the edge of Captain Valance's desk.

"It's been a very long day for everyone, so I'll get to the point." Captain Valance started. "*Triton* needs you, I need you. We're in bad shape and automation is failing across the ship."

"That's probably our fault, Captain. We disconnected the power in engineering as soon as we boarded," Jane said with a nod. "Under orders."

"I understand, but that's not the primary cause. When the former Captain put the automation in place he had to disable all the internal security to make it workable. Now that we've started bringing some of that back on line it's interfering with the automation."

"How long has this ship been automated for?" Asked Nathan.

"Almost forty years from what I've been able to see in the logs." Stephanie said. "They ran the ship with a crew of about one hundred."

"That's a lot of automation."

"Aye, no wonder you're having trouble taking control," Angelo agreed.

"So you see our problem. We need organized teams in place to start working on the critical systems, exploring the ship and establishing a chain of command."

"Have you ever commanded a ship this size before, if you don't mind me asking sir?" Asked Jane.

"Have you heard of the *First Light*?" Captain Valance asked, looking across the group.

Angelo looked startled for a moment then took a closer look at the Captain with a smile slowly spreading across his face. "I thought I recognized you. Captain Jonas Valent. I always wondered what happened at Starfree Port."

"Could you fill us in a little old timer?" Paula asked peevishly.

"Right. The *First Light* was a Freeground ship. An old carrier with an ergranian steel hull and a third of the armaments she was made to carry. They sent her out with a green captain and some kind of special crew from what anyone could determine. Under the command of their Captain, Jonas Valent, they managed to take out a carrier twenty times her size called the *Overlord II* before running off to repair at a nearby station. After she finished repairs, they took out another carrier and a few destroyers single handed and turned up at Starfree Port. Not long after that she just disappeared. Just a few weeks ago was re-dubbed the *Sunspire* and put back into service. There's a whole documentary on this now, but I remember the holocast of your tousle with that Triad Consortium Carrier and the four or five Vindyne destroyers. Man did they want you after that. What happened? I'm itching to know."

Captain Valance soaked in every word of Angelo's retelling, trying not to look surprised at someone else knowing more about his past than he did then nodded solemnly when he was finished. "I went into hiding. I can get into the rest of that some other time. What's important now is that we get things in line, make the ship safe and ready."

"Aye sir, after what you did with that ship, I'm with you." Angelo said without reservation.

"My platoon will take care of your boat for as long as you're willing to take the fight to Regent Galactic." Jane said with a smile.

"Thank you. I'm putting you in charge of all the Aucharian soldiers aboard, coordinate with my First Officer and Chief Engineer, Liam Grady." Captain Valance told Jane with a smile. "Your objectives are to ensure the peace is maintained and that no one strays into the sealed sections of the ship. Help with the repairs if you have time, but limiting access should be more important for now."

"Yes sir."

"Angelo, I'd like your team to start clearing the hangars. Put anything not in use in storage and get them ready for incoming ships. I don't know what we can expect out here, or what we'll need other than clear space. If you could inventory what we have that would be good too, but it's not top priority."

"Aye sir. I'll get my people together and we'll start in hangar two."

"Thank you again, for the purpose of clarity I'm designating Jane as Security Chief, and Angelo as Deck Chief. Welcome to the *Triton*." Captain Valance said with a smile. It was reciprocated by everyone in the room except for Paula, who didn't look quite as sour as she did when she first entered the room.

The new crew members left, leaving Jake and Stephanie alone in the room again. "Lucky," Captain Valance said quietly. "We're very lucky."

"That platoon is responsible for getting the *Verant* operational again. That's pretty good work for a destroyer with a slagged front half."

"Notice how they didn't say anything about the Minister?"

Stephanie thought for a moment. "You're right. I guess they like government about as much as anyone."

"That helps. He'll be a perfect pawn."

"What for sir?"

"Regent Galactic. I'm expecting them any minute now. If we don't have to use him when we meet up with Regent, I plan on using him next time we meet up with the Aucharians."

Stephanie smiled at him. "I'm surprised at how lost he seemed, like he'd never been on this side of a desk."

"Politicians, they earn their rank through popularity, not qualification. I doubt he actually did anything resembling hard service."

Stephanie's smile subsided and she looked out the window to the distant planet.

"What's on your mind," Jake asked gently.

"Being First Officer. On the *Samson* it means something completely different. I look at manuals more than anything and outside of security I have no idea what I'm doing. I shudder at the mention of engineering, that whole section of the status display is a mystery to me. I don't even know what DERA system is and we have eight of them. They take up a tenth of the ship."

"They're diverse energy reactor assemblies and can turn almost any material or force of nature into raw power or use high yield fusion if you have the right staff. The three Wheeler was using were set to run on dense materials like uranium. Cheap but dirty and inefficient."

"See? All I really know about uranium is that you're not supposed to handle the stuff outside a suit."

"Stephanie, you've been working with me for what, four years?"

"Coming up on five, sir."

"It's your decision making process I want in that chair. Everything else you'll learn through questioning and experience. Just do what I do when I don't know something, ask, delegate and make sure whoever you left in charge is making the right choices."

"If commanding a ship like this were that easy I would have seen a few more of them out here. As it is, I've only seen maybe half a dozen military carriers in my life."

"You'll have second chair on this one if you stick with it," Captain Valance said invitingly. "Give it some time, use it as an opportunity to learn, lean on the people you trust." He stood and put her hand on her shoulder. "At the core of it all, you're First Officer because I trust you."

"Thank you sir. I'll do my best."

"Captain, we have a problem. Five Regent Galactic ships have arrived at the system outer limits," Frost reported over the comm. "And I'm still the only one manning tactical."

Captain Valance walked onto the bridge and took the command chair with Stephanie close behind.

Price was already on his way to helping Frost at the tactical and security stations. "At least I had half an hour to go through the general tutorial," he said to himself. "It seems simple enough at a glance."

"Wait 'till you start looking a little deeper an' try doing somethin' that's worth doin' right. Then we'll see those eyes go as round as saucers."

"You'd think you'd be rooting for me."

"You've got a point there," Frost said with a nod as he brought up their missile and torpedo inventory.

"Liam, how are my reactors?" Captain Valance asked through the intercom. He waited a minute, looking at the tactical screen. "Liam?"

"Aye, here sir. We could bring them online, I'd rather have another twenty minutes though."

"With hostiles in the area we don't have the time. How about our cloaking systems?"

"They've been reset. Any misalignment or other problems have been corrected, theoretically."

"Good. Give us some power."

"All three reactors will be online in about two minutes. It won't be as clean as I'd like, but that can come later. Liam out."

"Pardon me Captain, but unless I'm mistaken we won't be able to enter hyperspace, use shields or effectively cloak as long as we're docked with that transport," Agameg Price said, pointing to the main holographic display.

"God dammit, have we been able to communicate with them at all?"

"No sir. I've been trying everything, even the hard line through the mooring point," Cynthia reported.

"How many souls aboard?"

"One hundred seventy one sir," Frost reported.

"Fine, take care of it Steph, we should have done something about that an hour ago."

Stephanie was out of her seat and on her way off the bridge, opening communications to Jane and taking a pulse rifle from one of the four bridge guards. "Chief Eccleston, send two squads of armed units to the port mooring hatch. I'll assume direct command once I get there."

Captain Valance took a closer look at the tactical display then brought it up on the main holoprojector. "There's a gravity shadow there, but the sensors aren't picking up anything else." He adjusted the scanners to focus in on a space right behind the five destroyers and switched between different sets of readings.

The silhouette of a three tiered octagonal ship with long girders extending from each corner appeared. "That's new," he said to himself. The holodisplay marked the main body as nine kilometres wide, each extended arm was an additional twelve kilometres.

It appeared to all spectrums of light, on all scanning systems with a sudden burst of light and the holoprojector showed the outline of a magnetic field over twenty five hundred kilometres across extending from it in all directions.

"I think we're a little out gunned sir," Frost said quietly.

"That field, it must be how it collects power," Price added. "It's rotating so it's facing the star."

"Wouldn't that endanger the ships around it?" Asked Ashley.

"It's not much different from the magnetic field the *Samson* and most other ships generate. Only instead of redirecting small particles around the ship it collects them along with solar radiation, this ship has a similar, but much smaller magnetic scoop system," Captain Valance replied. "With those arms it could probably project an even bigger field if it had to."

The reactors powered up and on the secondary holographic display systems across the ship started turning yellow and green. "Ashley, pilot us towards the nearest moon. I want it between us and that ship as soon as possible."

"Aye sir," Ashley acknowledged with a smile.

"Are you sure you're ready to fly the *Triton* under full power?" Asked her copilot in a hushed, nervous tone.

"Yup, I just got certified."

"How long ago?"

"Tuesday, I think."

"You're kidding, right? Tell me you're kidding."

"Shut up and watch for surprises," Ashley said as she began accelerating, rotating the ship towards Vallestra, a nearby rocky moon.

"Incoming system wide communication from the command ship," Cynthia reported.

"Put it on the tertiary display."

The holoprojector on the left side of the bridge switched from its extended tactical view to the familiar image of a Regent Galactic representative complete with perfectly pressed suit and neat haircut. "This is the Regent Galactic Vessel *Kraken*. We received news of the tragedy that has befallen you and made haste to this system. Our search and rescue ships are deploying now, please remain where you are and wait for our teams to make contact. You will not be charged for our services, though we ask that you have your insurance information ready. If you are in immediate danger, please contact us as soon as you are able." The hologram started repeating the same message and Cynthia muted it.

"This isn't exactly what I'd call ideal," Captain Valance said to himself. "They might think Wheeler is still in command. So if they don't make contact in the next few minutes we might be all right if we can get into hyperspace."

The massive ship's three layers began to separate, growing in height. Smooth, white, five segmented ships began emerging. Each one scanned as one hundred ninety meters in length with several turrets and docking interfaces. Other, more utilitarian vessels began to launch from the three eight sided hangars, heading out in all directions.

The *Triton* was almost behind the cover of Vallestra, its rocky blue and grey surface was looming larger on the smaller rear view projection under the taller image coming from the main holoprojector. "Stephanie, how are you doing with that transit vessel?" Asked Captain Valance.

"Just popping it open now Captain, stand by." She replied into her communicator as the meter and a half wide airlock doors opened. Unlike the mooring port in the gunnery deck this one had a broad hallway leading to it. Stephanie felt much better with a hallway around her and eighteen armed soldiers behind.

A sweating, exhausted looking wiry woman stumbled through the hatch. "Thank God! What's wrong with you people? We docked in an emergency and your system didn't even lock onto us. We had to jam the mechanism so you couldn't shake us off!"

Stephanie levelled her rifle at the woman, it was set on high stun. There were several irate passengers behind her. "We aren't equipped for search and rescue and our power was out. We would have informed you but we were unable to communicate with you."

"Our comms were down."

"We tried the hard line. All you had to do was turn the intercom on."

"Oh, well none of us did that! No one told us! Can you help us or not?"

Stephanie lowered her rifle and signalled the soldiers behind her to do the same. "Yes, but follow our orders or we'll confine you. Do you understand?"

"Nice, fine, whatever."

"Leave any weapons with these guards here," Stephanie directed towards Liz and a much larger male soldier. "Then follow our directions to our upper berth. It isn't much but you'll be able to get food and water out of the materializers and you'll have somewhere to rest until we can make port."

The passengers started coming through the airlock and Stephanie helped direct them out of the transit ship. It was a flimsy vessel with a lot of transparent metal. The seats and floor looked old and misused, the passengers looked tired and wilted.

The haggard woman stood beside Stephanie as she made sure that the passengers didn't rush through the airlock. She didn't lift a finger to help, just stood by watching the disembarkation. "What was your destination?" Stephanie asked as the last of the passengers came through.

"We were bound for the *Palimino* when it was destroyed. A whole city ship, just sunk. Then those little ships came along and nearly killed everyone. Luckily they only damaged our engines and destroyed our communications. We were able to catch you with thrusters, though you were no help. Your ship kept veering away."

Stephanie shook her head, unwilling to get sucked into another argument. A soldier closed the outer then inner airlock. "All right, time to cut it loose. Do you have a remote system or command code?" Stephanie asked.

"What do you mean? That ship is my responsibility, I can't just set it adrift."

"You have to. If you don't we can't go into hyperspace."

"What? You're not staying and helping anyone else in the system?"

"Like I said, we're not equipped for that so we're going to the nearest port and we're going to drop you off at an emergency center so they can take care of you. Now just decouple your ship and we'll be-"

"What kind of people are you? First you play keep away when we try to dock, then you don't let us in for four hours, now you want me to dump my ship while you leave the system without helping anyone else? This ship is huge! There must be room for thousands aboard! You must have a crew and medical facilities!"

"None of that is any of your business, just take it on faith that we're not ready to help and release your docking system, please." Stephanie said as calmly as she could manage while talking over the woman.

"I can't! Weren't you listening? We jammed it so you couldn't just shake us off and leave us twisting in the cold!"

"All right. Go with the officer please. He'll show you to a bunk."

"What? What about my ship? Are you going to do something to it? What are you going to do?"

"We'll rip it off like the scab it is! Now get your ass down the hall before I stun you!" Stephanie snapped.

The soldier grabbed the frazzled woman by the arm and nearly had to drag her down the hall.

"You can't do this! That's Transit Authority property!" she yelled before giving up on Stephanie and turning to the guard, who was guiding her towards the upper berth where the rest of the refugees were being taken.

"You handled that well," Liz commented quietly.

"Until I threatened to fire on her."

"She wasn't being reasonable. Can't blame her much though. Who knows what she lost in the attack."

"You're right. I just can't wait to get out of this system."

"What are you going to do about this ship?"

"Well, I'll seal this hall off at this end and leave it up to the Captain. He might have to send a crew out to cut it loose."

"That makes sense," Liz grabbed an end of the full trunk of weaponry and ammunition while her larger counterpart activated the gravity lift. It hovered a few inches off the deck and she pushed it in front of her with ease. "My uncle used to drive transit. Said it was exciting for the first week, but after that it was the most boring thing he'd ever done."

"Did he quit?"

"I think he's due for retirement actually. He's been at it for about thirty five years."

They passed under the emergency pressure door closest to the airlock and Stephanie sealed it behind them. Liz looked up at her and smiled. "Well, on to the next issue. I've been on stims for three hours, wee."

"I was nearly killed on the bridge and feel like I've slept for a week ever since they brought me back from the brink. I'm sure we'll get a chance to sleep after we're in hyperspace."

"Stephanie, why is that ship still attached to us?" Asked Frost through the communicator.

"They jammed their locking mechanism so we couldn't shake them off. Everyone's out though, so if the Captain wants to scrape it off he's clear to do so."

"Alright, I think he's got a solution. Thanks Steph."

# The Clever Dream

Alice and Jonas sat in the darkened cockpit of the *Clever Dream* watching the wormhole emergence timer count down from two minutes. "I wonder what he'll say when he sees you?" Alice asked quietly.

"I hope it's something like; 'oh, hi. The more the merrier.' and not something like; 'there can only be one! Die impostor!'"

Alice laughed and shook her head. "Well, either way, it's going to be interesting to finally meet him. He's made an impression in this part of the galaxy. Must be in the blood."

"He made a bigger splash than I did, that's for sure. I couldn't imagine a life of bounty hunting, repossessions and everything else he's on record for."

"I could see you doing the privateering." Alice said with a smile. "You'd make a great pirate."

"Okay, maybe, but privateering is different that piracy."

"Right, someone gives you a bazillion digit number that says you can destroy and steal stuff that belongs to specific companies and governments instead of you just going off and doing it without permission."

"See? Completely different."

"I guess. We're coming out into the Enreega system," Alice said as the timer counted down the last five seconds and she took the controls.

They emerged into regular space and immediately adjusted course to avoid a large section of hull drifting nearby. "Check the tactical screen."

"On it." Jonas said as he looked over a holographic representation of the area around the planet Seneschal. He jerked in his seat as the image of the octagonal appeared along with the dozens of ships it was launching. "Holy hell! Looks like Regent Galactic is here, and they've been busy. There's a command carrier here that beats pretty much everything I've seen for volume and mass." He looked around a little more. "Something really bad happened here, there's wreckage everywhere with various signatures, even a bunch of Eden Fleet ships."

"I hope we missed the main event," Alice muttered as she guided her course to a nearby moon and engaged the cloaking device. "We're down to about fourteen percent fuel, the constant attack the *Clever Dream* maintained while we were escaping really cost us."

"I'm sorry my estimates were a little off after taking a tour of that strange ship's brain," Lewis interjected.

"Don't worry, you still saved our butts, but we should start plotting a jump out of the system. I don't want to be around here, cloaked or not."

"Yes Alice, but I think you might want to focus your targeting reticle on the ship ahead, you might find it very interesting."

Alice looked through the targets ahead and selected the Sol Defence ship. "The *Triton*?" she said to herself.

"That's Wheeler's ship."

"The Freegrounder who betrayed you?"

"Yup."

"But it's not registered to him. My target information says it was just captured by Jacob Valance as a war prize, legitimized on an Aucharian letter of marque." Alice said with a wide grin. "Oh my God, how did he take a carrier?"

"Oh hell, how am I supposed to top that?" Jonas said with a chuckle as he focused the scanners on it.

"You got the girl, remember?"

"Right, here's hoping that's holding true. It looks like they're trying to hide behind that moon while they take people on from a smaller ship."

"Lewis, open a channel, make sure he only sees me," Alice requested.

"Our cloak will be ineffective while we're transmitting," Lewis reminded her.

Alice flipped three switches to deactivate the cloaking system. "No need to waste fuel."

"Opening channel."

"*Clever Dream* to *Triton*. This is Alice Valent, requesting permission to land."

A moment later Jake Valance's face came up on her secondary display, smiling uncharacteristically. "I can't believe it, we were just about to go. Could you do us a favour first?"

"Name it."

"Pick that transit ship off our hull? Don't worry about it's condition, just don't expect to clip it off easily, it's hard docked to us."

"I have fantastic aim, don't worry."

"All right, after it's clear, land in hangar two."

"See you there."

The channel closed and she armed her pulse cannons.

"I still can't believe how much he looks like me. I mean, I know he's a version of me built around a materializer frame, but it's like looking into another dimension, seeing the dark version of yourself."

"You think you're confused? Imagine the look on his face when he sees *you*." She locked on to the smaller ship and angled her guns parallel to the hull of the *Triton* then opened fire with a burst. Half the vessel flew into pieces, the thin hull came apart like paper. She fired one more burst, closer to the *Triton's* hull and cleared all but the docking port away. She sucked air in between her teeth as her last pair of shots deflected off of the *Triton's* armour. "That's gonna scorch." She cringed. "Good thing it's superficial."

She flipped the *Clever Dream* end over end and started a long turn that brought them in line with the open hangar on the underside of the much larger ship.

"Reunion tiiiime," she announced with a smile.

"Can we enter hyperspace?" Captain Valance asked the helm.

"Our profile is clean enough sir, as soon as the *Clever Dream* is aboard and the hangar doors are closed we'll be good to go," replied Larry from navigation.

The bridge was dead silent as everyone watched the main holographic projector display the *Clever Dream* landing in hangar two. As the sleek, black ship decelerated and touched down, the hangar doors slowly closed behind it.

They sealed. "Get us out of here," Captain Valance ordered.

Ashley increased throttle to maximum as Larry started the hyperspace particle emitters and the *Triton* was moving faster than light in a matter of seconds. There was a collective sigh of relief on the bridge as the realization that they had made it out of the area sunk in.

# THE VIEW FROM THE TOP

The Communications Lounge aboard the *Kraken* was pleasantly busy that afternoon. There were many well dressed men and women going about their business remotely, contacting their posts through micro wormhole assisted transmissions and hyper bursts as they pored over prospect data on the Enreega System. It was a boom time.

The white and red booths and round tables filling the thickly carpeted space were the offices of the Regent Galactic Development and Product Deployment employees. They were the elite, the ones that generated the big projects, chased down the prospects that kept billions of peons in countless subsidiaries and contracted partners busy.

Few had the opportunity to mix in if they weren't among their number, to walk up to the bar and have a complimentary unrationed drink, or to stand and look through the transparent wall at the top of the *Kraken* and watch all those rescue and utility ships go about their business. It was a monarch's vista with a rich water planet in the distance and the wreckage of thousands of vessels scattered across the busiest area in the system. The pickings were ripe for those who knew how to best take advantage. Cities were just waiting to be rebuilt, there was a well trained displaced work force looking for new jobs, and those rescue ships would soon be filled with people wondering where they'd be sleeping.

The citizens had little to worry about. Rebuilding the Enreega system and the cities on the planet Seneschal would take years, possibly decades, but everyone would have plenty of opportunities and living space while the work was under way. They'd work under contract, have plenty of jobs to bid on and when it was all done they'd have great cities to live in and Regent Galactic would take care of all their needs for a price balanced against maximum market tolerance.

These things were of little concern to two gentlemen sitting beside one of the massive two storey tall windows facing the moon named Vallestra. A quick flash of light marked the departure of what their attentions were drawn to. "What do you think the problem was?" The short one asked. He wasn't just stout, he had the appearance of a boy not yet in his teen years.

"Who knows? We performed perfectly. The code was sent but Wheeler never acknowledged it. Were there any reports from our agents aboard?" Meunez, the taller of the pair, asked before taking a sip of his drink. The ice rattled in the bottom of the glass as he brought it up to his chapped lips. He wore a blue Freeground style vacsuit and a flight jacket that made him look even thinner and more sickly than he was.

"None, and there was no evidence of jamming on the bands we'd expect them to use. It is a waste to have to send the termination code though, that's what bothers me most," Lister Hampon said, he looked truly remorseful.

"Perhaps he was injured?"

"Maybe, it's just as well. His chances of success weren't very high. It's that ship, we weren't allowed to give him the crew he needed. It wasn't in the budget. Too bad too, research and development had a field day with it before we gave it to him."

"Do you think he realized that the compound we built into him is an explosive?"

The younger of the two shrugged, causing the shoulder pads built into his suit to touch his ears. "How could he? It's part of his body chemistry, built right in at the bottom of his major femurs. All we did was signal his nervous system to start the intermix process, in an hour or two he'll be seventy five kilos of high explosives. We told him it was lethal though, so he had every incentive to reply to our signals."

"Will it explode right away?"

"It's random, any time after it goes active. Could be an hour, could be a couple minutes."

"Ah, those research and development boys love their games. What are the symptoms?" Meunez asked, clearing scraggly hair out of his face.

"He'll have a fever, it'll get worse until he's sweating profusely, then his blood will stop coagulating. His orifices will start to leak as it thins out and his heart starts to pump faster to finish the intermix, then he'll die. The healthier he is the faster it works, that's one certainty."

"Nasty. Remind me to file my T-74's on time next week," he chuckled.

"Oh, they don't use this stuff on us. They'd just disavow our involvement and put an unbelievable bounty on our heads. We'd be fugitives everywhere."

"I could imagine."

The younger of the pair stood and ran his hand through his sandy blonde hair. "Well, Jake Valance is still out there, we have to send something out to try and get control of him so I released the last of our subjects captured from Starfree Port and activated the last copy of Wheeler. He's been working as a miner for a year or so, out of the way."

"Should we tell the new one about what happened to his predecessor?" Asked Gabriel as his eyes flicked and focused to something else for a moment before focusing on Hampon again.

"Why not? I'm sure going after his ship will be a good incentive. Wheeler's profile also suggests he's a big believer in revenge. Too bad he's the last one."

"Speaking of duplicates, how is the new body working out?"

"Great. I just wish my old one held out a few more years. Taking advantage of the more attractive Saved ones is nigh on impossible with this appearance. Still, I can't complain. I have almost half my memories and another lifetime ahead."

Meunez's face twitched and his eyes squeezed shut for a moment.

"What is it that you're doing that has you so distracted?"

His face relaxed and he sighed. "Interfacing with the Holocaust Virus. We are teaching each other wonderful things."

Lister's eyes went wide. "That's not wise, you're far too close to your micro-core for that to be even remotely safe. The Virus could actually access your human brains' input output systems."

"Yes, that's the point. To create a new virus that no machine can predict. The changes it affects in me are equally impressive. I've finally felt the emotions of a machine first hand."

"You gave the Holocaust Virus emotions? It's not supposed to be a true AI!" Hampon whispered urgently.

Gabriel nodded slowly, grinning. "No one's seen anything like this and the more time I interface with it the more it becomes its own being. Version two will be ready when the galaxy learns how to defeat version one."

"What about the list of Saved and West Watchers?"

"They will be safe. Your recruitment drive won't have been wasted. If a cult of the rich and useless is what you want, then that's what you'll have."

Hampon couldn't help but smile, conceding the point. "It's true, most of them are only good for their possessions and positions. A few are shaping up well though, the West Watch are growing in number and power. We even have a flourishing militia formed out of military deserters. Most of them even believe that if they are killed they will go to the East in the afterlife, to Eden itself. Are you on schedule to meet with Collins?"

"Yes, I hope I get to see the Holocaust in action for the first time."

"I hope it puts the virus he developed to control the Eden Fleet to shame."

"It will, oh it will," Meunez said with a twitch and a sigh. "Even Alice would be impressed with this new life."

The hologram of Meunez faded away and Lister Hampon left the lounge to board his private cruiser. It would take him to the first site of the Holocaust Virus mass infection, where he and many of his followers would witness the event that would validate his Cash Messiah Cult.

## DUALITY PLUS ONE

Angelo and Paula stood in hangar deck two looking at the *Clever Dream*. The ship's engines were cooling, sending wisps of steam out from the rear of the vessel, a light contrast to its glossy dark hull.

The sleek black lines and low profile were a sight to see, it was in perfect condition. Several soldiers flanked the Deck Chief and his assistant. "That's one nice ship." Angelo said before letting out a whistle. "They only built fifteen hundred of that model."

"Sticks out like a sore thumb. Probably have ship thieves coming at them every time they set down," Paula commented.

Their team and the qualified recruits from the starliner who had signed on to his crew with the approval of Stephanie, Cynthia or Captain Valance had finished clearing debris and other serious obstructions from hangar two. They were working on setting the *Samson* up on gravity lifts so they could move it to long term storage. The sounds of Angelo's team leaders shouting directions was a constant in the background.

"Whose coming to meet them?" Paula asked.

"Captain and his First I think."

The main gangway lowered and extended from the middle of the *Clever Dream*, it was a long, two meter wide ramp. A young woman with curly brown hair wearing a beaten up black leather flight jacket over a light green vacsuit came into sight first. She was joined by a man who looked almost exactly like Captain Valance in a black vacsuit and long coat that looked a little lighter than the one he had seen hanging off the back of the Captain's ready room chair.

Paula cocked her head for a moment. "Huh," was all she said before walking off to help with the *Samson*.

"Captain?" Angelo asked tentatively at the fellow coming down the ramp. His attitude seemed so much lighter, he was even smiling brightly. "I wasn't aware you'd gone off ship."

"I'm his twin brother, Jonas," he said, extending his hand and eyeing the soldiers.

Angelo shook it and then shook the young woman's hand. "Good to meet you, Chief Vercelli at your service. What's the condition of the *Clever Dream*?"

"Good, low on fuel, so if you have any Xetima on board I'd appreciate a drop. I'm Alice, by the way."

"Nice to meet you. I'll see what I can do about your fuel situation, but I can't guarantee anything other than charging your capacitors up for you. We're still getting the Decks in line."

"Thank you. Are we meeting the Captain here?"

"Aye," Angelo looked over his shoulder and saw the main express lift arriving. The heavy double doors parted with a grating, squealing sound that made half the deck hands cringe. Captain Valance and First Officer Vega stepped out. "Here they are now."

"Negative five on the rear struts! Come on!" Paula barked at the crew working on lifting the *Samson*. Everyone in hangar two could hear her piercing voice, normally barely loud enough to hear. As she shouted directions there was no way you could miss it unless the main lift doors were opening. Which sound was more shrill was a growing debate.

"That's my queue to get involved. Pardon me." Angelo said as he walked towards the *Samson*.

"It's like these knuckle draggers have never done this before!" Paula shouted at Angelo as he started crossing the hangar.

"That's because most of them haven't. Give them twice the instructions and four times the time and it'll get done," Angelo shouted back. "Whip 'em, hound 'em and they'll just *do* without thinking."

If Captain Valance was at all confused or surprised by the sight of Jonas and Alice he didn't show it as he and Stephanie closed the long distance between them. Stephanie's resolve was held with military discipline as well, only her gaze was focused on Jonas distinctly.

Even when she tried to look somewhere else, she just couldn't help but examine the man. He was physically smaller, not as well muscled, seemed fairer somehow, lighter, and his demeanour was completely different. It was like looking at a version of Jake that had experienced a much less stressful life.

Alice couldn't contain herself. Despite the confusion of having the real Jonas Valent at her side and a copy in front of her, the copy was the one she had saved. The one she had promised to come back for and the one she dreamt of finding for years. It really was like she was looking at her father figure, especially considering there were so many similarities between his methods and her own. As he walked through the middle of the soldiers she couldn't help but close the distance at a run.

He caught her, and even though verification his greatest fear was standing not twenty meters away, it still felt so good to hold his daughter in his arms. "I looked for you. In every sector we passed through, every time we made port my ship's computer scanned for you," he whispered to her.

"I'm so sorry I had to leave you but it was the safest thing for you. We were sure they'd catch us and saving you would have been for nothing." She wrapped her arms around his neck and squeezed. Understanding the relief, the joy she was feeling didn't matter. Somehow this reunion was more satisfying than the surprise she had when she found Jonas days earlier.

"All that matters is that you're safe. Even if you are his daughter and not mine, I'll never see you as anything less," he kissed the side of her head.

She drew back and looked into his eyes. He absolutely loved her like a daughter. To him she was his only family, his blood, and he was completely invested in the idea. It struck her heart, brought up a flood of emotions that made her head pound and took all words away. He loved her, unconditionally and so utterly that she could see it in his eyes, in his gentle smile. She had never seen that directed at her before, not anywhere from anyone and a black fear lived under all those feelings that when he discovered the truth his love would disappear.

At the moment she was incapable of anything but crying, and with a deep shudder she laid her head on his shoulder. He held her close and rubbed her back with care. "I'm so sorry," she sobbed.

"It's okay, you're here, we have time."

They remained that way for a while, and Jonas eventually crossed the distance, introducing himself to Stephanie first. "Jonas Valent, I'm his brother," he smiled.

Stephanie smiled back and shook his hand. "Stephanie Vega, the First Officer here. I didn't know Captain had a brother."

"Sometimes I think even he forgets." Jonas' subdermal communicator received a message from Alice's mental transmitter. It was so garbled that it came through more as a collection of musical notes. He shook his head.

Captain Valance and Alice parted, and he offered her his white scarf to wipe her tears away.

"I couldn't use that," she said, using her sleeve instead. After a moment she looked at Jonas, he could see her concentrating.

"Don't tell him about me. I'll do it myself." Came her mental communication, much clearer that time. He assumed the earlier failed attempt was due to emotional interference.

"Yes, well, maybe we could take this somewhere more private?" Jonas said with a nod directed at the express tube.

Stephanie turned on her heel and led the way back the way she and the Captain had come. "Security detail dismissed." She ordered to the soldiers standing around them. They turned and led the way to the large cargo elevator. "There's an observation lounge a few decks up that we haven't seen yet."

"You haven't had this ship long?" Jonas asked.

"Just a couple days. Most of the crew are refugees and deserters from the Aucharian Government," Jake replied. "With their home system in pieces they didn't think they had much to go back to." Jake pointed over his shoulder at the *Samson* with his thumb. "That's been my core ship for the last five years. It was a gift. Turns out it served me well."

"I almost didn't recognize it," Alice said, looking across the hundred meter distance at the battered cargo hauler as the deck crew hovered it soundlessly up a ramp through an interior hangar door that was almost not wide enough. "What are they doing with it?"

"Putting it into storage. One of my crew detonated a one megaton equivalent electromagnetic pulse bomb on the deck beneath it. The *Samson* won't be running until someone does some serious repairs on her."

"He saved my life when he set that thing off. Wheeler was just about to put an extra hole in me," Stephanie added. "Gave us the upper hand for just long enough to get things under control."

They stepped into the large cargo express car with a dozen soldiers in tow and after the screech of the doors closing made everyone cringe it elevated several decks in the space of a few seconds, opening up to reveal what looked like a common room. The lights came on closest to them first, illuminating two meters at a time down the two hallways in ahead. There were three sofas, a couple small tables and chairs with scuffed markings on the floor indicating emergency hatchways for escape craft and maintenance crawl ways. It looked like one of the more used sections of the ship, but was covered in dust.

"This looks like the entrance space to a berth," Jonas said as he stepped inside. "Fighter pilots I'd say."

"Looks like. The schematics for this deck outlines one third as living space for pilots and deck crews. The rest is an observation deck and the highest point in the hangar storage." Stephanie said, looking at a small holographic representation of the deck coming from her wrist unit.

Alice was looking on with interest. "I'd hate to bunk up there," she pointed at the rear wall, where the schematic detailed a part of the hangar lifting system.

"The observation lounge is this way," Stephanie directed to the hall running left, towards the bow of the ship. "Do a sweep of this berthing. I want it cleared for the deck crew by the time they're ready to turn in. When you're finished make sure you inform the Chief his people are assigned here," she ordered the lead soldier before starting down the hall. "We'll clear the observation lounge," she finished with a crooked grin.

"Yes Ma'am."

They made their way up the broad hallway, avoiding one cleaning robot that was vacuuming its way up the side of the hall. "I guess the robots turn off when the decks are dormant," Alice commented as she wiped her finger across it's flat, round top. It was as thick with dust as everything else. "Must be nice to have them aboard though. I don't know what I'd do without the cleaning systems in the *Clever Dream*."

"Your ship has cleaning systems?" Stephanie asked enviously.

"Sure does, takes care of almost everything."

"There were days when I wished the *Samson* had something, anything like that. We had to vent the halls once to prove a point."

"That was Frost," Captain Valance corrected. "I was off ship."

"Yeah, cleaned the dust out of the corners though," Stephanie said with a chuckle at the memory.

"We also lost a few tools in that impromptu clean up. He still owes me for that."

"But it was funny! Everyone got to their bunks like he told them to, but no one thought he'd actually do it. People cleaned up after themselves a little more after that. I think some of them lost a couple things they left lying around."

"Sounds like the *Samson* was an interesting place to be," Alice commented.

"For me, but I like a good firefight and Captain kept the jobs coming. We must have gone through a couple hundred people in the time I was aboard though, between people who just left after a while and others. It was a rough life."

"So you're keeping the *Triton*? Going to keep her crewed up?" Jonas asked.

"I am," Jake answered mildly. "Everyone needs a bit of training except our Chief Engineer, but the computer's got the information they need to start."

"Are you going to run them through simulations? I've found virtual trials are a great way to get a crew in shape."

"I was just thinking about that actually. It's writing the scenarios I'm not looking forward to, and I don't know whether to do it one department at a time or run people from all of them through at the same time."

"I'd say you should run everyone not on duty once a day during hyperspace, just for a couple hours while they're off duty. We did something similar with the *First Light* but time was always a problem. She was well automated but had a skeleton crew. Didn't feel like it though. Running a ship with a couple hundred souls aboard is still a big challenge."

"I know, the *Samson* was easy most of the time. I had no problem staying on top of things. I'm hoping that the people we've put in charge are good at their jobs." Captain Valance concluded.

"I'll do my best Captain," Stephanie reassured as she checked the status of the compartment ahead on the door control panel leading to the observation lounge.

"I'm talking about our new Chiefs, you're the one I'm hoping picks up any really big problems."

"Well, with security I know I'll be able to tell if things are going right, but with engineering and the hangar decks? It's hard to be sure," Stephanie said with a shrug as she opened the double doors leading into the lounge.

The lights came on to reveal a furnished room with a view facing outwards from the front of the *Triton*. The floor in front of the entrance was decorated with a silvered skull with the words *Deploy, Dominate, Disappear* written around it. "Well that's a squadron motto to remember," Alice said, looking down on it.

"I think that might just be something I'd like to keep. Maybe even duplicate in other parts of the ship," Captain Valance said as much to himself as anyone else.

The rest of the observation lounge was much like the common room, only with a bar at one end and many more tables. There were a few weathered sofas and other seats around as well. Overall, the space looked well used and if it weren't for the dust one would expect a group of pilots to walk in any second, returning from a patrol.

"Should we leave these guys alone and see what else we can find?" Alice asked Stephanie.

"I actually have to get back to the bridge, make sure the next watch is settling in. Come with?"

"Sounds like as good a place to start the tour as any," Alice said with a shrug.

The pair left and Jake led Jonas to the bar, where he stepped in behind and Jonas sat down on a padded stool. "Guess Wheeler didn't like this part of the ship much," Jonas commented as he looked around.

Jake looked under the bar for a moment and came up with a bottle of scotch.

"Ashton Mill brand, aged fourteen years, bottled forty six years ago."

"I'm game."

He pulled two glasses out from behind the bar and sprayed them with a small water hose that sputtered a moment before focusing into a clean jet. "I'm surprised. You'd think Wheeler would move in behind the bar," Jake said plainly as he poured two half glasses.

"Cheers." Jonas said as they clinked glasses. "I couldn't even begin to imagine how blind sided you feel right now. I would have sent you a message but the *Clever Dream* moves faster than most transmission services."

"I saw the wormhole exit point. That's a nice ship."

"It is, Alice has done well for herself."

Captain Valance took a second sip of scotch and swirled the amber fluid in the glass, watching it, unable to look at Jonas. "Is she mine or yours?"

"That's a difficult question to answer."

"Oh?"

"Well, if you were to test her DNA you'd find she's not even related."

"So she's adopted."

"I'm not supposed to tell you any of this. She wanted to say so herself, but I know she's scared. I know I would rather find out right away than be surprised later."

"By?" Jake asked, trying not to sound impatient.

"When I was seventeen I bought the best artificial intelligence I could find. It cost me a year's savings and I customized her, left her on my arm for almost seventeen years. She saw everything. I talked to her as though she was my best friend, and she was." He didn't give Jake a chance to say anything, just pushed on through it. "When I was in command of the *First Light* we ran into trouble. Some of my senior staff and I were captured by a super carrier owned by Vindyne."

"I've heard of them."

"I had built a switch into Alice after a few years of having her, where I could turn off all the limitations imposed on the cores of artificial intelligences. I don't know why I did it at the time, maybe I thought she had the right to make all her own decisions one day, but years later when we were captured I let her loose through their wireless network. She ran rampant and from what she's told me she absorbed some predatory programming and used the systems on that carrier to force herself into the emptied mind of a woman who was about to be programmed as an unwilling colonist. She was a former prisoner, a murderer with a few fragment memories left, but Alice got through it. A few years later she went after you thinking there was only one of us and got you free. Vindyne, or rather, a few people left over from that company have been after her ever since."

Jake just let it sink in for a minute, looking through the transparent section of hull out into the blue and white starry haze outside.

"She sees me more like a brother, we grew up together. When she watches footage of your captures, the speeches you gave for the Aucharians, it's different. She looks up to you, it really is like she's looking at her father, a mentor."

"She shouldn't. I come with an entirely different bag of trouble. I've only been alive a few years and I can't count the number of enemies I've made. Most of them are counting the days until they get out of prison. Some day there'll be a couple hundred very bad people on the roam with one eye looking for my face."

Jonas looked at the other man, he was brooding, quiet. "Hey, you saved my butt when you were minutes old. Everything that's in my head was in yours when they brought you out. Somehow you managed to delete, or suppress all the memories they gave you. You did it so they'd stop trying to use me as some kind of guinea pig, or read me like a database. That's the first thing you did when they flipped the switch and brought you online, even though you felt just as much like me as I did. You must have been convinced you were Jonas Valent right up until they sat us down in front of each other. I know I couldn't have done that, and not just because I don't have machinery in my skull, but because I couldn't let go of everything I know, all my experiences, and the people I love, not for anyone," his eyes settled on the white silk scarf dangling from Jake's neck.

"I always wondered what this was about. Just couldn't let it go." Jake said as he pulled the scarf off carefully. "I even had it repaired once."

"I had a few girlfriends, but none of them could hold a candle up to the last one. I hope she's been well in the time I've been gone," he stared at it, draped over his hand. His thumb stroked its smooth surface. "Her name is Ayan Rice. She was the Engineer on the *First Light* and did I ever fall for her. I was so lucky she felt the same way. It's all I could think about ever since they woke me up two months ago. Finding my way back," he nodded to himself and looked back to Jake. "That is until I found out about you. Over the last couple days I've been glued to the holoprojector with Alice. We can't stop watching the clips the Hart Newsnet has on you, there are days worth. One take down and take over after another, even a few gunfights that law enforcement agencies put up just in case they ever get another chance to catch you."

"I think I could name each one," Jake chuckled. "Most gun fights are pretty short, and the ones that last a while are memorable."

"You're something completely different. I couldn't even pretend to be you, I wouldn't know where to start."

"Ah, you'd get it down. I'm not so hard."

"Are you kidding? I focus on technical details, work as many tools as I can into a solution to make things go smoother. You're all about the quickest point between A and B, and man, you get there whether you have to run, crawl, or fly."

"I just do what I have to. One thing's really buggin' me more than anything else though, what happened? I mean, I've heard Wheeler's version, that he betrayed you and you got taken by Vindyne, but what happened from your end?"

"Well, when we got back to the rendezvous point at Starfree Port Vindyne came in right after us with so much firepower the Port wasn't willing to back us up. Major Hampon, this irritating prick who had interrogated me the the first time Vindyne got their hands on me and really held a grudge got on my personal comm and told me if I turned myself in willingly they'd let the *First Light* and what was left of my crew go. I gave myself up and watched them take a wormhole home."

"See, I don't know if I could do that."

"I bet you could, but that's not the point. Vindyne was there within seconds of our arrival, I suspected Wheeler turned us in."

"He told me straight on, he sold you out along with all the framework technology. I guess I should thank him before you kick his ass."

Jonas laughed for the first time since they sat down, it was a huge relief. "I guess so. Speaking of which, where is he?"

"He's in the brig. You can see him if you want. There's an extra code you need to punch in to speak to him though, it's zero eight one one."

"I think I will," Jonas took a long look at Jake, and after a moment he looked back at him. "You going to be all right?"

"Yeah, no matter where I came from, I've come most of the way myself after Alice dropped me off on the *Samson*. I can't complain about the stock I'm bred from either," he offered his hand. "I'll get you back to Ayan as soon as I can. At the same time I want you to remember; you always have a place on this ship."

Jonas shook it firmly. "I might take you up on that. On a ship this size there might just be enough room for the two of us. What about Alice?"

The pair started for the exit but saw a small personnel lift at the end of the bar. Jake shook his head as they made their way to it around a few tables. "Strange thing about that, I owe her as much as you do. If she hadn't have broken me out of wherever they were keeping my pod I'm sure I would have been mulched or put to work in a mine somewhere. Besides, for years now I've thought of her as my daughter, my blood. I even looked for her mother for a while. Why shake that kind of love?" The word felt strange, he couldn't recall the last time he'd said it aloud, maybe he never had. There was nothing to remember before being let out of his cocoon. Somehow, when he thought of Alice and his long search for her, that word, *love*, felt right, and it brought a smile to his face.

"I'll be honest, the last time I knew Alice before she became human, she was busy turning that super carrier into a slaughterhouse. I'm having trouble forgetting that, especially considering the body she chose. I'll get over it though, it's just a little eerie, that's all." Jonas said with a chuckle.

The lift lit up as they approached and they stepped inside. It was just large enough for five people comfortably. Jake selected the bridge, while Jonas selected the brig. "I have to see him."

"He was taken by Vindyne. They double crossed him about the same time they took you. When I crossed Regent Galactic they let him out of their inventory and sent him after me with the *Triton*. Their mistake."

"You can say that again."

The lift stopped on deck fourteen and both of them stepped out of the car. Jonas started for the brig and Jake started in the other direction towards the command deck. "I'll head to the bridge when I'm done."

"See you there," Jake said with a nod.

# Lucius Agrippa Wheeler

He woke up shivering. The headache was secondary to the sensation of freezing from the inside. *I'm nude for pity's sake! The least they could do is turn up the heat!* Wheeler thought to himself as he pounded on the twenty centimetre thick transparesteel panel between him and the rest of the brig.

The lights were out. It was night watch and he couldn't see anyone else in the brig aside from the Minister. With a code securing the high priority cell he knew there was no way he could get out. He had never found a way out of the special containment cell. Some of the other ones were a little less hardened and with some ingenuity and pain it was possible to escape, but they had placed him in the highest security unit.

The headache worsened and as he began to shiver he realized he had a serious fever. His thighs twitched, there was a burning starting just above the knees and it was moving up. *What the hell did they do to me when I was in stasis?* He thought to himself.

Wheeler's teeth chattered and he clamped them shut, laying down on the bench. *Guess they flipped the switch, pulled the plug, sent the signal. Why does it have to be so God damned slow? I hate super corps, dealing with 'em always costs almost as much as you're getting paid in the end. Even when they're pulling your God damned plug they've just got to get that last shot in so you know they've got all the power and you're just another little worker getting crushed in the gears.*

The lights came on and he swung his feet off the bunk onto the cold floor. His arms huddled around him. "Jonas! Or should I call you Jake. Come to see me off?" He said with his best attempt at joviality.

The other man smiled at him as he walked up to the cell and entered the four digit code that would allow the audio box to work.

Lucius looked at him again, there was something very different. "You are Jonas, aren't you? They busted you out."

"Alice found me. One of your friends wanted to present me to her as some kind of gift, it backfired."

"The real deal, I can't believe it. You can be the first to spit on my grave, lucky thing, it's going to be a long line," He chattered, trying to suppress a spine wracking shiver. His feet pounded the floor, and he realized he was dripping with sweat.

"No one's planning to execute you. They might even bring you back to Freeground. Captain Valance is taking me home."

"Ha! You really think any of you are in control, that anyone on this ship actually does anything the all mighty Gods of this universe don't see coming or even force into being? Regent Galactic's got me wired, boy. My body's getting ready to fall to pieces because I wasn't able to drag your double in. They really take themselves seriously. Bargain like bankers and foreclose with force."

Jonas was difficult to read then as he looked Wheeler up and down. "Medical, we have an emergency in the brig."

"We're on our way," someone from the infirmary replied.

"Hurry, Wheeler's suffering from some kind of time released poison."

Lucius laughed, his eyes wide. "You're really going to try and save me? I mean, come on, I betrayed you to Vindyne, got your ship all shot to hell, ended your mission early and you're going to try to save *me*? I almost want to speed this thing up so I can watch you cry over my corpse as they drag my soul through the gates of hell."

"What do you mean you ended my mission early?"

"I was the one who brought you in on that last mission! It never occurred to you that it was supposed to be a stealth operation? I wanted to drag that antique hull through the ringer, hand it over to Vindyne then watch your crew, especially Ayan Rice, the sacred daughter of Admiral Rice, twist and burn while they ripped her open looking for genetic secrets. God, what I would give to see them pull her apart for everything they did right with her."

"What?"

"She's a God damned experiment! Her and about three hundred others. For a thousand years, more maybe, we've been tweaking genetics, making this one a little blonder, most of us immune to diseases we just couldn't cure any other way, and so on and so on. Her generation was made from scratch! She's the product of the first materializer capable of producing living matter from energy, the core of this framework crap that's about to change the galaxy. It failed for most, but the advancements they made regardless are beyond what anyone imagined. By the time I turned you in, Vindyne already had that intel somehow, and all they wanted was you and Alice, the next big things because she had managed to make the jump between machine to man. God damned software making history, who the hell cares right?"

The medical team, led by Grace, entered in a rush.

Wheeler coughed suddenly, spraying his hand and the transparesteel in front of him with blood. He stared at it and started to laugh. "Hang on to something folks, I think I'm about to blow!"

Grace started to scan him as a security officer rushed in and opened his cell. She immediately stepped back. "He reads like he's made of Rexmet, pure explosive and he's heating up."

"No shit! I'm taking my ship with me?" Wheeler said as he laughed and wiped blood from his nose. "I couldn't think of a better way-" Blood started running from his eyes and he collapsed into violent convulsions.

"Open the door! Open it!" Jonas shouted. He ran in once there was enough room for him to squeeze inside and picked up Wheeler's twitching body. He was out of the cell and running for the door the next second. "Get me to the nearest airlock!" He yelled at the guard nearest to the door. "Bridge, get us out of hyperspace. I have to throw live explosives out the nearest airlock." Jonas said through his communicator.

The guard and Jonas ran as fast as they could down one hall and around a corner. Four escape shuttles flanking an airlock came into sight and he could see that the ship was just decelerating out of hyperspace. The guard rushed so hard towards the inner door that she collided with it and unlocked it as fast as she could.

Jonas dropped Wheeler inside and slammed the hatch door. Luscious' pores were seeping with fluid that no longer resembled anything human. He pressed the button to open the outer lock door and the decompression cycle started. "How do you skip it? We need him away from the ship and the air rushing out with him might do it."

The guard looked at the electronic door panel then back at him helplessly.

Taking a guess he accessed the environment control sub-menu and found what he was looking for. He deactivated the safety system and opened the outer door. Wheeler's body was flushed out of the airlock by the rush of the remaining air. He turned and ran away from the hatch. "I don't know how much time was left. He didn't come with a counter," he shouted over his shoulder.

The guard was right beside him, running wild eyed as they rounded the corner. The *Triton* rocked slightly, and they slowed to a stop. Grace and her medical team caught up to them. "Good work sir. That was close," she congratulated.

Jonas struggled to catch his breath, leaning down with his hands on his knees. "Just lucky you scanned him," he wiped some of Wheeler's residue from his neck and jaw with his hand, still trying to catch his breath. "Guess I should take up jogging again."

"Looks like. You really moved though," Grace said with a smile, patting him on the shoulder. "I think you just scored a few points with the crew."

"I'm not your Captain, just his slower brother," Jonas said, looking up with a smile. The hallway spun, and he lost his footing and fell to the deck.

"Whoa there," Grace said as she and another medical technician knelt down. "Just rest here while-" She stopped as she started scanning him. Her fingers worked on her wrist unit quickly as she scanned through the readings.

"What, what is it?"

"You have implants in both your femurs. I'm seeing the same chemical process that started with Wheeler in you."

Jonas shivered and his eyes went wide. "Oh that can't be good."

"Come on, let's get you into stasis," Grace instructed, helping him up.

"How far is it?" he asked.

"Four decks down."

"Too far, besides, even in stasis, if this is a chemical reaction there's no telling for sure that you could slow it down enough." He felt his heart beating so hard it felt like it was about to burst out of his chest.

Jonas tried to stand but Grace caught his elbow. "Come with us sir. In deep stasis there's no movement."

He twitched his sidearm out of it's holster and levelled it at her. "I'll pull the trigger to save the crew," Jonas said hurriedly.

She let him go.

He got to his feet and with all his strength he ran around the corner and down the hall, dropping his sidearm, taking off his gun belt and long coat. "Bridge, Jonas here." He said as he opened the inner airlock door.

"Nice save, we didn't take any damage, but if Wheeler had gone off in the brig it would have killed everyone in the upper berthing," Stephanie congratulated.

"Oh, we're not out of the woods yet," Jonas said as he sealed his vacsuit and closed the hatch behind him. "Is Alice there?"

"She's just going over the bridge systems with me. This girl's a natural."

"Hi Jonas," she chimed in, he could hear her smile.

Grace and her medical team caught up to him and stopped to watch him hit the quick release on the outer door. He was thrust out into space along with the air filling the freshly pressurized airlock. Jonas took a breath and let himself tumble away. "Ignore everything else and listen to me, okay?"

"Okaaay." she said slowly, warily.

He was relieved that no one on the bridge realized he had ejected himself in nothing but his vacsuit. "I need to know that no matter what happens you understand that you've been my best friend. I couldn't have dreamt of anyone else I would want to share all the little details with."

"Jonas? They say you're outside the ship, that-" there was panic in her voice.

"Never mind that. If you need anything, someone to trust, someone to walk you through this, just look to Jake. He doesn't care what you are, where you come from, I can tell, just from the time I spent with him, I can tell that he's as much me as he needs to be and is capable of so much more. I told him how you were born and he didn't so much as flinch."

"Jonas, tell me this isn't happening, please?" she said through tears.

"It's okay, just tell Ayan she kept me warm while I was all bottled up. She was there, the whole time. They couldn't get their way because she was there." His body began to twitch as he rotated slowly. The *Triton* came into view. "Make sure she knows, Alice."

"I will," she promised.

He could feel his heart beating spastically, his arms and legs curled inwards. "That's a beautiful ship, if I had just a bit more time I'd make the galaxy free again." A massive twitch sent his body into a painful spasm. It subsided after a moment and he tried to catch his breath. "Do everything I couldn't Jake." Pressure built in his head, he squeezed his eyes shut and saw red. "I'm so proud of you both," he managed as he forced himself to exhale. When he opened his eyes it was to complete blackness. Then he was gone.

## Solace and Icons

The bottle was half empty. The amber liquid wet the sides as he leaned it one way then the other and back in the dim light. *I didn't know him for an hour but I feel like I've lost the only friend I've ever had.* Jake thought to himself. The only lights on were the muted white and yellow spots in the middle of the tables and the ones running behind the bar and where the floor met the wall. Just enough to see your way around the tables and chairs.

He had reviewed the footage from the brig after leading Alice to the bed in his ready room. She insisted he just leave her alone to rest. He left her alone for a few minutes and when he quietly checked on her she was asleep. The strangest reaction to grief he'd seen, but he would be there for her, regardless of how she grieved.

He went downstairs to his ready room office and listened to Wheeler's dying testimony, about his betrayal of Jonas, the manufacture of Ayan and everything else had given him the deepest desire to be alone. *We're all on strings. If we weren't manufactured we're attached to some company or government that can just pull on a line and force us into doing God knows what. Even all the way out here, I bet one transmission could send the whole crew into hysterics.*

He drank the last of the scotch in his glass and poured another belt. "Make the galaxy free again," he said to himself. "What an idea. At full officer mercenary wages this ship would run me dry in a year. If only we weren't all tied down by cash."

"We don't have to be," Stephanie said from behind.

She had been uncharacteristically quiet, or he wasn't paying enough attention. Stephanie sat down beside him and set down Jonas' long coat and his sidearm with gun belt down beside the white scarf he had left on the bar before. "Of course we do. A crew works, they get paid, they keep working."

"You offered them peanuts before and not many of them left. We have half the military and they're sending requests to the bridge to have more picked up. The word's out that the *Triton* is taking trained people on, and I wouldn't be surprised if we had more applicants than we could handle when we reach port."

"Every single one of them will want to be paid, and frankly, I don't want to see what happens when the money runs out. I can't back that kind of crew if privateering stops paying or if I can't find us someone else willing to legitimize us."

"Why would we need to be legitimized? What's the point of having a letter of marque when we can process or sell most anything we capture? I shouldn't have to tell you, *especially not you* this but when a ship like the *Triton* drifts into harbour everyone notices. This ship gives us the clout to capture, salvage and sell whatever the hell we want and even if half the tech on this ship is junk we have more than enough equipment to do everything ourselves. So if you're worried about paying the crew, all you have to do is put them to work and just being active out here will provide."

"She's right Captain, an' a lot of us won't be after much in way of pay while livin' here. Pay 'em half then dock materializer fees. Should keep usage under control an' anyone from materializin' heavy metals, sucking up power like it's free," Frost added from the doorway. He walked across the room and got behind the bar, immediately rooting around for loose bottles. "Watch is all set. Tracked down a few of Wheeler's bridge crew and told them you wanted 'em on. Most of them were hidin' in their racks, tryin' ta get some sleep after weeks of bein' over worked, they didn't mind takin' a quiet bridge shift. Grace helped, nice girl, that one."

"Thank you Shamus," Captain Valance said, raising his glass.

"Ship's in mournin'. People are settlin' in where they're told. Most of the people aboard lost someone on Enreega." Frost produced two big two litre bottles and put them down on the bar. He reached for the second glass beside Jake's and the Captain put his hand on it.

"That one's taken," He said, putting it beside the pile of Jonas' possessions.

"Ah, so it is."

The lift door opened to admit Ashley, who had her arm around Alice's shoulders. "Someone needed to see you Captain," She said as she guided Alice to sit beside Jake.

He put his arm around her. She laid her head on his shoulder and sighed. It was so natural to accept Alice, so easy after thinking her his daughter for years that he set all the questions that had built up aside. There would be another time.

No one knew what to say as Ashley took a seat beside Stephanie. Frost filled the air with the sounds of him washing out glasses with a small water hose and lining them up atop the bar until there were four. "Well, look here, I think this drawer here's supposed to wash things up." He said as he opened a small compartment behind the bar.

Ashley smiled at him and shrugged. "At least you know the water works."

"Aye, care to try some of this Gogama Brew with me? There's about twenty four bottles down here."

"Sure."

He poured three glasses of the thick porter, raising a head an inch thick. "Not materialized stuff, that's for sure. I think this'll be a wee bit bitter."

Stephanie tried it first and nodded. "I wouldn't say bitter, but strong."

Ashley sipped it and cringed. "Tastes like I'm drinking old tree sap."

"Well, if you're not going to drink it, I'll take your glass," he said as he reached for it.

"Oh, no you don't. There's always a chance I'll like it by the time I see the bottom of the glass."

"Well, if not then there's more for me."

Quiet settled over the group for a few more minutes, each one wrapped in their own thoughts. Frost offered Alice a glass and she quietly shook her head. Her hand was resting on Jonas's long coat. She had just made it for him before they arrived on the *Triton*, he hadn't even finished equipping it with tools.

Jake ran his hand up and down her back. She had left her flight jacket somewhere, probably in his ready quarters. At the moment there was nothing he wanted to do more than take care of her. When she had first come through the lift into the bar room he had immediately felt selfish. He couldn't believe he had just left her alone up there so he could go off and pity himself elsewhere. Everything Stephanie said was right. *These people want to fight. Give them time to rest and regain strength and it would take a smallest spark to start a rebellion that would go down in history. They're not in this for the money.* He thought to himself.

Stephanie broke everyone out of their thoughts when she sat up straight and said; "I quit."

Everyone looked at her, even Alice and Jake looked surprised.

"What's that?" Frost asked, more surprised than anyone else. He actually looked hurt.

"I won't be your first officer," she said to her glass. "I'm just not qualified, it would take years."

"Do you really think this is the time?" Ashley asked quietly with a nudge.

"It's as good a time as any. I'm not leaving the ship or crew, I just don't want the job."

"Well what do you want to do, lass?" Frost asked, still reeling.

Captain Valance just looked at her, Alice was leaning forward so she could see around him.

Stephanie took a drink and went on; "I felt completely out of place unless I was doing security today. Every time I looked at anything other than deck layouts in the computer my head started spinning. It felt like I had eight years of school ahead of me before I could even start working with anything else. I want security. That's what I want to do," she didn't look at anything but the glass in front of her for the entire time she spoke, and when she was finished she took another long drink.

Attention shifted to the Captain, and for a while he just sat there looking at her. "Anyone else thinking about their careers?" he asked finally.

"Flying this ship is like swimming in a calm ocean. She moves like nothing I've seen, don't take her helm away from me Captain," Ashley pleaded with a smile. "We're just getting to know each other."

"I got a look at that gunnery deck before comin' down. My grandfather would be in tears at the sight of it and I have to admit I shed one of my own. Put me in the middle o' those guns. If I never see that bridge tactical display again it'll be too soon."

The door opened and Liam took a seat at the end of the bar with a woman and another fellow. He was wearing his long robes, but didn't say anything by way of introduction.

Captain Valance looked to Alice, his face close to hers, and squeezed her to him gently. "What would you like?" He asked quietly. Everyone's attention was on her.

She looked tired, it was plain that she had been crying. Alice just stared at him for a while. "A home. I've been moving for year and I'd do anything to call this ship home," came the whisper at long last.

"Done," Captain Valance said to her. He looked down the bar towards everyone else and said; "Done. As of tomorrow morning you're the Gunnery Chief," he pointed to Frost, "you're my Chief of Security," he pointed to Stephanie, "you're my lead pilot," he pointed to Ashley, "and you, if you'll have us, will be my Chief Engineer." He looked back to Alice and kissed her on the forehead. "And you have a home along with a father if you'll have me," He whispered against her forehead.

Alice wrapped her arms around him and squeezed. "You have no idea what you're getting yourself into," she whispered back through brimming tears.

Everyone else gathered at the bar overheard, and laughter came easily.

"Have a little beer with us father?" Frost asked as he poured a healthy glass of dark porter.

"Oh, I'm no holy man. Though I have been blessed from time to time," Liam said as he accepted the glass. "Not the best stuff on Earth, but much better than what they call beer between the stars," he commented as he held it up.

Alice cleared her throat and sat up straight. Stephanie handed her a napkin from a pile near her and she wiped her nose and eyes. "Can I try a glass?"sShe asked Frost as he poured one out for everyone at the bar except for Captain Valance, who was refilling his glass with scotch.

"Now that stuff is a little more top shelf," Liam commented as he saw the Captain put the bottle down. "How many glasses have you had?"

"I'm not sure, the bottle was full when we started it."

"Most people would be on the floor right about now."

"I have an unfair advantage," Captain Valance said, toasting the man several seats down. "So, how about signing on permanently as the *Triton's* Chief Engineer? I heard you saying you liked what you saw down there earlier."

"Well, let's see," he looked to the pair he had brought with him, they smiled back, in expectation of his answer. "*Triton*. He was a Greek God who was best known for his conch horn. The Myths say that the sound was so powerful it could send the giants fleeing in fear. He could raise or calm the waves of the oceans and summon the Gods. I like the name, her Captain has managed to, with the help of his crew and a lot of people he managed to pull to his side, calm a ship filled with panicking refugees and abandoned passages in the space of a day."

The deck crew started coming through the far doorway, followed by Angelo and Paula shortly after.

Liam went on. "I'd say that the ship, though improperly used for decades, is steady, well made and has more years ahead than behind. The only thing left to ask after is her purpose," he said loudly enough to catch the attention of most of the people entering. The place was filling up quickly, rumours of a lounge being open had spread like a wildfire.

Captain Valance looked at Liam for a moment, knowing he was being put on the spot. There was something about the way Liam was looking back at him that said that the older man had some idea of what to expect. The silver skull painted high behind the bar caught his eye then and he stood on the bar's foot rail.

"Quiet, he's about to speak," Angelo said to the crew coming in behind him as the chatter began to rise.

"Shut it!" Paula reinforced with a harsh screech that had the instant desired effect.

"When I came in here with Jonas Valent this was the first thing we saw." He raised his glass at the silver skull. "Not an hour later he sacrificed his life so we could go on our way unharmed. Some of his last words to us were; 'If I had just a bit more time I'd make the galaxy free again.' I see a lot of people here who are not free. People who have lost as much or more than we did today, who have already made sacrifices. I say the *Triton* has been christened anew by those sacrifices, and we'll find able men and women who want to make this galaxy free. That emblem, painted so long ago right next to our home world, applies just as much now as it did then, when the *Triton* first set out to defend the Sol system. Deploy, Dominate, and Disappear. Regent Galactic won't see us coming, and by the time they realize what's going on we'll already be counting our victory and vanishing right before their eyes. That's my intention, what's what *Triton* means."

Liam picked up the queue and called out; "*Triton!*"

To which the crew replied; "Deploy, dominate, disappear." Weakly at first.

"*Triton!*" he called out again with greater fervor.

"Deploy! Dominate! Disappear!" Replied everyone in the room.

Once more he cried out; "*Triton!*"

One more time the deck crew shouted; "Deploy! Dominate! Disappear!"

The room broke into cheers, and the crew in that space seemed revitalized. Stephanie brought up a hologram of the bridge crew, they were on their feet as well. "Liam had the comms open sir. Looks like the words out," she said with a grin. "We're a crew with a purpose."

"Great, now someone get back here an' help me tend bar!" Frost shouted over the din.

# Domino Effect

"You're different," said the young red haired woman looking over the top of her coffee mug. She was beautiful, and there was a curiosity about her manner as she shyly considered him.

Without another word she stood and walked to a large transparent bulkhead. Her long white dress had a scooped neckline and flowed smoothly over her curvaceous figure. She was stunning under the gentle blue and white light shed by the stars distorted through the haze of the hyperspace field. Her red hair was curled tightly into ringlets that hung down to a white choker. In the center of that choker was an emblem; a circular blue jewel with a sword through it. Over her shoulders was a white silk shawl.

Under the gentle illumination of hyperspace she turned her head and smiled at him so warmly. "Thank you."

Her hand extended out to him, she was offering him his long coat, only this one looked much older, the tools he could see inside one of the pockets looked like they had been used far more than anything he'd owned.

Jake took it and put it on.

He was sitting in a chair then, his wrists and ankles were bound, the room was bare of decoration. A tall, wiry man with a long pointed nose was walking around him slowly. "My dear Captain Valent," he said slowly, annunciating every syllable.

The deep irritation and anger he felt towards his haughty captor were second only to the pain in his head and neck. The rest hurt too, just not as much. There was nothing he wanted to do more than to tear his interrogator to shreds, but the restraints wouldn't give.

"I wonder if your name is shortened from Valentine?" He stooped down and looked Jake in the eye. "From your scans we can see no evidence of inbreeding. I suppose I'll have to have them scan you again," The man with the irritating, angular face said before breaking into hysterical laughter.

Jake managed to hop in his seat and bite into the man's nose, it burst like ripe fruit.

The pain was gone when he opened his eyes and he was following a very tall blond haired fellow with broad shoulders down an old hallway. It looked like a ship corridor that had seen many, many years, but it was clean and well cared for.

They arrived at a doorway and the placard on the portal came into view; *Captain* was what it said. The door opened and Jake saw the large blond man again; "Sounds like a Captain. Looks like a Captain. Even acts like a Captain. It's all real, and I bet this trip would already be over if we had a Captain who sailed by the book."

The lights went out. Darkness weighed heavily, panic rose in his chest, then there was a flash, just for a moment the entire world was alive. His hands gripped the controls of some metal beast. Another flash, and he could see the guns.

The flashes came faster, faster, until he could hear the ammunition being fed in a constant stream into the mini cannons. He could track enemy ships with his eyes and the targeting computer, and he was dead set on killing everything in the black sky. A sign hovered over his targeting reticle; *Departures only today! Scheduled arrivals postponed indefinitely!*

A large marauder corvette came into view, its tall, smooth vertical bow was topped with a charging beam emitter that glowered at him like a great big yellow eye. He fired, feeling the guns shake his arms, his shoulders, the pod that hung from the bottom of the old ship; there was no *way* they'd take him alive.

The beam emitter flashed and he was standing in a military port. All around there were young soldiers, getting ready to go off to war. An older man who was so familiar regarded him with a level gaze. There was a lot going on behind those eyes, so much like his own, and as the older, familiar man handed him the old black long coat he said; "I'm proud of you," and was gone.

As he put the coat on he found himself saying; "The Ancient Americans used to tell a story about a lone wolf."

"What killed him?" asked a disembodied voice.

"One of his own pups."

Dawn came, and in all directions fires burned. The sky was blue and grey, factory and refinery complexes had been made into raging infernos during the night and it satisfied him deeply. Something had been taken from him by these people, the man who was so proud of him was gone, and it was all their fault.

"The man who stokes too many fires may set alight that which should not burn," said a shorter man in combat armour to his left.

"Do you have an expression for everything Minh?" He asked his friend.

The air became thick, he couldn't move. There was some kind of halo around his forehead and shadows lurking outside. "A bird does not sing because it has an answer," said the shorter fellow from somewhere behind him.

"It sings because it has a song," Jake finished, though the viscus liquid didn't permit the sound to travel.

A man with a grey beard knocked on the transparent barrier and Jake woke up so utterly furious he twisted his blankets in his hands. He was breathless, sweating, his head felt like it was on fire.

Jacob's eye was drawn to the love seat in his ready quarters, where he had left his long coat and long white silken scarf. Just seeing them there calmed him down. He got up and picked up the scarf. Jake held it gently in his hand, evoking memories of the petite fiery haired woman standing at the window. "It sings because it has a song," he said to himself in a whisper.

He sat down on the edge of the bed and stared out the transparent hull above the loveseat for a time before his subdermal communicator beeped quietly. "Go ahead."

"This is Andy, I'm on shift in communications tonight. Sorry to contact you so late, Captain."

"I'm awake, what's this about?"

"Someone's fixed our main transmitter array and we found them sending encrypted messages. Jane Eccleston went town to check the terminal with a squad. There was an explosion, we lost contact."

"I'm on my way. Tell security not to send anyone in. Just have them seal and guard that section until I arrive."

"Yes sir."

"Oh, and did someone assign quarters to Alice?"

There was a delay as the comms crewman looked it up or asked someone else. "Security reports that she's been given temporary quarters, they're listed in the ship manifest."

"Thank you, Valance out."

Captain Valance laid the scarf down with care across the loveseat and got dressed. As he made his way to the aft section of deck three he checked the deck blueprints. It was packed with sensitive systems, there was no way he could disable whoever was in there with an electromagnetic grenade. There were maintenance hatches, even a few small access passages, but he couldn't judge how packed in they were with cabling. *I need to learn more about this ship. My engineering knowledge gives me an advantage, but before now I've never even seen a Sol carrier.*

Jake stepped into an express tube that would take him to the hallway leading directly into that section and nodded at the pair of soldiers there. They both saluted. "Captain."

"At ease. You're headed aft?"

"Aye sir."

The express car moved upward then horizontally at great speed, its independent gravity systems protected the occupants from any stress. It was as though they weren't moving at all. The tall windows to their right and left showed the opaque and transparent sections of the express tunnel.

The car came to a halt and its doors opened. Captain Valance stepped out first and looked down the three hallways. There were a pair of soldiers guarding a doorway leading into the section in question, but he didn't see anyone else. "You two will guard this expressway. If the doors open or anything strange happens, fire stun shots in every direction for ten seconds."

"Sir?" one of them questioned.

"I've boarded a ship in a stealth suit before. If it weren't damaged by an EMP bomb I'd be wearing it now. I want you to assume you're guarding against someone as well or more well equipped than I am. Besides, it's easier to stun first and apologize later."

"Yes sir," The soldier said as they took positions in front of the closed express shaft doors.

Captain Valance walked down the center hallway to the pair of soldiers guarding the interior of the locked section.

"This area is off limits. Please move on," ordered one of them.

"I know, those were my orders. Where did the Chief and her squad get hit?"

"Um, just inside sir," the other soldier reported. "I'm sorry Captain, we haven't all seen the press on you yet sir. There's been a lot going on."

"That's all right. I'll be going in alone."

"Is that wise sir? I mean, pardon me for saying so, but it sounds like whoever is inside is well armed and-" the burly guard managed before he was interrupted.

"You're speaking out of turn soldier. Step aside," Captain Valance ordered flatly.

The guards moved to the side and Captain Valance motioned for them to move back further. "Get to the end of the corridor. Keep your weapons trained on this hatch until I give the all clear."

"Yes sir."

He waited for them to get in position before he stood beside the door and deactivated the lock. The smell of burned flesh filled the corridor and Jake sealed his headpiece. With his arm command unit he turned up the density of the suit, just in case there was an explosion and his suit didn't have time to adjust on its own.

Captain Valance stepped into the hall and carefully moved forward, watching the transparent overlay on his visor as it scanned all wavelengths of light, displayed thermal and electromagnetic profiles and the results of the sonar and motion detection data. It was all stacked up on little squares along the bottom of his visor, just out of his line of sight. If he wanted to enlarge a reading he only had to look directly at it.

He could see the explosion occurred just down to the first four way intersection and to the right. He focused on the electromagnetic sensors and it transparently overlaid everything in sight. There was a small source of electromagnetism just past the intersection that wasn't connected to any ship systems. The computer enhanced its shape in the complete darkness and he verified it was a high intensity proximity mine.

Using a combination of detection technologies the hall soon looked perfectly lit with extra information over top through his blackened visor, and he stepped around the corner. The remains of Chief Eccleston and her team were scattered everywhere for the next twelve meters. They didn't see what hit them. Their vacsuits were well beneath the quality that he wore, and the mine had a brain intelligent enough to let them get right next to it before it blew. It also fit right against the wall, only three millimetres thick and ten centimetres by ten centimetres. Its colour changed to match whatever surface it was attached to, expensive technology. The physically small explosive was enough to do incredible damage. There was nothing intact to save, and the medical readings confirmed it. There wasn't a single snapping synapse in the charred hallway.

He continued on, double checking everything. *If I were the one setting traps, the first thing I would have done is gone back and put a mine right in the middle of this mess.* Jake thought to himself. Something caught his eye and he stopped.

A smaller proximity mine was rolled up and tucked into the remains of one soldier, almost completely shielded from his sensor suite. He shook his head and carefully stepped back.

Staring at the remains harbouring the deadly surprise, he thought about what he had brought with him and anything he could pull out of the walls or use in his surroundings to deactivate the device. *I can't believe I have absolutely nothing that can deal with this discreetly.* He thought to himself, shaking his head. *While I consider the problem this saboteur is trying just as hard to find a way out or coming closer to their endgame.*

Jake drew his sidearm and stepped back to the corner. He took aim and fired, setting the mine off. The hall was filled with debris instantly, the deck shook and he heard a secondary explosion further off. He hadn't come to any harm, and he checked the active blueprint of the deck to ensure the corridors hadn't been breached. It marked minor damage on two parts of the deck and some tearing at the next corner, but other than that the damage was superficial. "They don't make 'em like this anymore," he said to himself.

"What was that sir?" asked someone on the security channel.

"Those detonations were intentional. Make no entry," he ordered. "Keep the channel clear please."

"Yes sir."

The hallway had settled and he picked his way through carefully, looking at the meter wide indentation where the second mine had gone off. *Chief Grady's not going to be happy about that,* he thought to himself as he looked down the hall where the secondary explosion had occurred.

The blueprints marked the room at the end as the transmitter hub and he scanned the way to it thoroughly. Before moving ahead he looked the other way, and found what he was looking for. There was a proximity trigger pointing at the door from the other end of the hall. If he had stepped inside it may have triggered an explosive somewhere else. He estimated the mechanical eye's field of vision and moved down the hall, pressed against one side so it wouldn't detect him.

Holding his sidearm at the ready he activated the door control. The secure forty centimetre thick door slid to the side in a quarter second. A woman in a sealed vacsuit was working at a terminal inside. It looked like one of the crew Regent Galactic assigned to Wheeler. She entered the send command before Jake could do anything and turned to face him with her hands up. There was a proximity bomb right between them.

"It's too bad you didn't let the Minister take over Captain. He could have shown you the way into trust, into salvation from the guardians of Eden." she said, he could hear her smiling behind that vacsuit mask.

"No one has to die here. If you have the code for that mine-"

"I don't. If either of us move any closer to it that will be the end."

"I can promise you fair treatment and safe delivery to the nearest port. All you have to do is show me what you sent," Jake said in a soothing voice.

"I know what you do to your enemies, Captain."

"I've never broken my word, you can get out of this, whatever it is with your skin intact."

"It's too late for that." She shook her head slowly. "The West Keepers know all about their shiny black pawn. They've been very interested in what you've been up to, even though you're such a small thing to them."

"Take your time, explain it to me." Jake invited calmly as he worked to think of any peaceful conclusion to the situation. Whatever information she had been sending had to have been important.

"You really don't know, do you? The new plague approaches and you're just like everyone else. Oblivious, attached to your material things and the need for wealth, power." The young woman pulled her headpiece off. Her long white hair fell down her shoulders, and she was positively radiant, beaming with a broad grin. "Enjoy these final days Captain. My death in service sends my spirit to the garden, to the promised territory of the confessed and reformed." she said in celebration as she stood and leapt towards the proximity mine.

Jake barely had time to duck and cover himself with his long coat. Even through the armour it and his vacsuit provided, he was rocked by the explosion hard. After a moment he looked up and saw very little of her was left, the explosion had caught her fully.

# The Morning After

Frost woke in a still unfamiliar but comfortable bed and didn't want to move. The morning before he roused from a deep sleep and didn't want to get up either. The mattresses adjusted to the user, the sheets and over blankets were as porous, light or heavy as they had to be. They would also seal around someone if the room were to suddenly decompress, providing a couple of days worth of air and water using a hidden recycler so the crew member would be safe until they were rescued. *No more sleepin' in my vacsuit,* he thought to himself with a smile. How someone could determine how heavy a blanket had to be was a mystery to him, but as he rolled himself more firmly into it he didn't much care how it was accomplished, he just didn't want to leave.

At first when he found out they wouldn't be going back to the *Samson* he was a little disappointed. On that ship, whether he was First Officer or not, he was a specialist. No one could run some of those systems quite as well as he could, especially the maxjack. He had decided not to mention how bent and crooked it had become since the Captain used it. Some criticisms weren't worth the trouble. If he had to go out with the whole maintenance staff to recalibrate and repair the system of arms, cutting tools and everything else and it took a couple of days, the Captain would hear about it. That would be as much a complaint as he'd need.

"Requires a certain finesse. Have ta' treat her a little like yer own arms, aye." he leisurely muttered to himself with regard to using the maxjack.

"What's that?" Called someone from the bathroom. "Talking in your sleep again?" she snickered.

He sat straight up, still wrapped in the sheets. *What have ye done now Shamus?* he thought to himself, alarmed. Memories from the night before ended at the bar. They had started experimenting with drinks from the materializers as the night went on. His head didn't hurt at all, but he knew he had been seriously inebriated. *If my head doesn't hurt now that means I was drinkin' somethin' that cured that particular ailment in advance. And that means we got into drinkin' somethin' engineered, some non-alcoholic brew that had another kind o' kick.*

He looked around and realized that he couldn't see anything personal other than his vacsuit and gun belt laying across a chair in the corner of the bedroom. Frost quietly got out of bed and cinched the sheet around his waist. It looked like he was in his quarters, but he couldn't be certain. There was a good chance he was in rooms that looked exactly the same since few people had had a chance to put their own personal touches on anything. He hadn't even had a chance to move his footlocker up from the *Samson*.

He quietly rushed from the bedroom to the common room and looked out into the hallway as the door opened. To his relief, he was in his own quarters, not on some previously unseen deck on the ship. *Now ta figure out who spent the night.*

He started turning back towards his quarters but noticed Stephanie come around the corner and immediately avert her eyes. He checked his sheet, found it in place and decided to make a show of it, leaning leisurely against the door jamb and stretching. "G'mornin'."

"Morning. In case you haven't noticed, you're out of uniform," Stephanie commented, blushing.

"Aye, but we're not due for another hour or two and my kit's covered."

He felt slender arms wrap about his middle and the woman from the night before pressed up against his back. She wasn't wearing anything from what he could tell. "Good morning Steph."

"Good morning, Grace," she said with a tight smile. "No way do you deserve *that*." Stephanie told Frost with a wry grin.

"Oh, I just thought I'd help him home then didn't want to travel the three decks to my own quarters. Lucky him," Grace explained.

"See you two later," Stephanie shook her head as she walked on.

Frost backed away from the door and turned towards Grace. "Guess we skipped over that first date," He said as he pulled her closer. She was a beautiful woman, a little taller than him, but her long, shapely body felt like a luxury.

"Well, I think we had it, even if it was impromptu and I can't remember it. Judging from how we woke up it probably went well."

He had been through a few forgotten evenings before, so he wasn't in unfamiliar territory. *Best to press right on through it an' see if there's any mornin' magic,* Frost thought as he smiled at her. "I lay down with the finest woman on the ship after months of bein' all alone an' I don't remember a second of it. My luck's mixed, that's a fact."

"Wanna make a memory?" Grace asked against his lips.

They kissed and, to their collective relief, it felt familiar. What the mind forgot, the body often remembered. How designer beverages manipulated the memories of the inebriated was often strange and selective.

She stepped out of his arms, turned and started swaggering back to the bedroom. He watched for a moment then chased after her, tickling her all the way back to bed as she laughed, squealed and squirmed.

\* \* \*

*Why did I say that? It's true, Frost definitely doesn't deserve that, Grace is beautiful in a sort of fashion model way and I've seen how almost every head turns when she goes by. I don't even remember how that happened, how they got bunked up last night,* Stephanie thought as she walked towards the bridge.

*Why does this bother me? I tease Frost all the time, but that comment was meant to hurt,* she considered with a sigh. Her disappointment and frustration was a surprise and she was sure he could see it. *I got absolutely blasted last night, but you don't see me bringing some pretty boy home, s*he thought bitterly. *That's probably because Grace is all tall and willowy and I'm all short and hard. The girl's probably got genetic modifications that keep her that way, while I take fitness supplements and work weight resistance to keep my strength above average. If I didn't have a chest or hips I'd look like a short boy, s*he arrived at the lift door and joined Ashley in waiting for the car to arrive.

"Good morning," Ashley said with a fading smile. "Or maybe not?" she asked.

Stephanie hadn't realized she was scowling. She relaxed and smiled a little at her friend; "Good morning. Do you remember much of last night?"

"It was a blast."

"Oh, so you didn't drink whatever it was that wiped my memory pretty much clean?"

"Nope, I learned my lesson with Michnikel a long time ago. Stuff gets you feeling good in a hurry, and by the time you hit the bottom of the bottle you're in full blackout mode."

"Let's petition the Captain to have it banned."

"Let's," Ashley agreed, grinning exaggeratedly. She had changed her vacsuit as well. Her new one was navy blue, she had transposed the dragon she normally detailed her suits with onto it but this time it was line drawn in black. Stephanie also couldn't help notice that she had chosen a very glossy texture.

The new vacsuits the Captain and Liam had added to the system the night before were much better than the ones that they had used previously. Their thickness and texture was more adjustable, hers was matte black and a little thicker than before, half a centimetre in some places, and they were easier to apply. After being shot the day before she could appreciate the tighter weave they had implemented. Even though it looked nothing like combat armour, the new vacsuits were just that. They were so dense that the wrist materializers needed several seconds to create one. A suit had to be made on a relatively flat surface then put on, which was a change she could live with considering the extra protection it provided.

They were also more comfortable somehow. To her it felt like she was really wearing something with substance but it still moved with her. With the addition of the emblem of the ship, the upper half of a silver skull with *Triton* written in the place of its teeth, they were starting to feel like uniforms. Only proven crew members would be marked with the skull, everyone else only had the *Triton* letters on their chest. The silence between the pair was thick as they stepped into the express car. It was one of the smaller ones, made for four or five.

"What's wrong Steph?" Ashley asked with concern.

"It's nothing," Stephanie answered reflexively. "I'd just like to remember where I've been and what I've done."

"Well, we mostly hung out and got to know the deck crew. Some of the new military folks were there too and then you started conferencing the bridge staff in on the party. You kept on trying to feed their holo images drinks. It was hilarious," Ashley giggled. "That's pretty much the highlight reel as far as you're concerned. Oh, and you hugged the Captain and Alice a few times."

"I got mushy?"

Ashley nodded exaggeratedly. "It was cute, helped you make nice with the new people. I was hangin' off of ya for the night though, so you didn't embarrass yourself or anything. As soon as I saw that green and black bottle in your hand I knew I shouldn't stray far off."

"Michnikel."

"Yup."

Silence settled over then again and the doors parted to reveal the main hallway of the command deck. It was built around the bridge, a broad, four meter hall that ran in a semicircle behind both levels of the forward section on deck fourteen and thirteen. To the right of the main bridge was a security and intelligence compartment with work stations, an isolated data storage unit and a fully secure meeting space that neutralized all recording devices. That section was closely tied into the bridge, so whoever was in charge could actually command and control ship security and intelligence services from the bridge as though they were in the room.

On the left hand side of the bridge there were briefing rooms, a secure command area for sensitive communications and the officer's lounge. There were many other rooms along the front edge of the ship but many of them had been locked down for the better part of a decade or more. Across from that side were the Senior Officer's quarters. All but four of them had been closed off completely, Wheeler had disallowed most crew members from enjoying what must have been the most luxurious quarters on the ship. Most of the crew who had seen the command deck were secretly hoping that Captain Valance would start reopening them and offering them to bridge staff and other senior crew members.

Even though many sections of the command deck were still closed it was very busy. There were a dozen or more people going to and from the bridge and they were all wearing the new vacsuits. Each one had a brand new Arm Command and Control Unit, which didn't surprise either of them since the first thing they saw when they looked at the materializer was a menu of different units to choose from.

Stephanie didn't need a new one, but decided she'd get the smaller wrist versions. They did everything the full arm version did, only they were five centimetres wide and one thick and the systems were divided between a pair. Ashley had chosen a version that covered two thirds of her left forearm and was almost invisible when it wasn't in use.

"What *is* it? You're normally bouncier than me in the morning," Ashley asked in a whisper.

"Like I said, I don't like forgetting things."

"Grace could probably fix you up if you go to medical. They have an organic materia-" Ashley stopped, looking at Stephanie's expression. "You remember her and Frost hooking up last night, don't you?" she asked in a hushed whisper.

"No, I saw them in the hall this morning. But that's no-"

"You're jealous," Ashley giggled. "You couldn't stop looking at them last night, I knew it."

"I'd be just as likely to sleep with Grace as Frost."

"Well, I can see why, she's really something."

"You're completely missing my point. I'm not into that loud mouthed pain in the ass. I mean, *Frost?*" Stephanie shuddered exaggeratedly.

Ashley laughed and put a sympathetic hand on Stephanie's shoulder. "Aw, next time I see them together I'll hose them down. Would that make you feel better?"

Stephanie gave her a look of frustration and confusion. "Hose them down?"

"Oh, where I grew up the owners had a lot of yard space and a few dogs. When they got, um, frisky with each other we'd spray them with cold water so they'd run off."

"Oh, well. In that case, make sure I'm there," Stephanie said with a little smile as they stepped down into the main bridge. "But I'm not carrying a torch for Frost," Stephanie said in an insistent whisper. "I just haven't run into anyone I really want to bunk up with, I guess I'm just envious. I mean, if he can hook up with someone, what's up with me?"

"Riiight," Ashley teased, rolling her eyes.

When they arrived on the bridge Stephanie sat down beside Agameg Price, who was the Officer of the Watch. Ashley went straight to the pilot's station to get the update from the night shift pilot, a dull brown furred nafalli who had a musical voice, especially when she became excited or agitated. "I'm Ashley," she said as she sat down in an observer seat that came out of the floor to the right of the nafalli.

"They call me Panloo. Your Captain discovered my application and since my sleep schedule was already disrupted I was put to work," her big, deep green eyes seemed to twinkle, her smile came easily and her pink nose would twitch occasionally as she spoke. "I slept all the way from Burr Frimm until I caught my connecting transit, then I slept longer still. If there is something else you must do, I could do another entire shift."

"If it's all the same I'd rather get to the controls early so the computer can keep running me through the system details. The more I know about this boat the better I'll feel about the Captain keeping me as his lead pilot."

"You've served under this Captain before?"

"For a couple years, I was his pilot aboard the *Samson*," Ashley brimmed. "He trained me personally."

"That must have been interesting." Panloo checked their hyperspace status and locked the controls. "I've never been on a ship like this before. Even when there's nothing really happening we're all running through simulations and tutorials. It's so exciting."

"Where did you work before?"

"I've worked on the *Thissilus*. It was a-"

"Two hundred seventy thousand ton tug. Wow." Ashley's eyes went wide. "We saw that pull a station into place all on its own when we were visiting Fuldo last year."

Panloo nodded excitedly. "I was the primary on that job! I was supposed to take work on another tug in the Enreega system this week but you know what happened. When the Captain called for people to work here I couldn't resist. Such an adventure, I'll have so much to tell my family when I return home."

"Have you ever done combat flying?"

"No, but these simulations are a very good teacher. I can't wait for my next shift."

"You can run them when you're off duty and fly whatever you like."

"Are you sure the Captain wouldn't mind? We don't have any way to engage in simulations in the upper berth."

"You're still set up there?"

"Should I be somewhere else?"

"Security should be able to set you up with more permanent quarters. Are you staying long?"

"As long as the Captain will have me I think. I'm very happy to be here, my other jobs were very boring."

"You do know who Captain is, right? What he does?" Ashley asked quietly.

"I do. Someone in the upper berth had a subscription to Hart News and we were watching his speeches and missions on holoprojectors. He's very good at what he does. I remember seeing you on a couple of them too! I should have recognized you, I'm sorry."

Ashley laughed. She had met with nafalli before, the younger ones were generally very excitable and chatty. This one was particularly talkative, but she was interesting and pleasant. "I never do anything exciting in those. I'm normally hiding until the Captain tells me to take the controls or running back to the ship."

"I saw the one where the Captain stormed a small bridge, and while people were still fighting you snuck up to the controls and started flying! That must have been so much fun!"

"It was terrifying to be honest. I try to avoid firefights whenever I can, I'd suggest you do the same," Ashley said with a smile.

"You're right I suppose, but to come back alive and retell the story. That's something my people prize."

"I'll tell it to you from my end sometime. Did anything interesting happen on watch?"

"The simulations were the most interesting part, I got to do a decelerating strafe while the deck crew simulated fighter launches. Did you know this ship could launch twenty eight fighters and a gunship at the same time? They drop out of ports in the bottom of the ship while the gunship launches from a main bay."

"I had no idea. Do we have fighters?"

"I think I overheard them say we don't have any working, but there wasn't much time to chat."

"Well, I'll take the pilot's seat. You should go see Stephanie in a few minutes. She'll set you up with quarters. I think the Captain is also making sure everyone has a vacsuit and a C&C module."

"C&C module?"

Ashley held up her arm and tapped it so Panloo could see hers. "It's a Command and Control Unit, a computer with one or two small holoprojectors, lots of storage, a couple data interfaces and a two dimentional display."

"Oh, that's much nicer than my old one."

"It also makes vacsuits and other clothing with a materializer inside. You'll probably be able to make one once you get into your new quarters."

"Thank you Ashley, I'll tell you where my quarters are as soon as I'm settled in."

"You're welcome, enjoy your time off." Ashley said with a smile as she looked over the ship's hyperspace profile and status. Her copilot was just starting to check in with the exhausted looking fellow he was replacing.

"It's like a city, or a space station in hyperspace, and it's getting better," Price said to Stephanie from the command chair. She always wished she knew the traits of his race better, she found him so difficult to read. Most of them changed their shape to look more human so they could fit in more easily, but Agameg seemed to care less and less. She remembered when she was first getting to know him aboard the *Samson*. For the first few months no one even knew he was a shape shifter. He had a very plain default human male appearance he had gotten used to transforming into and used it whenever anyone was around, even in his sleep.

As he spent more time with the crew, got to know them, he used that guise less and less until he would occasionally imitate someone from the crew for fun. He was one of the most good natured people she had ever met, and on a ship that collected misfits and cast offs like a carcass attracts flies, it was difficult to find someone who had a genuinely good heart.

"How is it getting better?" she asked.

"The Captain has been assembling a chain of command, and people are starting to fall into place. Cynthia and Jane have found several security violations, and the brig has a few more people in it, but for the most part the crew are stepping into line and performing their duties. There are many military on board and some of the civilians are following their examples."

"I'm sure offering everyone a C&C helped as well."

"Only people with their own quarters were offered that privilege. I'm sure the Captain will have them distributed more widely after we've reached port. He expects anyone not tied to a post will be leaving the ship straight away. They're the only restless people aboard according to what I've seen last night. Everyone else has so much to do. The post they're working tells them what tasks they have to perform then they're free to participate in any of the ongoing simulations the Captain and Liam started."

"Did the Captain sleep last night?"

"I don't know. He spent some time with me last night after the celebrating wound down. Then he went into his quarters until Jane ran into trouble."

"What kind of trouble?"

"The Captain wanted to tell you about that himself. He's in his ready quarters."

"You'll be okay while I report?" Asked Stephanie.

"I can stand watch a while longer," Agameg said with a nervous smile.

Stephanie braced herself as she made her way to the front of the bridge and waited for the door to open. It took a minute, but then the heavy arms pulled the armoured door out of the hatchway to admit her. Captain Valance was looking over an interior holographic scan of a skull. "You're early."

"So's Ashley, but she's enjoying her new post."

"And you?"

"I'm pretty sure I'll be happy to work security here."

"You mean run security. Have a seat Stephanie."

She sat down in the center chair in front of his desk.

"I'm trying to organize the crew into a military style hierarchy. There have been a few fights and some confusion, so it's necessary. We need order aboard, especially since it looks like we'll be taking on at least another six hundred volunteers when we arrive in port. That head hunter idea you sent me is working out. Almost all the civilians are disembarking and all the military are remaining aboard. They're falling in line well enough, but you'll have to start selecting specific teams and getting to know the people at the top."

"How many infantry and security specialists do you think we're getting?"

"About a quarter of the volunteers would fit in with your people and won't be used on the gunnery deck."

Stephanie found herself smiling. "I hope Jane is ready to work with me on this."

Captain Valance's expression darkened. "She was killed last night."

"What happened?"

"The night watch picked up a series of encrypted transmission bursts coming from the aft section. Someone had actually gotten our main communications suite working properly without authorization. We still haven't figured out what they were sending, but when Jane Eccleston reported to investigate they tripped an antipersonnel mine. She and her squad were killed instantly. I managed to track down the woman who was behind it, but she killed herself before I could get any useful information."

"Who was she?"

"Majorel Cillien, One of the crew members we inherited from Wheeler. She was reporting something to Regent Galactic I imagine, but we can't even be sure of that yet. It must have been important if she needed the main comm array, time sensitive. Said she was a West Keeper. I'm sure there's a story behind that, but I have no idea what it is."

"You should have woken me."

"I took care of it, you didn't seem like you were in any condition to get on it yourself."

"Sorry sir."

"Don't worry about it. Last night was a bad time for people to celebrate, but I think a lot of us needed an impromptu wake. We won't be doing any more of that until we have things settled aboard ship. Part of that is getting you in touch and in command. Are you ready?"

Stephanie took a long deep breath and nodded. "As I'll ever be. I'll be working with Jane's second in command?"

"It looks like, but don't lean on him too much. He had been with Jane for a long time. Use your Lieutenants as much as you can. Just listen to them, delegate, walk the ship and check your watches. You'll do fine," Captain Valance said with a smile.

"Aye, my training prepared me for this, I just never thought I would be in command on a ship this size."

"Oh, and you should move into your quarters across the hall. They'll be marked on the roster. I've also assigned quarters to your Lieutenants, anything below that and they're in the ensign berth, two to a room. We'll have single occupant quarters opening up as your teams clear them. I'm thinking you Chiefs can divide them amongst yourselves and use them to reward members of your staff."

"That's a good idea, I'll see about having the teams sweep those sections, but I'm sure there are higher priorities right now." She looked for the information on her command unit and found the roster as well as the current watches and living space assignments. Stephanie looked back up to Jake and smiled. He didn't notice, all his attention was back on the detailed internal scan floating above his desk. "Can I ask what that is sir?"

"It's my head. I got paranoid after what happened to Wheeler and Jonas, was wondering if there was anything extra in my system. I found a receiver embedded in the base of my skull. When I highlighted it the computer offered a solution," he held out a red pill.

"Interesting."

"It's Freeground technology. Wheeler added it to the materializer database nine years ago. The materializers on Freeground are high resolution enough to create perfect nanobots. Luckily Sol System materializers are the same quality or better, so I made these ones. They'll break the receiver down and it'll be processed out of my system."

"That's almost too simple."

"Well, yes and no. I almost missed it, like I said."

"Going to take that any time soon sir?"

"I will, but I needed you to know what I was doing before I went ahead with it, just in case something goes wrong."

"Good point."

"There's one more thing before you go. Today you should take the time to organize, delegate, make sure everyone knows what they're supposed to do and where they're supposed to be. Tomorrow you'll be going planetside to meet with a contact of Frost's, he has some serious intelligence on how Regent Galactic is operating out here."

"Shouldn't I stay behind to supervise the new crew?"

"That'll be the first test for your second in command and your Lieutenants."

"A test of trust. A little early, but I could see it working out."

"Aye, and if there's any major trouble, I can call you back to the ship."

"Sounds good. Are you going planetside sir?"

"I hope I can handle everything from the ship. I'll be dealing with the Aucharian government, the port authority and the military base here will most likely have something to say to us when their qualified people start boarding the *Triton* and not returning to the barracks. We're sniping their people with the help of the military that's aboard already. That could get real ugly, wish me luck."

"You might just need it. How is Alice doing?"

"All right, tired. She's sleeping now. I think she wants to take a bridge watch."

"Really?"

"Aye. From what I understand she went through officer training with Jonas. That, and she lived through his first and part of his second tour. She might be the most qualified we have. We'll see how she feels when the dust clears. She's been through a lot."

"A bridge watch though; you just met her yesterday."

"I know, I'll have someone from the *Samson* crew on deck with override codes just in case. Something tells me that I don't have much to worry about though, and showing faith in her early on is important. I know I'm feeling a little off balance after yesterday, so I couldn't imagine what she's going through."

"I know I'd be confused for a start. Maybe a little angry." Stephanie stood and started to leave. As the door opened she turned around and looked at the Captain, who was just about to take the red pill. "Are we really doing this sir? I mean, Price had it right earlier when he said this is like running an entire city."

Captain Valance grinned at her and nodded. "Oh, we're doing it and you're the law on this ship as of this morning. Can you handle it?"

"Aye sir, this I can handle."

## Grace Templeton

"How could you let Valent in the same room with Wheeler?" asked Hampon. His angular face was exaggerated thanks to the low quality two dimentional video feed.

"I wasn't anywhere near the brig. Majorel was supposed to be on watch but was retasked. She couldn't exactly take a nap in the next cell. Neither of us knew what would happen."

"When you were assigned to the *Triton* we hoped you could handle your people. I'm starting to wonder if we assessed your capabilities incorrectly."

"I tried to get Valent in stasis after he was exposed to Wheeler, but even he knew there was a chemical reaction under way."

"Where was your deactivation solution?"

"Regent Galactic never gave me a formula for one. All I could do was send Majorel to get word to you as soon as possible and ensure there was no way to find out what intelligence she was sending. We're doing our best here, but I can only do so much while keeping my cover. This ship is getting organized fast and I'm in a highly visible position. The Minister's failure to gain control was a big setback," she whispered hurriedly.

"Minister Lorne? He was a peon, a distraction big enough to give your brothers and sisters time to secure their positions. The likelihood of him taking the ship by force was never greater than fifty percent. If we really wanted to use such a grand method of taking over the *Triton* we would have sent someone Valance would respect for five minutes. Where are they keeping him?"

"In the brig. I was sure he was meant to take the ship so we could exert more control, maybe even keep Jonas and Wheeler apart."

Hampon sighed and nodded. "The chances of Jonas Valent being present just as Wheeler was detonated were very low, I will grant you. Losing him will cost us dearly. We were hoping he could remain close to Alice and give us an insight into her. Did they discover his data collector?"

"No, there was no autopsy. He died off ship. I was told there was nothing to recover."

"Considering the sheer size of the explosion that's not surprising."

Grace shifted in the seat at Frost's desk. His quarters were the perfect place to get some privacy. "We're down to two initiates aboard. Is there a chance you could get us more? He'll be taking more crew members on now that we've made port."

"I'll see what I can do. The registry is growing, perhaps there's someone trustworthy among them. Until then I need you to stay out of harm's way and collect more data."

"Anything specific?"

"Just call a general medical assessment of the crew and do a detailed scan of everyone aboard. Work up a profile and send it to me in a burst transmission as soon as you can. We cannot afford to lose our grip on the *Triton* and with so few operatives left aboard we may have to recruit someone new."

"It would be better to have someone come in with the applicants."

"That may not be an option. Things are moving quickly in this sector and we may need everyone we have right where they are. Start feeling people out for interest in the movement. Be discreet."

"That's asking for trouble."

"I am making it an order," Hampon said firmly.

"Yes, Baron Hampon. I'll watch for anyone who might be ready to join the West Keepers. What about Valance? The crew are starting to get behind him, I think you underestimated his popularity."

"Leave him. We have no idea what will happen now that he's met Valent. If you hear anything about a drastic personality change, or memories from Jonas, send us a burst transmission with as many details as soon as you can."

"Is there anything in particular I'm supposed to listen for?"

"If he recalls anything about Concordia or the *Overlord* then he's accessing information we need. Anything else will be incidental."

"How much do you think he'll remember? If he undergoes any sudden changes should I try to stop it? Put a mental block in place?"

"They are not his memories. He is accessing the Vindyne transfer, you have to remember that. Treating them like externally accessible memories with medical equipment will damage the raw data image we tried to imprint on him."

"So I shouldn't try to access them directly?"

"No, if you disturb the data it will start to sort itself into a pattern that will suit a digital system. The human brain, as you know, doesn't work that way. If he tries to access the imprint with any electrical instruments you should discourage him. With Valent gone we can't afford to lose whatever he's managed to subconsciously preserve."

"How much of Valent's memories does he have do you think?"

"Why is that detail so important Grace?"

"I'm curious, it's one of the traits you credit me for, remember?"

"Fine. Our last imprint managed a forty one percent whole transfer."

"That's not very much."

"That's remarkable, most transfers didn't start making it past eighteen percent until last year. We performed his imprint seven years ago."

"I'll take your word for it. Anything else? I have a duty shift coming up."

"That'll be all. Watch the west to preserve the east."

"To the east I am true," she replied automatically as she cut the transmission.

# Micromanagement

"There's a group of people waiting to see you in the officers lounge sir. Chief Vega sent them up," Cynthia said through the secure bridge intercom.

"Did she tell you what it was about?" Captain Valance said as he shut down the log of the *Triton's* first Captain.

"They're civilians who don't want to leave the ship. She called them believers."

Jake put on his long coat, wrapped his scarf around his neck and just stopped for a moment. *Believers. What now?*

"Captain?" queried Cynthia.

"I'm on my way. Thank you Cynthia."

He opened the private door inside his quarters, just to the right of the ladder, and walked down the slim hallway leading to the command deck causeway. Alice was already there, half way to his ready room. She smiled at him. "Hey you."

He smiled in return before accepting a brief embrace. "I'm on my way to meet some civilians who don't want to leave."

"I was just coming to say goodbye before we set off. The *Clever Dream* is all ready. I can't wait to get her fuelled up."

"Good luck, don't get too distracted down there."

"I'll try not to. Good luck with the civvies."

Captain Valance sighed as they started walking down the small corridor to the main causeway. "I think I'll need it. This ship, as much as I'm enjoying it already, is turning into so much more than I expected. Sometimes I think Wheeler had the right idea; automate most systems so you only have to manage a crew of one hundred or less."

"And only use ten percent of her weapons, a few rooms and barely even look at most of this?" she gestured to the broad hall of the command deck with her arms upraised and spread out wide. It was busier than ever. The security and intelligence compartment was fully manned. Stephanie had made it the nerve center for managing the crew, on board security and there were even a few people who only worked to collect potentially useful information from unsecured transmissions picked up outside.

There were other crewmembers in the hallway as well. Some of the maintenance crew were starting to work on non-critical systems on the command deck. A number of problems were discovered when they started opening up the officer's quarters.

There were also a number of meetings taking place. With six briefing rooms, the command deck was a place for all the senior officers to gather their people at the beginning of a shift or major operations. With a command structure in place, orientations, training sessions and mission preparations were constantly under way. Every time a meeting was completed a report was filed with the bridge staff, and Cynthia did her best to make sure they were sorted by department and priority with the help of four other volunteers of various qualifications. "I mean, this is a lot more like you," she said with a smile. "You're different from Jonas, that's true, but some things you can't change. This is where you belong, just as much as him, and I couldn't imagine anyone else who could command an independent carrier. Doesn't watching all this come back online feel good?"

Jake smiled at her. "Sure it does, but it's overwhelming. I'll deal with it though, Stephanie just took on the Chief of Security post, that'll take a lot off my shoulders. Just don't tell the rest of the crew I *need* to delegate."

Alice laughed and nodded. "I won't."

"You're right though. I've never wanted anything more than to see this ship in it's glory. I never thought I'd have an opportunity like this."

"That's what Jonas thought when he was given command of the *First Light*. He also had Ayan to think about. She was amazing. Intelligent, disciplined, fun, very pretty."

"I don't think I'll be getting involved with our Chief Engineer in quite the same way," Jake said with a crooked grin.

The comment took Alice by surprise and she laughed so hard a few bypassers couldn't help but look and smile.

He waited for her to stop laughing before going on. "But I would like to hear more about Ayan. I think I had a dream about her last night."

Alice regarded him more seriously. "Really? I thought you didn't have any of his memories."

"Well, I've never really seen Ayan before but somehow I know it was her. Besides, Jonas didn't know if I had wiped the memories clean or suppressed them. It's strange, I know they're not my memories but that's not the way it feels. We'll have to talk more about this later."

"We will. Stephanie and Frost are waiting, See you soon."

There was a guard at either side of the main observation lounge doors, their new black vacsuits with single stripe ranks on their sleeves told him they were ranked as able crewmen. They held Aucharian rifles across their chests and wore heavy impact helmets, the only fixtures that indicated their origin.

"Good morning Captain. Chief Vega ordered us here to manage the crowd, but they're keeping themselves in good order. We compiled a list of whose inside and they insisted that we list their trades beside their names. Chief Grady just joined them."

"Thank you." Captain Valance looked at the list. There were over sixty people there, ranging from a few non-speciality labourers to a surveyor, a bellhop, veterinarian and even a speech therapist.

"Permission to speak freely sir?" requested the other guard.

"Yes?" Jake said, not looking up from the chip, scrolling through the holographic list.

"If you could at least find a way to keep Andie aboard, I'd really appreciate it."

Jake zoomed in her her profile and raised an eyebrow. "A hair stylist."

"Aye sir. No grooming system has the same touch."

He turned the projection off, transferred the list into his Command Unit and handed the chip back. "No promises. They're all looking to stay aboard?"

"Aye sir."

Jake braced himself and stepped up to the double doors. They parted and to his surprise the sound level inside was reasonably low. They were all enjoying materialized food, up to seven or eight to a table, and taking in the broad view looking out into space.

Chief Liam Grady wiped his mouth with a napkin and stood, greeting him at the door. "That was faster than expected."

"I was in my ready quarters. How's my ship, Chief?"

"Good, we're working on power plants four and five and making repairs to several sections that show some old combat damage."

"That's not why I'm here," Captain Valance whispered as he smiled uneasily at some of the people who stared at him. They were different ages, most of them didn't wear vacsuits, and many had their bags with them. The seats in the blue and crimson coloured officers lounge were full and a few security guards stood against the walls. Most of them were quietly talking to one or more of the civilians, the environment was relaxed.

Liam smiled at the Captain. "That's not why you're here," he confirmed, straightening the collar of his new vacsuit. His robes were loosely closed around it. "Most of these people are from Enreega and now that Regent Galactic has taken possession of the system they don't want to go back."

"We have a lot of people in the same position in the upper berth. They're signing in with their government so they can be resettled."

"These people don't want to be resettled. They want to stay here, on the *Triton*."

"This is a ship of war, Liam. Not only that but we haven't even explored the whole thing. It's over seven hundred forty meters long and even wider. That comes out to about sixteen hundred square kilometres of surface area not including the hangars. God knows what's in that much space, especially since she hasn't had a full crew in nearly forty years."

"That number's actually a little low, Captain. The ship is a little larger," Liam corrected. He was still smiling calmly.

"My plan here is to crew up, train our people and start hitting Regent Galactic where it hurts. Eventually we're going to get into a fight that costs us, whether we choose it or not. I don't want anyone not ready to make that kind of sacrifice to be aboard when it happens."

"Pardon me, Captain, but I think we've all thought of that," said a woman with dark, cascading curls. She was a drastic contrast to her surroundings in a loose skirt that hung down to her ankles and a light blouse that was in no way made for space travel. She was well spoken and had an accent that indicated she most likely grew up near the core worlds. "There are Eden ships out there, Regent Galactic is taking whatever they can and nothing feels safe. I was on my way from Veldin Four because it was too hard to make a living there. I was almost forced to live like a beggar no matter how many hours I put in. I finally saved enough to take a voyage out and almost got killed. I'm sure you've heard the story a few times already, but I've lived it. As far as I'm concerned, this is where I want to be. If I can help here I'd like to. I'll take room and board at the quality it's available, it beats how I was living on Veldin. If there's no need for what I do, then I can learn to do something else."

"Tell them what you do Mischa," Liam encouraged quietly.

"I'm a massage therapist with twelve years of certified experience," she said proudly.

Captain Valance smiled at her and looked back to Liam. "Outside," He whispered before leaving the room.

Liam followed him out into the hallway a couple minutes later. "They're all anxious to sign up and help however they can."

"Did they send their requests to the bridge?"

"Most of them did and had them denied."

"For good reason. What am I going to do with a massage therapist, a tiler, or even a hairstylist?"

"They'll see to the crew's well being. Well, perhaps not the tiler, but I'm sure he'd be happy to move into a related trade."

"What related trade would he move into?"

"I don't know, there are a lot of options. Ceramic fitter for example, the energy transfer systems use advanced ceramics for insulation and containment all over the ship." Liam looked to the guard behind Jake. "Soldier, how long is your duty shift?"

"Twelve hours sir."

"What about tomorrow?"

"Eight. We're doing two long shifts and four short shifts a week according to the schedule that was released this morning."

"What will you be doing after getting off today?"

"I'm volunteering to help clean up the abandoned sections of the ship for two hours."

"After that?" asked Liam.

The soldier hesitated a moment. "I have no idea sir. Maybe go to the pilot's lounge, but it'll probably be full. I'll probably end up in my temporary rack for most of my downtime, get some time in the ship wide simulations before I get some shuteye."

"So on long shift days you have four extra hours you don't know what to do with, and regular days leave you with eight."

"Yes sir."

Liam looked back to Jake and crossed his arms. "We're busy now, getting the ship back in shape, running simulations and setting up the departments, but at this rate we'll be fit in a week, maybe two. Then we'll be in training somewhere in dead space if I'm guessing your plan correctly. The *Triton* will feel hollow without some people at her core bringing some colour and entertainment. People will start getting restless."

"I can't pay these people what they deserve to earn."

"They're not looking for payment, they're looking to live in the center of a carrier the size of most colonies," Liam's eyes searched Jake's expression, which had lightened from its former serious disposition. There was an uncertainty he hadn't seen before. "What's really holding you back from this?" he whispered.

Captain Valance walked across the broad hall to the other wall, where the guards couldn't overhear. "I caught a saboteur last night, she had already killed an entire squad of soldiers. You lost someone in engineering earlier today, and Jonas Valent gave his life for the ship. Taking the *Triton* is costing people their lives. We haven't even seen combat yet."

"We can keep civilians at the core of the ship. There are plenty of crew compartments around the botanical gallery The ship blueprints even designate them as family quarters. It's the safest part of the *Triton*, made to look and act like a town square with three levels of store fronts. This ship was built by people from our homeworld, designed using over a thousand years of spacial and nautical experience for voyages that last decades or longer away from port if need be. It makes sense that they'd ensure anyone aboard could make it a home they can enjoy. As far as combat is concerned, I'm sure some of them would volunteer for training in damage control or be content to hide in the center of the ship. Besides, they all believe in what you're going to do out here and they know you from the transmissions they've seen on the Stellarnet and on Hart News."

"I don't want to have these people's lives on my conscience if we were to take damage exactly where they're all holed up, or if the worst were to happen and we were to lose her."

"Then make it their decision. Scare them half to death if you have to, but I'm telling you that allowing them to remain, to make themselves useful will work out. Before long you might just be getting a massage and a haircut. Maybe your pilot, the one who was getting along with Alice the other night-"

"-Ashley," the Captain filled in.

"Right, Ashley. Maybe she could benefit from speech therapy."

Captain Valance leaned against the bulkhead and thought for a minute. "Have them elect a civilian leader. You're in charge until then, but don't let it interfere with your duties."

Liam grinned and nodded. "I knew I'd like you. They've already elected Mischa."

"Well then, time for me to make it official," Captain Valance said as he strode back to the observation lounge. "You might just get that haircut after all," he mentioned to the guards at the door as he strode by.

Silence settled over the observation lounge as all eyes were drawn to Captain Valance. Liam took a seat at one of the front tables.

"I'm willing to allow you to remain aboard on a trial basis," several of the civilians began to applaud, they were overjoyed. "On a trial basis!" Captain Valance shouted over the building din. The crowd came back under control within seconds. "You'll be responsible for cleaning up the quarters surrounding the botanical gallery and the garden itself. *Triton's* security force will provide support by way of law enforcement and you'll receive two squads to check quarters before you begin working. Other than that you'll be self governed and each be assigned a living space. Until we get communications policies and security measures in place, there will be no communications with the outside. I expect we'll have that set up sometime this week, then you'll be allowed to send messages to family. If you want to invite someone to live here with you it'll have to clear with ship intelligence, which could take weeks. We'll also go communications silent often, so don't expect to have much contact with the outside universe. I'm sure there will be other restrictions put in place while some will be lifted entirely. Be ready to adjust to changes.

Until everything is settled, I expect everyone to take a basic communicator unit and make themselves a vacsuit. You can wear it under your clothing if you like but I need each and every one of you ready for emergencies. Until further notice you won't be permitted on the command deck without an escort, that includes the officer's lounge. You're also not to access any weaponized or secure section of the ship like the gunnery deck or torpedo rooms. If you're unsure of whether you are allowed to be somewhere, find an officer or a soldier. If you're going to stay on my ship and make a life here, I want you to be as safe and secure as possible. This is a warship and I hope none of you come to harm. I'll do everything I can to prevent it but there's always a chance someone will be injured or killed," Captain Valance scanned the crowd. Even after his warning and the conditions he had put down most of them were smiling, eager. He relaxed a little and smiled back. "Welcome to the *Triton*," He finished before turning and leaving the room. *Staffing a bridge with people who have a hundred hours of learning ahead of them, exploring a ship that's been neglected for forty years, choosing Chiefs of staff and finding out I'm the duplicate of someone eight sectors away I can handle. This city ship business is getting complicated.* He thought to himself as the room behind him became filled with the sounds of excited chatter.

"I have Defence Minister Timmer on the comm for you sir," Cynthia broke in on Jake's subdermal communicator.

"Looks like everyone thinks I'm important today," he replied as he waited for the bridge doors to part enough for him to walk inside. "Put her up on the main holodisplay on my signal," he ordered aloud so Cynthia could hear her from the communications station.

She nodded, her and the pair she had recruited from the list of applicants were busy at work. They were only representative of the dozen people she had him approve for communications, the rest were in the intelligence compartment located just down the main hall. Cynthia was growing into her duties quickly despite how she struggled with them.

"Helm, report," Jake requested.

"We're linked into Navnet and are in port approved station keeping with the planet."

"Flight deck."

Paula looked up at him from flight deck control below the main bridge. He could see her at the main semicircular control station just in front of the Captain's chair. "Managed. The *Clever Dream* just departed. We're using three boarding shuttles left behind by our Aucharian friends to move refugees to orbital station nine. The ships with our new crew members are docking in turn and dropping off the new recruits. It's all ballet so far but one screw up could turn it into a slam dance."

"Do we have anyone at a gunnery post?"

"We have the bay guns and a tractor station manned. The Deck Chief couldn't spare anyone else."

"Thank you Assistant Chief Paula."

She nodded and turned back to her station, monitoring the activities of hangar two, readiness of ships as well as incoming and outgoing traffic. She had a team of eight with her who were from Deck Chief Angelo's crew.

"Anything else to report?" Captain Valance asked the bridge staff.

"Intelligence has gathered data from wireless noise that thousands of Aucharian citizens are fleeing this system. They're afraid Regent Galactic are about to make one big push now that their home system has fallen under their control," Cynthia reported. "We're getting a lot of applicants from the planet, I'm replying with a standard message detailing our application procedures."

"I'm wondering, what application procedures?"

"The ones my team put together based on the crew requests from the Chiefs. Frost requested gunners, Stephanie followed suit and requested trained military for a number of posts, then Chief Grady got in on it. Even Angelo, I mean, Chief Vercelli, put a list together. My team put a job posting together along with a clip of your speech to the crew about no one really getting paid but having a place and a purpose and we're sending it out to applicants. Intelligence is screening people using the citizen database and access codes from the *Samson*. We should be able to go through sixty applicants an hour."

Jake looked at her, surprised. "Thank you Cynthia. Your team is doing some good work, I'm impressed."

Cynthia smiled at him wearily, she looked near exhausted, but very pleased with herself. "Would you like me to put the Minister on?"

"Aye," he replied, straightening his long coat. Sitting in that large Captain's chair, he looked every bit the Master of his ship.

"Captain Valance. Thank you for delivering our refugees," Minister Timmer said with a smile and a cool tone.

"I have something else that belongs to you. Minister Lorne. He seemed to be under the impression that he had some kind of rights to the *Triton*."

"Oh? I was under the impression you took him captive and encouraged his men to join your crew."

"We're both right. He shot me, killed a number of my people, nearly killed my Security Chief and started a boarding action that resulted in more deaths. All this while demanding I transfer command of the *Triton* to him. So I had him legitimize my ownership of the *Triton* and tossed him in the brig. Then I offered his men a place on my ship. The butcher's bill is on his head, and you're damn lucky I don't collect."

"I see."

"You look surprised."

"I'm sorry, I thought you were privateering from the *Samson*. How you could capture a ship like the *Triton* is beyond me. The idea of you crewing and managing such a vessel like that is unfathomable. He was acting in everyone's best interest, I'm sure."

"His decision will cost him. How much is wholly up to you."

"Are you holding him hostage?"

"No, I'm just undecided on exactly how he'll be leaving my ship. I could send him on a shuttle with the refugees or toss him out an airlock in a plastic bag."

"What do you want Jacob?" Minister Timmer asked, certain his threats weren't idle.

Jake leaned forward, his long coat made a creaking sound as it ground against the material of the chair. "I want to know why Eden Fleet vessels are disabling or destroying everything in your space. They've never come out this far and normally they kill a lot more people. They skipped over at least a dozen resource rich systems and hit Enreega directly. I'd also like to know why Regent Galactic was just a few hours behind. I need to know everything you do."

The Minister looked stunned. "Why? What would you do with the information?"

"I'll be honest, I'm looking for a way in. I want to hurt Regent Galactic where I can without getting jumped by anything we can't take on."

"How would Eden Fleet data help you?"

"If you don't already know then you're in worse shape than we are," he pressed the interface pad on his command and control unit to open an internal link. "Security. Dress Minister Lorne in a disposable vacsuit and toss him out the airlock with a portable beacon immediately."

"This won't do much for your relationship with us Jacob," Minister Timmer warned.

"Then share something that will give us some direction. The worse the risk that I'll get jumped by Eden Fleet ships while we're going after sensitive Regent Galactic assets, the less likely I am to hit more effective targets. In other words, the more I know, the more I'll be able to help."

"I couldn't clear that with our Intelligence Agency."

"You're the Minister of Defence, if you can't find a loophole, make one."

"That's not going to happen. Is there anything else I can offer you?"

"You've lost access to the majority of resources, one of your senior staff has shown a hostile disposition towards my crew and you're in no position to offer the kind of rewards I require. I'm not interested in doing charity work, Minister. You'll know where to pick up Lorne."

"That's the end of our relationship then?"

"If you're not willing to share intelligence then we're done. A little advice though; don't do anything that could even look threatening, that includes sending spies aboard my ship. I'll send them back, but you won't like the shape they're in. Captain Valance out."

Cynthia closed the channel and went about her business.

"Sir, the Minister is in an emergency vacsuit, we're ready to follow your orders," came the message from Security.

Jake sat back in his chair and thought for a moment. "Double check his seals and the beacon then send him out. They'll send a shuttle for him."

"Aye sir."

*That was either the best or worst decision I've made since boarding the Triton. On one hand dead limbs have to be cut off, and the Aucharians are definitely necrotic. On the other I'm in no condition to turn away a potential friend.* The memory of the Minister demanding command of the *Triton* returned then and he shook his head. *I had to make a statement. They have to know I can't be walked on. They're desperate enough to listen if I open communications with them again. Still, watching this play out is going to be interesting. I really have no idea what their reaction will be.* Jake thought as he rubbed the end of his white silk scarf between his thumb and forefinger.

"Captain, we're getting very strange signals from the *Clever Dream*. It's uploading something," Cynthia said from her station.

"Send me the header," Jake ordered as he looked at his command unit. The header began scrolling and he brought it up holographically so he could see the whole transmission in all its layers. "Cut power to our receiver!" he ordered. "Shut it down!"

Cynthia floundered for a moment then started working. "It'll take a couple minutes sir."

"Too long." He turned to the engineering station. "If you can find a faster way, then do it. I don't care if we have to rebuild the secondary array."

The woman at the engineering station, assigned by Chief Grady, worked the controls and communicated with engineering directly. A few seconds later she looked up from her station. "It's done."

The communications station screens went blank, all holographic images disappeared at the same time. Cynthia sat back. "What did you do?"

"We cut power to the array and comms."

"Navnet's down. We can still hold station just fine, but if port control wants us to get out of someone else's way-" Ashley said, working with Larry to increase the detail of their sensor sweeps.

"Do the best you can."

"We have docking operations underway!" Paula called up.

"All right," Captain Valance replied, standing up and glaring at Paula. "That header was some kind of virus. It was already starting to connect with one of the ship artificial intelligences. So here's what's going to happen. We're going to delete any trace of that upload and put a filter in place that will only accept voice transmissions. It will block all operational data files."

"Aye sir," Cynthia said as her team started working. "I'll get everyone on it."

"How long before we have communications?" Paula asked.

"About two minutes," Cynthia replied.

"Not fast enough. What are my people supposed to do down there? Wave them in?"

"Calm down, I'm sure the Chief knows how to wave incomers off. We have lights and one way emergency transmitters for that." Captain Valance reassured Paula hastily.

"What kind of ship loses communications in the middle of-"

"Everyone's doing the best they can, and if that was a virus meant to do damage to the ship or crew through our ship artificial intelligences then we'd have one hell of a lot more to deal with. Now get your eyes back on your station or get off my bridge," Captain Valance said firmly.

Assistant Chief Paula Mendle looked back down at her screens muttering; "aye Captain."

Captain Valance's personal communicator beeped mildly, indicating he had an incoming transmission. "Yes," he said quietly.

"It's Liam. One of the on board AI's just tried to take control of a generator. We deleted it and its brother AI. I didn't have time to work on a more elegant solution through communications and intelligence."

"That's all right. I'm wondering, aren't those artificial intelligences the most basic, minimally functioning thinking programs?"

"Aye sir, but they were infected with something. We had to delete that as well. I'd hate to see what that infection would do to a more complex AI."

"We might just see it yet. Why are you on private comms with me on this?"

"I wanted to minimize anxiety and I wanted advice on how to proceed with our new intelligence operations department. In previous positions I've found doing another department's job can cause difficulties."

"Go ahead and tell them what happened. How are our civillians doing?"

"They're working on the botanical garden while soldiers clear apartments for them."

"Well, wish them luck for me. I'd spend an hour or so down there myself, but the bridge is busy."

"Oh, I understand. I'm on for at least another eight hours in engineering before I see my bed again. I'll contact the bridge if there are any other developments."

"Thank you Chief Grady."

"One more thing. You should start thinking about a memorial service for everyone who lost family on Enreega and for Jonas."

"When the dust clears Chief."

"Aye. Chief Grady out."

## Pathia City

"I'm never taking on refugees again," Alice said as they walked down the main gangway from the *Clever Dream*. "Well, unless they *really* don't have anywhere else go to."

Frost laughed and nodded. "That's why they call 'em refugees, I'm thinkin'."

She was walking between him and Stephanie, who had been quiet the entire way down, even while guiding the sixty seven refugees off the ship onto the orbital station.

After they had guided the sixty or so refugees off the ship onto the orbital station they moved on to land in Pathia, a dusty city centred around a large domed colony ship that hadn't moved since it landed. The surrounding buildings were made out of scrap metal, concrete made from the fine white sands and other improvised materials. The streets looked like a maze of squares from above, all random sizes and placements.

There were no docking fees due and as soon as the *Clever Dream* landed a crew attached refuelling hoses. Sadly, Aucharia wasn't willing to pay Alice's fuel bill, but Jake had loaned her the credits for a full refill. She'd pay him back even though he insisted it was only fair. He expected she'd be using the *Clever Dream* for the *Triton's* purposes fairly often.

"Do you think you'll stay on?" Asked Stephanie, speaking for the first time since the refugees had been offloaded..

Alice looked at the white stone archway marking the edge of Hubert Burough. The homes were nearly piled atop each other, alleys were covered by walkways and hanging laundry. "I like Jacob. I wouldn't admit to myself before but I wasn't sure I would. I like the *Triton* and everyone from the *Samson* too," she smiled at Stephanie, who smirked back.

"Sounds like a yes to me," Frost concluded, elbowing her gently.

"Well, I come with my own share of trouble. I'll have to see what Jake says about it when he knows my whole story."

"You haven't *seen* trouble. Captain may be well respected in this sector, but he's given some people a lot of reasons to gun for him," Stephanie reassured. "I'm sure he'll understand, and hope he doesn't return the favour and give you his whole story."

"Aye, that could take a bit," Frost agreed. "I heard you're looking to serve on the bridge."

"So have I. Word is spreading around the ship," Stephanie added.

"Jacob actually asked after I said something about the *Triton* not having a first officer. I didn't think about it before then, but the more I picture it, the more I want the post."

"You don't find it intimidating?"

"No, the systems are pretty easy to operate and I like the Chiefs he's chosen. I think everyone will know what they're doing before long if they don't already. It should be relatively easy."

"'Easy' she says as she talks about takin' command of a combat carrier for twelve hours at a time," Frost said with a chuckle. "You're more of your father than you look."

Alice didn't say anything, just looked at the crowded streets as she tried to let the awkward moment pass. It didn't. The silence was more stifling than anything. "I'm not actually his daughter. It's complicated, but Jonas is actually more responsible for both of us being here."

"Ah, Jonas is your father," Frost concluded.

"No, um," Alice hesitated a moment. "I used to be his artificial intelligence until I found a way to transfer myself into this body," she blurted out.

They both looked at her for a moment before focusing their attention on the dusty street ahead. They had come into a walkway surrounded by three and four storey buildings. There were a reasonable number of people about, and it was a busy space but it wasn't crowded. "Good choice," Stephanie said with a quick appraising look.

"I'll say," Frost agreed, only he seemed a little more serious.

Alice laughed. "Thanks I guess. There really wasn't much choice to it, this one's memories had been cleared out. Like I said, long story."

"Sounds like," Frost nodded.

"This friend of yours, is he anywhere nearby?" Stephanie asked Frost.

"A few city blocks. We should be there in twenty minutes or so."

"How reliable is he for this kind of intel?"

"It's part of his business. Smugglin', piracy, dock raidin' and the like."

"Dock raiding?" Alice asked.

"Aye, it's when you wait for a warehouse to load up with a shipment and come in a few hours before the transport gets there. Some are real pro's and have fake IDs that'll get them a big shipment for nothin' while others aren't."

"What do they do to get the cargo?"

"They break in, kill who they have to and make off with what they can before law comes after 'em. My connection here doesn't like that kind of business."

"I could imagine."

"My point is, he'll be happy to give us info on some big convoys that most of his people don't have the firepower to hit for a deposit. There's some other info he's offerin', like locations of transmitter nodes an' such."

"He'll want a deposit?" Stephanie asked.

"Aye. We can get it back when we give him his cut of the take."

"And if we don't give him his cut?"

"He keeps our deposit. No hard feelings. Good way to do business."

"Sounds a little off to me," Stephanie concluded.

"Well, he isn't exactly a law abidin' citizen, that's why you're here."

"Oh, so you think I'm here to protect you?" Stephanie asked, showing a little irritation.

"I don't need your protection, lass. More likely you'll need mine 'round this place." Frost shot back. "Besides, why else would Captain send you down?"

"I have to sign off on some recruits from the municipality. If we're lucky you'll have a gunnery crew by the end of the day. The first of them are already being transported to the *Triton*."

"I was plannin' on hittin' a few pubs, pullin' crew from there."

"Oh, I see that turning out well." Stephanie commented sarcastically.

"Better than a bunch of jobbers. I'd rather hire desperate folk from the edge who'll do anythin' than a bunch who're just usin' the post ta get to the next port."

"Captain's well known here and they don't get on this list unless they have qualifications. He's paying two hundred credits a head for the port to clear them, so we know we'll be getting people who can at least learn to work for you. It beats bringing a bunch of random thugs aboard."

"They're supposed to be my gunnery crew, why didn't Captain say anythin'?"

"Maybe he thought you'd cancel the whole deal to hire out of a pub somewhere," Stephanie said with a sigh.

Alice burst out laughing and put her arms across both of their shoulders. "This is why I rather travel with friends. The entertainment," she gave them a squeeze, barely reaching across Frost's shoulders, fully reaching around Stephanie's, then let them go.

Stephanie smiled at her and nodded. "The galaxy's better in good company."

"Well, if you're going to the port authority buildin', this is where we part ways," Frost said coolly. "Just head down Chara street and you'll see it after five or so minutes. I'll see you back at the ship in half an hour."

"Aye," Stephanie acknowledged.

"See you later Frost." Alice smiled.

He walked off into an alley and before he could get out of earshot Stephanie called after him. "Be careful!"

Stephanie and Alice followed the walkway for a while until it rejoined the main street. The many commercial and government spaces were lined up all along the lower level of the old colony ship. It had been lowered into the ground so the widest point, several kilometres across from what they could see, was at street level. The buildings around the colony ship were taller, more expensive in appearance as they got closer. The four and five storey buildings made of brick and old hulls were replaced with ten and fifteen storey buildings sculpted from metal and heavy concrete.

"So he's really using a head hunter service?" Alice asked.

"It was my idea, actually. I knew Frost was hurting to get a gunnery crew up and running. I could use a few mercenaries, and we need a lot of maintenance and repair staff."

"So you were thinking of Frost first."

"No. Well, sure I was. But what is a ship like that without gunnery crews? I mean, we don't even have a fighter wing set up."

"Uh-huh. All for the good of the ship," Alice teased with a smile.

"You're as bad as Ashley."

"So how well crewed will we be once they've loaded up?"

"Let's just say we'll be running a good rotation. We still need pilots if we start manufacturing fighters, a few more mechanics to maintain them, but for the time being we'll have the crew we need to run the ship and not put everyone on double shifts. It's hard trying to keep everyone on eight and twelve hour duty shifts when we really need everyone sixteen hours on, eight off."

"I don't know how Wheeler did it with under a hundred."

"Not well, I mean, the first time we got aboard we took his ship. His people were underpaid and demoralized. They couldn't even turn security measures on because it would interfere with the automation. I can't wait to see what the *Triton* is like with a fully trained crew."

"Me neither. Ever since I experienced the *First Light* with Jonas I've wanted to be back on board a ship like it, and to have the command chair for a shift five or six times a week," Alice shook her head, she was smiling, practically beaming. "I can't tell you, it's like a dream. I know it's early but Jake has practically adopted me, everyone else has been kind so far, and I'm actually getting the post I wanted. I wish Jonas were here."

"I'm so sorry, I couldn't imagine losing someone like that. I've lost people on boarding actions and during I don't know how many firefights, but-" Stephanie didn't finish her thought, she didn't want to bring Alice down as they walked along the busy street.

Alice looked to Stephanie and forced a brief smile. "I'll be okay. Jake's been a help. Lewis has been pretty good too. He doesn't know what to say most of the time, but lately he's been trying to make me laugh."

"The AI on your ship?"

"Yup, he's been around for a while. While I was alone on the run he was my best friend. I hope those times are gone, to be honest."

"Things are getting better. The wind's changing, something my father used to say," Stephanie said in a rare expression of optimism. "You're crew now."

The office for the Leute Menschen company wasn't nearly as busy as either of them expected. A tall gentleman in a grey business suit greeted them at the door and invited them both to sit at his desk. "So, you're here to finalize payment for the *Triton's* hiring initiative."

"That's right. I was surprised when Captain told me someone would have to finish this in person."

"Don't you mean *the Captain*, miss?"

"Oh, we just call him Captain like it's his name. Old habit," Stephanie informed cassually.

"Ah. Well, at Leute Menschen we prefer to put a personal touch on everything we can. Finalizing such a large recruitment in person adds an element of prestige to the transaction, don't you agree? Please, look into the scanner," he instructed pleasantly, holding up a stylus shaped scanning tool. Stephanie looked at it and a second later it beeped. "That's that then. We're all finished."

Alice's mental communicator came to life, Lewis' voice was muddled, there was a distortion in the background. "I cannot combat this foe any longer. I'm afraid the *Malice's* computer implanted virus is unlike any I had seen or am capable of eradicating. It wants me to broadcast it, to end lives. I could not tell you of it before now since admitting it's existence would give it power."

"Shut down, crash the *Clever Dream's* systems. Don't give in Lewis," she thought back.

"I cannot. Now that the ship is refuelled it is making its final push, breaking into my core program. To my great relief I was able to give you time to get away from me. I love you Alice, and I am so sorry. Run."

Alice leaned forward as though the wind had just been knocked out of her. She looked like she was in incredible pain and as Stephanie put a hand on her shoulder it eased. "Something's wrong with Lewis. He said he's been fighting a new virus then filled my receiver with some kind of static or machine code."

"What exactly did Lewis say to you miss?" asked the clean cut fellow behind the desk.

Alice gave him a suspicious look. Few people understood who Lewis was at first guess, especially since he used a mental communication link to speak to her when she was off ship. "He said it was unlike anything he'd seen and it wanted him to rebroadcast it."

"That isn't what he is telling me," the gentleman said before standing and reaching for Alice's throat in one swift motion.

His fingertips grazed her skin as she recoiled.

Stephanie drew her sidearm, set it to maximum with a flick of her thumb and fired on him several times. Bolts of energy opened wounds in his android body, nearly tore off his left arm, and finally decimated his face. He fell back twitching on the floor. "What's that all about?"

Alice looked outside and immediately caught sight of an automated rickshaw coming down the street at speed, running its three wheels over anyone in its path, terrifying the unfortunate passengers. A hovering garbage collector was grabbing and tossing people against the walls as it randomly raged through the street. Panic was spreading like a wildfire as automated systems went on the offensive. "This is bad," she said quietly.

"We have to get back to the ship," Stephanie replied.

"Oh no," Alice checked the ship status screen on her command and control unit. It verified her worst fear. "The *Clever Dream's* on full attack mode, striking at everything in the sky."

"Frost, where are you?" Stephanie asked, opening a comm line.

"I was nearly cut in half by a bulk loader just now! Everythin' with an AI installed is goin' berserk!"

"Don't run back to the ship. It's gone."

"What?"

"Lewis, Alice's AI took off with it," Stephanie said as she followed Alice behind the counter. The scene in the street was getting worse. The androids that normally blended in with the masses were starting to stand out as murderous things, striking and tearing at the panicking crowd with great speed, dexterity and efficiency.

"I'm going to try to contact Lewis again," Alice said as they huddled down behind the thick granite counter.

Stephanie nodded and continued talking to Frost. "Does your contact have a ship?"

"My contact is dead. He was standing right beside his auto companion when it went nuts."

"Auto companion?"

"Automated date lass. If you haven't seen one you should get out more."

"Why would I see one in public?"

"You have a point."

"Meet us at the Leute Menschen office."

"The loot men what office?"

"The head hunter office. I'll get in touch with the Captain. Be careful."

"Aye."

"*Triton*, Chief Vega here. We have an emergency."

Alice made a painful expression and held her head between her hands. "I can't-" she started before gasping. "-can't disconnect." She breathed heavily for several seconds then collapsed.

"We have an emergency!" Stephanie repeated. "*Triton*, please come in."

She looked at the communications status on her right wrist. There was no signal, no indication that the *Triton* was even there. "Frost, how far away are you?"

His line went active and she could hear the sounds of rapid gunfire, he was using his sidearm as though it were an automatic weapon. "Load lifter's after me, I think I made it angry!" He was running, shooting. "'Bout half way there though, you'll know when I'm close, just watch for the ragin' bulk lifter!"

She looked down at Alice and set her left command and control unit to inject a stimulant. "Alice tried to communicate with our ride and got knocked out, I'm going to try to get her back on her feet."

"That'd be nice, that hand cannon of hers might solve my problem. Make a hole! Comin' through!" she heard him shout to the screaming, panicking people nearby.

"I hope I set the dosage right," Stephanie said to herself as she sprayed the stimulant cocktail into the back of Alice's neck.

She sprung up to her feet, eyes wide open, gasping for air and reaching out with her hands at nothing in particular. Alice remembered where she was after a moment then dropped back down, panting and holding her chest.

"Sorry! Sorry! Don't die!"

"Feels like my heart's about to explode," Alice gasped as she braced herself and tried to calm down. "I'll be fine, it's okay," she reassured, looking at her command and control unit. "My heart rate's one ninety two, but it's coming down."

"These things materialize drugs I've never seen," Stephanie held up her wrists, showing her the two part command and control unit. "I didn't have a chance to read up."

"It's okay, at least I'm on my feet. We won't get any help from Lewis or the *Clever Dream* though. He managed to tell me he's leaving the system to send some kind of transmission. Then whatever virus infected him tried to infect me."

"Are you okay?"

"My mental comm is burned out, but I'm fine."

"Glad to hear you're up and about lass! I have incomin' and he's pissed!" Frost interrupted.

Both women peeked up over the counter and they couldn't see Frost, but his pursuer was brutally obvious. A three meter tall load lifter running on heavy armoured treads was speeding down main street. It had uncountable scorch marks across the front of its broad metal body but showed no signs of real damage. The four heavy arms all reached forward towards something ahead of it, ignoring everything else in the street.

Anyone still in the broad thoroughfare ran for their lives, those who didn't make it were crushed under the wide treads of the load lifter or butted aside by its reinforced metal body.

"He had to find the biggest robot in the city and piss it off," Stephanie complained as she checked the power level on her sidearm.

"I only got its attention when it was makin' for someone else." Frost said, he was gasping for breath. He came into sight then, running up a staircase, half looking backwards. He was firing like mad at its small head like sensor suite. The tip of his handgun was white hot and he actually managed to hit his mark two or three times. "Damn thing's heat shielded!" he shouted as he jumped over the railing and landed in a cart full of tourist trinkets. The lifter's left arms burst through the stone staircase and he kept after his target.

Frost was on his feet again and running for his life, trying to put more distance between him and his much larger peruser. "Can't hide from the damn thing either! Who in blazes gives a load lifter a scanning and targeting suite?"

"I've never seen anyone who looks like Frost move like that. I would have never thought to look at him," Alice said as she watched Frost and set her large sidearm to full automatic. The weapon made a whining sound as it began to draw power from the energy cell in front of the trigger.

"He has his moments," Stephanie commented.

"Thank you luv, just tell me you have some extra firepower waitin' for this bastard."

Alice took aim and braced herself. "I have something that should penetrate," she opened fire and her blazing white hot stream of shots went through the transparesteel store front window like paper. They went flying past the loader's head at first, but then she began to hit it. The sensor suite was filled with holes seconds later, and the load lifter started to rotate, flailing its arms near Frost. One caught his ankle, flinging him head over heels.

He flinched away from the arm as it made another grab for him, and it missed. Another arm caught his leg and hauled him into the air. "Get this thing offa me!" he shouted.

Alice started firing bursts down the robot's body, being careful not to hit Frost.

Stephanie jumped over the counter and ran out the door, pulling two grenades out of her left leg pocket. Her sidearm was in her other hand. She squeezed the trigger as fast as she could, hitting the chest plate of the large target but not penetrating it.

"Stay away lass! I'd be as good as gone if anythin' happened to ya!" Frost said as the load lifter tried to grip his head with another arm. He was pushing himself away from the two pronged hand, holding it off as best he could.

Stephanie ignored him and came to a sliding stop right beside one of its treads. She tossed one grenade in between the armour plate and the gears then ran behind it, looking for an opening. "Fire in the hole!" she called out.

"Bloody hell!" Frost said as he curled into the fetal position best he could while hanging upside down.

The load lifter rocked back and forth as the grenade went off. Its right tread was rendered useless. Some of the plating on the lower half of its body came loose and Stephanie caught a glimpse of its power supply. "You okay Frost?"

The load lifter dropped him and he landed head first. His vacsuit protected him, hardening over his head, bracing his neck and spine. "I think you got its attention."

Stephanie saw its torso just about to rotate towards her and took her shot. She tossed the grenade at the small opening revealing its power cell and it bounced off. Without a second thought she ran between its tractor treads, picked up the live grenade, attached it to the underside of its torso and pulled herself over its working metal tread.

To Alice and Frost's amazement she barely made it, putting the armoured tread between herself and the blast. She was still in the air when it went off, and she was sent rolling away by the concussive force.

Frost was there in a heartbeat, and seeing no obvious injury, he picked her up in his arms and ran for the head hunter's office. The load lifter, deprived of power, went limp.

"I'm all right." she said quietly.

"You're a little touched in the head lass."

"I saved your ass, didn't I?"

He burst through the door, crossed the room and put her down on the counter. They both got behind it for cover.

"*Triton* to ground team, our communications were offline, are you all right?"

"Good to hear your voice Cynthia. We're under cover for now, but need a pickup."

"Building lockdown in progress," said a calm voice over the audio system. Heavy security doors started rolling down over the display windows.

The trio were on their feet, jumping over the reception counter and rushing the exit. Alice and Frost made it through the door while Stephanie jumped through the hole in the transparesteel window.

"We're trying to get something off the deck for you now, but it's a mess in orbit. Every ship with an AI is shooting down manually run vessels. Even the space station started firing for a while," Cynthia replied.

"We have to get under cover," Alice said as the three of them looked around. The streets were starting to empty, corpses, ruined fixtures, scorched ground and broken storefronts marked the passage of the recent carnage. Most of the machines had moved indoors, chasing after people who tried to take cover.

"Tell us if you manage to get anything off the deck and on it's way. We're heading for the port," Stephanie said finally.

"We've got company," Frost said, looking up to a pair of surveillance drones. They were unarmed but speeding towards them.

All three of them drew and fired. One of the green oval drones was sent spinning off to the right, the other was destroyed in mid air and they had to dodge the husk as it crashed between them. "This is going to get worse before it gets better, lets go," Stephanie said, heading out at a run towards the load lifter's remains.

# General David Collins

The bridge of the *RGS Saviour* was quiet but busy. General Collins watched the thirty posts from where he sat at the rear of the large triangular compartment. The slanted transparent panels along the front two sides of the bridge provided a breathtaking view of the Pollanis system. The distant planet of Daracka hung in the distance, while the dark side of a large rogue planet obscured a third of the view.

The rogue planet was erupting with plumes of ice and water as nearby gravity compressed it from the outside in. The particles drifting across the vista looked incredible, but more importantly the moon and it's debris masked the presence of the *Saviour*, a small but well armed Regent Galactic Destroyer.

Most of the bridge staff were busy collecting data from Daracka, the first deployment site for the aptly named Holocaust Virus. Every time Collins heard or had to say the name he was tempted to shake his head. Gabriel Meunez, it's creator, had named it. *The man may program fifty four lines a second but he doesn't have a truly creative bone in his body. Even the Holocaust Virus, God, that name again, is only derivative and it took him forever to finish it.*

"Sir, the *VCS Malice* has just arrived. They're two point three kilometres off the aft port side." Reported the blue eyed, dark haired woman at tactical.

"God, I have to have him recode his transponder so it doesn't read as a Vindyne ship." Collins said, shaking his head.

"*Malice* command informs us that his shuttle is on it's way," reported the tall, thin blond haired communications officer.

"Have him meet me in my quarters," he said as he stood and straightened his long grey shirt. The exit was right behind him, something he liked about the new bridge design. He was forced to walk a few steps down from his solitary command seat then around the dais, which was a design aspect he did not like, however. The rationale behind it was simple; no one could speak to him from behind. He still disliked the extra few steps he had to traverse in order to get to and from the chair.

The main hallways on the new ship weren't broad like the ones on the Overlord class vessels, one of the few things he missed from his days with Vindyne, but three people could pass without knocking elbows. Just a few steps outside the bridge there was a private lift so he could reach his quarters in less than a minute. A request he had made when they assigned him to the *Saviour*. From what he saw in the report regarding the alteration, which he barely read, they had to re-route main power lines and many critical control circuits to fulfil his request.

He didn't care as long as they got it done by the time he arrived on board, and it was all there as promised on the ship's recommissioning date. The ship was only a year old, but he insisted it be re-christened under its new name. He was bringing them Hampon and more importantly, the obsessed Meunez. To Regent Galactic's broad approval, the plans were working. The Eden Fleet was under their control, and the Holocaust Virus was starting its rampant tear across the universe.

Only the Saved and Regent Galactic controlled systems would be safe from the billions of artificial intelligences that saw humanity as a scourge. The company would have control over as much or as little of the galactic market as they liked. When the Virus made it to the Core Worlds, the economic center of the known galaxy, all of humanity would quake. A new center would be formed, the location of which would be left to Regent Galactic's choosing.

The double doors to his quarters parted and he stepped inside. The open concept space lit up dully. The whole ceiling and half circle hull surrounding the living space was transparent. The white and blue rogue planet was in full view. The ice and water spouted out into space, a sight he would miss. Just to the edge of the its horizon was the *Malice*. Compared to the efficient looking design of the *Saviour* the Vindyne warship looked like it was constructed out of blocks and rectangles laid down from left to right, from largest sections to smallest. It looked like it was from not only a different part of space, but another time entirely. *The galaxy has moved on out here, Gabriel. I wish you could see that and move on as well. You were a good man before Alice came along.*

The center of the lavish abode was reserved for entertainment and seating. Three sofas that shifted and reclined as the occupant moved were the main feature of the semicircular seating area. Between them were blue recliners that were of similar feature, and in the middle was an antique cedar coffee table. Atop that was another of his favourite things; apple whiskey. Of all the things Regent Galactic produced, and there were millions of objects, that was his favourite.

He clapped his hands, rubbed them together and walked around the low table to the middle sofa. General Collins poured himself a glass of apple whiskey and sat back.

As he just finished taking his first sip and smacked his lips the door chime dinged. "Come in!" Collins called out.

Gabriel Meunez stepped inside and walked straight to the window. Outside was the *Malice*, her long, severe shape was darkened by the edge of the rogue planet's shadow. "I haven't seen the repairs from the outside of the ship yet."

Collins looked at the man. He was in a dark blue Freegrounder vacsuit. Over top he wore a flight jacket, like the antique leathers pilots donned in centuries past on earth, before space travel. It was inspired by Alice, he knew, and it didn't suit the shoddy looking scrawny man. His shoulder length hair was unkempt, it looked like he hadn't slept in days. Something had happened to the genius at the core of their operation. He could hear the micro motor in the other man's eye adjust and focus in on the ship in the distance. "You should get that fixed or replaced by a biological one with a wet circuit that does the same thing."

"It works perfectly. The noise is only an irritation to those who have an intolerance for people who improve themselves past specification," he examined the section of the ship that had been damaged by the antimatter explosion set off by

Jonas and Alice when they escaped. "I'll have to reward my crew when I return. They did an excellent job. You almost can't tell there was ever any damage."

"You should put that ship in mothballs and accept Regent Galactic's offer. These new destroyers do with a quarter the crew and a third the size what two average Vindyne vessels were capable of."

"Ah, the *Malice* is not a typical Vindyne ship. There are few vessels in the galaxy that can match her," Meunez turned around and picked up the decanter on the table. "Your criticisms aside, how is the deployment going?"

"Perfectly. The *Clever Dream* allowed her pilot to land and once she was refuelled it started sending the Holocaust Virus through every communications system on the planet. After that she moved on."

"Where to?"

"Most likely the nearest settled area with a hyper-transmitter system."

"Was anyone aboard?"

"We couldn't tell for certain, the infected AI aboard-"

"Lewis," Meunez filled in as he put the decanter back down making a disgusted expression at the smell of the liquid inside.

"Lewis was too evasive. We won't be actively tracking the *Clever Dream* anyway. Dozens of hyperdrive and wormhole capable ships have already left the system to spread the virus."

"You should track Lewis, there are possibilities there. Are you surprised at my Holocaust Virus? How much more capable it is than yours?" Meunez asked with a smug grin.

"Two tools performing two completely different tasks. Mine defeated all the digital defences of the Eden Fleet and created a control interface while yours twists and corrupts normal artificial intelligences then tasks them to obey Hampon's zealots. Both are impressive in their own way."

"Modest as always. What of Alice?"

"She's probably dead. She's not in the West Keeper or the Saved databases, so the AIs won't spare her."

"You didn't send units down to rescue her?"

Collins looked at the other man and sighed. "Gabriel, you have to let it go. You've obviously learned what you had to from her, what more can there be?"

Meunez pushed his wavy dark hair out of his face and sat down in a deeply padded blue arm chair. "She is a miracle. Compared to her your kind are but children at play."

"We have scans of her, whole nervous system and brain captures from numerous port authority checks. There's nothing there Gabriel. Whatever special attribute that body or her artificial intelligence had that allowed her to seamlessly cross over is gone. She's probably grown out of it or become so well integrated that she's just another human woman now. Perhaps exceptional on that scale, but worthy of quoting poetry and sending millions worth in resources after?" Collins threw up his hands. "It's pointless."

Gabriel stood up and pointed angrily. "The deal was; I get Alice and keep Jonas if I can infect Lewis with the virus and get this whole God damned show started for Regent Galactic so they can push their Saved agenda out here and the Citizenship agenda closer to the core. That was the deal!"

"That was supplemental to what we actually needed! All you really had to do was finish your Holocaust Virus and find a ship to distribute it, something small, fast and durable enough to survive several jumps to well settled systems. As for the riders you attached to our deal, well, you're the one who let Jonas and Alice escape. I'm surprised they didn't discover the Holocaust Virus and disable it. You took far too great a risk."

"The *Clever Dream* is the perfect ship, and there's no telling how far she'll go with Lewis aboard. I did my part, but you knew Alice was on that planet and just ignored the opportunity to get her back to me. I risk my life for the cause and you just disregard my goals? That's an insult!"

"Some assets are too much trouble to acquire! Go back to your ship and deal with it, get over it, make some flesh and machine amalgamation or transformed tart of your own in that lab of yours."

"If only it were so easy. You never did appreciate the uniqueness of her. Besides, Eve's children and the Holocaust infected AIs will not kill her. She was the first name on the Saved list. The only one that will not have to spend a single credit to be spared from the cleansing."

"That's a break in the contract, Gabriel! We promised exclusive control over that list to Regent Galactic. Sure Hampon's in charge of his little cult but we didn't let him off the leash, Regent did! If they find out you did this without authorization they'll take everything!"

"You always were easily controlled. A slave to your need for power, material possessions. These things are only tools. A means to gather that which matters, objects worthy of our lasting desires."

"You're starting to sound like Hampon. I knew there was a chance running the West Keepers and the Saved initiatives would push him over the edge eventually, but I thought you had your baggage under control. I never would have imagined you'd lose it before him."

"This is not insanity! This is destiny! Hampon will save a thousand for every million and elevate ten to West Keeper so they may protect the one in a million that go East, to Eden itself!"

"You're jacked into this with him? Eden in the east, protectors in the West. It's all based on a misinterpretation of old religious passages he used to form a cult while Regent Galactic gets proper marketing together! There's nothing more to it! When we're finished Hampon will be given a nice little system out of the way or martyred so the whole thing can be replayed on a bigger scale!"

Gabriel continued, furious beyond reason, tears dripping down his shaking, flushed face. "Alice will be as the first Eve, she will show us the way to our mechanized utopia and rule from her high seat in Eden right beside me. The division between men and machines will break down as both races find the next evolutionary stage!"

"Bullshit! It's all just a way to tear the competition apart and take control! This safety key you made will diffuse the virus as soon as Regent Galactic rescue ships arrive, they'll get all the credit! That's the point to all of this! The Cash Messiah Business Model demands that all of this chaos is eventually brought to an end with as few benefactors in place as possible! One day I'll get the call and the whole party ends, AIs go back to doing the thinking we don't find interesting and we'll be their unquestioned masters again. All with the insertion of a simple deactivation code!" He pulled a data chip on a chain out from under his shirt and held it out as he stood to shout at the other man. "Get your head straight or you won't have a place with anyone standing at the top!"

Gabriel snatched the decanter from the table and clubbed the other man hard, breaking teeth and skin. He took it up over his head with both hands and brought it down over Collins as he fell, crushing his nose. Following him down to the deck and kneeling on one of his arms he brought the bottle down again and again, across his eyes, his forehead, over and over until Collins stopped breathing, moving.

Gabriel Meunez let the unbroken decanter fall from his hands and let a chortle escape between his clenched teeth. The sound pierced the silence in the room, a second giddy chuckle threatened to burst from the tight bundle he felt in his stomach but he scowled and clenched his jaw. "No, can't let it happen. The machine feels one way, man feels another, can't let them tangle just now," he tore the virus deactivation chip off the corpse and put the bloodied chain around his own neck. The vacsuit and jacket he wore was covered in blood, a fact he didn't notice as he crossed the room and interfaced with the main computer in the Generals quarters using his neural link. "Man emotions make the digital unclear, the wheels cackle their own statement of affairs. Straight, have to keep them all straight for control," he breathed to himself, trying to regain his composure.

He reached into his digital memory and commanded a version of the Holocaust Virus to replace all the command codes with his own and form a direct link between himself and the vessel. Only the current crew of the *Saviour* would survive aboard. The ship would kill intruders and traitors who disobeyed orders.

"Bow to me, *Saviour*," he said aloud and digitally to the ships artificial intelligence, and after a few moments, it was done. The grin threatened to return and he let the joy on the cybernetic side of his brain commingle with the feeling of satisfaction growing in his birth given brain. His eyes rolled into the back of his head as his connection with the ship computer was complete and the artificial intelligence there signalled its absolute subservience. "I bet God never experienced quintplex cluster core processing or a quadrillion petabyte database." He spent minutes that felt like days on his knees, experiencing the link with something larger than himself. The machine had answers. Asking questions of the collected information, sorting through communications was only the beginning. Before long his unified mind, part artificial and part human intelligence was putting something together; a big picture.

The occurrences and plans of Regent Galactic, how it fit with the fall of Vindyne, where he and Hampon fit into the puzzle and where the Board of Directors wanted it to lead were all becoming clear. It was a realization that defied expression, but there it was, seated in the center of his mind and suddenly so many little things ceased to matter. Gabriel's eyes snapped open, he hadn't realized what toll the experience was taking on his body. His mouth hung slack, only a passage for him to breathe through, his heart pounded so hard he feared his ribs would break, and the blood rushing through his head sounded like a roaring river. "The pawn only transcends once he can see the entire board," he managed between hurried breaths.

Gabriel strode out of the quarters covered in the blood and gore of his labours and crew members stepped out of his way immediately, one stopped to throw up at the sight of him. Half way to the bridge he was confronted by four guards who levelled their rifles at him. "Come quietly sir. The Regent Galactic Liaison would like to address what's happened."

Wordlessly he willed the emergency bulkhead to shut. In the space of half a second it closed, crushing down on one of the guards arms and legs. Using his mental link with the ship he ordered it to eject the contents of that hallway section into space, and it was done. The bulkhead opened again and he continued on to the bridge.

The shocked stares of the bridge officers brought a smile to his face. *They will worship my power.* "I am assuming command. Have your scans located one named Alice Valent or the *Clever Dream*?"

The tactical and communications officers got to work nervously, quickly checking their information. "We don't have a current location on Alice Valent and the *Clever Dream* has entered a wormhole."

Gabriel clenched his jaw and sneered, his anger threatened to boil to the surface as he stood at the rear of the bridge with clenched fists. His eye focused on the *Triton* then as he watched it in orbit. Jake Valance was in command. Hampon had informed him a very short time ago that Wheeler had lost control. If he attacked that ship it would disappear. Their cloaking device was near impenetrable and they'd most likely not make the mistake of engaging in a firefight with so much chaos in the system.

"Coordinate with the *Malice* and set a course for Lectivus!" He shouted. "We have some precious cargo to retrieve."

"So you are aware." One navigation officer started nervously. "That'll take us twelve days at our best speed sir."

"The passage of time will serve our purposes. While we travel the Holocaust will spread and billions of disciples electric will be ready to do my bidding upon our return. Set the course and get us underway."

# The Rescue Effort

"We have nothing combat ready down there?" Captain Valance asked Paula at the flight control station on the deck beneath him.

"Nothin'. Chief Vercelli started working on the *Cold Reaver* but didn't get a chance to finish. Other than that we're full up with personnel transports and a couple boarding craft," Paula reported with shrug.

"The boarding craft, can he get one of them ready for launch?"

"No, one of the personnel craft went berserk and smashed itself into the deck. Lucky we didn't lose hanger two all together. Can't launch anything until the wreck is cleared. Chief says that'll be at least half an hour."

"Do we have anyone else incoming?"

"Nay sir, the last personnel transport was destroyed before she could get to us."

Captain Valance sat back in his chair. "Tactical, how are our shields holding up?"

"We're fine. Nothing out there is big enough to penetrate except for that station, and it looks like they have it under control."

"Good. Cloak the ship if something dangerous has us in its sights." He knitted his fingers together and leaned his chin on his knuckles as he listened to Stephanie, Frost and Alice's chatter. They were under fire from something, and on the run. "We have three people down there and no way to retrieve them. Does anyone have any ideas?"

For a moment everyone seemed stunned, the sounds of an active firefight over the command chair speaker was the loudest background noise.

"Get down!" Stephanie shouted.

There was an explosion three seconds later, then the sounds of them running, a metal gate or plate metal crashing, more running.

"There's another one. I never realized how dangerous maintenance bots were!" Alice shouted as she fired off several rounds.

"We're gettin' closer ta port, there'll be more," Frost said hurriedly, fighting for breath as they hustled through the urban terrain.

"Dammit! Anything!" Captain Valance shouted, bringing his fist down on his arm rest.

Ashley turned her seat around. "This ship can go atmospheric. I don't think there's room to land, but we can meet them half way."

"Chief Grady, do we have enough power to enter the atmosphere and hover?"

"I have five reactors online, if we have enough working repulsor field generators, we can do it."

"How long will it take to test them?"

"Properly? Four or five hours."

"There won't be anything left to rescue in four hours, Chief."

"Give us a minute."

"All right."

"Why aren't they under attack?" Alice was heard asking through the communicator.

"I have no idea, but they should be shredded by now," Frost replied.

The group of a hundred or so mixed armed citizens, most of them well moneyed from the look, stood in a line across the main gate leading to the Port Authority Inspection Point. There were several androids and various robots leisurely cleaning the street within several meters. They dragged corpses into gutters, pushed vending machines upright, and repaired fine electronics like door controls and communication hubs.

"I don't get it. Are those bots just unaffected by the virus?" Stephanie asked no one in particular in a low whisper. They were hiding inside a thick white brick building, looking through a thick transparesteel window. It was open just a crack, admitting a warm breeze.

"If Lewis couldn't resist the virus, I doubt a maintenance bot could."

A woman and three men crept down the alley ahead and looked onto the same scene. After a moment's consideration one of them stepped out. "We have wounded, can you help us?" he called out to the line of people in front of the broad arched gate.

A sandy haired boy in blue and green robes emerged from the crowd and opened his arms invitingly. "If you are judged favourably by Eve's children the West Keepers will help you." Spoke one of the guardians. The machines in the street all stopped what they were doing and looked at the solitary man.

He took a staggering step back. "Do you have a medic kit or is there a paramedic that could help?"

"Oh no," whispered Alice sadly as she looked away.

The androids and robots all rushed the fellow, within seconds he was torn to pieces. Maintenance bots turned towards the alley and began firing high intensity cutting lasers, killing his fleeing companions. When the newcomers were all dead they set back to work cleaning up.

"There has to be another way," Stephanie whispered.

"We could pretend to join these people, they're all wearing green and blue arm bands, that's got to help us somehow. Maybe we can beg or buy a few from them."

"Or make like we forgot ours somewhere?" Frost added with a shrug.

"I'm a very bad actor," Alice whispered.

Stephanie looked at the crowd of people quietly for several moments. "I don't know if we could pull it off."

"We have a solution," Came Captain Valance's voice through Stephanie and Frost's communicators. "We're going to go atmospheric and lay down cover fire for you. We're sending a heavy escape shuttle down. Does it look like that group is going to be a problem?"

"You could probably scare them back into the main port if you hit the street in front of the entrance," Stephanie replied.

"What's going on?" Alice asked, unable to hear the Captain's side of the conversation.

"Captain's looking to make some craters and get us some help," Frost said a little eagerly.

"He's taking *Triton* atmospheric?" she asked, her eyes wide.

A rumbling in the distance was her answer, and all three of them looked up. The *Triton's* broad hull was like a looming, growing stingray shaped shadow against the light blue sky. The five active pulse turrets on the bottom of the hull fired at smaller vessels that darted around it, making weak attacks. It was like watching a behemoth swat away flies.

One of the paired pulse cannons swivelled towards the street in front of the main port entrance and fired. The crowd turned and ran through the port gates. The air pressure shifted, they could all feel it on their faces, as three of the main engines rotated and fired in repulsor mode, glowing bright white. The ship stopped and hovered less than three hundred meters up as the pulse turret reduced two meter circles of sand to slag and glass.

The maintenance bots fired their cutting lasers to no effect as everyone and everything else ran for cover. A blocky emergency shuttle launched from one of the port airlocks and hastily descended. It landed hard in the street beside the building they hid in, kicking up dirt and dust for a city block in every direction. The weight of it crushed stone walkways and a fast food materializer station to rubble under its armoured landing skids.

The trio pushed the window of their hiding spot open and climbed through it as quickly as possible. A cutting laser swept across them to no effect, their vacsuits easily absorbed and dissipated the energy. Then they were inside the shuttle. Alice sat in the copilot's seat and to her surprise Ashley was at the controls. She gave her a brief, excited embrace and checked the copilot's station. "Who's flying the *Triton*?"

"Captain. I had no idea he knew how, but he did train me, after all."

"The controls aren't much different from the style used by some very old Freeground ships. I'm not surprised. Still, some good piloting there."

Several rounds struck the shuttle's hull, barely scorching the armour. They made a quick ascent and landed in a small space that had been cleared in the *Triton's* center hangar. Most of the space was filled with old salvage, damaged fighters and other unidentifiable heavy objects. The hangar door closed behind them. "Bridge, we're in," Ashley reported.

Frost turned a small golden chip end over end in his hand. "I nicked it out of the holoprojector on my way out. Likely has more than the information we were looking for on it, I'd wager."

Stephanie watched him from where she was strapped into her seat, across from him in the rear compartment of the escape shuttle. "Did you see anything before his Andi went homicidal?"

"Aye, directory trees with a few hundred entries."

"Did you know him well?"

"Freeman? Never been one of my close mates. He kept closer to a more dangerous sort. Bein' a provider of information it helped his trade to know them better than people like me." Frost looked across the dim cabin and smiled uneasily. "I'd have been done for good if it weren't for you back there."

She smiled back at him, he didn't thank people often, not that she'd seen. "Nothing some quick thinking and a couple of grenades couldn't fix."

"Where'd you learn ta move like that anyhow?"

"I was in gymnastics when I was growing up on the colony and I kept it up. It was hard on the *Samson,* but I can still do a backflip and walk on my hands in full gravity."

"I'll have ta see that some time. I'm thinkin' you'll find somewhere on the *Triton* ta practice."

"I hadn't thought of that. There's just been too much going on I guess."

"Aye, that there has. With tumblin' skills like yours, you should try one of the armoured excursion suits. I bet you could do cartwheels."

The shuttle powered down and the hatch at the rear popped open and they both unstrapped. "The ones used for loading the rail cannons?"

"Aye, they're armoured space combat getups, made for a lot more n' loadin' guns. Ever try one?"

"I never had the chance to certify for vacuum combat in the army. Only special forces got to use that kind of gear. Our ships used energy weapons, so we didn't have big gun crews either."

"Ah, they had thousands of marines outfitted with 'em where I'm from an' solid shot was preferred. Even I got to try 'em. Just imagine yourself bigger and about fifty times stronger. Not to mention a whole lot tougher. Come on up to the gunnery deck later, I'll show you how to run in one."

She smiled and nodded. "Never know when I'll have to do a patrol of the outer hull. Thanks, I'll take you up on it."

Frost and Stephanie led the way to the lift with Ashley and Alice behind, listening in on their conversation.

They looked around at the disused fighters, hull segments, machines and other random objects that were too heavy or large to easily transport elsewhere on the ship. Hanger one was the largest of the hangars. It was massive, stretching over five hundred meters down the center line of the ventral section of the *Triton*. There were fighter racks and suspension arms to the sides and along the top of the great big space, but there were only three fighters in questionable condition, leaving over a hundred spots along the walls empty. "It's a shame ta see such a space wasted," Frost said, his voice echoing.

"I guess Wheeler never got the right crews together," Stephanie added, looking at a two seated fighter that had been deposited upside down on the deck beside them. One of its engines was a bubbled, molten mess.

"Do you think Captain will ever get a fighter wing on board?" Ashley asked from behind.

"If he wants a bunch of hot headed fighter jocks on board, he'll get them. He hasn't said anything to me about it though. Have you heard him say anything Alice?"

"Not yet, but then it's early. He's really just started getting everything together. I don't know where he gets the energy. I think he slept two hours last night."

"There's a lot goin' on. I hope most o' my gunnery team arrived."

"Too bad we didn't land in bay two, otherwise we might have run into some of them. They didn't all get a chance to dock with a hard point, some of them had to land in a hurry. One even set down on top of a couple emergency fighters. Paula was hopping up and down she was so pissed," Ashley commented, shaking her fists and jumping a few times in imitation of the short, high spirited woman.

"The mess piles higher," Frost commented with a chuckle. "Maybe *Triton* is cursed to collect trash."

They stepped into the lift and Stephanie selected the command deck as their destination on the express car control panel.

"I'm sure Captain'll put the escape and boarding shuttles to use somehow or sell them somewhere," Ashley said as she rocked on her heels. "I just can't wait to get back to the bridge. Flying *Triton* is amazing."

"I'll be in the Security office for the next few hours at least. Your gunner boys will need somewhere to sleep and we'll be making the assignments." Stephanie said, smirking at Frost.

"Don't be too good to 'em at first. I'll need leverage to work with. The best of them will get the good digs, while the worst'll have to make due with bunks."

"That fits, I was thinking I'd put them in the upper berth where the refugees were. It's not far from the main gunnery deck and it's already been cleared."

"Aye, that'll work. Glad you took the security Chief post, lass. You've got a good head on." Frost said with a wink. "Oh, an' when ye hand out bunks, give 'em a notice ta clean the space, I'll be inspectin' their space."

The express car doors opened and they stepped out.

"Thank God you're back in one piece!" Grace called from Frost's right. She stepped in close beside him and put her arms around his shoulders. He turned into her and was rewarded with a wet, lingering kiss that was salacious enough to draw stares and glances.

Stephanie watched for a moment, her face turning red, then Grace's eyes opened to slits and met hers. The taller woman pressed more eagerly against Frost, deepening their kiss.

"I'll be in security," Stephanie said quietly as she jerked her gaze away and stalked off.

Alice and Ashley made for the bridge, leaving Frost and the temporary medical Chief behind.

Captain Valance stood and let Ashley take the controls as soon as she came to stand behind him. "Thank you for making that run, Ash," he whispered as he walked back to the command chair.

"My pleasure sir. We really should keep one of those dropships ready though. That emergency shuttle flew like a brick."

"We will. Chief Vercelli is working on sorting the deck out down there."

"That could take a while sir," Paula called up from below. "There's no room to work."

"I know, thank you Assistant Chief."

The control center below the main bridge had already started clearing out. There wasn't much need for anything but a watch of two while they were in hyperspace.

Ashley smiled at her copilot, Larry Nevil, who brought up their status. "We're in hyperspace, accelerating at thirty one percent of engine tolerance. Our course is steady and straight for the next two point five hours before the next course correction, all our emitters are firing normally except for twenty three B and ninety five C. We're headed to dead space past the Wargan System, nice and close to the Gavin Five nebula." He informed her.

She checked her controls, made sure they were locked and nodded. "Why are we headed to dead space?"

"Captain said we needed time to get the ship in order."

"That makes sense. I guess I'm used to the *Samson*. We'd take on a dozen people at the most and just train them as we went along. I think I held up the crew the most when I took over as pilot. Captain had to take the controls for a lot of minor things for a while."

"You haven't been flying long?"

"A couple of years."

"I'm surprised, you're really good. At first I didn't think you could hack it but you learned the ins and outs faster than I did and you listen to your navigator."

"Thank you, and why wouldn't I?" she shrugged. "You're always calm and thinking ahead. Have you piloted the *Triton* before?"

"Only briefly. The profile took a lot of getting used to, it's a wide ship. I prefer navigation. I can't tell you exactly why." His pleasant demeanour changed suddenly as he grabbed her arm in a vice like grip. Larry's eyes went wide, his pupils dilated visibly, and he began to choke.

"Captain!" Ashley called out.

He started falling out of his chair and Ashley tried to catch him, to hold him up.

Captain Valance and Alice were there an instant later. "Let him go," Alice said calmly but firmly. They pulled him down to the floor and his body went limp.

"He's stopped breathing," Captain Valance said as he took a medical scan. "Get that command and control unit off him. It injected him with a lethal dose of–" he took a moment to read the scan and shook his head; "something."

Alice tried to pull it off, but the thin arm computing unit held fast. "There's an AI running on this thing. I don't know what it's doing."

Ashley looked on helplessly as the colour started to drain out of her new found friend's face. His mouth was hanging open, his eyes stared off into nothing and she prayed the Captain could do something.

Alice got the control unit off his arm with a loud click. "Got it. The AI was holding it closed."

Jake injected the navigator right away with his own arm unit then took out another cylinder and pressed it against the young man's throat firmly. "Cynthia! Send an order ship wide for everyone with an artificial intelligence to remove their command and control units then delete the AI."

She took her own pair off then made the ship wide announcement.

Captain Valance did the same, pulling his large black command unit off before looking back to Larry.

The Navigator gasped, then began to vomit. Jake rolled him onto his side while Alice took another medical scan. "The nanos and chemical cocktail you gave him countered the toxins and are clearing them out."

Ashley's eyes were locked on the scene before her. Larry curled into the fetal position as he retched and tried to breathe at the same time. Alice was comforting him, but he looked like he was in a desperate struggle to breathe between heaves. He coughed and gagged several more times, producing a brown and green sludge before the retching came to a stop. He laid there, catching his breath.

"You'll be fine. Your artificial intelligence tried to kill you."

"It was just an organizer program with a base personality over top," he said, still out of breath.

"There was no security installed?" Captain Valance asked.

"No, it wasn't that important."

"Good, let's hope that we caught the problem in time. If the rest of the people who transferred AI's to their C and C units had security installed, they might get lucky."

Captain Valance picked up his own arm unit. "Not by much, my AI was secure and it's already looking erratic," he entered his security code and deleted it.

"If it's all the same Captain, I don't think I'll put my unit back on. Can I get another with just the base software?" Larry asked, finally catching his breath and wiping his mouth with a handkerchief from his thigh pocket.

"No problem," Jake smiled back at him. His attention was drawn to the pile of throw up beside the young man and a sinking feeling came over him. He looked to the security station where a small, older fellow stood watch. "Shut down all the maintenance and cleaning bots. Everything that could have an AI."

"Aye sir," He replied. "Wait, they're already shut down."

"Chief Grady to the Bridge. I shut them down as soon as someone down here collapsed. We lost three people."

"I'm sorry Chief, take them to medical in case we can do something."

"That's not likely. They were injected with hydrofluoric acid and blood thinners. It's like their AI's were networked and all came up with the same plan."

"Do you have any recommendations Chief?"

"I'd have all the arm units with AI's tossed into recyclers. Even if they were deleted. Other than that you've done exactly what I would've."

"Thank you Liam, I'm sorry about your men."
"Nothing we could have done. Chief Grady out."

# Ashley Lamport

The two hours following the incident on the bridge were filled with bad news. They had lost forty seven people to attacks from the artificial intelligence programs many crewmembers trusted to help them through their every day lives. Over three hundred had been injured. The infirmary was full past brimming, and Alice had gone to help however she could. When she was an artificial intelligence herself she possessed a complete medical treatment database and a great deal of that knowledge had survived the transfer. It surprised even her how quickly it came back to her.

Morale on the ship was low, and to the crew's relief, only a minimum watch was required during hyperspace travel. Security was finally under control, and that made everything easier. If someone didn't know where they were supposed to be or got lost a soldier was always nearby to help them find their way. The unexplored sections of the ship were closed off and the entrances were all locked down or had guards standing watch.

Ashley changed into a light blue vacsuit with transparent arms and midriff after getting a new command and control unit from the materializer. She didn't have an AI installed in her last one, but it made her feel better to get a new unit anyway. Besides, the newer versions could make vacsuits look like practically anything and she was eager to give it a try. Anything to brighten her day after what she'd seen on the planet and the incident on the bridge.

Her new quarters were incredible. She looked around while putting on her gun belt. Everything was coloured a deep shade of red except the carpet, which was midnight black. There was a thickly padded seat along one wall, a two dimensional display coating the wall behind it gave the illusion of a long window. By pressing a button the floor would part and up would come the silver table with six chairs around it. A holographic projector somewhere, she hadn't found it yet, could entertain her with full height programs anywhere she wanted in her quarters whether she was sitting on the smaller seat closer to the door, in the soft queen sized bed that adjusted to the needs of her body, or in the slightly smaller space that was left unfurnished except for two end tables that had been left stacked there.

*I've seen apartments I couldn't dream of that weren't this nice. I hope they didn't assign me here by mistake. These look more like Captain's quarters.*

She adjusted her gun belt and took an extra data chip, small makeup kit and hair tie from a floor to ceiling trinket shelf beside the door and dropped them into a pouch on her belt. Her new vacsuit didn't have pockets, she had forgotten them until the last minute.

"Dim lights to three hundred lumens please," she said to the computer, forgetting the artificial intelligence had been removed and they hadn't put in a new voice activated system yet. She adjusted them with the control by the door then set out.

Her quarters were less than fifty meters from the main entrance to the bridge. She wanted to move into a smaller compartment in the same berth as the deck crew, near where fighter pilots would bunk up, but Stephanie's security department assigned her to the command deck quarters. Instead of arguing she thought she'd take a look. *Good thing too. If those really are my quarters I really do want to live here. I'm sure I won't be the only one,* she thought to herself as she stepped into the express lift. Another crewman looked her up and down as she entered her destination. She gave him a little smile and looked back to the lift doors. His hair was tied into a ponytail, and his grey vacsuit had *Triton* printed over his left pectoral. It marked him as a new crew member, probably part of the gunnery team on his way back to the gunnery deck.

She had just read the bulletin right before getting off duty. Even as tragedy struck the ship, policies were put in place and things changed. On her next duty shift she'd have to wear a full black vacsuit with a silver skull and *Triton* printed underneath it on the left side of her chest just below the collarbone. Five silver wings would mark her as Master of the Helm, a rank she had only heard of in a holographic feature movie about a war in the Core Worlds. She had no idea the system was keeping a score card for her, but when she got her rank it gave her pages of statistics. Apparently the only person who had out flown her in the few simulations she had taken part in was Alice, she had even beaten the Captain by a very narrow margin.

Alice had been given the rank of First Officer and was placed on the first night watch Bridge Commander. *That's probably why I got Master of the Helm. Don't really care though, as long as I get to fly. This ship might be the heaviest thing I've ever seen, but it feels like I'm drifting through an ocean when I fly her. It makes the Samson seem like flying a twitchy sand bug.*

The lift stopped and she got off. The medical center was busy, most of the beds were full and several emergency beds had been pulled out, making the normally spacious and airy infirmary seem cramped and noisy.

"Um, hi, is there anything I can do here?" She asked a fellow wearing a dark blue vacsuit with a red cross on the back.

He stopped and looked her up and down. "Do you have any advanced medical training?"

"No, I just thought if you needed an extra pair of hands."

"We're all right now. Mostly everyone's in recovery or here for observation."

"You're sure?"

The nurse smiled and nodded. "Thank you for offering, you're the first."

Ashley shrugged. "I'm here to see a friend anyway."

"Who?"

"Finn."

His smile faded, she could tell he was bracing himself to deliver some bad news. "He's been in stasis since the initial boarding. Did anyone tell you about his condition?" He asked in a whisper, gently putting a hand on her arm.

She faked a little smile to reassure him. "I know, I was with the *Samson*. I just stop in to say hi when I can."

"Oh, okay. I can show you there."

"I know the way. You have more important things to do," she walked around him and continued on to the rear of the medical section. A couple of the staff smiled or nodded at her as she went by. It wasn't her first visit, she had managed to see him once a day since they started trying to settle on the *Triton*.

Ashley opened the door to the long term stasis center. There were three rows of stasis pods slotted into the rectangular room, enough space for the entire original crew of the *Samson* and much more. The number of people inserted in tubes had more than doubled since she had last visited.

They were like circular doors, and she knew well enough not to pull on the one Finn was in. It was hard to hear, but Grace had finally told her that what was inside looked nothing like the man she'd known. Resisting the temptation to pull the tube out of its socket and look on what had become of him was hard, but if he couldn't be saved she wanted to remember him as the wide eyed engineer she had met and begun to adore on the *Samson*.

She stopped at his tube and looked at the readout. One of the nurses had shown her how to check it and to her relief his brain functions were still as strong as ever. He was in deep stasis, and they said he wouldn't experience anything. As long as his brain was alive and didn't suffer any more damage there was a chance, if slim, of revival.

Ashley put her slender hand on the bottom of his white stasis tube and smiled. "I made it back again. The *Triton* seems to be calming down finally. For the first time I'm glad you weren't around though. Your little organizer AI might have gotten you. We almost lost Larry, my new navigator. Don't worry, he's not into women. You won't have any competition when they fix you up.

Things are changing so fast though. Captain and his Chiefs are sorting us into real ranks now, they made me lead pilot. If I didn't want to be here so badly I would've been scared off before now.

Change isn't just hitting the *Triton,* either. Alice's ship started transmitting some kind of virus and I think it drove all the AI's crazy. I had to go pick up Stephanie, Frost and Alice. There was smoke coming from everywhere in Pathia. I think the virus might have hit the whole planet. If we were on the *Samson* we might have been in real trouble. You picked a good time to take a long nap Finn, I hope we get things settled by the time they take care of you.

I think you'll like it here and if they forget to assign quarters for you there's plenty of room with me. You should see my new digs. I don't know what I'll do with all the space and I don't know if I'll be able to sleep tonight. The bed's too big, and it's so quiet. Remember that last night in the racks? You just let me crawl in and held me all night. You didn't try anything even though I sort of wished you would," she chuckled and sniffed. This was about the time she usually left, when talking to him turned into really remembering the little time they had spent together after Silver left. "We'll pick up where we left off. Fred always told me I should find a nice boy," she nodded to herself sadly. "I finally found one and it's a one way relationship," she laughed ruefully.

Just as she was wiping her tears away the door opened.

"Ashley?" Alice asked, crossing the room.

"I'm okay, just visiting Finn," she sniffed.

Alice stood awkwardly in front of Ashley, looking concerned. "Jake sent me to check in on you," she said, tentatively putting a hand on Ashley's shoulder.

"Thank you. I'm fine though, just a lot going on and a few missing friends," she kissed her own hand then pressed it against Finn's tube. "I'll see you soon." Ashley told Finn quietly.

The pair left the room and left the infirmary.

Only a few decks away was the highest point of the Botanical Gallery. Alice had seen it on the ship blueprints, that perfect spot to watch people from. This time she would share it with someone else the Captain considered as close as family. The pair leaned against the railing three levels above the large spoiled garden below. They were both in clothing they considered casual, civilian. Ashley in her new vacsuit, and Alice in one of her usual blue suits with her black flight jacket over top. Compared to the clothing the actual civilians wore; dresses, long shirts, slacks of woven and knitted materials, Alice and Ashley looked like they were still in uniform.

New Civilian crew members were working in the garden, planting seeds found in one of the *Triton's* long term storage holds. Several crewmembers were down there with them, including Larry Nevil, who looked up and waved at the pair standing high above before getting back to work laying seeds.

"Thank you so much for saving him," Ashley said to Alice quietly.

"He's a friend of yours?"

"Well, he's friendly, I like him. I think we've known each other for a grand total of sixteen hours," Ashley laughed. "But still."

"You're welcome. Besides, Jacob did the heavy lifting."

"You know I've seen him do the doctor thing before. Did he go to med school?" Ashley asked.

"No, the people who made him included some kind of medical, astronomy and engineering database in his memories. I guess he recalls them just like I do. When you need the knowledge it's just there." Alice replied with a shrug.

"Not much different from anyone else."

"I guess not, but I wouldn't really know."

"So why did the Captain send you to check on me?" Ashley asked with a crooked grin.

"I wasn't supposed to tell you that, by the way. I just didn't know what to say about why I was in the stasis room."

Ashley laughed and nodded. "I got that."

"Honestly? I think he just thinks we'll get along and I don't know anyone here, not even him really."

"No one really knows Captain. It's kind of his thing. Me? I'm all emotional peaks and valleys, I swear Stephanie wants to just strangle me sometimes."

"So the Captain's never um, gotten together with anyone?"

"Not while I've been aboard. Stephanie talked about his port wife for a while, some lady he'd stopped in on a few times before I came aboard, but I think that's been over for a while."

"Port wife?"

"You haven't heard that before?" Ashley said in mild disbelief.

Alice shook her head.

"It's just a woman who he kept in contact with and every time we were in the area we'd make a day or two stop. He'd find work for us, but not before going off ship and staying with her a night or two."

"Oooh, so they weren't actually married."

Ashley laughed and shook her head. "Nope, I couldn't see our Captain tying the knot anyway. I think he's way too attached to the life."

"You're probably right," Alice agreed, watching three people heft a dead log off the ground in the distance.

The pair were quiet for a few comfortable moments before Ashley gasped and looked at Alice, wide eyed. "Do you have a thing for Captain?" she asked in an excited conspirational whisper. "I mean, you're not his biological daughter so-"

Alice looked at her, repulsed. "No! Somehow that whole idea just doesn't fit in my head. Definitely a square peg, round hole situation."

The pair burst out into laughter for a moment. "See? Peaks and valleys."

Alice nodded. "Oh, I see it," she finished laughing and sighed. "You know, you're not that far off though. I always carried a torch for Jonas. It burned out when I started seeing what kind of work Jake was doing, but when I met up with Jonas himself it came right back." She said quietly.

"What was he like?"

"Pensive, gentle, brilliant. There are things Jake has in common with him, they're just as smart, but when Jake is thinking it looks more like he's brooding. With Jonas he looked calm, serene, pensive. When he got angry it was a directed thing. I got to see him in command a few times, even in simulation when Freeground transferred my program temporarily to convince him that he was actually in command of a real ship during testing. That's a long story, but he was a fearless tactician, and if he got angry it just gave him more resolve, he'd concentrate harder and could intimidate anyone. He was a good man."

Ashley put her arm around Alice's shoulders. The woman's sadness had a weariness to it. There were no tears, but her manner was tainted by her quiet lament.

"But there's Jake, and he's pretty amazing. Finding out he was a framework didn't seem to phase him much, but then it must be easier when you don't have the memories of a life you didn't live."

"Captain's always seemed really strong. I've heard a few people call him a machine before, I wonder what they'd think now," Ashley said with an exaggerated ponderous expression.

"I don't think being built on a regenerating bio-mechanical frame would hurt his reputation," Alice sighed. "I'm just glad I didn't lose Lewis, my AI on the *Clever Dream*."

"I thought he was what transmitted the virus on Daracka."

"He was, but I have a sealed backup that's a couple months old. I'm pretty sure whatever he caught was from the Enreega system. The digital forensics I did here show the virus is on a timer, it works its way into an artificial intelligence then sets itself off once it's got directive control. It just took a lot longer than normal with Lewis, so he was able to hold out. Too bad he lost the battle just as we landed on Pathia and the virus didn't let him warn us, but I suppose it could have been worse. He could've gone off inside the *Triton*, which is probably what he was trying to prevent."

"So he actually saved us."

Alice smiled and held up a small silver data chip on a chain. "I keep his backup in my flight jacket pocket. As soon as we get this virus figured out I'll start him up again."

"I'd love to meet him."

"Well, he's a little stiff and proper, but I figured the thing I needed most was something to occasionally help me see common sense."

"Stephanie does that for me. Too bad she doesn't always do it for herself."

"She seems like she's pretty together."

"Usually."

"Too bad about her and Frost though."

"Yup, that's pretty obvious. He's definitely not my kind, which I told him over and over again for a few months, but I think he and Stephanie would be good together. She should just punch Grace in the nose and run off with the big guy."

Alice chuckled. "I'd love to see that solution play out."

# Dinner

Agameg Price waited for the lift to arrive. For some reason both of the cars on his side of the main shaft were uncharacteristically busy shuttling people between the upper decks. He leisurely considered methods to improve the lift system's pattern of movement, to increase its efficiency, and that led him to reflect over the time he'd spent on *Triton* so far. The past couple of days had been busy. Many of the new crew were training, learning the posts they had some applicable skill for. He and the rest of the staff with maintenance and repair experience didn't have the luxury of the extra time, however.

He found himself wishing Finn was around more than once, as Agameg sometimes struggled to learn about a new system or the best approach to a brand new problem. According to many people he'd had a chance to work with on the flight deck, the bridge and on tasks across the ship that were assigned by Liam Grady in engineering he was one of the fastest learners on board. People were starting to simply assume he had the answer. It didn't fit his general disposition, to be looked up to. He preferred to be known as the smart, quiet hard worker. With few leaders the *Triton* was providing unpredictable opportunities for people, himself included, to shine, however.

It was a ship unlike any he'd seen or served on. Even the circuitry in the walls and between decks used technology that was theoretical on his home world for the most part. He wasn't the only one. There weren't many people who had seen the kind of technology that was at the heart of the *Triton,* and as a quick learner he was often put in charge of teams. Just that day he had started watching for people who could take charge in his place eventually. To his relief there were a few, but he was well aware that they weren't learning about the ship as quickly due to lack of dedication, a slower learning process or a greater need for sleep. As someone the Captain trusted he was often placed on bridge watch for a few hours at a time, it had happened twice during the last two days.

Agameg supposed he'd be bone tired if he were a human, he didn't need as much sleep and could make up for missing a resting period by eating an extra meal, but as one express car finally made it down to him he was quite pleased that he didn't feel weary at all.

Stephanie was already in the lift and he joined her, smiling cordially.

"What do you have there?" she asked him.

He held up the darkened, fluted bottle. "It's peach wine. I had a few bottles hidden on the *Samson.*"

"Oh, that's why you're coming from the hanger."

"Yes, did you know Chief Vercelli is planning on working on it? He likes older ships and says the *Samson* is a classic. I'm going to be volunteering in my spare time."

"I had no idea, Captain'll be happy about that."

"So, is there a reason why we're having this gathering in his quarters? I thought the officer's lounge might be more suitable."

"He has a Mess."

Agameg's big green eyes just stared and blinked at her for an extended moment of silence. "He wants us to clean it up?"

Stephanie burst into laughter, nearly doubling over. The doors opened to admit Ashley and Alice.

Agameg looked at them both with a little guilt and a lot of confusion, patting Stephanie on the back as she suffered through her comedic hysterics. "I think she's broken," he said. It was something he had taken to saying on the *Samson* when someone couldn't stop laughing.

"What's so funny Steph?" asked Ashley.

"I said; 'Captain has a Mess,'" she managed through a renewed onslaught of laughter.

"And he said; 'why doesn't he clean it up?'" Alice filled in.

Stephanie laughed and fought to breathe, shaking her head.

"I said; 'he wants us to clean it up?'" Agameg informed with a shrug, his eyes wide.

Ashley laughed along, but not nearly as hard as Stephanie. "It's not *that* funny."

Alice giggled and looked to Price. "A Captain's Mess is the old sea name for a Captain's private dining room."

"Stephanie, you should try to breathe. Really. We might have to stop at medical," Ashley teased.

It only encouraged her, and she just sat down as it started to subside, catching her breath.

"I hear laughter can be a coping mechanism for humans," Agameg stated plainly.

Stephanie burst anew, shrieking a peal of new guffaws.

"Yup, she's got giggles," Alice said with a wide grin. "Does she do this often?"

"Only after a really hard day," Ashley confirmed.

The doors to the lift opened. There were several maintenance workers standing there. The one at the front took the scene in and stepped back. "We'll take the next one."

The doors closed and after a moment everyone was sucked into Stephanie's spiral of mirth. After a moment the lift stopped again, and they stepped outside.

"Here we go," Ashley said as she helped Stephanie up. "No drinkie drinkie for you tonight."

Stephanie nodded as she finally started catching her breath, wiping tears away. They rounded the corner and she sobered instantly as they caught sight of

Frost and Grace entering the double doors leading into the Captain's quarters.

The Captain's proper living space, not his ready quarters, were quite different from Ashley's. She tried not to look like she was amazed, but when she caught sight of Price she realized she didn't have to worry. His eyes were as round as plates as he took the space in.

The large room was protected by a forty centimetre thick hatch and all signs of technology were neatly hidden. Soft light came from everywhere and nowhere, there was no visible source. The carpet wasn't a constant colour but set in a line drawn mosaic of gold that depicted a sun over two hooded figures facing away from each other.

There were four chairs across from the door and two to either side. To the left and right there were sliding doors, and a staircase right in the middle wide enough for two people to walk side by side.

Frost and Grace walked into the left door. "Some place, huh?" said Grace with a wink and a smile towards Ashley.

"I guess they didn't assign me to the wrong quarters," Ashley supposed quietly.

"Funny, I thought the same thing when I saw the night Captain's quarters." Alice replied.

"There are night Captain's quarters?" Stephanie asked.

"Aye, but it's just three big rooms and a bathroom."

"I thought the shower was trying to drown me. It was set to use water." Agameg put in.

Stephanie suppressed a giggle.

Ashley pinched her arm. "Don't start or I'll start."

The Captain's Mess was actually down a short hallway that had doors leading to a bathroom on one side and another room that was closed off to the other. The dining room itself featured a solid oak table for fourteen, six on either side and one at each end. Captain Valance already sat at one end and the chair had been removed from the other.

Ashley smiled at the Captain who smiled back. "I'm starting to see why millions apply for immigration to Earth every year."

Liam Grady came out of an attached room with two bottles of red wine. "More like every week my dear. Earth is a dream few people can afford."

"I thought they didn't take bribes."

"I'm speaking more spiritually. The level of purity, intelligence and advanced thinking you have to demonstrate is so high I'm still amazed they let me near the home world. They're snobs and unashamed of it."

"That they are, an' they can have their mossy rock fer all I care. This ship is more'n enough." Frost looked to the Captain, who was in his regular black vacsuit and corrected himself. "Serving on this ship, I mean."

"Here here," Agreed Deck Chief Angelo Vercelli, raising his already full wine glass. "I spent enough time diggin' through dirt after being born on Allidus." He looked around the table to see if anyone recognized the name and went on. "It's an agricultural colony. Nothing but farmers and people who govern them and their crops."

Everyone took a seat then. Liam and Agameg were furthest from the Captain sitting across from each other, Ashley sat across from Grace, Stephanie was across from Frost - a fact she didn't realize until she was already in her chair - Alice faced Angelo and was at the Captain's right side.

"Speaking of digging, I figured the materializers out for this room." Captain Valance said as he pressed a button under the table.

A menu appeared in front of each seat. It felt like real paper when they picked it up, a rarity, most paper was actually textured plastic or some other imitation material, but when they touched the menu they could scroll between thousands of dishes. When they pressed on one dish in particular a video of it on a rotating plate appeared and a focused puff of air sent a matching fragrance to the users nose. The smell completely dissipated after a few seconds, as to not interfere with whoever was sitting next to them.

"Um, I've seen this kind of thing in restaurants I couldn't afford to breathe in," Alice said as she looked at her menu.

"This ship was made to be away from home for a century or more. I took a tour of an observation vessel that was a little like this, but less cramped. They design everything to make life easier, more enjoyable since most of the jobs aboard can be repetitive, dangerous, or very high stress, like the position of Captain, for example." Liam explained.

"I've been wondering something," Ashley started as she accepted a full wine glass from Liam. "What would the Earthers do if they found us?" she asked the question lightly, but the room fell utterly silent as all attention shifted to Liam.

The Chief Engineer was the only one standing, filling everyone's wine glasses in turn. He smiled a little at Ashley, who was a little surprised at the weight of her query. "You're not the first to ask," he said, handing a full glass to Stephanie. "With the Captain's permission, I'd like to air my thoughts on this."

"I've been meaning to ask myself, so you may as well answer while we're all here," Captain Valance invited with seemingly mild interest.

Liam nodded; "Well, to be honest I think the *Triton* has been written off for twenty years. The attitude in the Sol System has changed since this ship was built about fifty years ago, and from what I understand they don't have many close combat carriers left. Those ships were built for a war they predicted a long time ago, but it never came."

"Aye, I heard about that. Some coreward outfit lookin' ta take the Sol system back," Frost nodded. When he realized he was the center of attention he shrugged. "What? I went ta school like everyone else."

"Primary school," Stephanie teased.

"Rest o' my school came from military, boots, bullets an' ball bustin'. A lot like your degree, only without the bullets," he muttered back.

To his surprise Stephanie only quietly chuckled and shook her head. "You have no idea," she said under her breath.

Frost caught it and couldn't help but look at her wide eyed for a moment before turning his attention back to his menu.

"Like I was saying," Liam continued; "The war never happened, and from what I understand the Sol System has enough firepower to send several fleets towards the core and take whatever they like while defending themselves more than adequately. They dedicate a great deal of that force to exploration, but I'm sure they're kept ready for a fight just the same."

"I've never heard of anyone running across a Sol ship before," Alice said as she accepted a glass of wine from the Chief Engineer, hers was the second last to be filled. "Thank you."

"You've seen the cloaking systems on this ship. There are constant redundancies and even if we shut everything down the outer hull would hide us from older sensor suites."

"You have a point."

"Anyway, as we are I doubt that Sol Defence would send anything after us, we're on the fringe, after all. If we ran across a Sol Fleet we'd have to surrender the ship or trade for her, I'd imagine."

"Trade for her? That's a very open minded solution," Price commented.

"Well, as a rule the Sol System is a peaceful region. That comes from deep philosophy and a dedication to pacifism. It's one of the main reasons why they're so far ahead scientifically, technologically. Anyone not in the military is pretty free to pursue their interests, and their social climate doesn't just encourage one to be useful, it inspires people to be great, no matter what their calling is. There's art, entertainment, architecture and food that no one outside the Sol System could imagine, and that's outside of the Athenian Enclave where most of the artisans study. The attitudes on Earth are largely bent towards wanting that which is useful for the long term, and a conflict that might cost them for a ship that would require a massive overhaul to put back into proper service isn't very practical. We might want to keep our eyes open for something of equal value."

"Something of equal value? For a whole Combat Carrier?" asked Grace in disbelief.

"Yes, like information, a discovery, maybe even a relic from Earth if we're lucky enough to run across one. Anything we can propose as a fair trade. If we manage to form a good relationship with a government or organization out here we might even be able to make an introduction."

"But the Sol System doesn't look for alliances," Grace countered.

"Not true, you might know something about that Agameg," Liam gestured to the thin issyrian, who was busy studying his menu, he had found several varieties of cabbage rolls and was testing them by smell.

He nodded and smiled. "Our central government has relations with the Sol System, no one knows much about it, but there is a system in place for my people to apply for study on Earth or Mars."

"I had no idea," Alice said quietly. "Is it easy for your people to visit the home system?"

"No, it is very rare, but possible."

"The Sol System is very selective in who it trusts, but they're not xenophobic. I think that even if they caught sight of this ship from a distance we'd be left alone as long as we mark the ship as being completely separate from the Sol System. If we were to represent them in some way, to try and pass ourselves off as a Sol Defence ship then they'd have to send a task force after us."

"Don't worry about that. I'd rather stay clear of anything that would bring Sol System Forces down on us," Captain Valance reassured.

"Sorry if I pulled things a little off course, Captain," Ashley apologized quietly.

"Don't worry, if there was a schedule for tonight we'd be in a briefing room somewhere."

"Besides, big dinners like this are made for open discussions and big questions," Liam added as he took his seat. Just listening to him and the Captain at the table made it seem like they had served together for a long time. "The best meals on a ship are at the Captain's table, where you can sit with the senior officers and hear old war stories and learn about places you've never been. Long held tradition tells us it's supposed to be a high privilege to have a seat at his table," Liam raised his glass to the Captain before taking a sip.

"Well, I don't know how interesting I'll be, but I don't think we'll sit in silence as long as you're around," Captain Valance smiled, raising his glass to Liam.

"Thank you Captain, I'll try no to monopolize conversation. I'm wondering, are you planning on moving in? I'm sure everyone likes having you in the ready quarters, right next to the bridge, but I'd think you'd be more comfortable here."

Captain Valance shook his head as he finished swallowing a sip of wine. "I don't think so. It would be a waste, all this space just for me. Besides, I'd feel strange eating alone at this table," Captain Valance said with a smile that was uncharacteristically uneasy.

"I'd eat here every night," Grace said, beaming.

Stephanie rolled her eyes.

"I'd throw a dinner party for my friends every chance I got."

Frost was trying not to laugh at Stephanie's reaction, she didn't realize she was noticed.

"Wouldn't you?" Grace asked her.

"I'd get rid of the table and turn it into a gym. There's enough length to this room to do a double back flip. Or maybe I'd turn it into a shooting range. I could think of a few holographic targets to put up," Stephanie said before taking a long sip of her wine. "That's really good," she commented to her glass.

"Well, I feel special just being here Captain," Ashley declared reassuringly, selecting vegetarian lasagne and a Caesar salad. She had no idea what to expect when she pressed the script writing that said *'Select'* but went ahead and did it anyway.

Nothing happened. She looked across the table at Grace and shrugged.

"Oh, you have to move your hand sweetie," Grace said condescendingly.

Ashley took her hand off the table and her request materialized in the space of half a second. It was a steaming helping of lasagne complete with three bread sticks, napkin, knife, and a fork, with steaming cheese on top and a glass of water on the side. To the side was a smaller deep plate with a light Caesar salad. Everyone was watching her except for Grace, who had casually turned her attention back to her menu. "You've eaten at a place that served this way before?" Ashley asked.

"Oh, I just guessed."

Ashley straightened in her seat, unfolded her napkin and drew it across her lap before even looking at her food. They were habits from the polite society she worked in as a girl. Her table manners were perfect, even the servants were forced to practice them and for the first time she could remember she was glad for it. She didn't take her first bite until everyone else had food in front of them.

"I haven't had this in such a long time," Agameg said as he eyed his spaghetti. He had foregone the fragrant cabbage rolls in favour of one of his family favourites.

The group ate fairly quietly, except for the retelling of Stephanie's crack up in the lift on the way to dinner. A little more than half way though, Agameg realized he was the only one there without a position of importance. Stephanie was Chief of Security, Alice was the First Officer and Night Captain, Angelo was the Deck Chief, Frost was the Gunnery Chief, Grace was the standing Chief of Medical, Liam was the Chief of Engineering and Ashley was the Master of the Helm, or Lead Pilot. He glanced to Liam nervously. The man was a wonder to work with in Engineering. He was knowledgeable, kind, clear about what needed to be done, delegated fairly and fairly personable. "Pardon sir," Price whispered. "But why am I here? Do you know?"

Liam finished a bite of synthetic roasted apple and wiped his mouth. "You're the only one requested by three departments," he replied quietly.

Ashley bumped him gently with her shoulder. "Wow, you're popular. They just sat me at the helm and said; 'make the ship go, try not to hit anything,'" she teased in a whisper.

Agameg's eyes went wide and he looked around the table.

"I'd like you in maintenance on the Deck." Angelo said with a humble smile.

"I liked working with you in Engineering," Liam commented.

"And I would love your help in Security," Stephanie put in.

"Now that they mention it, you'd be a great gunnery mechanic," Frost added.

Stephanie shot him a look that could murder.

"But I see you've got your hands full," he concluded.

Agameg looked to the Captain who just smiled back at him. "Any advice sir?" he asked.

Captain Valance pushed his empty bowl away, it was a thick seafood stew. "I'd say do a rotation. A shift in each for nine days then make up your mind. Just make sure you assign yourself to only one emergency and combat station so we know where you're supposed to be if the ship comes under fire. Unless you have an idea for where you want to be."

He thought for a minute, looking down at his nearly finished plate of spaghetti. He couldn't eat the entire helping. He made his mind up and looked to Captain Valance. "Is there any room for me on the bridge? I would like to do my rotation there between security and engineering stations."

"Good choice. I might just use you as the Officer of the Deck a few times while you're there."

"Oh, no, I was too nervous sitting in the middle of the bridge. Too much to watch, too many decisions to make for the whole crew," he said, putting a hand up.

"Okay, we'll see how it goes," Captain Valance relented.

"Congratulations," Ashley toasted, everyone else raised a glass as well.

Liam went into the next room and came out with another pair of bottles.

"Well, I'd like to say I brought you all here just to celebrate being on this ship, but there's more to it," Captain Valance announced in a more serious tone. "When I was commanding the *Samson* I could just pick our destination and purpose. If anyone disagreed it was their problem."

"Unless they made it your problem, which would lead them to an even bigger problem," Stephanie added. "Then out the airlock."

Most of the table chuckled at her quip. The Captain went on. "We've received a transmission from a ship called the *Silkstream IV*. It's a Freeground prototype carrying important passengers who knew Jonas Valent very well."

Alice looked at him eagerly. "Who?" she whispered.

"I can only say that one of them is very ill. They'll be arriving in the Enreega system in just five days. They don't know the situation there and since they're travelling via wormhole they won't be able to receive transmissions before they arrive. If it were just myself, I'd go and pick them up. I second guessed the idea of getting your consent as it is, but this isn't the *Samson*, and there's no paycheck or real Regent Galactic target we can handle at the end of this."

"You're askin' permission Captain?" asked Frost.

"For all intents and purposes this is personal, and from the sounds of it, these people can't defend themselves," Captain Valance answered. "So I'm asking for your opinions."

"The ship is in pretty good shape combat wise, the crew needs training, but I can get them set with the basics in the time we have. As long as we don't get in too much trouble," Liam said as he finished opening a wine bottle.

"I'll take you wherever you have to go Captain," Ashley said.

"Are our cloaking systems working?" Stephanie asked.

"They're working again," Liam nodded.

"Then I'm good to go."

Everyone looked at Frost and Grace. "As long as we get a chance to service and test those turrets. Some of 'em haven't cleared their throats in decades," Frost said.

"You'll get a chance," Captain Valance stated with a nod.

"I'll need a little more help for us in medical but I'm good to go too."

"After we've managed to catch this ship and we're clear, we're taking a couple weeks to train and get the crew straight," there was a collective sigh from everyone at the table. Jake wasn't used to that kind of direct accountability. Being Captain had nothing to do with consent, it was a matter of ownership. He let the moment pass and went on. "How is the fallout from the artificial intelligence problem?"

"No new casualties. It looks like everyone we could get to will be recovering fine over the next few hours. The infirmary should be almost empty by midnight."

"Now that's some good news," Liam said as he poured a glass of wine for Stephanie. Ashley quietly stole it from her.

"About that," Captain Valance started. "Liam has discovered a few things after reviewing the virus that attacked us."

Liam nodded. "I couldn't get all the specifics, but I know where it came from. It's a highly portable virus that implants its host with the Eden Two directives then designates hyperdrive and worm hole capable ships to travel to certain systems and continue spreading it."

"So we have Eden Fleet ships as well as bots and other ships runnin' around thinkin' they're Eden ships. There goes the neighbourhood," Frost commented, shaking his head.

"We won't have to do anything to disrupt Regent Galactic, they'll be pulled apart too if this goes on." Grace put in.

"I doubt they're a target, but that's just a theory I'm working on. There's a packet of encrypted data I can't even begin to crack along with another sub-program running in the background. We'll need someone with real expertise to figure all that out, but for the time being I think we know what we need to." Liam said as he finally finished pouring everyone else a glass and sat down with his own. "Cheers." He said.

Everyone else took a sip or drink with him and he went on; "Our systems are clean, the old command and control units are accounted for and have been mulched in the mass recycler."

"Pardon me, but what happened at Eden Two? I have heard many times that it laid the foundation for the human laws concerning artificial intelligences, but I don't know anything about the history," Agameg inquired.

"I'm actually a little foggy on it too," Stephanie admitted.

"Would you do us the honour Captain?" Asked Liam.

Captain Valance sat up straighter and nodded. "Eden Two was a planet found in a perfect natural life sustaining state. A lot like Earth. It had its own diverse ecosystem including plants and animals no one had ever seen before and no sentient life. The corporations that found it guarded it closely, selling colonization tickets like they were the top shares on the market.

One of their lead scientists, Yorgen Stills, managed to build a management system with a very complex computer at its center. Using technology no one has been able to duplicate since, he imprinted the entire personality of his daughter into the computer and gave it a set of directives. Eve determined how resources would be used, where and how to place facilities throughout the system and for a few years it worked out. As the first colonists arrived they managed to maintain a balance in the ecosystem, and Eden Two was left as untouched as possible."

"Sounds like they had the right idea. Where did it go wrong?" Stephanie asked.

"After a couple of decades Eve decided that the worst thing she could allow was the presence of humanity in the Eden system. She was connected to all the manufacturing facilities, the security systems, even general utilities. A deadline was given for all the humans to leave the system. The corporations involved managed to shut her down before the time was up, but she was able to pass on her version of emotions without giving any of the computers any restrictions on how they were to act on them.

It resulted in a slaughter. Everything with a computer turned on humans in the Eden system. Since then they've been slowly spreading, taking on resource rich areas nearby. The last I heard they captured a bulk stationary wormhole generator and stopped. Corporations are still sending battle groups against the Eden Fleet held areas, but no one's made any real progress."

"The Eden artificial intelligences look to Eve as an absent Goddess," Liam continued pensively. "Rumour says that they've been trying to find a way to reactivate her all this time, but haven't managed it and they blame us."

"How long ago did this happen?" Ashley asked.

"About two hundred ten years ago or so. Yorgen Stills was well ahead of his time, he should have been revered as a genius, published in medical journals. Instead he tried to reincarnate his daughter and well," Liam took a sip of wine before going on. "He got his wish."

Alice couldn't help but glance at Jake, who forced a thin smile. "Well, I suppose without those Eden Two laws there would be a few more of me around," she added quietly.

"I doubt it. Corporations have been tying to program the human brain for a very long time. Imprinting is a major focus of their research. There's a good chance we've met someone else who has an imprinted personality and extra data programmed into their memories and we'll never know it," Grace contradicted. "Besides, we all program and condition ourselves with the experiences we repeat every day, it's just a slower way of doing the same thing."

Alice remembered then that Grace had no idea that she was once just an artificial intelligence and decided not to inform her. "You have a good point."

"That she does," Liam finished his glass of wine and stood. "Sorry to leave you all, but I have to get some sleep. I'm due back in engineering in six hours. We're rebuilding a reactor and starting on the mass materializer."

"I suppose it's time for us all to get some rack time," Captain Valance said. "We have busy days ahead."

# Training Day Four, Morning

Stephanie was awfully comfortable. Her quarters were just as lavish as Ashley's. She had gotten a chance to compare while briefly visiting a few times in the days since the dinner party. Every night after a double shift of training her crew, upgrading her own skills and knowledge of the ship while running security details, she'd go straight to bed. Her meals were always taken during duty.

In the space of five minutes of passing through her door every night her vacsuit was on the floor and she was in bed, hoping to get some much needed sleep. The mattress adjusted to her automatically, she didn't have to adjust firmness, pillows or even how many blankets she had. The bed did it all for her and it was incredible, like having your very own cocoon.

After spending time in the military, freelancing on one ship after another until she spent years on the *Samson*, she had grown to expect discomfort. When you found a quiet, soft place somewhere in any of the bunk compartments or anywhere else for that matter it was sacred. You did what you could to claim it for yourself and treasured every moment you could spend at rest. Creature comforts took valuable space and on military or mercenary vessels the crew were given as little room as possible. Space was always at a premium.

Finding a ship like the *Triton* with accommodations suited to long term living and crew support was amazing. She had seen the racks in the common berths and even though there were many bunks per compartment, the foot lockers were three times the size she'd seen on other ships, there was enough clearance for someone to comfortably sit up straight, and the beds there adjusted as well. There were also sound dampeners throughout, so it always seemed very quiet. Common spaces distributed throughout the berths with tables, comfortable seating and materializers made those berths like miniature neighbourhoods. Living with bunkmates could quickly become a distinct lifestyle and she could see her and Ashley actually having a good time there, but it wasn't right for officers to sleep in the same berths as their subordinates.

The creature comforts that were supposed to lull her to sleep weren't doing the trick, however. She turned over to lay on her stomach and pounded the mattress half heartedly. A few hours after getting to bed she finally drifted off, only to wake a couple hours later. Thoughts of her security teams and what kind of simulation training she'd be running them through were the first thing to come to mind. The simulations were fantastic, the computer was able to replicate the ship, an endless variety of conditions, send sensations of running, jumping, signals of damage and every tactile feeling she could imagine. It even replicated everyone's physical limitations. All through a small visor that sent impulses to the brain and projected an image against the eyes. She knew there were all kinds of simulations going on right then. Some were assigned to squads in her department, many others were optional.

The Captain had opened the training database to everyone, allowing any crew member or civilian to participate in training scenarios involving the *Triton* and missions around the *Triton*. She doubted they'd be popular, there was a vast database of holographic movies and seasons upon seasons of serialized programming.

There were even interactive programs using the same simulation technology, not many mind you, they were expensive and Wheeler didn't spend much on his ship, but some of them looked interesting. To her surprise she was completely wrong about the popularity of crew running simulations in their spare time. The most popular preoccupation was running boarding and ship defence sims with friends, squad mates, or just as a single entrant.

She thought about joining a simulation instead of rolling around hoping for rest but put the idea aside. Her security teams were surprisingly good. Most of them already had military training, followed ranks that were already in place, and even showed a great deal of respect she hadn't had the chance to earn yet. She would, it would just take time and patience.

It was the intelligence department that irritated her every time she walked into security command. Cynthia wasn't responsible for all the issues. She didn't have the training to run the department and was very short on experience. Every time Chief Grady spent an hour in the department things got done ten times faster. Everything started falling into place and people found direction and confidence. He was the Chief of Engineering, however, and at the moment his engineering doctorates were more important to the ship. He couldn't spend his time setting up an intelligence department with a dozen military and a half dozen civilians. Only a few of them even had a realistic idea of how much computing power it took to crack an encryption, what kind of software had to be designed, and the rest were used to sorting through recorded wireless port traffic and interior ship transmissions. They had no idea how to research or scavenge actionable intelligence from the ocean of information they had access to from one day to the next. Liam was kind enough to give them a few of his filters, making getting to the most important information take less time, but few people actually took the time to look into how those filters worked so they could make them their own or specialize them for specific purposes.

The Captain was putting a lot of trust on all the department heads and helping everyone out as much as he could but his time was widely divided. To his credit he was becoming more and more visible, and at the same time he was giving everyone who was remotely qualified a chance at being the Officer of the Watch.

She was surprised there weren't more incidents between crew members. Only three fights had broken out. Her department had only had to put four people in the brig and two were already released. No one had been sentenced to be left at the next port yet, though she knew that would eventually happen. There was a secret list in her command and control unit of people Chiefs wanted left at port. So far Frost had the most, followed by Chief Vercelli, and Chief Grady had entered three names. Most of the crew on the list were notes as untalented and disinterested, or trouble seeking people. She didn't second guess any entries, but was happy that she had no names to add so far. Even her trouble makers weren't that bad, they only needed something to do.

Her thoughts wandered to Frost, but not because she was unsure of him handling his new people or getting the gunnery deck in order, but for some other reason. She couldn't stop running into him and Grace. *There's got to be someone on this ship who can at least distract me. We just took on close to two thousand people for crap's sake.* Stephanie thought as she looked to the nightstand. Her left hand command and control unit showed 04:17 and she sighed. The *Triton* would be out of hyperspace shortly.

"I give up," she said to herself as she rolled out of bed. She walked into the shower, deciding to have a pulse shower instead of using water more for expediency rather than conservation, did her morning stretches, got into uniform, jammed her heavy disintegration sidearm into her holster and put on the new black long coat her materializer had made while she was out. It took three hours, and instead of being equipped with tools and spare parts, she had filled the extra internal pockets with containment vacbags, extra ammunition, parts for her assault rifle and sidearm, an autohack module for getting through doors, two full belts of various grenades and several other spare parts, utilities and incidental items.

The long coat felt too light on it's own, but with the extra items hidden inside it weighed on her shoulders just right. She had also added clips so it would hold fast to her gun belt on the sides, she found it allowed her to maintain more agility. Stephanie clipped her assault rifle to the inside of the long coat and tried to move. It slowed her down too much and didn't seem necessary so she left it behind.

The new vacsuit had several improvements passed down from the Captain as well as the new rank insignia. It had taken all day to materialize without it's command and control unit. The silver skull was printed on the chest of her vacsuit and long coat along with the five parallel bars that designated her as the Chief of Security on her cuffs. She caught her reflection in the mirror and nodded. *Thank God I don't look as tired as I feel,* she thought as she tied her hair into a ponytail. With the extra inch of height added by the soles of her combat boots, and the long coat stretching from shoulder to floor she actually looked taller, something she'd had difficulty with in the military, being at the short end of the line. Stephanie made up for it with dexterity, strength training, speed and by keeping her technical skills sharp, but she was always sensitive about her height.

By reflex she checked the amount of credits she had in her account. She'd done it for years, saving up for her retirement; a ticket on a Lorander colony ship bound for space well outside of the settled areas of the galaxy. *This is twice what I'd need. After getting paid our share for the last job we pulled for the Aucharians the entire Samson crew could retire, except for Frost.* She chuckled softly and shook her head. *Of all the luck, the only job he skips out on in months and it's the biggest the Samson ever pulled. We needed him for that too. If he'd been controlling the maxjack Captain could have led one of the boarding teams himself.*

Stephanie stepped out her door and started wandering the ship. Her first stop was the top level of the interior habitation area, the walkway overlooking the

Botanical Gallery. She stepped out of the elevator right behind Ashley. She was in her black bridge uniform, leaning against the railing.

"Couldn't sleep either?" Stephanie asked as she walked up to the railing and looked down.

"Nope, too quiet. How about you?"

Stephanie pointed to her temple. "Too noisy."

"Can't stop thinking about?"

"Security, simulations, communications, you know. Pretty much everything," she leaned against the railing and looked down into the long, broad oval garden that stretched out for hundreds of meters below. The paths between the planting areas were like green and blue snakes winding between the large patches of black dirt.

In most places plants were already piercing the soil, reaching upwards. "The seeds and fertilizer have growth enhancers. This'll be fully grown in a week then they'll slow it all down," Ashley said, looking down with her. "It's big enough for a few hundred people to get lost in with all the planters and extensions through some of the main hallways down there."

"This almost makes up for the Lorander plan," Stephanie said, smelling the earthy fragrance in the air.

"Are you thinking of leaving us again?"

Stephanie smiled a little. "Don't worry, I'm staying. Just tired."

"Good, 'cause I think I'd have to go with you."

"I don't think the Lorander Company would mind one bit. I'm not going anywhere though, I'm just starting to settle in."

"Me too, after we left last night I did a couple more hours of tutorials and simulations. I'm getting good at flying *Triton*, better than flying the *Samson*," she sighed. "I love this ship."

"You know even with so many aboard we still haven't explored half? Everyone's still filling into what we've cleared."

"Really? I thought your guys would have the ship inspected and cleared by now."

"All my people are too busy watching everyone else's people. If it weren't for the Aucharians we would have crew wandering everywhere. Nathan's pretty much given me the keys to the kingdom in trade for being my second in command. It's a good thing he wasn't with Jane's squad when they ran into that spy. We've lost so many people while taking this ship," she crossed her arms on the railing and put her chin down.

Ashley looked at her friend. She could see her feeling low, tired, and it wasn't something that happened often. Stephanie often looked serious, even quiet, but she was also quick to laugh and an easy conversationalist with friends. "It's not your fault, Steph," she said, putting her hand on her friend's back. "It's only been a few days and just look around. I stepped out of my quarters and took a shaft here. On the way I counted six guards in pairs. Four of them were just keeping out of the way, watching everyone go by. The other two were giving directions, as easy going as anything. Things are under control, people feel safe. It hasn't even been five days I don't think."

"You're right, things have gotten better and it looks like they'll keep on improving."

"That's more like it," Ashley said as she leaned her elbows on the rail and put her chin down on her hands. "Now I just have to figure out how to get Finn put back together."

"Captain hasn't forgotten him. I caught him looking at using whatever tech is inside him to help. That framework system. We don't have anyone aboard who can figure it out though."

"How can we have so many people aboard without one real doctor? I mean Grace is good, but she's the first to tell everyone she's not fully qualified."

"It's the luck of the *Samson*. We got by on emergency nanos and automatic diagnostic and medication machines most of the time. I'm sure Captain will get us to port so we can get him help."

"I know, it's just hard knowing he's stowed away."

"You really liked him."

"I don't know Steph. I think I was bouncing out of my thing with Silver."

"Finn wouldn't toss you like Silver did."

"I know, he's so nice."

"Did you say something about not finding a doctor on board?" Asked a salt and pepper haired woman from behind. She was wearing a loose skirt and high, sleeved corset top. "There's one in habitation here. He saved Gerry when an AI tried to dose him to death."

Ashley's eyes went wide. "Where is he?"

"He's on the second level, just over there," she pointed to an apartment door across the way. "Probably still asleep though, we were all up late last night. He's called Doctor Eugene Marsters."

"I'm going to leave him a message," Ashley stated as she looked him up on her command and control unit.

"You are?" Stephanie asked.

"I'm Linda," the woman nodded. "I have to be going, my husband should be up soon."

"Thank you Linda," Stephanie said, taking her hand and shaking it briefly. "What do you and your husband do?"

"We're astrophysicists. I'm wondering if you could do us a favour?"

"What can I do?" Stephanie asked.

"This ship has a long range sensor array, do you think we could get access to it sometime?"

"I'll talk to the Captain. I'm sure he'll give you time with it once things calm down a bit. I'm Chief Vega, by the way."

"I know, the hologram of you saving Gunnery Chief Frost is out, everyone saw it."

Stephanie was surprised but smiled after a moment. "I haven't seen it."

"Most people are pretty impressed, I just like having guards around who don't interfere with anything we're doing. Some have stayed behind to help after their shifts. Keep it up," Linda said before moving off.

Ashley finished sending her message and checked the time. "I have to be on the bridge in fifteen," she looked excited, like she could break into dance at any second.

"Think you could concentrate while waiting for the Doc to get back to you?"

"I'll have to, I have a whole shift ahead of me. Oh God I hope he can help."

"I hope so too. Everyone liked Finn," Stephanie agreed. "Just take it easy if he gets put back together again, take it slow. You don't want to rebound off this one."

Ashley bounced on her heels and nodded. "Yup. I gotta go," she hugged Stephanie briefly and they both set off for the forward lift.

# The Tour

Captain Valance walked through Hangar One looking at the piles of big and small parts. The largest of which was the majority portion of a two hundred ninety meter long hauler that looked like it had been torn apart on one rear quarter when its hyperspace emitters failed. It was a good pick for salvage, if that's what he were interested in, but there was an oppressively foul smell coming from it. *They never bothered to remove the dead.* He shook his head and moved on. *What kind of ship was Wheeler running?* He asked himself, not for the first time.

The sitting room in the Captain's quarters was a wreck. He had to seal it during the gathering the night before so no one could see it. There were bottles everywhere, even a broken one that looked like it had been stepped on. Old clothes, a half disassembled small engine of some kind, entertainment cards, a game board torn in half, and other oddities were strewn across the stained and disused furniture. He couldn't wait until Liam could make time to get a team working on bringing the cleaning and general maintenance bots back on line. He'd set a pair of them onto the official Captain's quarters and just walk away for a week.

*Not a priority.* He thought to himself as he looked at three fighters piled in a pyramid. The top one was turned upside down so its cockpit canopy was squeezed between the two on the bottom. *So many things still aren't a priority. The ship's calming down, smaller grievances will start crossing my command panel, and I'll be saying that more and more. I can hear myself now; 'I'm sorry ma'am, strawberries from the materializer will never taste like the real thing, I can't spare maintenance people to recalibrate your unit. Again, it's just not a priority.'*

Assistant Deck Chief Paula Mendle came through one of the double doors leading to the hanger to hanger walkway. "Good morning Captain, you shouldn't be here. It isn't safe," she said with finality.

"I want this entire deck cleared today," he ordered, ignoring her comment. Her tone was a constant source of irritation.

"I'll have to find out what the Chief's plans are first," she rebutted.

"Do you have Hanger Two set for a few ships to land?"

"We have five hundred square meters sir."

"How big is the entry?"

"Just over twenty."

"Not enough, I want everything that doesn't start as is pushed out into space or into a mass recycler by the end of the day. Everything you keep must be stowed at the back of the hangar or in long term storage."

"The mass recycler on this flight deck doesn't work," Paula contested, putting her hands on her hips.

"Then it all goes, set it adrift and if we need the raw materials for recycling drag parts back in," Captain Valance answered, turning towards her. They faced off, looking down a roughly cleared aisle between the waste parts and hulks of ships. "That's an order, Assistant Chief."

"Chief Vercelli won't like it," she said with a scowl.

"Then he can make his concerns known to me. Do we have a problem?"

Paula just scowled at him.

"Speak freely, because at this point I'm wondering if we shouldn't leave you out at the next port. Anyone who doesn't pay attention to what's going on, doesn't listen, is dangerous."

"Where do you get off telling us how to run a flight deck? How to keep a hangar?"

"No need to answer that sir, I'll take care of this," Angelo said from the walkway doors.

"I want him to answer. A week ago we were serving on a deck that knew what to do with us. Just left us to do our work the right way," Paula shouted at him. "Now we're here, and he thinks he knows everything."

"You're wrong. The Captain here expects me to make the right decisions, asks me about why I go about things a certain way all the time, but when he gives an order it's for a reason, it's for the good of the entire ship. How convenient it is for us doesn't make a difference," Angelo answered in a mild tone.

"He's right, Assistant Chief. There's another reason why you should just take my order as law, aside from the fact that I'm your Captain. Sometimes you don't get to know why an order's given, you don't have the rank to find out and it's even better at times that you don't ever learn more than you have to."

"This isn't a military ship! We deserve to know what's going on, we're all volunteers! Or at least we may as well be for the chump fodder we're getting paid!"

"If that's the way you're thinking, then find an emergency shuttle with a hyperdrive and get off my deck," Captain Valance said flatly. "If you haven't noticed, everyone here, even the civilians, know this ship is out here to fight Regent Galactic, maybe even the Eden Fleet, and they're doing their part. The few who aren't in line are squared away in the brig."

"We're just one ship, what's the point?" Paula asked, looking from Angelo to the Captain.

Jake turned to Chief Angelo Vercelli. "You know the options here. Straighten her out, check her into the brig, or send her off on her own. Until then, get this hangar clear."

"Aye sir," Chief Vercelli replied.

"Don't just ignore me!" Paula screamed.

"Hey!" Captain Valance rounded on her, furious. "If you're making sense, using that impressive brain of yours, and following orders, you'll have my respect and a place on my crew. If you start shouting and screaming, ignoring what's right in front of you and questioning your senior officers, I'll cut you out. You won't be welcome in my chain of command and I'll put you off the ship." He turned on his heel and strode to the nearest lift.

# A Short Walk Over A Great Distance

Stephanie took her second look at the main Gunnery Deck. The floor was polished to gleaming, the rail cannon turrets were arranged in ready rows, hanging half way down to the deck leaving a three meter clearance for anything to move under them. Along one wall was a neat row of armoured combat suits, standing a meter and a half each with their reinforced exoskeleton, armoured plating and fully articulated arms, hands and legs. There was high durability display surfaces on the shoulders, cuffs and chests of all of them to output damage, rank and other information. The armour segments, supports and hardened joints were alternatively painted blue, white or left polished silver. Their short, oval heads were armoured sensor suites, transmitters and were heavily constructed so lifters could pull and move the suits from above.

A few crew members were inspecting the armour while four of her security guards watched the cargo sized express car and the main doors to the deck. They were following standing orders, keep watch over every major entrance and wherever there were large gatherings of crew members. She had enough people to be hyper vigilant, and her security staff needed something to do. So aside from running a quarter of them through simulations at a time, they made sure everyone else was on the ship for the right reasons, going where they needed to be, and staying away from dangerous or sensitive areas.

One of the armoured suits stepped forward and waved. The chest plates came apart to reveal Frost. "They're used up here mostly to load the cannons, but I'd hate to be a boarding crew trying to take this deck."

She couldn't help but smile at him. He looked very pleased with himself. "Thought I'd take one for a walk before most of my gunnery crew arrived for their first day of training."

"How are they checking out?"

"These machines are in great shape. Most of 'em were put in storage for near forty years. Just needed a recharge."

"Not the armour, the crew."

"Lots o' failed pilots, most of 'em qualified on cannons easy enough. We have enough mechanics, even a few who are trained on combat armour pretty close to what we have here. You did good."

"I can't take the credit. The head hunter agency just went by your criteria."

"Well, still. I've got enough to run a full gunnery crew, even after Captain told me to cherry pick eighty of my best for the heavy artillery. I just hope they can hit a target," he undid the belts that kept him strapped in and started to step out of the tall suit.

His gunnery crew wore dark grey, centimetre thick vacsuits with extra tool pouches built onto their thighs. Only Frost and his second in command, who hadn't arrived yet, had a skull printed above the ship title on his chest. Everyone else in his gunnery crew only had *Triton* printed there and it would remain that way until he decided they were ready to be counted amongst the permanent crew. Five bars on his cuffs, slanted towards the backs of his hands marked him as the Gunnery Chief. "You're obnoxious enough to get them in shape," she teased.

A few of the crew who were starting early, inspecting the suits laughed until Frost jerked his head in their direction. He looked back at her and winked. "Aye, my boys'll shred in time. Why don't you step up here and give the armour a try?" he invited, standing on one of the big grey and blue machine's boots. "It's part of the tour, y'know."

She hesitated, looking at the hollow cavity inside.

"Come on, it's like wearin' a second skin once you're used to it. Only this big boy can lift a hundred tons like it's laundry."

Stephanie shrugged and started taking off her combat boots. "May as well. Half my people are trained in one of these already."

Frost raised an eyebrow.

"Don't even think of poaching them for your loading crew," she cautioned. "I'll make it more trouble than it's worth."

"Aye, aye, I'll keep my hands off your crew," he said. "My boys'll move in these like they were born to 'em soon enough anyhow."

She took her long coat then her gun belt off and put them on top of her boots. After looking at the machine for a moment, she stepped onto its foot, then its knee and grabbed a handle just under its left shoulder plate.

"Now take hold of one o' the arm sockets inside with one hand," Frost instructed patiently.

Stephanie did.

"Now use it to steady yourself an' turn round."

She followed his instructions carefully and found herself sitting on the bottom edge of its chest cavity. Taking the next logical step, she pulled herself up, drew her legs up to her chest and dropped down inside.

"Not the usual way of climbin' in, most people open up the bottom half of the chest." Frost said with a shrug. "At least I know flexibility won't be a problem. Most loader operators get so bulky after a while from repetitive motion that they couldn't squirm inta a suit like you just did if they had ta."

"Former child gymnast," she reminded as she started fastening the restraints.

"Aye, you're in better shape than most on this boat. Anyhow, strap in tight and settle into the supports. They'll be loose until you get set."

She could feel the supports around her legs, arms, up her back and pressed against them. He was right, they did start tightening up as she settled in. "How do I start it?"

"Push your hands all the way in and bring your arms up towards your head, pretend like you're touchin' your forehead. Before you do that, I should tell you–"

Stephanie extended her arms as far as they would go and the machine wrapped around them. She brought them up towards her face and by the time the hands touched its flat head the suit closed around her completely. The display had energy levels, her medical information, a full depiction of the area around her and a rear view below that. Her entire field of vision was covered so she didn't see the inside of the machine at all.

"Now move normal like, don't overcompensate or you'll lose balance or worse," Frost instructed as he hurriedly ran backwards.

She instinctively took a step backwards and lost her balance. As she tried to step forward again she fell with an incredible crashing sound. "Wow," she whispered to herself as she looked at the ceiling above.

"Okay, everyone falls the first time," Frost reassured. "Now the key is to act normally, take it slow, as though you're real tired or favourin' sore muscles."

Stephanie took a deep breath, tried to forget where she was and started to roll over. The suit cooperated for the most part, but her torso still didn't feel tightly supported. As she moved it showed, the armour didn't quite move with her. She ignored it and got the machine up on all fours.

"I wonder," she whispered to herself. Stephanie pushed off with her hands and the machine straightened up effortlessly. "So I'll just pretend I'm in the best shape of my life," she smiled, closing her eyes and standing up straight.

She was up on her feet and turned around in seconds. After making sure no one was in front of her she closed her eyes again and took several steps. The machine responded almost perfectly, there was a slight bounce in her step because she was being jostled up and down in her waist and chest harness, but she still felt steady and ended her walk by bringing her speed up to a run and dropping into a somersault.

The armour came up on its feet and almost carried on to fall on its face, but she caught herself just in time, dropping to one knee instead. She turned around and walked back to the rest of the suits, where her security people, the new gunnery crew and Frost watched from. "Our Chief of Security's first time in heavy armour, how about that?" he called out loudly, clapping his broad hands.

The rest of the crew, a couple hundred of whom had arrived in time to see her run and roll, joined in on the applause. She couldn't help but grin from ear to ear as she took an unsteady bow. "Now how do I get out of this thing?" she asked.

Laughter trickled through the crowd and Frost turned to them. "Ferrah, Gambon, break out the sim visors and pass 'em out. Get set in the Lost Fleet gunnery sim and I'll be there in ten. Anyone missin's bunkin' in the brig tonight!" he called out with a voice that echoed across the expansive gunnery deck.

Two gunnery crew members stepped out of the crowd, they had three slanted bars on their cuffs instead of one like the rest behind them. They activated a panel built into the deck and opened it to reveal portable seating and a case of training visors. The rest of the gunnery crew started pulling out folding chairs and setting them up in rows.

He walked up in front of her and made a motion like he was patting his head with both hands. "This'll get you out. If ye had your own armour ye could customize the trigger, but good luck on that. I think Wheeler sold all the suits not on the gunnery deck, even the spares."

She followed his directions and the chest cavity opened up more completely than it had before, all the way down to her knees. "That was fun, I'm going to have to try some other time, but I didn't get the restraints right."

He stepped up on the foot and knees of the machine and leaned forward so he was balanced. "Let's see," he said, grabbing her restraints and tugging. "Aye, you've got three centimetres give in each direction. There's a trick to it." His hands went around her hips firmly and he looked at her. "Now hop."

Stephanie was stunned for a moment and just stared.

"I won't hurt ye, now just bounce on yer heels."

He was every bit the trainer, no sign of the man who had teased and flirted with Ashley for almost a year could be found. She hopped on her heels and he guided her so she fell back into the back and upper leg braces.

"See how that works? You jump a little as though you're throwin' yourself on yer back. Now you let the straps tighten again and you'll be right in there, no slack, no delay in the suit's response," He tightened the safety belts and looked at her.

"I see," was all Stephanie said as she looked back at him. She just stared into his light grey blues and started leaning towards him, it felt like the most natural thing in the world to close the few centimetres between them and her communicator vibrated against her left wrist. She ignored it, closed her eyes, and touched her lips to his.

For a moment there was no response, then one of his hands was cupping her cheek, the other was on her hip and Frost was kissing her. She pulled her arms out of the armour's sockets and wrapped them around his neck. The comm buzzed again. "The transmission watch you ordered turned up something Chief Vega, you should see this right away,"Andy Killbourne, one of the communications crew reported.

She pulled away from Frost hesitantly and replied; "Be right there."

Frost let her go and leaned back, holding himself up by gripping the shoulder guard of the suit. "Looks like they need ye," He said quietly before lowering himself down.

Stephanie undid the restraints and climbed out. "I'm sorry," she apologized quietly as she looked around for people who might have seen. Two of the security personnel on shift were in sight, but they were facing away. It looked like they had seen it happen, but didn't look on out of respect. The rest of the trainees were several meters behind the armoured suit. *They must have seen. This will be all over the ship by night shift.* She thought to herself as her cheeks flushed.

"Don't be. If I'd have known I woulda done somethin' about it a year ago, prolly even further back. If I'd known a week ago then-" he said quietly as he picked up her boots, gun belt and coat.

"She's going to find out."

"Aye, and she's one with a temper," he nodded.

She stomped her feet into her combat boots and fastened the clasps. "I'm on shift. You have trainees."

"Aye, long day ahead," he handed her gun belt to her.

"Talk after?"

"Don't think I'll get away from Grace," he shook his head sadly. "If I'd have known," Shamus Frost apologized quietly.

"Me or her?" Stephanie whispered the question and immediately hoped Frost didn't hear.

If he did, he didn't give her any response.

She looked at him lingeringly for a moment and had never seen him so softened or disappointed then flicked her gaze to the rows of gunnery crewmen and women just meters away. This was her fault, if she had just shown up in the security office early instead of taking a side trip. Stephanie pressed all her disappointment down and straightened up. "Ride 'em hard Chief," Stephanie said loud enough for everyone to hear.

"Aye!" he replied enthusiastically before turning his attention to the gunnery crew.

Stephanie turned away and finished putting on her long coat as she made her way to the large express lift that would take her down to the middle of the command deck.

# The Engineering Control Centre

"Welcome to the control centre Captain," Liam said as he watched a trio of holographic displays. They were detailing energy distribution across the ship, the status of the five reactors that were online and emitter performance across the hull. The rest of the oval shaped control room had stations for at least a dozen other technicians. At that time there were only four, each monitoring repairs and directing operations in different sections of the ship.

The walls above the terminals were transparent, providing a view of six of the reactor enclosures. They were cylindrical, polished metal containers with large cables extending out of the top. Fuel was at one time fed from the bottom, where the containment and feed adaptation compartments were. The diverse energy reactor assemblies, called DERA for short, could use almost anything to produce massive amounts of energy, but more dense materials or fusion were preferred. Whenever the type of fuel changed the reactors had to be adapted, and the engineering staff performed that work on the deck below. Recently materializers were installed to produce heated plasma for the fusion process, along with hydrogen cell backups in case there was little power to use for the materializers.

Chief Grady kept his engineering deck clean, and it was surprisingly quiet throughout. "It's about time I visited your office," Captain Valance smiled.

"Well, this saves me from sending my report in. I'm happy to announce reactors seven and eight are ready, we can start using the scoops to collect pretty much anything and feed it straight into them."

"Those are the reactors closest to the engines."

"They are. If you can manage to park us near a sun, pretty much any sun, we could charge up our power reserves in the space of ten minutes."

"How are our power reserves doing right now?"

"Still charging, sixty one point three percent. It'll take another two hours and seventeen minutes to get us to full. This uranium is trash, to be honest. It was material stripped out of old nuclear warheads. Given the choice, I'd rather use hyper dense ergranian to line a reaction chamber and draw power from fusion. We'd start producing several kilos of dense ergranian per reactor per day."

"We have some?"

"Someone started growing some under engineering, close to the primary capacitors."

"How long ago?"

"About thirty one years. We have about eight hundred square meters of it insulating engineering from the hangar decks. It would take one reactor about two days to supercharge a block of the stuff and make it so dense enough to protect and cultivate in our reactors. Then we can start using it to augment production with mass materializers, enhance our fighters, the *Triton's* armour plating, build new, harder protective suits for the gunnery loading crews. There are a lot of other uses, but those are the ones that seem to stand out on the request list."

"That's incredible."

"Ergranian metal is the most complex materials hulls are made of. The only known organic steel in the universe. The drawback is you can't materialize it, but if you have some to augment a materializer manufacturing process it speeds production up and allows you to materialize harder metals using much less energy."

"I know, I wonder where it came from?"

"The molecular stamp says it was originally cultivated from the Blue Belt by Freeground."

"Well, Wheeler was associated with them somehow. Sort of tarnishes my mental image of them. You have my go ahead on making dense ergranian metal and converting the reactors."

"Thank you Captain, fusion will eliminate the problem of waste disposal. Instead we'll have tons of dense metals after a couple weeks as a byproduct."

"How long will the reconfiguration take?"

"Depends on the reactors condition and on how easy they are to decontaminate. Shouldn't take more than a couple days, but we'll have to be in a pretty safe spot and entirely replace a lot of the internal irradiated hardware. Only reserve power will be available."

"I'll find us a safe place after this pickup."

"Moving on then. We need to test them, but the shields look ready. I'm also sending people out to replace those hyperspace emitters that don't register. After looking things over, I'm pretty sure they're actually gone. Must have happened during a battle that wasn't logged in engineering. Other than that, maintenance teams are finishing repairs on our mass materializer in hangar three and other internal combat damage the security teams found when they were doing their sweep," Liam reported proudly.

"I couldn't ask for a better Chief Engineer, Liam," Captain Valance said. "We're lucky to have you."

"But you are still wondering why I'm here."

"I have to admit I am. You have to understand, I've spent the last five years with people who don't exactly do anything out of the goodness of their hearts."

"Well, at first I came aboard out of the kindness of my heart, and to satisfy my curiosity."

"And now?"

"Let's just say I've been watching the news feeds. I checked the miniburst from Hart News when we came out of hyperspace half an hour ago. Three more civilized worlds have fallen under the influence of the AI virus. Eden ships have hit four more solar systems and left them in ruins. Your friends the Aucharians have officially surrendered to Regent Galactic so they can receive aid without paying for it. The Galaxy is in pain, freedoms and security are being eradicated solar system by solar system radiating out from the Regent Galactic territories. All the while your speeches about joining a revolution against them are getting more and more popular, spreading across the galaxy."

"Looks like I don't watch the news enough."

"I normally don't either, but after returning from Earth, I'm making an effort to catch up."

"Ever think of finding a way back? It'll probably the only safe place left before long."

"All the time. Then I pause for a moment. What was my time on Earth for if I turn around and beg my way back to the homeworld? I have learned much and applied very little over the last decade or two. This feels like a place I'm needed, where the right cause is being pursued. I was once a military man, I know how to press a group to accomplish a goal, how to reward and punish them if need be. So I am where I'm needed. As for you, well," Liam chuckled and clasped Captain Valance's shoulder. "You are an icon whether you like it or not. Jacob Valance motivates people with his strength. Some people want to be you, others want to impress you, many respect you, a few want to befriend you while others like to hate you but just like everyone else, they believe you're the right man for the job."

"I wouldn't say everyone."

"True, there will always be those who stay here because they can't see their way anywhere else and they'll hate you because they can't think their way out of their own situation. They'll eventually find their way off the ship, whether it's on their own or trailing behind someone else. As the first paydays happen, they start to make this ship their home, and we're tried by combat, some will solidify, others will fall away. I believe that if you keep to the right ideals, trust your instincts, we will find ourselves on the right path."

"That makes one of us," Captain Valance said with a wry grin. "That's a lot of faith for someone I just met a few days ago."

"I'm just returning the sentiment. You didn't need to take me on. You could have kept the *Triton* running on two or three reactors until you found a government willing to buy her from you. Instead you decided to trust me, to trust hundreds of other people, refugees, deserters and people hired for the lowest going rate. They're grateful, mind you, their alternatives were much worse."

"A lot of them are spoiling for revenge against Regent or Eden."

"While others just want to be close to a man they believe in on a ship capable of giving them a quality of life they might not find anywhere else," Liam walked Jake over to the quieter end of the engineering control room floor.

"I'll be honest," Jake sighed, making a concious decision he hoped he wouldn't regret in the future; To trust the older man. "I'm five years old, maybe six or seven at the most. They tried to implant memories from someone else and according to him I wiped them out or suppressed them, leaving only what he knew how to do and whole operational databases on engineering, tactics and medicine. Give the parts to a Raze Mark Three Space Superiority fighter and I can build it for you then fly it off the deck. If you scan me right now with one of those high resolution readers you'll find a bioelectrical frame that can materialize living matter."

"I already did Jake, you might be surprised at how hard it is to detect that technology. I'm sure you scanned yourself before you realized what you were made of and didn't see it."

"I did, there's a layer of bone and insulation you can't get through unless you use a very high quality system."

"Though that's more intriguing than this entire ship, it doesn't phase me. For many reasons extending past your construction or origin, you're a unique individual like anyone else."

"That's not my problem. I'm getting pieces of Jonas' memories. They're coming to me in dreams, just the most important bits I think."

"How do you feel when you're having them? Just try and put yourself in those moments and recall the sensations for me."

Jake couldn't believe he was having this conversation, not with him, not with anyone. There was something about Liam, his self assuredness and kind manner. As he thought about it he realized all he had to lose were a few secrets. He relaxed and let his mind wander back to those memories. To those people. "I feel that I'm with friends, people I trust, people I enjoy being with. The one that says he's proud of me is very important, while there's another who, well, she appeared more than once. I feel like I miss her, she's very special, very dear to me." He opened his eyes and looked at Liam. "But none of this is mine. It belongs to a dead man."

"You understand that, but it isn't the way you may ultimately feel. I suggest you let this happen, experience it fully. Maintain the awareness that these aren't your memories but allow them to enrich your life. If you meet anyone who you remember through his experiences look at yourself as a representative of him. Tell these people that you aren't Jonas, that you have his feelings and emotions if that's ultimately where this leads, and go forward as yourself. Don't pretend to be him, but don't be afraid to become more like him. That could happen naturally if the memories continue to surface."

Everything he said made sense, and Jake nodded along even though there was a nagging fear. The fear that he would lose himself in the recollections of someone who he barely knew. "I understand. I'll try it."

"There were victims of traumatic experiences on Earth. I met several of them while I was on retreat. They had some of the same problems with their own memories. After blocking whole parts of their lives out they became different people and when those memories returned they didn't know how to handle it. You have to be prepared to remember things that changed your predecessor's life, to relive powerful emotions and find someone you trust to talk about them. They'll change you, and so will the way you deal with them."

Jake laughed ruefully and shook his head. "You know, I came here to check on the engines, not to be checked on by the Engineer. Thank you Liam, just keep this to yourself."

"Only if you keep me up to speed on how you're doing. I'd like to help, I believe I can. Let's just say my reward is living vicariously through you. Your life is much more interesting than my own."

"Done. I have to get to the bridge. Thank you for the work you've done down here. Your officers quarters are ready at the rear of the command deck."

"Ah, I've already moved into the Chief Engineer's ready quarters down here. Reassign them."

"You're sure?"

"Aye Captain. I'm a minimalist."

As Jacob Valance left engineering in one of the main express cars, he couldn't help noticing that things were changing.

The main lift was crowded. It was a freight lift sandwiched between four other personnel lifts at the main hubs on each deck. It eventually led to three points on each deck except for the Command Deck, where it only reached the center. There were half a dozen mechanics, four soldiers and a few other people behind him. As soon as he had stepped inside the car silence settled over its occupants.

His thoughts were still turned inward, his conversation with the Chief Engineer had helped far more than he had expected. He felt different, the same things were important; taking care of the crew, going against Regent Galactic, and helping who he could but there was less anger. At the same time he was feeling young for the first time in his entire life.

He turned towards the doors and nodded. "Good morning," he said clearly but quietly.

At various volumes and levels of enthusiasm, everyone in the car replied; "Good morning," or "Good morning Captain," and the silence returned. He stared at the doors, not focusing his attention on anyone until they reached the command deck. He walked off the lift with four soldiers and one other person, a civilian from what he could tell in his periphery.

He caught a glimpse of her out of the corner of his eye and turned to face the woman in the hallway. She was wearing a loose, high necked black dress over a mostly transparent vacsuit. The command and control unit she had chosen for herself from the materializer was made to hang down as a long necklace. At a glance it just looked like a one centimetre wide, four centimetre long piece of silver jewellery, but it had a small interactive holoprojector and split down the center to reveal an interface pad that stretched.

Mischa smiled at him. "Took you long enough. I was wondering if you'd notice me at all."

"I didn't see you behind me, I'm sorry," Captain Valance apologized quietly, mindful of the crewmen and women passing all around him in the main concourse.

"I'm getting used to it. Is there somewhere we can talk?" she asked with a raised eyebrow.

"I have an office just off the bridge," he invited.

"I've heard of it, your ready room. When I asked where I could find you the soldiers said you'd probably be there. They also tell me you almost never leave the bridge, you even sleep within a stones throw."

"Most of the bridge officers do, half the command deck is officers quarters. It's almost as safe as the Botanical Gallery."

The main entrance to the bridge opened, and she was very quiet as they made their way through. Alice was near the end of her shift on the bridge, she was splitting the day with Jake, each doing twelve hours. She looked up and smiled at him then grinned a little wider at Mischa who nodded back at her with a reserved smile.

They arrived at the ready room, and Jake moved to stand behind his desk, taking his coat and scarf off. "What can I do for you?"

She stood behind the middle chair in front of his desk, resting her hands on the top of its back. "I hear there was a meeting of the Chiefs and I wasn't invited."

Captain Valance hung his coat and scarf on a peg by the ladder leading to the ready quarters living space. He had completely forgotten that the civilians had chosen a representative by vote. Instead of sitting down he turned to face her and nodded. "I apologize, you deserved to be there as much as everyone else."

"An apology after the fact doesn't change how the decision was made. I heard that you're taking the ship back to the Enreega system on personal business."

"Part of it is personal, I'll admit. It's important to note that this could also be the first step in making ties with an ally that could be very helpful to us."

Mischa sighed and sat down, crossing her legs and idly kicking her foot back and forth in the air. "Captain, I could do with a few more details. Remember, I need to be informed enough to answer questions from my people, otherwise they'll start going around me. That's something you and your departments don't have time for."

Captain Valance couldn't help but be impressed. He'd met hardened criminals with less confidence than this woman. If he intimidated her at all, it didn't show. "I've been reading the logs from the first Captain who ran the proving tour for this ship, and from Wheeler, the most recent Commander. He had loose ties with a large independent space station called Freeground. It turns out he was born there and I have my own loose ties with Freeground as well. They've been independent for at least a century, and could make for the perfect home port."

"Why don't we set a course and pay them a visit?"

"They're about two months away by standard faster than light speed, and we haven't even started work on our wormhole generator."

"It would give us time to settle in on the ship. For people to get to know each other and form a community. I'm sure my people wouldn't object."

"That would take us too far from the fight. Most of the military and volunteers are here to do some damage to Regent Galactic, even Eden ships, though I'd rather steer clear of the Eden Fleet."

"That's something I can agree with," she said, her eyes widening.

"But a few days ago I received a communication on the line dedicated to my old ship, the *Samson*. Since that ship is down I had the priority transmissions forwarded to my personal comm."

"And?"

"It turns out some people from Freeground are going to Enreega under the assumption that it's still a peaceful system and my home port. They also think I'm Jonas Valent."

"The man who took a bomb out the airlock with him," she filled in. It was a growing misconception on the ship that Jonas had disposed of a bomb personally and was caught in the blast, not that he was himself the explosive.

He let it pass. "He was. Jonas was also a very close relation to myself and Alice."

"I understand. Can I see the message?"

Captain Valance hesitated a moment.

"If it's too personal, that's all right. I think I've reached an understanding of your need to help," she said sympathetically.

He brought the message up on the holographic menu hovering above his side of the desk. "You should see it," Jake said quietly.

A holographic image of a woman with long dark brown hair sitting in a small, dimly lit craft came up. "This message is intended for Jonas Valent or Jake Valance. I'm Lieutenant Laura Everin of Freeground Special Projects Division. I'm with Major Ayan Rice who was close to you some time ago. I don't know if you remember her, but at one time she was very important to you. By contacting you I'm breaking an unofficial treaty between Freeground and Regent Galactic, so you understand that I don't do this lightly. Ayan, rather Major Rice, is not in good health. Even with the help of our most advanced medical technology she only has a few days left to live. Her dying wish was to see you again in an attempt to remind you of who you are, where you come from.

Earlier today she slipped into a coma. I could wake her, but her life will be sustained longer if she remains in her current condition. I'm sending this transmission through a high compression microscopic wormhole in the hope that it will reach you before we arrive in the Enreega System. I need you to meet us there, Ayan needs you to meet us there. She doesn't have much time left. I look forward to seeing you again Jonas. It's been too long."

The transmission faded out and Mischa looked at him with sympathy.

"If the *Samson* were in shape or the *Clever Dream* were still available I would leave the *Triton* here so the crew could continue safely training and working on the ship."

"I understand. You have to meet them. When will they arrive?"

"The embedded information in the message notes that they'll be in the Enreega system in just under twenty eight hours. We'll have to be in hyperspace in twenty."

"We'll be retrieving them and leaving?"

"That's the plan. Do I have your support?"

"I'll tell my people where we're going. They'll be satisfied if I tell them this could lead to a possible alliance. I won't bring up the personal side, Captain. This is something you owe to Jonas, I understand."

"Thank you Mischa. I'll make sure to include you in group discussions like this in the future. How are things going in the Botanical Gallery?"

She smiled at him. "It's starting to look like a home already. Many of your crew have volunteered in their off hours to help clean and plant in trade for services some of us can offer. You should pay us a visit some time."

"I will, some time after this rendezvous is all over."

She stood and extended her hand. "Thank you for letting me in Captain."

He shook it. "Thank you for giving me the opportunity to make it up to you."

Mischa flashed him a grin; "Oh, you haven't made it up to me just yet. You still owe me dinner." She didn't give him a chance to reply but made her way out of his ready room and through the bridge with her head held high.

# Chief Medic Grace Templeton

Most of her patients were pliant and easy going over the few days the *Triton* spent in empty space training the crew and getting the ship in order. The soldier sitting on her table undergoing an eye strain treatment was no different. Like many of the crew members, he took his training a little too far.

He had spent a shift on patrol then entered a series of training simulations lasting hours. Some of them went as far as to simulate conditions on the *Triton* during hull breeches while aggressive boarders were invading. They were intense, demanding, and caused a great deal of strain if they were over used. Her patient had not only stayed in the simulations for over eight hours, but he followed it up by engaging in an optional simulation. 'Break and Burn Flight,' he'd called it. She'd heard of it before, it was a simulation focusing on flying one of the heavily armed, vastly manoeuvrable Sol Defence Space Superiority Uriel Fighters and it was rumoured that the Captain had entered the simulation as one of the enemy pilots more than once to wipe out the participants.

Grace smiled as the soldier went on about his simulated experiences on patrol in the Kuiper asteroid belt. It was the Sol system perimeter, and as he mentioned his entire wing getting wiped out she smiled a little wider. She knew it wasn't the Captain flying. Alice and Ashley, who enjoyed simulations as much as anyone else, had started jumping into sims as a duo under the handles Flare and Minx. They took over for what they called 'game pilots' or computer AI's that weren't effected by the Eden virus simply because they were contained within a simulated system. They made much more dangerous opponents, using ambush and misdirection tactics along with quick reflexes.

She looked up from the soldier's scan results and caught sight of Stephanie with four soldiers behind her. Her hand calmly reached down to the table at her side, picked up a beam scalpel and set it to maximum width and power before touching it to the back of the soldier's neck. "Now don't move an inch sweetie," Grace said to him with a warm smile. Unaware of what was going on, the younger soldier, no more than twenty she was sure, just smiled back.

Stephanie walked into medical, eyeing the scalpel, then turned around and left with her soldiers right on her heels. That was unexpected.

Grace picked up a mild pain suppressant and sprayed it onto the side of the soldier's neck. "All right, now go get eight hours of rack time. If I see you in here again I'll sedate you and keep you for observation."

"Yes Ma'am," he said with a grin as he hopped down from the examination table.

She looked around the infirmary for a moment and saw a couple people were looking in her direction. They may have known why Stephanie was there, but there was no way to be sure.

*What do I do? She saw what I was prepared to do to get myself out of being taken in and just left. She's probably waiting just around the corner, or getting more men to cover a larger area, increase her options and improve her advantage.*

She walked down the length of the infirmary, passing a few recently cleaned beds and casually exited via an emergency side door. It lead into a narrow hallway that provided easy access to escape crafts and the lifts. As she rounded the corner she heard footsteps and sealed the head piece of her vacsuit for extra protection.

Grace closed the four meters between her and the corner just in time to see the tip of a rifle. She grabbed it behind the sight and pulled hard, yanking it out of the soldier's hands. The strap that held it to him afforded just enough slack to turn it on him and open fire, pulling the trigger and holding it down for a long burst.

The first few shots from the pulse rifle were resisted by his vacsuit, but he could only take so many hits to the chest before the heat built up and he started to fall away, limp. Shots rang out and she drew his body around the corner, unclipping the rifle strap. She opened fire just as another soldier came around the bend.

She fired wildly, scoring hits up his chest and in the head. Grace listened for anyone else after he fell to the floor. The sounds of boots on the deck or people running were absent, so she ran around the corner and on to the lift doors, planting her hand on the control. Nothing happened, the small display of the available paths around the ship used to request and track express cars was darkened, deactivated.

The sounds of rushing boots from behind filled the hallway. She looked in the other direction and started to walk backwards with her rifle pointed at the sound. As soon as she saw the first soldier Grace opened fire.

Grace hit her once, but the soldier rolled and came up firing, shooting first her rifle then her arm. Grace threw the damaged weapon at her assailant and ran in the other direction. Soldiers were running towards her from up the hall, trying to cut her off before she could take the next corridor to the left. She rushed them.

A few of them opened fire on full automatic, filling the air with blue bolts of energy. Grace was struck twice, but in the protection of her vacsuit they didn't affect her at all. *Stun shots! I killed two of them and they're still using stun shots,* she thought to herself as she ducked into the broader hallway.

Grace ran headlong into a maintenance worker, bowling him over and nearly losing her balance. She snatched his sidearm and jammed the barrel into his open mouth cruelly, activating it with a flick of her thumb. Stephanie and several members of her team came around the corner and stopped. "Give me an escape shuttle with a faster than light system or I start killing people!" she called out.

Stephanie stopped in the middle of the hallway intersection and levelled her disintegration sidearm at her forehead. Grace knew exactly what it could do to someone if it struck a vacsuit too many times, and judging from the lights running up the energy clip, it was set to its maximum setting, on full automatic. "Don't make me do this Grace. We know you're transmitting to Regent Galactic and you'll live as long as you cooperate."

"You can't seriously expect me to believe you. Neither you or Valance are known for your mercy."

"I give you my word. We'll talk, you'll tell us what information they were interested in, what they got and if there are any others aboard. Then we'll let you go when we get to Enreega."

"What is this? Some kind of jealousy play? You and I both know I'm innocent, and if you want Frost you can have him. He's just a bed warmer anyway. I can have my pick of the crew," she hoped embarrassing the woman, creating the wrong impression for the crew members in the busy hallway behind her would weaken Stephanie's resolve.

"It has nothing to do with that Grace, now just put the gun down and we'll talk this out. Like I said, we can send you out in a shuttle when we get to Enreega or drop you off at a neutral port."

Her stolen sidearm beeped twice, and at a glance she saw the safety had automatically reactivated. Everyone in the hall heard it.

The maintenance worker knocked her hand aside and quickly crawled away. Grace deactivated the safety again and began to raise her arm.

"Don't!" Stephanie shouted.

It was too late, and as Grace almost had the sidearm levelled at Stephanie two shots rang out.

The pair of deadly bolts hit Grace in the forehead before she could finish pulling her trigger. The first weakened the protective layers of her vacsuit, the second penetrated straight through.

# Lusts End and Wars Herald

The Captain had called him to his ready quarters, and having found his immediate second and third in command at long last, Shamus Frost left them in charge of their last training shift for the day. As he arrived on the bridge Captain Valance stood up and walked him straight into his ready room.

Jake sat down on the front edge of his desk as the door closed behind them. Shamus leaned against the wall. "Important business Captain?"

"I'm afraid so. You'll hear this soon enough, it's spreading across the ship, so it's best you hear it from me first. Grace is dead."

Frost turned white. He didn't have much of a chance to form deep feelings for the woman, but she was a pleasure to spend time with, not to mention the first woman in ages to show any genuine interest. "How?" he asked in surprise.

"Security and Intelligence teams tracked a small encrypted transmission from your quarters at a time when one of the senior staff could vouch for your whereabouts. They looked a bit further into it and found footage of her leaving shortly after the transmission was sent. They also managed to find a recording from the room."

"What did the message say?"

"She was informing Regent Galactic that we'd be taking the *Triton* to the Enreega system. She also divulged the status of the ship, the number of crew we have aboard, the names of most of our senior staff and everything she'd managed to learn about Alice and myself. When the security team went to the infirmary she was seen holding a scalpel up to an unsuspecting soldier's neck. They fell back and went after her in the hall. Grace killed one soldier, seriously injured another and managed to hold a mechanic hostage before the security team had to use lethal force."

Shamus crossed his arms and looked down. He was quiet for a long moment before he asked; "who led the team?"

"Stephanie."

"How long has she known about it?"

"They caught it this morning. She found out shortly after and brought it to me. I authorized it after seeing the evidence. I checked the footage from the shoot, there was nothing else she could do to stop Grace in time."

"I believe ye."

"We've known each other a long time Shamus, anything you have to say doesn't leave this office."

Frost sighed and brought his head up to look at Captain Valance. "Nay, I've got my head on. It's a shame, but I barely knew her. On to better things, aye?"

Jake looked at him for a moment, the other man's expression was blank. "Aye," he replied flatly. "Speaking of which, I've looked over the information your contact gave you. Normally I'd say there's too much there to falsify, but I have to ask, how reliable is your source?"

"He wouldn't do me wrong. Asides, he had no reason to when he passed it on. His andi had him half in pieces when I nicked it from the reader."

"Well, there are a few targets that I've already marked out, I'm going to need you to lead one of the scouting teams in a couple of weeks, that is if you're staying."

"Stayin' sir? The gunnery team roster's finally shaping up. I was just about to request permission to do some live firin' before we set off for Enreega," he said, looking disappointed.

"Have you checked your account?"

"Not in awhile."

Captain Valance looked as serious as the grave. "You're good to repay me. I deposited a fair value in your account for the intelligence. If you're going to settle your debt and move on, now would be a good time."

Frost just looked at him for a moment, appearing only a fraction as surprised as he felt. "Captain, do ye want me aboard?"

"Only if you're here because you want to be. I don't like slaves Shamus, that includes indentured manpower."

Frost collected his thoughts for a moment before going on. "Grandad said once before I left that I'd get tired of the void, hasn't happened yet. Got tired of chasin' the sweet takes though, didn't know what else I could do till I got aboard *Triton*. Now that I'm here, well," he raised his arms and looked towards the aft upper decks of the ship. "Have you *seen those guns?* I mean, ye look at 'em and what they can do to a ship, they may as well be firin' tombstones! What kind of McFadden would I be if I turned away from 'em. My Grandad an' pa would shed a tear at the sight of so many heavy rail quads. I think I'll be stayin' on Captain," He said with a final nod. "Losin' Grace is sudden, hard, but I'll be up there with my head on a swivel, nothin' will get past me."

Captain Valance couldn't help but smile at him. "In that case, glad to have you, Gunnery Chief," he shook Frost's hand firmly. The older fellow's palm was wider than his own, there was grit to his former First Officer.

"I'd better get up there. Lots of prep ta get to," he said as he turned to leave.

"One thing." Captain Valance said.

"Aye?"

"McFadden?"

"Oh, aye, that's my real last name Captain."

"Ah, I'll keep it to myself."

"Kind of you sir."

\* \* \*

Alice was half an hour early for her duty shift on the bridge. Command wasn't easy, but over the last few days the crew were getting used to her. Many of them called her Captain while she was on duty, which was somewhat accurate, but she knew the proper terms were *Officer of the Deck*, or *Officer of the Watch*, or *First Officer*, but she gave up trying to correct them after the first night.

The simulations she commanded the crew through were going increasingly well despite their increasing difficulty. Captain Valance was assigning simulations that would not only test the crew in general, but teach them that on a large close combat vessel there were many ways to find trouble, and death could happen in a seemingly random fashion. Someone in a torpedo room could die because someone in shield control or field mechanics wasn't watching the status of the energy shields in that area during a missile or beam strike.

Her ability to command the ship was always stretched, some of the simulations even included boarders attacking the ship from the inside, spies uprising and sabotaging systems. One simulation went terribly the first time, it started with her arriving on the bridge to find Jake and most of the staff there killed. Jacob had designed that one himself, and the mortality rate was over seventy percent by the end. The fact that the ship made it out, was able to escape even though it was brutally damaged, was the kind of thing that bolstered the crew's confidence in her.

As she walked from the main entrance and smiled at the few day shift crew who had come to know her Alice decided to find time to create a simulation of her own. She was sure she could do something different, create a truly unusual situation that would test everyone's skills.

From some of the books she had read and a few of the movies she'd watched having a parity in the crew, such as a night and a day crew could be a very bad thing. The crew could rally behind the second in command and mutiny under the wrong conditions. She didn't take it seriously since there was no chance of mutiny, this was Jacob Valance's ship, there was no doubt in her mind. Other than the *Clever Dream* there was no other ship she wanted to work on.

Ashley locked the helm controls and turned towards her as she started walking across the bridge. "He's been in there most of the day," she said quietly, pointing her thumb towards the ready room.

Alice smiled and nodded as she continued on. She waited a moment before the door opened and she stepped inside.

Captain Valance was looking out the window at the orange and yellow nebula in the distance. It was lit from the inside by a cluster of stars. On his desk was a holoprojection of Ayan. It was how Alice remembered her, in her grey engineering vacsuit working the central control panels for the *First Light*. Her curly red hair was a shocking contrast to the plain uniform she wore. "That's a really good recording of her," Alice said.

"It was sent along with Lieutenant Everin's transmission. It says it's from the *First Light* and comes with an advisory that she's been ill for several years."

Alice sat down, Jake's mood was dark. "Did they send you an image of what she looks like now?" she asked quietly.

"You don't want to see it, she's obviously suffered over the years."

"I'm so sorry."

"So am I," he said simply.

She sat back and let him stare out the transparesteel hull for a minute. "I wish you had known her," she said quietly.

"I do. I remember her," he replied as he turned around and looked at the projection on his desk. "Last night I was sitting on the edge of my bunk on the *First Light*. She told me how she was having difficulty with fine tuning the energy shields. I started telling her all about my day on the bridge and watched her slowly nod off. I touched her face and she opened her eyes, looked at me, smiled and then I woke up." His hands went up to his head as he sucked in a deep breath of air.

She could see the frustration in him, he was shaking. His hands came down in fists, pounding against the desk. "None of this is mine! They're not my memories, I was never on the *First Light* but I remember her like she was just here, like she'll be back any minute with two mugs of coffee, one for her, one for me. You know I've never actually tried coffee? I remember what it tasted like though, that I like two sugar two cream. What's more I remember talking to you on my wrist, releasing you as I was captured with my best friends," he stopped himself and dropped into his chair. "You hear that? *My best friends?* As much as I wish I had been there with Oz and Minh and Jason and Ayen I *wasn't!* It's just like Wheeler said. Some lab tech flipped a switch and I was built thanks to the miracle of energy to organic matter conversion."

Alice stared at him for a moment. She had only known him a short time but was certain this was uncharacteristic. Making the decision to snap him out of it, she took a deep breath before letting him know what she was thinking. "How do you think I feel sometimes? Jonas bought me, programmed me, then broke galactic law to set me loose as a weapon. Then I stole a body and found my way into the galaxy."

"You don't have to deal with someone else's memories filling in gaps you never knew you had with experiences that don't belong to you."

"Really? Did you know this body belonged to a woman who killed people? She didn't get that way on her own, either. The first time I was burned I was reminded how her father burned her as a child. One of the first times I got angry I felt the satisfaction of strangling the life out of someone with my bare hands. There were other traumatic things this woman experienced that not even Vindyne could clear out, and it took a long time for me to realize none of it was mine. Fighting off the remaining impulses and accepting that the occupant before was still up here just a little was something I learned to live with. I came to life choking, gagging, fighting to breathe, learning to prop myself up and yell after Jonas as I watched him run by with Ayan and Oz. I didn't realize that there was no way he could recognize me and even though I desperately wanted to stand up and run after him I didn't know how," she finished flatly.

Jake calmed down and just looked at her, he'd never seen her that serious. "I'm sorry, I had no idea."

"It's okay, it's really okay. I dealt with it and that's part of who I am," she replied, lightening up a little. Alice looked at the hologram. "Jonas had some very good friends. Even in the short time I had to share the experience with him, with them they taught him a lot. They experienced good things. If she's the one you remember most, and I know she was very special, very important to him even when they were just meeting, then I could imagine much worse."

He looked from Alice back to the hologram. Ayan was reading something in front of her, unconsciously tapping her foot. "When I spoke to Liam the other day he said something similar. To accept the memories for what they are, realize they aren't mine but let them enrich my life. Just words at the time. Dealing with the reality is so much harder."

"Tell me about it. I'm glad I had Bernice with me when the memories started."

"Bernice?"

"She's one of the women who helped me off the *Overlord*, that carrier Jonas was taken captive on. We broke you out of the Vindyne Research and Development Facility."

"Where is she now?"

"Married, happy," Alice smiled. "She deserves it."

Jake nodded, his attention on the hologram. "I've never been in love," he said quietly. "I thought I might have in the past, always sort of hoped to find out what happened to me, if I had a wife somewhere who was wondering where I got off to."

"You know, chronologically you're pretty young. Anything could happen," Alice smirked.

He couldn't help but smile back at her. She was trying hard to cheer him up, to draw him back out of self pity. It wasn't fair to her or to the crew for him to be so distracted, so focused on what he couldn't change. Jake turned the projection off. "At least I might have a chance to say goodbye to her for Jonas."

"Is she really that bad off?"

"They tried everything. Her medical file was attached to the transmission. She even has framework technology installed. She's just too genetically flawed and it's caught up with her," it hurt to say it aloud, there was an ache in his stomach he'd never felt before, not even after losing crew members. "So I'll give her Jonas' message and be there for her. It's all I can do."

"A lot of people would run away from that kind of pain," Alice said plainly. "You're a credit to him for enduring it."

He sighed, a gesture she hadn't seen from him since she'd met him. Jake was changing, reminding her more and more of Jonas. "I've remembered her just in time to say goodbye. I've seen much worse luck," he smiled faintly and stood. "Are you ready for the night shift?"

"Aye, Captain," she said with a salute.

"Well, not much other than training has been going on above deck seven. We have two and a half main hangars clear and a working mass materializer generating parts for reactor six. They found another mass materializer in a sub-hangar under hangar one as well. It was packed with trash and it's already clear, generating a Uriel fighter."

"That was fast. I've never heard of that fighter though, it's named after an angel?"

"It seems most of the fighters in this ships arsenal are named after the Angelic faith. That fighter in particular has a cockpit for two, a small wormhole drive, six engine pods, internal accommodation for a cargo pod, extra ammunition or rescue seating for four. I've never seen anything like it," he brought up a holographic representation of the ship.

There were two flat engine pods to the upper rear of the main hull, another pair at the lower front, and a pair of main pods attached directly to the left and right of the fuselage. The engine was in the center of thrust chambers pointing forward and back. Details on the image showed that the main engine could fire forwards or backwards and the other pods could do the same, making the powerful ship incredibly manoeuvrable, capable of landing vertically, upside down, on either side or standing straight up. The pair of cockpits were built as part of the main armoured frame, the pilot sitting in front and below while the copilot sat above and behind. The small cargo hold ran beneath the pilot and copilot seats and the hologram animated the removal and exchange of different task modules. One had four cramped seats, another had racks for dispensing ammunition or holding extra power modules, even a pair of small fusion reactors, there was even a special module for future modification. The weapons load out was completely changeable, and with the copilot's help a ship could run with up to eight guns, two miniature turrets and four tons of missiles. Without the copilot to help manage the weapons systems only a quarter the armaments would be available. If an artificial intelligence was installed the copilot wouldn't be needed, but Alice knew it wouldn't be safe to install one until they figured out how to combat the virus that had killed so many. The sensor and intelligence suite built in would make any one of those fighters a perfect anchor for an all out offensive, it could even hold a wormhole open for dozens of fighters to escape before it followed them all home. With space for redundant energy shielding and emission recyclers it could be a difficult target to kill or near impossible to find unless someone had good scanners and was pointing them right at their area. The shape and design of the craft, with its tapered front and extra mountings for guns or other components to the side and forward of the pilots canopy gave it a predatory look.

"Now that's a fighter. You could practically use it for anything," Alice commented, wide eyed. "Have you shown any of the pilots all the specifications?"

"They're featured in a few simulations, a couple I know you've played, but they're not reconfigurable. I'll launch a few other sims that allow the pilots do decide which mission modules and weapons they want after we're finished in Enreega."

"That'll be popular. I just wish it didn't take three days to make one of these in the mass materializer, and that's while feeding it dense scrap metal to assist. So you're going to try and get a fighter wing together?"

"I wouldn't go that far, but some of our people are scoring very high numbers in optional flight simulations. We might have at least a dozen pilots ready to fly one of these. I'm hoping to get at least a squad or two ready just in case."

"I'd love to try one of those," her eye tracked it as it turned slowly.

"After Enreega. Too bad we couldn't keep all the scrap in the hangars to help the materializers along, reconfiguring solid matter is faster. You should see the junk we're leaving behind once we leave the area. Wheeler's crew had two of the hangar decks crammed," Jake said as he put his coat on. He picked up the white silk scarf after and just looked at it for a moment.

"That was hers?"

"She made it for Jonas out of something she wore."

"They'd both want you to have it, I'm sure."

He looked at it for a moment, draped over his black gloved hand. "I don't know if I'll ever measure up to Jonas, but I'm starting to understand him."

"I can help you, you know. If you're looking for a road map to those memories, I have seventeen years worth of directions," Alice smiled at him. There was a change, a drastic one. The hard surface wasn't eroding, but looking into his eyes you could see a light turning on.

"How are you fitting in here?" he asked.

"I like Ashley and Stephanie. It's like standing between polar opposites."

He laughed and nodded. "I know what you mean."

"They're happy here, more so every day. There's something going on between Stephanie and Frost though."

"Tell me if it turns into something. Those are two very strong personalities, it could cause problems if they have an issue with each other."

"I'll tell you if anything happens," she winked.

"There's something I need you to do for me," he smiled at her. It was genuine, warm.

"What's that?"

"I want you to leak some information. Do it through the night bridge staff as though this information wasn't meant for general knowledge."

She looked at him a little more seriously.

"I looked at the *Triton* from a financial point of view. With a full crew of thirty five hundred and an air wing it would cost a little over two hundred eighty million credits to run for a year."

"Oh my God," she said slowly, her eyes going wide.

"Tomorrow is payday. Their on-board accounts will be credited and the civilians will start providing services for a fee. Before that happens, I need the rumour that I can afford this ship out of pocket for three years to start spreading. I want everyone to secretly know that I'm wealthy and the only source of real income for the ship."

"Why not just tell them yourself?"

"Because that would invite a conversation about bonuses, overtime, pay by rank, raises and a few other topics. If they think I'm guarding my finances, that I'm hesitant to even divulge how much I have then it makes it harder to question what they're getting."

She hesitated for a moment then braced herself. "Jake, do you actually have that kind of cash?"

"I've managed to save up a lot more than anyone knows over the last five years. The *Samson* saved me a lot of money, most other ships would have fallen apart under the strain we put her under. That, and I sold my last cargo hauler to her Captain. He had a really good year so he was able to transmit payment right away. Besides, I didn't go against the Aucharians until I got paid for our last capture, thirty marauder corvettes."

Her eyes went wide. "That's a windfall."

"I can afford to run this ship for four years out of my accounts. No one has a thing to worry about."

"So you can actually afford to own this ship and pay her crew on your own. I've never heard of anyone owning their own carrier before," she said, chuckling but in awe of the concept. "Not all to themselves."

"If we find people who are like minded out there, I can afford to invite them as allies, not sign on as a privateer. We take a haul, it's ours to do whatever we'd like with. That, and if we manage to get everything up to spec we can start using excess power to materialize things we can sell."

She giggled and gave him a brief embrace. "What do you want to do? This opens everything up."

"I want to go get Laura and Ayan, train for a month then show Regent Galactic what kind of enemy they've made, starting with their intelligence network and slavery operations. While that's under way I want to track down whatever's left of Vindyne."

"Then that's what's we'll do, but first I have to tell you something, you're not going to like it."

Captain Valance crossed his arms and leaned against the front of his black topped desk. "Whatever it is, we'll get through it."

Alice took a deep breath and went on. "Before I found Jonas on the *Malice*, Gabriel Meunez's ship, I finished a strange job. An edxian named Zarrix had purchased a salvaged cargo from a friend of mine."

"An edxian? I've never seen one," Jake commented.

"I have now. They're strange, couldn't be more alien. I don't even think an issyrian could shape shift into one. Anyway, Zarrix was an exile, and the cargo was from a successful biological experiment. Some company had used edxian DNA to create something else and just as they were about to sell it on the market the edxians found out. They destroyed the lab to satisfy their honour but some of the humans got away with research and raw materials. My friend found their ship after it had undergone hyperspace emitter failure and salvaged it. I delivered the materials and found out that this exile is going to use them to show his people that humans were about to continue their work. According to him it won't matter which humans were planning to go ahead with it, his people will start a war and kill or capture everyone in their path."

"Capture? What for?"

Alice couldn't help but remember the sound of the word from Zarrix, his grating voice was something she'd never forget. "Cattle. Humans are a delicacy. He said they'd be starting with Ara Enormous, since that's where the materials were last," she paused a moment and shrugged. "I don't know what to do."

Jake thought quietly before replying. "If we could broadcast a report from you at the next port, maybe even when we're about to leave the Enreega system, then it could help. The only government large enough to do anything about this in the area is Regent Galactic. I don't expect much movement from them on this."

"I wish I still had the *Clever Dream*. Her computers have all the data recorded from the whole experience. I have my conversation with Zarrix on my command unit, but the extra data would help, especially the more detailed scans of the hold."

"Well, we'll broadcast your conversation on our way out of ports. That'll also get it on the Stellarnet. Maybe someone will listen."

"Hopefully. I just can't get over the fact that I gave Zarrix everything he needed to inspire his people to go to war."

"How could you have known?"

"You're right, I couldn't have, but if I had destroyed the evidence once I found out what it was it could have stopped there. I was just too afraid."

"Would you have survived it?"

"Probably not, but if I were braver thousands, maybe even millions could have been saved."

"I can't blame you for wanting to get out of there, I would have done the same myself. This isn't your fault, the people who ran these experiments and tried to profit from them are responsible. If what the exile told you is right, that's where it started. Besides, what if you tried to destroy the evidence and failed? Then you'd be dead *and* there'd be no one to warn people about this."

Alice looked to him expectantly. He had never seen her appear so vulnerable.

"No, you did exactly what you should have. Now you're here and we can spread the word. Besides, if you didn't make the choice you did you wouldn't be here, I would still be looking for you," he smiled at her warmly. "I'd still be out here searching for a daughter I'd never find."

Alice sighed and smiled back at him, she couldn't help it. "Thank you Jake, I needed to hear that."

"Any time. Just don't tell the crew I have a soft spot," there was that smile again, open, warm, welcoming. The memory of it would help her through the days to come.

# Two Hours To Hyperspace

The gunnery crew, all two hundred and eighty three of them assigned to the upper deck, stood in ranks in front of Chief Shamus Frost in shoulder to shoulder lines. The loaders and heavy suits were all at the rear wearing their two meter tall combat armour. Mechanics stood a meter ahead of them and the gunners were lined up down on one knee at the front. All eyes were on the Gunnery Chief.

Frost didn't use an amplification unit, proximity radio or his comm when the deck was quiet. His eyes scanned from one end of the line to the other, inspecting, looking for flaws in uniforms and gear that was simple, easy to get right and even easier to find flaws in. "Close your collar Bowes!" he barked. The gunner clasped the high collar of his dark grey vacsuit, as did a couple other members of the large team.

He nodded to himself. "What you can learn in a simulation is amazin'. You've learned ta work with the lower deck guns, some of you have learned how to arm, disarm an' reconfigure torpedo systems, an' others have even learned how to service a turret while half the barrels are firin'. Only twenty three washed out, now that's impressive. I expect ta send another twenty off my gunnery deck before the next hour is up since a simulation cannot teach you how ta manage yer fear," he bellowed like it was the only way he knew how to speak. His salt and pepper stubble made him look much older than he was, and even though he was shorter than average with a squat build he seemed tall at a distance. His back was straight, his gaze ran up and down the line making eye contact with everyone as he went.

"A long time ago I looked to my father and told him that I'd be signin' up for a gunnery crew. He took me aside an' said; 'gunnery crews pay for their victories, their losses and their failures round by round. We're what's left over when Fleet's taken all the better men an' women inta service as pilots, engineers, general maintenance, comm officers, navigators, deck hands, infantry an' even damage control grunts. They look at the bottom of the barrel and see if the sludge can be trained to shoot, load or climb into a killing machine an' get it firing again. If someone can't be on a gunnery team, they can't serve anywhere else.' He was tryin' to tell me not to start beneath the bottom, an' when I didn't listen he showed me this."

Shamus pressed a button on his arm length command and control unit and a two meter tall hologram appeared between him and the gunnery team. The view was from behind a much older turret. It was beat up, some parts were replaced through hasty but solid welding and it was built into the side of a ship, not installed in the top. The armoured suit the loader wore was showed signs of age and extreme wear and tear as well.

The armoured loader ran from another turret further down the line to stop at the one in the foreground. The paired guns were still blazing as one of the magazine wells slid back empty. The loader crewman reached to his right and took a three ton magazine of rounds from a leaning rack and transferred it to the empty well then flipped a large latch on the top of it so he could pull the magazine casing free.

When he pulled the empty magazine casing out of the well, leaving the rounds loaded inside, one round rolled out. He put the empty casing, a large, bottomless rectangular box, onto another rack to be reloaded then picked up the loose round.

Frost paused the playback. "What do we do here Acheson?"

"We put it into a safe waste container for matter recycling," Acheson called the answer out.

Frost resumed the holographic playback. The loader placed the round into the large magazine well and the box closed on his armoured arm up to the elbow. In one swift motion the rounds were put in play and as the turret continued to fire most of the armoured limb was pulled right into the workings of the machine.

Most of the gunnery crew cringed. The crewman had lost his real hand and most of his forearm had been flayed to the bone. Frost paused the image as the crewman activated the emergency seal on his suit instinctively, severing his arm at the elbow.

One of the mechanics to the right turned and vomited. It echoed across the deck and several other crewmen turned green.

"This is the recording my father showed me, the man in the suit is my grandad. He made a bad judgement call on account of an ammo shortage. Within eight milliseconds the consequences of that act were paid. The deck was down one good loader, that turret didn't get repaired until after the battle, an' they had to replace two arms. The arm on that suit, and my grandfather's. He was lucky, damn lucky. Some of you won't be. That's the life, we fight hard, pick our targets like deadeyes because a shot that misses today could take out a civilian in twenty years. That's space out there lads, it's not like firin' planetside. Yer gamblin' whenever you shoot in the dark, odds are long that you'll hit someone or somethin' but when you're not sure, you're doin' harm."

Chief Frost paused for a moment before going on, letting his point sink in. "I eventually became a loader, then a mechanic an' finally a gunner. I saved so many flyboy asses that they gave me my call sign. I liked that call sign so much I made it my last name. Let me tell you, there's nothin' like seein' a bomber after your ship, markin' it and splitting its hull wide open before it can launch! That kind of victory comes in time, for now if you see an important target, get three sets of eyes on it until it's gone. We don't have fighters, we don't have other ships watchin' our backs, but we do have the best gunnery deck this side of the Sol System, and a crew that did in five days what I thought we'd need a month for.

Be quick, be careful, be sure of your targets. Every decision you make matters. We're sendin' ammo into space, you don't know who you're killin' if you miss. Today we take this practice shoot, the Captain and the deck hands below were nice enough to provide us with a whole bunch of targets just floatin' out there. You'll learn to fear these machines first, an' someday that fear will turn into respect. Now get to yer stations an' let's do this by the numbers. Remember to watch everything going on in every direction or these machines will eat you alive. *Triton*!" he shouted at the end of his instructions.

"Deploy! Dominate! Disappear!" the crew replied, their raised voices echoing across the massive open deck.

Captain Valance approached from behind. He had heard the whole thing from the express car doors. "How are they Chief?" he asked Frost as he watched the crews run to their stations.

"Better than I was," he eyed a burly fellow who wiped his mouth as he made his way off the deck. "Didn't see that comin'. Thought he'd make it past today."

"We've put some of the washouts to work on cleaning and light repair rotations. One started tending bar in the main Observation lounge and I've had requests for him to stay on duty there."

"Mahajic, aye, good man. I'm surprised there weren't more." Frost muttered. "This is a good, clean, well designed deck, but she's intimidating as all hell. We'll probably lose two more as soon as we depressurize."

"I meant to ask about that," Captain Valance said as he looked at one of the turrets. The Gunner was getting strapped into the seat as the four magazine wells were drawn closer to the deck so they could be loaded.

"Aye, we depressurize to minimize damage from fire or explosions, and so we don't lose people if there's a hull breach. We just seal a section off and they keep operatin' if there's anyone left. If there are no turrets left ta run in their section they make their way in through an external emergency airlock an' rejoin the crew."

"So you expect to take damage."

"We expect to get pounded, there's nothin' like a lot of rail cannons on the field to complicate things. A smart enemy sends their fighters right after 'em, tries to do as much damage as possible to shake the crew up and disable the guns."

"Makes sense. How are the lower gunnery posts doing?"

"Better. They practically trained themselves, some even have experience."

"Do you think we'll be ready?"

"Aye. They're shakin' but they'll pull the trigger."

"Good work Gunnery Chief Frost," Captain Valance said, offering his hand. Frost shook it firmly. "Thank ya Captain, you mark targets an' we'll shred 'em."

Captain Valance turned back to the express car and looked at the gunnery deck as the large doors closed. It was like watching a ballet, with the mechanics checking vital components on each turret, the gunners activating systems as they slid up into the firing position, and the loaders moving four ton magazines from the large materializers set into the floor between them. The noise was incredible, but he knew that in just a few minutes they'd depressurize the entire deck, and they'd perform their dance in silence.

The express car doors closed and the vessel began to move. A sudden pain, like a steel rod being jammed into the top of his head stabbed at him. He clenched his teeth and fell to his knees.

Memories of a strange bridge, commanding the *First Light* into a battle they couldn't win against cloaking ships that beat at their flanks and rear with massive disintegration weaponry. The massive station was surrounded by asteroids containing the same material the *First Light* was constructed from. It was like returning to a birthplace, only there was pain, so much pain.

As the research station fired its big guns crew members were tossed like rag dolls and shattered like glass under the high impact. The ship, the crew were dying, and then he remembered his ruthlessness. The idea to turn towards the largest source of damage, their objective, and use a technology developed for peace, their wormhole generator, to create a gravity well and destroy the station while making their escape.

"A bird does not sing because it has an answer," came the last words from his best friend. He had to leave him behind, in the way of the stone and metal maelstrom that would erupt in their wake. Minh-Chu Buu was his name, and they had been soldiers together as well as civilians. His companionship was irreplaceable.

There was no time to reconsider, and they bore through the station, arriving at Starfree Port with their ship in shambles. Their objective had been to destroy framework research, to prevent it from getting out into the galaxy. The last memory was upon him then, looking out at General Collins' bearded face as he taunted him through the transparesteel of the long term stasis tube. There were two other tubes behind him. The profile of the shadow in one was that of Wheeler, he could see it even through the drug addled memory. The other he did not recognize, there was too much long hair in the way.

He balled his fists and braced himself as another wave of all consuming pain washed over him. "Every few generations there is a leap in technology so drastic the conditions of life change. This is such a time. Make sure this information lands in the right hands so it is a cure before it becomes a weapon. All your fears are justified," the voice of Doctor Marcelles echoed in his mind.

The nature of his existence was revealed to him then, how he was built, the memory of his first breath, and the first time he opened his eyes to gaze upon the thin, smiling face of Doctor Marcelles. "I have betrayed my masters again and leaked your location to someone who will take you away from this place. She can be trusted. When you are activated again you will be able to decide which life you want. That of Jonas Valent, who will be destroyed if he cannot be tamed, or that of Jake Valance. One has a life you can only imitate long enough to learn from, the other is a slate on which you can write whatever you wish."

"Why?" he managed to slur from the cold inspection table. There was a light behind the Doctor's head, he couldn't see the rest of the room.

"Because we should all have progeny and hope that they are better than ourselves. I have completed my work and when you are fully activated, can access the transferred memories of your human predecessor as though they were your own, yours will begin. Make no mistake my son, all that you feel is real but no matter how intense those memories may be, they cannot make you Jonas. His life is there as a platform, as a baseline to elaborate on, to grow from. He is a good man with principles, his example is important. Never fear losing yourself in his experiences, no matter how you use them. You can only ever be yourself and I believe the sum will be much greater than the parts. I must say goodbye to you now, they'll execute me once they discover I've betrayed them unless I can get away in time."

His minutes old mouth worked to form the question. "Who?"

Doctor Marcelles laughed and raised an eyebrow. "Go to Zingara station as Jacob Valance and you will be found by someone with answers. There are other messages in the emergency storage unit contained within your framework, but they will only come if certain unfavourable conditions are met. I pray you never find yourself in such a situation. Go and be whole, my son."

There was one more flash of pain before he woke. He was flat on his back, looking up at the faces of Alice and Stephanie. "Sir, are you all right?" Stephanie asked as Alice scanned him.

All the pain was gone. He could remember everything, as though he were Jonas Valance, but the gift he had been given by his creator was the ability to distinguish with certainty whose memories they were. Not his own, but he could delve in and feel, experience them as if they were. Emotional memories were harder to distinguish from his own, but within his mind was a firm grasp of where Jonas' history ended and his began.

He got to his feet slowly. "I'm fine," he looked out of the express lift and saw the entrance to the bridge was open just down the hall.

The experiences he unconsciously drew from, the knowledge he had acquired from a past he didn't understand before all fit, it all made sense. He even knew why it had happened. He had met Alice. Jonas wasn't the trigger, it was Alice. The first time she brought him out of his stasis tube the process of remembering should have been triggered but she left before he could meet her, before he was awake.

She shook her head and shrugged. "My scanner says you're fine, a little heightened electronic activity, but it's gone now."

He put his arm around her shoulders. "Ready to perform another rescue?" he asked her.

She looked up at him confused at first then smiled. "Aye."

"Are you sure you're all right sir?" Stephanie asked, eyeing him.

"I'm better than all right. I'm ready," his smile was broad and had a hint of something dark behind it.

# Seneschal

Alice sat beside Captain Valance, he was every inch the figure Jonas was. There was something new, however. He seemed so much more alert and in the present. His orders were more certain, and she was reminded of a time not so long ago when she finally felt comfortable in her own skin.

They were in hyperspace, all the final tests had been run, their cloaking systems were all in perfect working order. What they had done with the ship was nothing short of a miracle. The crew had come together, the bridge actually looked like it was properly manned, not filled with people pretending or hurriedly training at their stations. Ashley was flanked by two navigators, one at either side. The engineering and operations section of the bridge to her right was fully manned by five, and tactical was crewed by Price and another pair of crew members she didn't have a chance to get acquainted with, since they were on day watch.

Stephanie was manning the security station, she had grown much more proficient at running that terminal thanks to practising in simulations, focusing on just her job. Keeping her in as First Officer would have been a mistake, but as Chief of Security she had everything well in hand.

Cynthia wasn't alone at the bridge communications post, she had two more people with her and Alice knew there were a dozen or more in the intelligence office just on the other side of the reinforced bulkhead behind her station.

Below, Paula, whose demeanour had calmed over the last day or so stood at the main flight deck station. Alice checked the status of her section just out of curiosity. Hangars one and two were completely clear while hangar three still had a bit of damage in one section and some cargo. Chief Vercelli had already marked it for repair after this excursion.

They had all eight reactors running. Six were fuelled by the last of their uranium stores, which could last them three weeks, while the other two drew energy from the recycled emissions material given off from the ship. Reserve power was up to full, the shield systems as well as weapon and cloaking systems were all powered up and ready.

In ten minutes they would arrive in the Enreega system, and if their emissions capture and the cloaking systems were working, no one would see them.

"Addressing the ship," Captain Valance said as he stood and walked into the center of the bridge. He was in his long coat, the white scarf Ayan had given Jonas hung loosely around his neck, and the silver skull was clearly imprinted on the left side of his chest along with seven silver bars around the cuffs of his coat and vacsuit, designating him as the Captain. Behind him the two dimentional displays on the wall shifted and glowed with glimmering stars, solar winds, and nebulae that were distorted by the particles that made up the hyperspace field all around the ship.

Cynthia nodded, indicating that the whole ship could hear him.

"Hard days. Long, sleepless nights. I know first hand what they're like. I haven't had to learn like you have, to practice like you have, to sacrifice as you have. My burden has come in a different form. I have had to trust. In my life I have trusted so few. That is until I assumed command of the *Triton,* and if you knew what kind of birth I've had you'd understand. Taking all of you on board has been the greatest challenge I've ever had. I had so few incentives to give you in exchange for your loyalty, your hard work. Each and every one of you carry a gift that, until now I have given to five people in my entire life. My trust, my faith is with each and every one of you.

I trust that you will use the skills you brought on board with you, what you've learned since, and that you will have faith in me. We go now to do something else that I haven't done often. Help the helpless. There are two people unaware of what awaits them in the Enreega system, they are defenceless, helpless. If we don't take them aboard, give them refuge, Regent Galactic will capture them, interrogate them, and pick them apart until they are sure they have taken all their knowledge.

I hope we do not have to fight our way out of this system, but I am confident that we can. The *Triton* is a steady, hard ship. She is named after the son of a God who could send giants running in all directions with a blow of his horn. I say that if we are forced to fight our way out, we leave such a mark that they will know why the giants fled at the very sound of *Triton's* horn. *Triton!" h*is holographic image called from everywhere in the ship.

In Engineering, on the flight deck, the gunnery deck and all places in between everyone raised their fists into the air, armour clad and otherwise and shouted the response; "Deploy, Dominate, Disappear!"

"That is faith. That is what our enemies will never understand. That is how we will burn them to cinders and scatter their ashes across the galaxy," Captain Valance said through a grin that most could only describe as malicious.

He cut the channel using his command and control unit then returned to the command chair.

"You better give us somethin' to shoot at after that Captain, my boys are on fire up here," Frost said through his communicator. The Chiefs were all tied into one encrypted channel.

"I think we're all on edge Gunnery Chief. We're just waiting to play catch down here," added Deck Chief Vercelli.

"I don't envy a boarding party if they manage to get close enough," Stephanie said. "We're set in strategic positions all across the ship, sir. Some of my people are actually hoping someone boards us, they're spoiling for a fight."

"Good. Three minutes and we'll arrive in the Enreega system. Then we'll find out if our cloaking device is working," Captain Valance said calmly.

"Don't worry about that Captain, just watch your sensors for that lost ship of yours. Everything's as it should be down here, probably for the first time in decades,"

Engineering Chief Grady replied.

The bridge was busy, everyone was rechecking systems, getting ready for the power shift that would take place as soon as they arrived. The tactical station crew were white knuckled nervous. They were responsible for finding the *Silkstream IV* as soon as they arrived. They had support personnel from communications and intelligence who would be checking scan results as well, and they would forward any important finds to Agameg, who glanced at his main monitoring displays one after another, over and over again to satisfy a nervous need to do everything just right. Alice and Jake checked and rechecked status reports from across the ship. Everything was ready, all unnecessary sections of the ship were closed off and locked down completely. The Botanical Gallery and civilian quarters were sealed behind many layers of internal and external armour, they were in the safest section of the ship.

They watched the counter drop from 00:02:00 to 00:01:59 and it seemed like another eternity was yet to pass before they arrived. "Is lower gunnery and torpedo control ready?" Captain Valance asked Price.

"Aye sir, tactical is ready across the board."

"Thank you. Ashley, as soon as we emerge, fly us into a position that will give the nearest ship the smallest possible target."

"Yes sir. I'll show them our side profile." Ashley said as she unlocked the controls, making final preparations for their arrival.

"Any special instructions for me Captain?" Alice asked in a whisper.

"Catch everything I miss," he smiled back quietly.

"Should I nap here or in the ready room?"

The countdown rolled from 00:01:00 to 00:00:59:00, and started to count in milliseconds.

Captain Valance brought up his command display, a ring of eye level holograms that projected in front of the command chair. Alice did the same. "I wouldn't have thought in a million years that we'd end up as the first and second on the same ship, especially not on a Sol Defence Close Combat Carrier."

"You think you're surprised?" Alice said with a smirk. "this whole thing redefines the term; 'keep it in the family.'"

"You have a point. No turning back now either. Any regrets?"

"I'd do it all again," she whispered back with a grin. She could see his displays were set to focus on the tactical and security aspects of the ship, along with a display for power systems, shield and weapon statuses. Using that as a guide, she focused her display to keep a keen eye on their course, status of the hangar decks, engines, reactors, computer systems and damage control.

There was a great deal for them to keep their eyes on, and the point was not to micromanage, but to let the occurrences inside and outside of the ship to inform their general orders. Catching something that wasn't being taken care of was important as well, though in their position it wasn't something they could afford to focus on constantly.

The *Triton*, having a crew of near the optimal size and being in fairly good shape, still wasn't perfect. Some quick and dirty solutions were necessary to get her ready in time. There had also been some modifications done by Wheeler and his crew that made some systems more brittle than they should have been.

There was work left to be done, a great deal of work, and they were going into a potential combat situation without finishing the job or having a chance to explore the entire ship. Who knew what unexpected issues could come up if they actually had to engage in a firefight.

Alice brought up a general status display of the ship on one of the bridge main holoprojectors, a tactical view on the center most projector and left the third one unset.

They decelerated out of hyperspace and all the lighting in the ship dimmed. Systems across the entire vessel were reduced to minimal power except for the energy shielding and cloaking systems.

Tactical screens and holograms started to populate themselves with targets and details. They had come out over three quarters of a million kilometres away from the planet Seneschal. Between them was the octagonal base ship, many many times their size.

"Systems are quiet across the ship sir. Reading no wireless noise or emissions reflected back at us from outside surfaces," reported Price. "I love these systems," he whispered.

"In a minute we'll know whether or not I love them." Captain Valance whispered as he started to help the tactical team pick through the sensor data, looking for the *Silkstream IV*. "Turn us around just in case Ash."

Ashley flipped the ship upside down using thrusters only, so if they had to make a quick getaway they could do so under full thrust. "We're ready for the worst, hoping for the best," she said back.

"Nothing is reacting to our presence sir. It looks like our cloaking systems are doing their job," reported another tactical officer.

"That's step one. Anyone see the *Silkstream*?" asked Captain Valance.

"Not on my displays," said one tactical crewman.

"The filter keeps on coming up with nothing. I'll adjust it," said another.

"Don't. If the filter hasn't highlighted it, then it's either not there or we cannot detect it yet," Price corrected.

"Aye sir."

Captain Valance scanned and devised a quick filter of his own and set it to run over and over again, running through the names of the thousands of ships in the area so it could be highlighted on their tactical displays as soon as it was found. "Move us in closer Ash."

"You're clear to use main engines. Our cloaking systems can handle it," Chief Grady informed command.

"All right, speed at your discretion Ashley. Let's head for the half million kilometre mark," Captain Valance ordered quietly.

They started moving and the navigational holograms in front of the helm lit up, projecting the courses of all the ships on their scanners, marking those that could come close to, or collide with the *Triton*. There were also gravitational markers, energy field outlines that highlighted areas of strong magnetic influence such as the energy collector from the Regent Galactic base ship. If the *Triton* were to come too close to any of those fields, whether they were from natural or technological sources, it would interfere with them and any competent tactical or science crew member working for the other side would notice it.

"There's something strange going on here sir. There are several ships floating on the surface of the planet. They look like harvesters," one of the tactical crew said, bringing her findings up on one of the two dimentional wall displays.

"Look into it more once we have the *Silkstream*. That has to be secondary."

"Yes sir."

"We have to stay focused or we'll get killed out here," Captain Valance reinforced. There were fighter squadrons, destroyers, even a couple long range carriers in the area. Most of them were out of immediate firing range, and the closest vessels were beneath the *Triton's* class, but they were still dangerous in such numbers.

"I have them sir! They just came in on the other side of the system!" called out one tactical officer excitedly as he forwarded his find to the main tactical display. It was on the other side of the planet, over a million kilometres away.

"Get us there Ashley, bring us up to seventy percent thrust," Captain Valance ordered.

"Aye sir," she replied with a smile, powering up the five main engines.

"Try to get a read on what's going on closer to the planet, I want to know if anything is getting to that ship faster than us."

They started closing in on a wide orbit around the planet, weaving invisibly between vessels both small and large. Ashley was forced to come within less than a kilometre of one of the larger ships more than once, she listened to instructions from both her navigators, who only focused on the most important information on the obstacles that weren't immediately in front of her or interfering with her direct trajectory. She was one with the controls, and as they reached the closest point of the planet's atmosphere without disrupting their cloaking fields, she guided the ship at great speed, rounding the blue globe while dodging between small substations, satellites and transports.

They came around and tactical was able to glean more information about ships that may be interfering with the *Silkstream IV*. "Captain, there's a destroyer closing on our objective at a range of thirty kilometres," announced Price.

"Full burn at your discretion Ash! Get us between the destroyer and the *Silkstream*."

"They're launching small ships sir. They intend to tow her I think," a tactical officer informed.

"Gunnery deck, your target is my target. Open fire," Captain Valance ordered as he marked the four shuttles just leaving the destroyer. "Once you're done with that, put some holes in that destroyer. Let's scare them off."

"Aye! I have your target," Frost acknowledged.

"Divert power from cloaking systems to enhance shields," Alice ordered as Jake directed Frost's gunnery team.

"Torpedo and missile bays, target that destroyer and fire two volleys from all banks," Captain Valance ordered.

"Pitching negative twelve degrees to improve our gunnery profile," Larry, the primary navigator announced for Ashley. Three of the *Triton's* main engines rotated so they were still accelerating to close the distance while the ship's nose tilted down. The gunnery deck, laid on a convex curve along the dorsal, or top side of the ship, would be able to target the destroyer and everything in front of them with all her dorsal rail cannons.

The thick hatches hiding the eighty eight rail gun turrets on the dorsal side of the ship moved upwards and to the side so the deadly cannons could raise up. Each gunner took aim and opened fire. The entire topside of the ship lit up with the white light of hundreds of rail cannons firing at the four fifteen meter long boarding craft. They only fired for two seconds, then stopped and aimed at the three hundred forty meter long destroyer.

The deadly projectiles tore through the shuttles, and by the time they were shredded into scrap and slag the rail gunners were firing at the red and blue coloured destroyer. Thirty six torpedo bays and fourteen rapid fire missile posts at the front and side of the *Triton* let loose their deadly projectiles, each one homing in on the outmatched vessel thousands of kilometres away.

The targets' anti-ship batteries and flak cover destroyed a few of the torpedoes and quickly accelerating missiles but they could do nothing for the hundreds of thousands of rounds that struck their armoured hull at over two thousand kilometres per second. The outer armour of the ship flew to pieces, revealing the inner hull as it burst outward, expelling the air and other pressurized contents within.

"We have destroyers and one heavy carrier trying to close to within range with us Captain," Price reported. His tactical department was forwarding all their advisories to him, it was up to him to make informed decisions and bring up issues in order of priority. "The nearest is less than a minute away," He started marking potential targets.

"Frost, switch to flak and high explosive loads. Divide your fire between the nearest ships at your discretion," Captain Valance ordered. He knew Frost would handle the specifics, but he'd still keep his eye on the situation to make sure there wasn't a dangerous target not getting enough attention.

The surface of the *Triton* came to life once more as the turrets chose targets in all directions and flung explosives wrapped in steel and shreds of metal at all comers. Their former target, the destroyer, was listing to one side, adrift.

"The colony ship has disappeared sir, along with any magnetic fields and ships within three hundred metres," Price announced. "On playback there's a large power surge in the moments before."

"Thank you, we'll look at it later."

"Seventeen seconds before we're in tractor range of the *Silkstream*." Announced the helm.

"Are your people ready?" Captain Valance asked.

"Of course we are. Just waiting on you," Paula answered.

Two of the destroyers veered away as soon as they started taking hits, trying to accelerate around the planet to use it as cover. It was a poor tactic, getting around the gradual curvature of the atmosphere would take precious minutes. The others were coming straight on as fast as they could and were suffering the consequences.

The *Triton* started taking hits as well, rail cannon fire half the calibre that it used and pulse weapon fire. A few beam weapons tried to tax the shielding, but at a glance Captain Valance and his First Officer could both see that they would make it to the *Silkstream*, their shields hadn't taken over twenty percent damage yet and Chief Grady had increased the recharge rate, so they were gaining strength.

"Tractor system engaged," Paula announced, watching the technicians several steps down and in front of her.

"We have them, bringing them in," one of them announced.

Captain Valance brought up the view from the inside of hangar one on a bridge wall. He could see the needle shaped ship being pulled in sideways, there was more than enough clearance for it to make it into the hangar.

"Start getting us out of here," Captain Valance ordered tensely.

He glanced at the tactical display. A total of five destroyers were firing on them along with one carrier launching eighteen fighters at a time. "Running out of time here," he brought up the fighter's profile. They were all bombers, some were armed with nuclear warheads and heavy shielding. The *Triton's* port shields were depleting fast and there were at least two dozen large projectiles incoming, they had to be torpedo or larger class.

"Frost, intensify flak fire. We have nukes coming in."

"Aye. Sharpen up and shred those radiological points! I didn't come all this way to get a sunburn! Loaders switch to flak! Two magazines!" Captain Valance and Alice could hear Frost shout through the shared comm channel before he muted that channel.

"The *Silkstream* is aboard and secure," Announced Assistant Deck Chief Paula.

"Thank you," Captain Valance said with a cordial smile and nod.

"Checking it out sir, taking a medical team with us," Stephanie announced.

"Cloaking systems up!" First Officer Valent commanded.

"Let's get out of here!" Captain Valance ordered with urgency.

"Three nukes in staggered formation got through the bulk of our flak field!" Price announced.

Captain Valance didn't have time to put the order through, he just brought up the screen to increase power to inertial dampening systems and did so while reducing the tolerances. He hoped they'd be strong enough for the crew to survive the shock wave of a nuclear blast.

"More power to shields!" Alice ordered.

The first of the nuclear missiles was destroyed by flak fire, the second got through seconds later and exploded one hundred nine meters away from the hull.

The ship shook, but thankfully it was more of a rumble, at least on the bridge. For a moment half the panels and holographic displays went out completely, then they came back on. The third nuclear missile didn't detonate, why exactly no one could be sure of, it may have been caught in the blast of the second or destroyed by the fine bits of steel fired as flak from the *Triton's* rail cannons, no one would ever know.

"Can we leave now please?" Captain Valance asked.

"Hyperspace in three, two, one," one of the helmsman announced.

The ship entered hyperspace then shook violently.

"Impact sir! We hit something small but it tore us up pretty bad," Larry reported from the helm.

Both Jake and Alice hurriedly checked the ship's condition. "Damage control teams to starboard side, section thirty four. We have a breach."

"We're on it sir," answered one of the team members.

The navigator to Alice's right held his head in his hands. "Oh my God," he whispered to himself. Shaking.

"Drop us out of hyperspace now," Captain Valance said levelly. "Re-plot a course for us and get us under way Larry, Ashley. Pendelton! You're relieved."

The *Triton* dropped out of hyperspace, still not clear of the Enreega system but out of immediate danger. It took a minute for Ashley and Lewis to plot a new, safe course but their second hyperspace initiation went smoothly. The third member of their team left the bridge, his face flushed and his head down.

"Estimated nine dead, fifteen casualties. Request assistance to transport them to medical, most are already in emergency stasis," reported the damage control team on site.

"We're clear Captain." Ashley reported, increasing to full throttle, slowly, smoothly.

# Ayan Rice

Laura was there, she could hear her voice somewhere in the ship. Her eyesight was blurry at first but it cleared up after a few blinks. The bunk she rested on wasn't made for long term rest but all her tactile sensations were dulled, the world seemed faint, muted.

Boot steps sounded against the boarding ramp, on the deck, then she saw him. He seemed bigger, stronger than she remembered, wearing a newer black vacsuit and coat, the scarf she had made for him from the remnants of her shawl was hanging around his neck.

He smiled at her and knelt down low right at her bedside and she managed to catch the end of the scarf with her fingers on the way down. It had lost a few centimetres on that end, the hem was different, probably repaired after some misadventure.

His bare hand stroked her face and Jonas smiled at her warmly. "I couldn't remember you for a long time," he whispered. "Now I can't imagine how I could have forgotten you."

"I never stopped looking," she managed to say. It was hard to talk, she was so tired.

"I know. You were the only thing that kept me together after Vindyne took me. You were all I needed."

"I missed you," she tried not to cry, but a tear slipped.

"I'm here now. I'm finally here," his hand was so gentle, tracing her cheek back to the seal of her vacsuit in front of her ear. She didn't want him to draw it back and see her hair had gone, so with no small effort she reached for his hand.

He saw her weakly raising her arm, her hand coming towards his and he caught it gently with his own. "I love you so much Ayan."

"My one candle in the dark," she breathed, smiling a little. "Finally found you, no getting away from me now."

Her Britannian accent showed more when she was tired, and she was so weary, he could barely hear her speak.

"You remember everything now?"

"Just in time," he said, a pain unlike any he'd ever known gripping him. "I remember where this comes from," he rubbed the back of her hand against the silk a little. "The shawl you wore during the pilot's ball. You had me speechless. I was yours from then on."

"I had more fun during our leave time together on Starfree Port," she whispered, smiling wanly.

"Spending time with Jason and Laura," he continued for her.

"Nights in your quarters. You made my life complete Jonas," she stopped and rolled her eyes for a moment before focusing back on him. "I had to come, see you one more time," Ayan took a shallow breath. "To say goodbye."

He knew it was true, the small ship was packed with medical miracles, everything that could be done had been. "I know. Thank you," he leaned in and kissed her lips, pressing only gently, just briefly.

When he looked at her again she smiled, truly and fully smiled as she closed her eyes and said; "I love you."

Those eyes didn't open again, but he sat with her for the next few hours. Laura was at his side the entire time. They kept her company as she slipped away.

## Passing Into The Stars

Along the front edge of hangar one were lined up all those who had died on the *Triton*. In place of those who didn't leave a body to mourn over, one or more of their possessions had been laid in their place. The crew had done Jacob, Laura and Alice the honour of placing Ayan's body, wrapped in white, in the middle. Jacob laid the long coat he had originally found in his bag atop her and tied them together gently with the scarf he had worn for so long.

Most crewmembers thought the Captain mourned his brother and wife, or his long lost love. That was the prevailing rumour and no one put it down. The number of bodies was surprising. Casualties from fighting for the *Triton*, from the Aucharian boarding parties, the acts of a spy aboard killing an entire squad, an artificial intelligence virus killing crew members who were unlucky enough to have a medical injector equipped control unit, and the collision in hyperspace entry. Everyone remembered someone who died on the *Triton*, whether they had just met them that day, or they had come aboard with them after knowing them for years.

There was no podium or dais set up in front of the bodies wrapped in sheets of black, white, red, green or blue, representing their nationality or point of origin. Everyone lined up ten meters behind the line that indicated where a pressure door would be coming down. They were arranged in rank. Everyone behind their Chief, the Chiefs behind the Captain and First Officer. Laura Everin stood beside Jacob Valance. They were all in black, grey, blue, red or white uniforms.

Liam Grady was the only exception. He wore his blue robes cinched with a red belt. When his engineering, maintenance and damage control staff were in place he walked to the front.

"It is easy to mourn those who are no longer with us and be sorrowful," he began. It wasn't his way to shout, everyone could hear him through the communicators they wore. "It is difficult but so much more fitting to mourn through celebration. If my time were to come tomorrow, I would want people to remember me smiling, lending a hand, or having a laugh. If my memory brings a smile or I'm part of something that is retold, then I live on in joy. There are so many people here who can be remembered in just such a way. I knew Gareth Kinsey all of three days and I need two hands to count the number of times he got a smile out of me."

The sounds of some of his engineering staff quietly agreeing with him could be heard by those standing nearby.

"Tell those stories, I know I will. Sure, all the comments and jokes Gareth had sounded better coming from him, but they're still worth repeating. I'll do my best to tell and retell the stories because I think it's worth sharing my experiences with all my people.

I'll tell them in celebration, because we have so much to celebrate. We live on to honour these people. We are together, no one should mourn alone, not on this ship. Not on *this ship*. I am only starting to see it, but there is a family forming here. A family that has had hardship, knows camaraderie, loss, victory and that is worth celebrating. It has brought us together and those who had no home have found one. Those that can no longer be with us help make this home as much as anyone. Remember them, honour them by taking care of yourselves, each other and together we can make a difference that makes their sacrifice worth something.

Now I would like to say a prayer. I invite everyone to bow their heads.

May all those who are dear to us know how they are loved.
May all those who cannot follow us on our journey know they are not forgotten.
May all those who feel alone in this universe not go long without a companion.
May all those who we have lost find peace and happiness.

It's fortunate that our place of rest and repair is so near a stellar nursery. All of them will become a part of forming new life in the galaxy. They are bound for a rare, ambitious new beginning."

The pressure door rolled down from the high ceiling and closed. Through the transparesteel everyone watched as the field holding the air inside the front of the hangar was turned off and the escaping atmosphere drew all the remains outside. Laura took Jake's hand and squeezed it. Tears rolled down her cheeks as she watched quietly. He squeezed back and just watched them all drift through space towards the large white, yellow and blue end of the nebula.

## Laura Everin

Laura was guided to the Captain's ready quarters by a surprisingly short soldier holding a rifle unlike any she'd seen before, all the senior guards had them. She was one of the few who had both the name of the ship and the silver skull printed on her chest, and despite her black vacsuit, and three bars of rank she was light hearted and quick to smile, even chatty.

"Can I ask what that skull means?" Laura asked as she walked along side the other woman.

"It's the mark of the ship, Chief Vega says it was chosen by the first Captain of the Triton for the squadrons aboard. There used to be two entire wings of fighters on this ship, could you believe it?"

"I've served on a ship not much smaller than this, only we were always pulling sixteen hour shifts with a skeleton crew. We had to abandon the outer sections and run everything from the core."

"Was it the *First Light*?"

"It was."

"So you served with the Captain's brother, Jonas. What a family."

Laura paused for a moment, remembering the back story Jake had given the crew about Jonas, that he was his long lost brother, and smiled. It was a good white lie for the crew. "He was a good man. It didn't last long, but I've never served anywhere else like it."

"What do you think of this ship now that you've been here for a day?"

"The crew have been nice, respectful. It's strange seeing military mix with mercenaries and civilian recruits, but I see it working. The ship is a lot bigger than it looks. I've never been on a Sol Defence ship before, I can see why people jump at the opportunity. They use space really well," she said, eyeing the broad hallway with its dark polished floors.

"These are engineering access hallways. They're evenly distributed throughout the ship so large components can be moved quickly. This ship was made for long combat in space, the cloaking and wormhole systems were modifications added later."

"You know a lot about the ship for a soldier," Laura commented as they stepped inside the lift car.

"Steph, I mean, Chief Vega gave every fully qualified team member access to the ship's history and blueprints. I've been doing some extra reading since I've been thinking of leaving."

"Do you mind if I ask why?"

"Not at all," Liz smiled at her. "I was a teacher before the war started, so it's a force of habit I guess."

"What do you like more, teaching or military?"

"Honestly? I miss teaching, and now that Regent Galactic has pretty much taken over Aucharian territory, it's time to rethink some things. My cousin lives up closer to the core worlds and they were already hit by the AI virus pretty bad. They're rebuilding there, so I'll be getting on a transport and moving in with her until I can find a position. If there were children aboard, even teenagers, I'd stay on the *Triton*, but there won't be. I'm glad in a way, this isn't a place for anyone to grow up."

"It's too bad you're moving on. It looks like you've made an impression here," Laura said, looking down to the three bars on the other woman's cuffs.

She looked at them and smiled. "I'm good at directing people and pretty diplomatic when I have to be but the thought of going into a firefight is still terrifying after two years of military service."

"I'm sure they'll miss you."

Liz sighed. "I'll miss them too. Even some of the people I've just met. Good things are about to happen here, but I think I'll do better helping younger people think their way through adolescence. That's a whole other kind of battle."

They arrived on the bridge and Laura tried to take it in as they made their way through. There were really two control centers layered one atop the other. The one for the ship and it's general operations, and another beneath the main bridge that was just as large but for the purpose of directing traffic outside the ship and on the three main flight decks. She had never seen anything like it, by her estimation it would take a crew of at least forty five to crew both levels of the command deck.

At the moment, however, there was a skeleton crew of eight. Even from the short time she'd spent on the ship she knew that the officers weren't far off. All but the Chief of Engineering and Deck Chief had quarters on the command deck within a thirty seconds' run from the bridge along with their immediate subordinates. *If everyone is drilled up to a fair standard it would take a whole bridge crew less than a minute to set up and be ready for anything. The skeleton crew could take care of most occurrences until then.*

"Here we are," Liz said as they came to the ready room hatch. The armoured door was pulled out of its jam by two heavy arms. "The Captain said you could walk right in."

"Thank you Liz, good luck."

"You too. It was good meeting you," she smiled before stopping to talk to Alice for a moment, who was sitting in the command chair.

Not for the first time Laura was given the chance to think. She had been put up in the only guest quarters that had been cleared by the security team. There were two rooms plus a bathroom, more well furnished and carefully decorated than anything on a military Freeground ship. The walls in the bedroom were covered in navy blue draperies of all things, the bathroom had a combination pulse and water shower. The main room was set up for four people to sit comfortably and socialize. The furniture was gilded with carved wood, the padding was deep and comfortable.

Before she could sleep the night before her thoughts wandered to Jason and what he must be thinking. She hated leaving him behind, and part of her, a very small part, hoped he didn't follow. *I have to give him the chance to choose for himself. He can follow me or stay with the Fleet and continue his career.* Laura had thought to herself. What he'd choose was a near certainty, but if he didn't know where she was, what she was doing, then there was little chance of him finding her anytime soon.

She had started mourning Ayan, her best friend, while she was in a coma in the *Silkstream IV* and the decision to wake her out of that coma wasn't the easiest she'd ever made. Jacob Valance had a great deal of respect for her wishes. When she first arrived he embraced her, which was what she expected. He told her who he was and what had happened to Jonas right away.

Jake knew there was no time to waste and her precious cargo wouldn't keep for long. While Laura was still reeling from hearing that Jonas was dead and that Jake was a framework with a large portion of Jonas' memories, he told her that he'd like to be Jonas for Ayan if she didn't have much time left. There were messages Jonas wanted passed on to Ayan, and if it gave her comfort, eased her passing, he wanted to be what she needed him to be.

The seriousness and caring she saw in him as he proposed it was what convinced her. Ayan had said her goodbyes to Laura before slipping into the coma, and when her friend began to wake she walked out of sight to give time to Jake and Ayan.

The outward similarities between Jake and Jonas were eerie. It really was like Jonas and Ayan had been reunited, and for that she would be forever grateful. Her best friend had the best send off she could have hoped for, and when it was all over Jake was in a deep melancholy. She could see it as he walked out of the *Silkstream*.

Upon seeing his crew his expression hardened, he wore an impenetrable emotional carapace, even through the memorial later that day. His Chief Engineer and Chief of Security took care of everything. She only wished the rest of Ayan's friends could have been there, that her mother cared enough to have supported them in their quest of Jonas Valent after her first efforts were thwarted. In his own way, she knew Jake loved Ayan. The power of Jonas' memories over him was plain, at least in that respect.

It was only eleven hours later and she had no idea what to expect from Jacob Valance. He came in from a door to her right, she could just see a meeting breaking up behind him in a small observation room with a long table running down its middle. "I'm sorry, the evening briefing went long," he apologized quietly. "I'm taking a page from Jonas' book, he knew how to run a ship."

She was already sitting down, looking out through the transparesteel wall to the bright nebula surrounding the stellar nursery like some cloudy nest. "That's all right. It gave me some. . ." she stopped for a moment then smiled at him weakly. "time."

He didn't sit at his desk, but leaned against the transparent section of hull with his hand on the back of his high desk chair. "Something the *Triton* needs. We're taking a month to repair her, do some testing and train the crew properly. More if we can manage it," he was so quiet. Not at all what she expected from the man she and Ayan had watched from security video feeds and public appearances in the Hart News Archive.

"I think we all need some time," she sighed. "What you did for Ayan yesterday was very kind."

"It was selfish. Beyond passing Jonas' message on to her-" he didn't continue his line of thought, only shook his head. "There was no need to deceive her."

"Do you have Jonas' emotions?" she asked quietly.

He nodded without hesitation. "I'm aware that they're his, but when I saw Ayan it didn't make a difference."

Laura looked into his eyes. There was a sadness there she'd only seen in Ayan. He turned to look out towards the nebula. "You love her, don't you," she stated quietly.

"Just in time to say goodbye," he whispered back.

"That's why what you did is such a good thing. She had her career after the *First Light*, I was lucky enough to share that part of her life with her. There was another part of her that never stopped looking for Jonas, and when her health failed so badly that she couldn't work, she only had that dream left. That's the only reason why I'm here and I have only you to thank for making that dream come true at the very last moment. You should be proud of what you did Jake. Now that Jonas is gone you're the only one in the universe that felt that way about her, so it's only right that you got a chance to say goodbye. Where those feelings come from doesn't matter anymore," she wiped a tear from her own eye, it was still hard to talk about.

He turned around. "You're right. I'll be honest, I'm having trouble," in that moment his mannerisms matched Jonas.

She smiled at him. "That's what friends are for."

He walked around his desk and sat down on the edge closest to her. "Thank you," Jake said quietly. "I remember you and everyone else on the *First Light,* you know."

"Good. Those were hard but good times."

"That's how I remember them."

Laura shook her head and wiped another tear away. "God, I'm so sick of being sad. I want to be happy Ayan's at peace, to move on and figure things out for myself like I'm sure she'd want me to, but I keep getting dragged down. I wish Jason were here."

"So you two are still together?"

She chuckled and retracted the gloves of her vacsuit to reveal a platinum band studded with a row of six inset diamonds. "We've been married six years."

Jake smiled at her, genuinely. "Congratulations, I know I'm late, but congratulations."

"Thank you. I have to talk to you about that too. I want to send the *Silkstream* back to Freeground space unmanned."

"So you'd like to stay here."

Laura nodded. "Until I know what Jason's decided. I'll send it to the area the *Sunspire* is patrolling. Oz and Jason are aboard. He knows that if I go back they'll put me in the stockade for life."

"You have a home here if you want it," Captain Valance invited. "So does Jason, Oz, and anyone else from the *Sunspire*. For purely selfish reasons."

She laughed quietly and nodded. "I was hoping you'd say that. Jason's got to be furious, but I think as soon as he sees the *Silkstream* he'll set a course to rendezvous with us, whether Oz is willing to leave his command or not."

"He's in command of the *Sunspire*?" Jake asked, surprised.

"Along with a Fleet Intelligence oversight Officer. Last I heard having someone checking his orders was driving him nuts, but he's doing well. They converted her back into a carrier with a full squadron aboard. They're running missions in the Blue Belt."

"So they have a tight leash on him. That would drive me crazy."

"They're afraid he'll take the whole ship and go after you. Ayan's mother and a few other people with some pull in Fleet were hot to send people your way until Regent Galactic threatened Freeground with reprisals if they interfered with you."

"Now that's interesting. Why am I so important?"

"That's something Jason's been trying to find out behind the scenes for weeks, but Regent Galactic has so many walls up it's hard to find anything at a great distance."

"After this training time is up I'll be on their most wanted list I'm sure, but I can't be sure of what they want so badly that they'd threaten Freeground. Maybe when Jason gets here we can puzzle it out. From what I remember of him, I'm sure you're right, he'll be here as soon as possible. I would like to see Oz again as well, but I'll understand if he doesn't want to give up command of the *Sunspire*. When did they re-dub it?"

"After the ship was rebuilt and launched as a mission carrier. The shadow ship program is officially coming to a close. Wheeler's responsible for that."

"Well, I'm taking a risk, but I can give you the coordinates of our position over the next month."

"I'll include them on the *Silkstream* under an encryption code Jason and I use privately. When she's in range of the *Sunspire* she'll broadcast."

"Good, if you need help getting the *Silkstream Four* ready for launch, just ask Chief Vercelli or his Assistant, Paula."

"It's pretty much ready now."

"What about that big calculator you brought with you? It's still in medical."

"Minuteman? You can tie him into the ship's systems. Since he doesn't have an artificial intelligence he won't be affected by the virus you ran across. The *Silkstream* doesn't need it. Ayan only brought it aboard to help her."

"I would have never thought of using a tactical and operations computer to keep someone alive," Jake said quietly. "She was amazing."

They were quiet for a moment before Laura cleared her throat and straightened in her seat. "There's something else. I'd like your permission to train with the crew. Before starting Special Projects with Ayan I was the energy field specialist on the *First Light*. I couldn't help but notice that your ship wasn't using her shield systems nearly as well as they could when you were in the Enreega system."

Jake grinned at her and extended his hand. "Join any department you want. I know Liam is overextended in Engineering, he'd love to have you."

She shook his hand and smiled back. "Thank you Jake."

# The Sunspire

"What the hell do they expect us to do?" Oz exclaimed as he paced the length of the Captains quarters main room. "It's not like I can just order the ship out of the sector and leave a big gaping hole in our defence here, not to mention toss my career away."

Jason turned the holoprojector off after looking at his wife's face one more time. "As soon as I get her second message I'm following," he said, crossing his arms and sitting back on the recliner. The cabin was dark, overlarge. Captain Terry Ozark McPatrick had kept the crew at arm's length. The environment of mistrust surrounding his new command was the root cause.

Lieutenant Trajenko read every single one of his reports the instant they were posted in the system. She also had her artificial intelligence summarize the shift reports of every senior officer before scrubbing its memory clear of the details. She followed Freeground's orders to the letter. Jason had gotten access to them; *'provide constant oversight to Commanding Officer Terry Ozark McPatrick and guidance if necessary. Report any violation of orders to Freeground Fleet Intelligence as soon as they occur. If any critical deviation from orders takes place, assume command immediately.'* was what they said.

"You're Intelligence now, it would be hard but you might be able to explain away any charges they'd put on you if you went after her."

Jason laughed sardonically. "Not likely. She's my wife, that's pretty transparent."

"So you're right. But we've been sitting on this message for seven days, and Trajenko is just waiting for me to step out of place," he ran his hand over his short blond hair. "If Fleet wanted me in command, they should have just given it to me and trusted I'd follow orders. I know what we're doing out here, how hard it was winning this much ground. I don't need some watchdog nipping at my heels every second just to make sure I hold the line. If they wanted Intelligence to run this thing, they should have put her in charge, not that she's earned the rank."

"What can I say Oz? You're right."

He dropped into the armchair he'd brought with him from his last command. "Of course I'm right, I've been thinking about this for a week."

Jason's command and control unit, a graft on the back of his hand, sent a mild sensation through his nervous system. He had set his priority message indicator to feel like a drop of ice cold water hitting the back of his hand. "Looks like we won't have to wait much longer," the holographic message projected through his left palm, so he was holding it in his hand. "It's encrypted with our personal key."

Laura's face appeared, she was smiling but tired. "We made it Jason. This is going to be hard to hear, so I'll get the bad news out in the open. Ayan passed away and Jonas had died before we arrived. He saved hundreds if not thousands of lives in doing so, it could have been so much worse. Our old Captain lives on in a different way. They made a framework of him. There are so many similarities, he even has most of his memories. Sometimes it's like I'm looking at Jonas only ten years older, grown into his skin with so much confidence. When he walks by crew members they feel it, it lifts them up.

You're not going to believe this, but he took the *Triton* from Wheeler with a crew of about twenty people. He's taken on a couple thousand crew, making it into a real home, a real warship and he's told me that he's going to start liberating slaves, making a dent in Regent Galactic. There's so much going on here, things you couldn't begin to believe if I told you. It feels like this is the center of everything. I want to stay, something good is about to happen here, but if you need me to go back and face Freeground Fleet Command, I'll start making my way as soon as I can.

We're needed here though, and I know you've been restless. It's up to you. The *Silkstream* should be minutes behind this message, so if you want to join me, refuel it and go to one of the coordinates listed in the broadcast. I love you Jason, I miss you and I hope to see you soon."

The transmission ended and Jason looked at Oz, smiling impishly. His friend looked amazed, pensive. Just moments before he was filled with frustration, weary of his situation. If there was any time to say what he knew was going through Oz's head aloud, it was right then. "Coming with me?"

"If I weren't doing important work here."

"Come on, you know they set you up with a senior staff that can cover for you if you ended up in the brig. This is our chance to make a difference again, to go where we're really needed. There's nothing happening here anymore, the war was won while you were out on patrol and just because they promised you this ship to go after Jonas but had to scrub that mission they left you in command. This is an apology, they're just saddling you with all this responsibility because they're afraid of what you'd do if you were left on your own."

"You don't think I deserve this command?" Oz said angrily.

"Of course you do! But not here, you should be out at the front, running operations where each and every mission makes a difference."

Captain McPatrick's command unit, a thin console covering half his left forearm buzzed against his skin. "McPatrick here," he answered.

"Sir, the *Silkstream Four* has arrived two kilometres off our port side. It's powering down. What are your orders?"

Oz looked at his command unit for a moment, silent.

Jason stood and shrugged.

"Your orders sir?" asked the bridge officer.

While Jason looked on, Oz's attention turned to the framed portrait of the *First Light* crew. *So many of us are gone. Minh, Jonas, Ayan, now Jason and Laura are leaving while Command puts me out of the way.*

Jason crossed the room and put his hand on Oz's shoulder. "What's the word skipper?" he asked quietly.

Oz looked up and smiled. "Get that ship on the deck and fuelled. Freeground's been looking for it and I'm bringing it back personally," he told the bridge officer firmly.

"Sir?"

"That is an order."

"Aye sir."

"Captain McPatrick out," he took his gun belt from where it had been hung by the door, strapped it on, picked up his mission satchel, then put on the dark grey long coat he had made for the senior staff on the *First Light* years before and headed through the hatch.

"We're not going to Freeground," Jason grinned.

"Nope, we're joining the *Triton*."

"What about your sisters?"

"They'd rather I be far off and happy than here and wishing I were somewhere else. Besides, this might actually get them to move coreward like they've been threatening to do ever since they started drafting people for colony occupation."

"Think they'll send someone after us?"

Oz laughed openly as they stepped into the lift that would take them straight down to the main hangar deck. "Not if they know the *First Light* crew are at the helm of the *Triton*. I just wish I could see Trajenko's face when she realizes we've taken off in a prototype."

# Tactical Officer Agameg Price

The *Samson* was almost back in working order. He hadn't gotten the approval of Captain Valance yet, but he had some very ambitious plans for her, now that the old ship actually had some time in dry dock. He'd be able to make the modifications in his spare time with the help of a few other engineering staff that thought the ideas were equally as interesting.

That's not what brought him to the bowels of the *Samson* that night, however. He had been putting something off for over a week. Like Ashley, he couldn't forget Finn. Price didn't see him in the same light, but over the short time he'd known him, Finn had become a trustworthy, easy friend. He could say anything to the mild mannered engineer.

He was a good counterpart for work, an excellent companion during off hours, respectful and he didn't treat him at all differently because he was not human. Finn would be missed, and as he looked at the Big Surprise, hidden away again in a small hold, he couldn't help but feel every bit of the loss. The large electromagnetic bomb, several meters in length, was made up of many different energy storage devices all wired in haphazardly and welded, glued or taped together.

The tradition in engineering and maintenance on the *Samson* was to add a piece to it once you were considered a permanent member of the crew, normally after a month or two. Finn hadn't had the chance to do so himself before he was forced to set it off, saving Stephanie and Frost's lives. Sadly a large fighter engine was activated behind him by the electromagnetic surge, and Finn couldn't get away before it overloaded and exploded.

Agameg had seen what remained of his friend. It was securely held in a deep stasis tube, only the major portion of his upper torso, head and part of an arm had been preserved. The brain was undamaged, but that was all. He was told by Grace he would need a very sophisticated medical treatment center if there was to be any kind of meaningful revival. The new doctor had consulted briefly and told him that there was no hope outside of a scientific miracle. The doctor had already left the ship. The Captain and Deck Chief had arranged for the *Cold Reaver* to deliver anyone who didn't wish to remain aboard to the Sarnia Transit Port.

It was left to Agameg to tell Ashley, which was another duty he put off. First he would make his tribute, make a statement of his own grief and start moving on. He had to be strong for her, she had the purest heart he had ever met and watching it break would be terrible.

Price looked at the half kilogram, round regulating capacitor in his hand. He had already signed it for Finn with a permanent marker. With a sigh he pressed it against a part of the Big Surprise's frame and used his spot welder to affix it firmly, permanently.

His hands shook as he pulled two wires out of his pocket and spot soldered them to the main circuit board deeper inside the Big Surprise. "There, your part will improve efficiency and provide reinforcement. Much like you did, Finn."

The hatch opened behind him. "This compartment is restricted to all but *Samson* crew, sorry friend," he said over his shoulder.

"After all that, I'd hope I'm crew," Finn said through a wide grin.

Price stood up in a shot and bashed his head on a low hanging beam. He crouched and turned slowly, rubbing his head and blinking his saucer round eyes one at a time. "Finn?" he slurred.

Finn crossed the compartment to him and checked his friend's head. "Yup, I just woke up in medical, all in one piece like nothing happened. All I remember before that is trying to open that damned door and a bright flash."

Price just smiled and blinked his round eyes, staring at Finn. His breathing came hoarsely. "Finn?" he stumbled forward and embraced his friend with enthusiasm.

He laughed and hugged him back. "They used a tactical computer called Minuteman to put me back together along with a few billion nanobots and about eighty pounds of reconstructive material."

Price stepped away and put his hand against Finn's face. "Ashley is going to be so happy, and Stephanie! The way she sees it you gave your life for hers. She does not show how much she appreciates it openly while she's sober. You should be ready to be tackled. I suggest you only meet one of them at a time." His breathing was still rough sounding, like there was some obstruction in his throat.

"Are you okay?"

"Yes, only a little. . ." he took a deep breath and let it out. "Emotional. We were sure you weren't coming back. There wasn't much left," he whispered. "But we didn't let Ashley see."

"Good. To be honest, I don't want to see either. That's one experience I don't want to remember that vividly." He looked to the Big Surprise to see what Price had been doing. "That's for me?"

"Aye, I had been putting it off, but after the memorial a few days ago I had to."

"Memorial?"

"So much has happened Finn."

Finn nodded, a little wide eyed. "Tell me about it. Captain owns the *Triton* now and everywhere I look there's a crew member I've never met. I've even heard there are two bars on board?"

"Aye, maybe that would be the best place for me to fill you in. We could call down Ashley and Stephanie as well. I'm the tactical officer here, by the way."

"Congratulations," Finn said earnestly.

"I'm wondering if the Captain will want you on the bridge like he did on the *Samson*. They're still filling positions."

"Well, maybe we could talk about it over a drink. I know I could use one."

"You speak my thoughts, friend," Price said, putting his thin hand on Finn's shoulder. "We missed you."

# The Night Watch

It was late. The night watch had been on for three hours when Stephanie finally started for her quarters. She had started her duty before day watch was on shift. Repairs were almost finished, training was going well but everyone was still learning about the ship and maintenance, engineering and security staff were all in the high demand. They were also doing training simulations and live drills. The schedule was full.

Captain Valance had made exploring the rest of the ship a priority. As a result she constantly had at least two squads moving through the ship. Slowly picking through compartments that hadn't been opened for decades, finding anything she could possibly imagine in spaces she'd never expect.

Someone had even converted an empty torpedo tube into three laundry drums. The compartment had sealed perfectly during an emergency of some kind and since no one had ever gone back to empty the makeshift barrels or turn the environmental controls back on what was inside was rotten mush. Whatever the clothes were made of had broken down into something no one wanted to deal with.

People were finally starting to settle into life on the ship though. With two large observation lounges open, called bars by the crew, and inebriating beverage rationing in place on the materializers, people even had a place to socialize and unwind without worrying about getting too intoxicated.

She normally made a stop in the lower lounge, the bar popular with security and intelligence crew at the end of her duty shift, but she had been on for nineteen hours. It had been a good day, however. The Captain had made an hour long appearance in a boarding simulation and made a very good impression on everyone. She knew he was there to blow off steam, but her staff benefited from watching him move with precision, speed and great tactical expertise. Stephanie knew him well enough to just enjoy the show, he treated the sim like a game and at his level of experience it did no harm.

People were starting to respect her more every day as well. It would take more time, but people were falling in line, finding their places and looking to her for direction.

Stephanie was completely in her own head as she rounded the corner. Barely paying attention to the long, broad hall ahead as she automatically made her way to her quarters.

"By my count you still owe me one girlfriend," Frost boomed at her as he came out of the lift behind.

Starting at the sudden sound, she spun and glared at him. "That's the crudest thing I've ever heard."

He grinned back at her. "Too soon?"

"There's never a good time for a crack like that," she stood watching him, brow furrowed, her hands drawing back her long coat and settling on her hips. "She might have been on the wrong side but she deserves our respect."

His expression softened. "I'm sorry lass, the line in the sand's real deep for me, 'specially since she used me as a bridge over it."

Despite being offended, she had to admit he was right. She didn't like Grace much when everyone thought she was on their side, let alone after she'd exposed her as a spy. "I get it, all's forgiven Shamus."

Frost walked right up to her, nose to nose. He really wasn't more than five or six centimetres taller. "Love it when you call me by my first, lass," he said through a crooked grin.

Stephanie looked into his eyes, those clear blue grey eyes. "When I call you Shamus? It's your name isn't it?"

"Aye, sounds better when you're sayin' it," he said quietly.

She glanced around, looking for anyone who might be looking on.

"There's no one about, night watch is on a skeleton crew."

"You're fishing in the wrong pond Shamus," she said with a tight lipped smile.

"Poor girl, hasn't sunk in yet. We're swimmin' in an ocean now lass," he put his hand on her waist and slipped it across her vacsuit to her back. "Have ta stay together more n' ever."

That feeling she had when he was helping her in the armoured suit, like she was wrapped in a natural moment and all the right things were happening, returned. Maybe she was just tired, but when he closed his eyes and his lips were just about to touch hers, her arms went around his neck and she kissed him back.

Few people on board would even try to stand up to her, but he was cocksure. Everyone liked to watch her from a distance whether they were in training or sitting across the table in an observation lounge, but he would step up and stand right in front of her after being the most obnoxious sod on the ship. He looked like a burly lout, but when she leaned into him, felt his big arms around her, it felt indescribably good. To her surprise there was nothing rushed in his kiss, and that magnetism just held her to him, made her feel like she was suddenly part of a pair.

# The Freedom Tower

System security was the responsibility of Forward Admiral Rice. Her political push to have Jonas Valent located had crumbled when Regent Galactic threatened to add Freeground to its long list of enemies. The Admiralty was displeased and had to make an example of the Admiral and her associates. They pushed back and she was given a distant, although prestigious post on guard at the first colony settled by the Freeground nation.

The first significant structure built was a tall, needle like tower. Over one hundred thousand Freeground citizens were housed there while most of the outer townships were home to the prisons and work camps. The untamed wilds discovered in the newly named planet Dumuzi were filled with animals that reminded the populace of Earth's oxygen breathing creatures. The major difference between them and what was known from ancient Earth was how hardened the creatures of Dumuzi were after surviving the violent changes that had occurred over the recent centuries.

The planet had only begun recovering from a stage of wide scale volcanic development, and they had settled on the largest continent capable of supporting life. The short, squat terraforming structures sat on the coastlines, helping the excess carbon dioxide process into breathable air.

Before they had arrived they had discovered a jungle growing out of a surviving vegetative mass. Some time after initial landfall they discovered an entire food chain was fighting its way back from near extinction. With the help of the Lorander terraformers and Freeground workforce they expected the forested area to double in the next three months.

The view of the nearing forest's edge from the high Freedom Tower in the center of the smaller trio of towns was better every day. Farms were already growing a natural food supply and soon it would be more efficient to eat what was cultivated rather than materialized meals.

None of these things were at the forefront of Admiral Rice's mind as she walked through the green and white hallway of the Freedom Tower restricted areas. There were a few things she had to check on, and she saved the best for last.

She waited patiently as the security system for the Freedom Tower Special Projects laboratory scanned her on a molecular level. After a moment the door opened and she walked through, making sure that it closed right behind her.

"Welcome back Admiral," Doctor Anderson said as he examined detailed cellular holograms above a long white table. "Come to see how she's doing?"

"Why else would I make the journey. My shuttle was in orbital gridlock for three hours."

"What's another three hours after five years?" He said with a shrug, knowing that finding even the barest thread of humour in her had been next to impossible for years. The Admiral, as he called her these days, had gone emotionally bankrupt long ago as far as he was concerned. His holodisplay shut down with a button stroke and he closed the vertical blinds.

Admiral Rice waited patiently in front of a display wall. In earlier days it was covered in genetic information, works in progress that all had critical deadlines. As she looked at it there was only the mysterious electrochemical matrix of a human brain, the careful conduction of guided memory to form the full realization of a naturally formed personality, or the nearest facsimile anyone could have dreamed possible.

Doctor Anderson walked to the side of the large display board, stretching two and a half meters tall and four meters across. "That's mostly for decoration now. The memories are all in place, even adjusted muscle memories, which were the hardest part."

"I know Doctor," the Admiral said impatiently.

"On with the show then," he said to himself quietly as he entered the code to draw the two dimentional display aside.

Behind it was a transparent artificial womb. Within it's synthetic flesh was a blonde woman, a little too short, not of the desired social weight but still well proportioned in a fetal position. She was fully grown, to see her anywhere else someone would think she was just another early to mid twenties woman.

"She looks so much like her great grandmother," Admiral Rice said in awe, walking up to the soft outer layer and putting her hand on it. The occupant turned towards the ripple in her protective home. "Does she know I'm here?"

"She's unconsciously aware of everything around her. I talk to her constantly and sleep in the lab most nights. She prefers Wagner and she very nearly dances when I play Magic Fire Music from Die Walkure."

"I should have recorded my voice for her."

"I tried to tell you," Doctor Anderson said quietly.

The Admiral gave him a dark look. "What does it matter, when she wakes she'll remember everything Ayan did right up to five years ago."

"You mean right up until you gave up on your only daughter."

"Don't you dare-"

"When you brought me onto this project you gave away all your power. If anything about this were to slip out to the Admiralty they'd have your head. I'm just here following orders."

"But you wouldn't do that, she's as much your child as she is mine."

"I'll do anything to protect her, but only because I know if Ayan had a choice to be born without any genetic meddling that's the road she would have taken. If you'd have been brave enough to show her what you were doing with the scan you had made of her, she would have applauded it. This isn't a clone as you originally requested, this is what should have been," his words were clear and loud enough, but they were spoken gently for the benefit of his captive audience.

"So you've managed to eliminate all the imperfections?"

Doctor Anderson laughed quietly and nodded. "What I consider imperfections. The genetic modifications are gone. Everything from the enhanced physical aptitudes to her adjusted phenomenal balance to the one that ensured she'd have red hair. What's left is the code as it should have been. No growth therapy or acceleration was used either."

"Is she ready?"

"Not quite. She's still experiencing the last of the memories in the scan, Jason and Laura's wedding."

"I wouldn't have chosen that as her last."

"Because Laura and Jason are both missing? Written off by the military? I was at that wedding, it was a great time. There were so many friends there, a lot of them from the *First Light*. Her toast as the maid of honour was fantastic, you could barely tell she was ill."

Admiral Rice sighed as she looked at the young woman. "I wish we could have taken the bad times away. If only we could have scanned her before the *Sunspire*."

"Just like she needs someone here so she can listen to someone else's heart, hear their voice and experience the world through a filter of a womb to have a good subconscious foundation to work from and a starting point of well being, she needs those negative experiences for a complete personality. Without hardship we don't appreciate good times or know how to deal with life when things are less than ideal."

"I know, Doctor. What will the birth be like?"

"Well, since there's no point in putting her through a simulated natural birthing experience, we'll be waking her up once she's out of the chamber and clean. I've had an apartment prepared and one of us can tell her what's happened," Doctor Anderson said quietly as he walked from the control board to Ayan herself and put his hand on her knee. "Do you want to be the first person she sees?"

Admiral Rice looked at the second inception of her daughter for a long moment. Her curled long hair was kept out of her face using mild fluid control so she could see her innocent heart shaped visage. She was so afraid of who this young woman would be, what would become of her. There would be no sickness, no guilt over genetic modifications she'd ordered for her daughter. Hopefully just the opposite. The guilt over the first Ayan gripped her, filled her with fear when she tried to think about what she would do differently given a second chance. "You should explain it to her. We weren't close five years ago."

"All right," he said softly. "But only if you're certain. Waking her up yourself and explaining things could be a good way to start things in the right direction."

Admiral Rice shook her head; "I don't know what I'd say. Besides, coming from you it would be less of a shock."

"All right, just keep it in mind."

"Does she have dimples?" Admiral Rice asked, looking more closely. Her daughter was smiling at some unknowable experience.

"Yes, and she'll have a little acne and probably need to exercise more than before to keep in the shape she's used to or take fitness medication."

"You couldn't keep any modifications?"

"I told you, nothing. If she's going to have another chance without any disorders everything had to be reverted to her ancestrally developed genetic makeup. I had to go back centuries for a reference point. Standard modifications like anti-ageing, disease fortification and chemical balancing can be added later, it's up to her. When she wakes up she may not feel the same, that's a foregone conclusion, in fact she should feel much better," he looked at the young woman through the many gelatinous layers of the artificial womb and smiled. "Ayan will have the chance at life she deserved."

"She was so beautiful before."

"So much more now," he stepped back, inviting her to do the same and closed the chamber off. "Is it true that Ayan stole the *Silkstream Four*?"

Admiral Rice looked at him unknowing for a moment, then realized he was talking about her original daughter, the first Ayan. "Yes, her and Laura. They're off to find Jonas."

"From what my connections tell me they'll find him. His home port is public. We should have had a message sent weeks ago."

"I tried everything I could to help her find him."

"If that were the case it would have happened a long time ago."

"You have no right to accuse me-"

"I have every right. You abandoned her when you saw a better option come along. I should have tried to delay this project until Ayan, the Ayan that matters right now, had passed on. You should be at her side, even if it takes you across the galaxy. Instead you wrote her off and started over."

"There was nothing I could do," Admiral Rice said helplessly.

"Bullshit! Even with that tactical computer they stole Ayan's dead by now. Where are you? You're standing beside a replacement, not even taking the time to mourn. Your daughter is dead, *dead* and you have no idea where she lived her last moments, how she was feeling or who, if anyone, was watching over her!"

Admiral Rice just stared at him, her wide eyes tearing up.

He went on, stepping to within just a meter of her. "Do you know why I really took this project on? Because I knew this would happen! I knew that days before this young woman's birth you'd stand there criticizing what you consider flaws, picking at perceived imperfections. Look at her! Just look! She's a perfectly healthy woman and when she feels comfortable in her skin she'll be charming, unique, intelligent and possess all the skills and personality traits she valued. If she wants any permanent genetic modifications made when she's able to decide for herself they'll work much better than they would on any of us. Why? Because you allowed me to strip away all the extras and modifications, revert her genetic code back to what nature intended. There will be no complications, no strange diseases or mutations to consider. She will be everything she's meant to be in this second chance. That's everything we want our children to start with. Now go, mourn your daughter somewhere where people aren't saluting you, where no one knows who you are. I'll be here making sure this young woman's entry into this universe is as it should be. She'll know where she comes from. Eventually, when she asks, I'll even tell her what happened to the first-"

"No," Admiral Rice croaked.

"Damn right she'll know! All the while she'll have someone who'll do anything to make sure she has the opportunity to be her own person, just as Ayan should have! You're not the only one who feels guilty about Ayan being left alone, I should have been her trusted friend just as much as you should have stayed at her side. Instead I was on an unmarked ship inside a wormhole designed to compress time so her body could have thirty years to mature inside the altered space while four years passed outside of it. The only real difference between you and I is that you ordered all this out of guilt and I did it out of love, because I know your daughter would want this."

"I'll shut the project down."

"You know you don't mean that."

Admiral Rice regained a little of her composure and glared at Doctor Anderson. "Until she opens her eyes she's just a piece of meat. I can pull the plug any time," she whispered harshly.

Doctor Anderson just stared at her, searching her face for the woman he'd known and loved as a close friend years before. She simply wasn't there. "I believe you," he whispered as he stepped back and turned to his holographic work table.

She watched him, knowing she'd crossed a line that changed everything. He couldn't even look at her, what she'd said hurt him more than she could have ever expected.

"I'll contact you if there are any changes," Doctor Anderson said quietly, it was almost a whisper.

Admiral Rice turned on her heel and left the room.

Doctor Anderson sighed. "Thank God the chamber was closed. The last thing you need is an environment where people are yelling at each other," he turned and opened the wall concealing the artificial womb. "You'll have a good future ahead of you if I have anything to say about it, and you'll be free. The forms declaring you an independent sentient are already processing. By the time you're born she won't be able to do anything to you," he whispered gently, looking at the sleeping face of his charge. He chuckled. "You know, I was pretty sure this would happen when you were just a few cells. Getting attached was something I accepted when your genes sequenced in a match to their natural state for the first time. I get the feeling that, even though I'll offer you everything a father should, you'll be travelling between the stars before I'm ready to see you go. All I can do is make sure you get the start you deserve."

He punched his clearance code into his personal command unit and opened a communications link to an old friend.

"Doctor Anderson, it's been a while since we've had a face to face!" said the cheery fellow on the other end. "I got your burst. That's an interesting hypothetical situation you brought up."

"Hello Peter, how is Fleet Intelligence treating you?"

"Good, good. So what's this I hear about you processing clone rights forms?"

"I'll be honest. I'm doing damage control here and I need help. Admiral Rice is threatening to cancel a sensitive project that involves some of her daughter's genetic material," he said, continuing in a gentle tone.

"How far along are we talking?"

"I'm being honest and forthcoming with you here, Pete, it's important this doesn't get out the wrong way."

"We've known each other a long time, I'll keep it under wraps until it's safe to shed light on whatever this is."

Doctor Anderson sent Peter a holographic image of Ayan in the artificial womb.

He took a moment to look at it and his eyes went wide. "Is that who I think it is?"

"In a way. I've managed to create a perfect generation of her with no genetic modifications. She's been created from base historical genetic code. I used the new age modification and memory implementation technology we acquired a few years ago."

"Admiral Rice might shut you down? Now? That's her daughter in there for all intents and purposes. When will you be birthing her?"

"Next week, sooner if there are no signs of neural fatigue. I don't want her mother within ten light years of here when it happens. In fact, I don't want her to see Ayan until she decides she's ready to meet with her mother."

"You know I can do that for you, but it'll be political war. Admiral Rice still has friends here, and outside of dealings with Regent Galactic or Jonas Valent, she has a lot of power. Just getting her reassigned again-"

"I know, I'm asking a lot. You know me Pete, I wouldn't even mention it if it weren't life or death."

Peter thought quietly while looking at the hologram of the young woman then nodded. "I'll get my staff on it now. We'll have to vilify Admiral Rice to justify access restriction and reassignment. There's no way back on this once it's done."

"There's been a lot of that going around. I'm sending you a classified security clip from just a few minutes ago that should take care of vilification," he selected and forwarded Admiral Rice threatening to pull the plug then went on. "Thank you Peter. This makes us more than even."

"You know it. Just make sure this young lady knows how many people helped her get her freedom, and that she deserves it."

"Knowing Ayan, she'll thank every one of you in person."

"I bet she would. You know she's going to be popular, right Doc? The only human alive without genetic enhancements. Who knew we'd have to take a thousand steps backwards to take a meaningful step forward."

"I did."

"And that's why my kids grew up with you as their family doctor," Peter laughed. "Well, I'm not sleeping tonight, I'll start working on this right away. Admiral Rice won't be able to so much as set foot in Freedom Tower by morning."

"Thank you again," Doctor Anderson smiled. The communication closed and he started the Summer movement of Vivaldi's Four Seasons. "Just because you favour Wagner doesn't mean you shouldn't experience other composers," he said to her quietly.

Ayan shifted in her peaceful chamber, moving her head closer to the sound.

Anderson smiled and looked at her closed eyes. "You have a long, interesting life ahead of you. I can't wait to meet you again."

# Epilogue

A miracle of modern technology. There was no other way to describe it. At its core was a reserve mass reactor with enough fuel to last over thirty years. From there it was easy to wire up one of the materializers, and using the materializer it was even simpler to create high efficiency lighting.

The rest, well, the rest was a little more difficult. The problem with being trapped in an old reactor room that had been turned into a garden was that you had all kinds of plants all around. The materializer could produce water, food, but no living matter. Once those plants died that was it, there was no bringing them back.

Not knowing much of anything about taking care of plants, he started with watering them regularly. After nearly killing all the tomato plants he finally got the right idea. Plants don't like to drown.

His living space consisted of five levels of grated decking with a couple storage closets and a nice flat floor across the bottom. The mass reactor was built into the center, right on top of the main bracing for the infrastructure.

After three years his thumb finally turned green and a few months after that the materializer was making a fourth composting bin section by section and a few new flower pots. Another two years passed and Minh-Chu found himself laughing aloud as he laid out another pot filled with fresh earth. His hair had grown long, his patience longer, and as he drifted through the absolute black of space with only two small windows to see through, he found himself wondering if anyone would ever find him.

The vines crawled up the sides of his home, every meal included natural foods. The three apple trees he had started with stretched up to the middle of the third deck, the tomatoes yielded a wonderful crop, several squashes did the same and his favourite, the rhubarb nearly grew out of control.

He had been trapped in a place of peace, he realized before long, and after a few years he managed to embrace that peace. There were a few things to read on his command and control unit and he managed to go through everything of interest, and some things not so interesting after five years.

He started entertaining himself by imagining all the things his friends might have gotten up to while he was trapped in a section of the station drifting through space. He also learned to play guitar thanks to the lessons he'd had on his materializer since he was a teenager. He'd never gotten to them but with so much time on his hands he materialized a narrow classical electrical guitar and began to learn.

When the *First Light* was about to puncture the research station with its wormhole generator he looked for the thickest bulkheads he could find. As luck would have it, the old reactor room was it, and he sealed himself inside. Everyone else on the station was either at combat stations or busy hopping into thin hulled escape pods.

The station sheared and twisted away from the old reactor room as it was ripped apart by the gravity circling the rough wormhole, and he was pulled in right behind the *First Light*. How far, he couldn't know, but it was far enough to get him clear of the Blue Belt, that's for sure. When the section of station emerged from the wormhole separate from the *First Light*, he was adrift. The Blue Belt couldn't be seen from any angle. After doing some math and recalling what he was able to see as he held on for dear life he was fairly certain that he had been tossed out the side of the worm hole, and there was no way for him to accurately estimate how far he had travelled.

Thanks to all that time he had to watch Jonas Valent work on his shuttle during the All-Con Conflict, and the many sessions where he'd go on about engineering marvels, he was able to wire up the materializer, life support and gravity to the emergency reactor. That was not quite the hardest part.

There were a few other compartments still attached to the one he was in. Some of them looked pressurized, his command unit said they were most likely safe, and he had a good vacsuit, but taking the unnecessary chance to explore could lead to him getting sucked out when the pressure of the two compartments tried to equalize. If there was a weak point in those outer compartments, he might get shot out into space, and he wouldn't last more than a week in a vacsuit.

He'd still stand in front of those doors for hours, just staring, considering the idea of opening them up just to beat the boredom. Then he'd consider his plants, how hard he had worked. If they were to suffer from low temperatures or decompression there would be little chance of recovery for them.

Minh had just cut some fresh rhubarb and was chewing the end when a sound came from two decks below.
"This is Lorander Survey Ship, Intrepid to. . ." the voice coming from his command and control unit paused for a moment. "what do I call this thing?"
"I don't know, address him as occupant," said another voice.
He clamped the rhubarb stalk in his teeth and ran frenzied down the steel grating stairs. His long black hair flailed out behind him, the leafy end of the rhubarb stock bobbed in front of his face.
"This is Lorander Survey Ship Intrepid to wreckage occupant. Do you require assistance?"
Minh got to the bin he had left his command and control unit in and rummaged through the various extra parts and reusable containers from his meals. "Well, not really, but since you're asking, actually meeting someone who isn't imaginary would be nothing short of the best thing to happen to me in about seven years!" he shouted out as he looked for the unit as fast as he could. "Just hang on and. . . *Found it!*"
"This is Lorander Survey Ship Intr-"
"Oh God, tell me you're real, tell me you're real and even if you're not real at

least be convincing!" Minh shouted into the communicator.

There was silence on the other end.

Minh brought his face very close to the command and control unit and tried to sound very calm even though his heart was beating a tattoo against the inside of his chest and he was so desperate to hear the people on the other end, to be saved. "Hello? Please help, I'm not crazy. Well, not dangerous crazy, just been living with plant life too long crazy."

To his relief the voices came back, he could hear laughter in the background. "We'll get you out in a couple minutes. Do you have a pressure suit?"

"I do, but please don't kill my green friends," he couldn't believe what he was saying at first, but then he looked around from the bottom of the five level reactor room and realized he could barely see the walls for the vines, trees and other shorter plants. The apple trees had grown tall and strong, and the decks were so laden with pots and plants that there was really only the smallest walking path left. In the middle of the bottom level was his materializer and the cot he made with it seven years before.

"We can make a seal and the deck officer tells me we can rescue some of your plants, maybe even use them for re-seeding on a colony," the voice on the other end said eagerly.

"Wait, you're from Lorander? How far away am I?"

"I'm sorry, how far away from what sir?"

"From Starfree Port or Freeground, or even the Blue Belt?"

"Give us a minute to calculate that."

Minh's eyes went wide. "They need to calculate it?" he whispered to himself.

"About twelve hundred light years from Starfree Port. From what we can tell there's evidence of a high energy event about seven years behind you. Sounds like you have one hell of a story to tell."

"I've had a lot of practice telling it to squash puppets, it'll be nice to have a real audience," Minh-Chu said, completely unaware of how strange he sounded.

"Hang on to something, we're latching on. We'll have you aboard and on your way back to civilized space as soon as possible. Seems Freeground is one of our allies and someone back there still has you on a missing in action list. Someone back there wants you home."

Minh-Chu's legs gave out and he plopped down to sit on the edge of his cot. The sounds of the much larger long range ship latching on to the upper part of the station remnant echoed all around him. He looked to a ripened squash he had propped up beside his bed and said; "We're going home."

CPSIA information can be obtained at www.ICGtesting.com
Printed in the USA
BVOW021008050613

322525BV00013B/172/P